ABLAZE

Books in the World of Raphtova

The Reawakening Trilogy
Spark

Ashes

Ablaze

Tales of the Inn
The Curse of the Stoneskin (coming soon)
Operation Brooch (coming soon)
The Wanderer (coming soon)

Leane Winger

ABLAZE

Book Three of the Reawakening Trilogy

1. Edition, 2023

ISBN 978-1-7389046-0-0

Published by Leane Winger, Mackenzie BC, Canada
leane.n.winger@gmail.com
leanewinger.com

Cover design by Aiden Walker

For Seth Einar

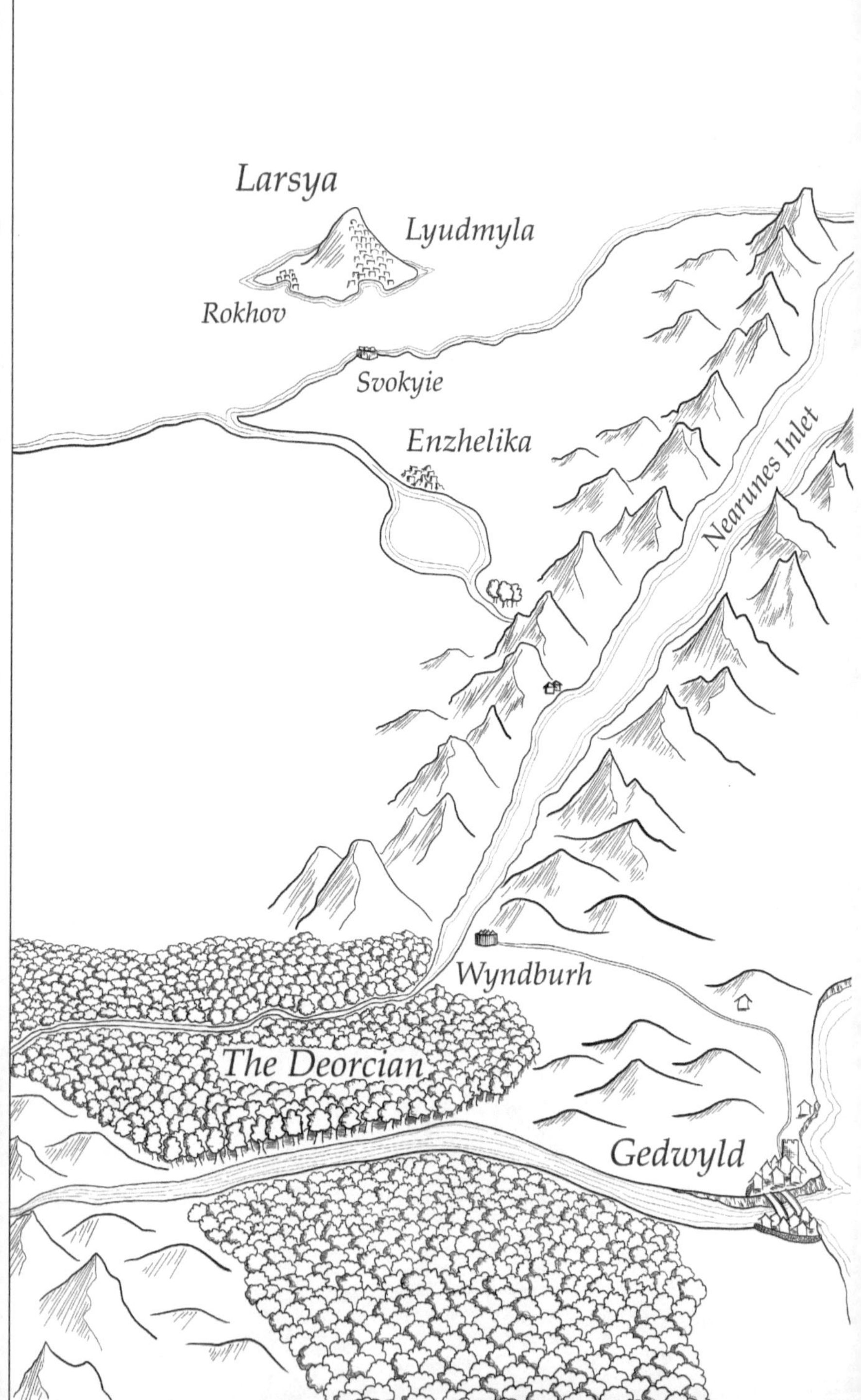

Larsya
Lyudmyla
Rokhov
Svokyie
Enzhelika
Nearunes Inlet
Wyndburh
The Deorcian
Gedwyld

The Glittering Sea
Thea's House

She opened her eyes.

Something was different in the cold stone surrounding her. The silence was quieter. There were no sounds of hammering metal or barked commands. A halt had been called on all actions until further orders came.

She stretched, her powerful muscles flexing effortlessly, her skin gleaming bronze in the dim light of her cell.

She was strong, and she knew it. Her people were made to be strong, grown in secret chambers beneath the mountains, fed with iron and steel until their skin was harder than any armour, training night and day for the moment when they would be needed. She lifted her axe and tested its weight. It was heavy and large, made to kill. Just like she was.

The gates opened, swinging silently on their hinges. Beyond them, light streamed, brighter than anything she had ever seen. The way had been opened.

She was made for this day, and now it had come. She crouched, her axe ready in her hands, every muscle tensed for action.

The orders came.

Go. Kill.

Chapter One

Thea ran through the trees, footsteps pounding across the thick moss that covered the ground. Sylica was just visible through the gloom ahead, running as if her life depended on it, her small metallic dragon galloping at her heels.

Ulfgar's giant pack creaked with every jogging step as he kept pace beside Thea, his wild beard splayed with the self-made breeze of momentum.

Overhead, the great planet Micai was already large in the sky. The light of Allumen flickered between its golden rings as the shadows of the Deorcian began closing in.

Thea ran, legs aching, breaths coming in heavy gasps. Even Sylica was slowing. As Thea and Ulfgar caught up, they found her breathing heavily.

"Time to sleep." Ulfgar gestured to the darkening sky. "I'll take watch."

Thea sank to the ground. Food was thrust into her hands and she ate. Beneath her, the ground was cold and hard. Wrapping her oilskin cloak around herself like a blanket, she lay down and closed her eyes.

Dimly, she became aware of someone shaking her. Daylight filtered through the trees and Ulfgar's beard. Was it morning already?

Thea forced herself to sit up. Her head pounded with exhaustion, as if she hadn't slept at all. Ulfgar rummaged in his pack, then sat down beside her, munching on a biscuit. Beyond him, Sylica snored, curled around Daisy's metallic form. Early morning light outlined each branch with a frosty glow. Thea shivered and pulled her cloak tight.

The ache of absence crept across her senses. Roland was not there. For the first time in so many days, she had been sleeping alone.

Ulfgar was watching her. "You going to check in?"

Thea looked away. She didn't want to face her General. How could she? Zanele and Hwasan were dead, the Resistance was betrayed and revealed to the enemy, and the person she loved most in the world was gone. She couldn't face Allulien's anger and condemnation. The anger and condemnation she carried for herself was already more than she could bear.

"You still have orders, you know."

Thea looked at Ulfgar. There was a gentleness in his eyes that she hadn't seen before. Taking orders under Micai had changed him. Or maybe he had changed, and that was why he took orders.

"And you gave your word."

Something ached, deep in Thea's chest. A promise to serve the Deity was a promise for life. Whatever might happen, she wouldn't be like the rest of her people who turned their back on the Deity. She would check in with her General, like she was supposed to.

Finding a private place not far away, Thea knelt on the cold ground and waited.

The warm glow of Allulien's presence washed over her, its brightness searing through her guilt and fear. Trembling, she looked up into her General's face.

It was not the joyful, piercing gaze that Thea was used to seeing, but it was not the vengeful, angry gaze she feared. Instead, the ethereal eyes that looked down on her were solemn and thoughtful. "We need to talk."

Tears filled Thea's eyes. "I know. I'm so sorry. I ruined everything and now the Resistance is in danger and it's all my fault."

"You do not have the power to ruin everything." Allulien's eyes gleamed. "You are one person among thousands on Raphtova. You do not have the power of a Tilaryn, or a full knowledge of the Deity's plans. Do you understand?"

Thea nodded.

Allulien's face grew stern. "The war is not lost. Because you chose to follow your own wisdom instead of what the Deity commanded you, the war has become harder."

Thea lowered her gaze. "I'm sorry, Allulien. I understand now."

Allulien placed a hand on Thea's head. "Accept your new orders: you must lay aside your own desires and do everything in your power to save the Resistance. The Fallen One is already moving, and there is not much time."

Thea felt, once again, the rush of tingling warmth that accompanied the presence of the Deity's power. She had her magic again, and from the moment of Allulien's touch, all her weariness and pain melted away.

When she opened her eyes, Allulien was gone.

Thea took a long, trembling breath. She would obey, and do all that she could to save the Resistance.

Jumping to her feet, Thea hurried back to the place

where Ulfgar waited.

He nodded a greeting. "Micai says hi."

Thea smiled. Her spirit felt lighter than it had before. "Did Micai say anything about what we should do?"

"Just run fast."

Thea nodded. "It will be a long run."

"We'll do the best we can." Ulfgar took a swig from his tankard. "Want some?"

Thea accepted a drink as Ulfgar shook Sylica awake.

"Up you get," Ulfgar muttered.

"Hm?" Sylica rolled over and blinked up at the forest canopy overhead.

"Morning. Lots of running to do today."

"Oh, I like running!" Sylica sat up, pushing her white and green hair out of her eyes. "I can run really fast!"

"That's good." Thea clipped her bow in place on its baldric. "Ready to go save the Fauns?"

"Yeah!" Sylica scrambled to her feet. "Which way do we go? That way?" Daisy yapped excitedly and ran circles around her feet, clanking with every bound.

"Just wait a breath or two," Thea laughed. "Don't you want to eat something?"

"I can eat and run at the same time. Once I ate a whole pie while I was running because if my mom caught me she would have taken the pie away and I wanted to eat it first." Sylica grinned. "I've had lots of practice."

"We're off, then?" Ulfgar grunted, heaving himself to his feet.

"I guess we are." Thea glanced around the forest. The trees weren't as large here as in the lower reaches of the Deorcian. If they were lucky they'd make good time and not encounter any monsters.

"Let's go!" Sylica cried, tearing off through the trees with Daisy at her heel.

"This way, Sylica!" Thea yelled.

"Oh." Sylica turned and sped past Thea and Ulfgar. "Come on, slowpokes! Let's go save the Fauns!"

Thea and Ulfgar followed, settling into a comfortable jog. Soon Thea's legs were aching, but she didn't dare to stop. Allulien said there wasn't much time.

Around them, the trees blurred and shifted. Thea shook her head as everything snapped back into focus again. She hadn't been dizzy. What was going on? A short while later, it happened again. It hadn't felt like magic, but something wasn't normal.

"Sylica," Thea called, hurrying to catch up to her green-skinned friend, "what are you doing to the trees?"

"Nothing." Sylica blinked innocently, without slackening her pace.

"But they're moving." Thea stared in alarm as the forest around them shifted again. "Trees aren't supposed to move like that."

"They're not moving," Sylica grinned, "*we're* moving. I mean—moving faster."

"You mean ..."

"I'm making us go faster with my magic. Then we can save the Fauns sooner!"

Thea smiled. "And you know what I can do?" Between panting breaths, she prayed a prayer of blessing over their journey. With a surge of magic, the weariness lifted from her limbs.

"That's better," Ulfgar grinned. "Double time!"

They ran on through the forest, into staph and beyond. Through a gap in the branches overhead, Thea caught a glimpse of mountain crags to the east.

In the shadows, something moved.

Thea hesitated, but Sylica ran on, with Daisy galloping along beside her.

Ulfgar stepped beside Thea, his great axe in his hands. "Something up there?" he muttered under his breath.

A roar tore through the silence of the forest as a tall, lizard-like creature emerged from between the trees. It towered above Sylica, baring its razor-sharp teeth.

Sylica froze. "Thea? My magic juice is all gone!"

"Then smash it!" Ulfgar yelled. Swinging his axe, he charged at the athexe, roaring at the top of his lungs.

The athexe startled, stared at Ulfgar, then stumbled back in its hurry to get away.

"Ha!" Ulfgar cried, in hot pursuit. "They haven't forgotten me yet!"

Two more athexes emerged from the shadows.

"Charge!" Sylica yelled, brandishing her mace.

Thea grabbed Raybow off her back as Sylica smashed the closest athexe in the stomach.

Thea shot. The arrow blazed with light as it struck the monster's shoulder.

The other athexe snarled and lashed out with a long clawed arm, striking sparks off Sylica's glittering armour.

With a roar, Ulfgar emerged from the undergrowth, running headfirst towards the remaining athexes. They froze for one brief moment, then turned and fled.

"Right. Off you go." Ulfgar muttered, waving them away. He turned to Thea and Sylica with a grin. "Well, then." His breath came in heavy gasps, but otherwise he seemed unharmed.

Thea couldn't help a smile. "We carry on?"

Ulfgar nodded and set off through the trees once again. They ran until the shadows engulfed the forest in the darkness of an overcast night.

"Right. Call it a night." Ulfgar muttered. He shoved a bit of jerky into Thea and Sylica's hands, then sat down with a clatter of chain mail and weaponry. "Stay close," he added. "I'll shield us in case more of those buggers show up."

Thea nodded, casting her own magic. A blessed sleep would give them the strength to run another day.

"Two shiny tents." Sylica hummed happily as she wrapped herself in her blanket and lay down to sleep. "I like seeing magic, it's so pretty and sparkly. Isn't it, Daisy? A pretty gold tent from Thea and a pretty green tent from Ulfgar. I wonder if I could make a tent too? It could be all sorts of colours ... like pink ... and yellow .... and ..."

A soft snore filled the silence of the forest.

Thea wrapped her cloak tight and lay down beside her. She was asleep as soon as her head touched the ground.

"Morning."

Thea opened her eyes. The first rays of daylight glimmered through the forest canopy overhead as Allumen emerged from its nightly eclipse.

"Hungry?" Ulfgar asked.

Thea forced herself to sit up. A dusting of snow had fallen overnight, leaving small white patches on the forest floor where the gaps in the branches had let the flakes through. Thea shivered and stretched her aching muscles.

"Oh! Pretty snow!" Sylica murmured. "Look, Daisy,

there's snow today."

The little metal dragon stretched, then trotted around the clearing, snuffling curiously at the delicate carpet of snow.

Sylica hopped up. "Ready to go?"

Thea shook her head. "I have to check in first."

"Me too." Ulfgar shrugged. "Doesn't have to take long."

Thea knelt where she was. Allulien did not appear or speak, but the warm rush of magic returned to replace what she had used the day before. She looked up to see Ulfgar waiting for her.

"How far do you think we've come?" he asked, munching on a piece of dried meat.

"I have no idea. The forest all looks the same to me."

Ulfgar glanced at Sylica. "That magic of yours. What can you do with it?"

"Whatever I want to. Kind of." Sylica frowned. "My body is full of magic juice, but my body isn't very big, so I can't do very big magic things. That's what Meiling said."

"How about dropping us right by the Resistance? That would be faster than running."

"I wanted to, but it was too big for my magic. And Meiling said I have to be careful not to break the world too much, because the world doesn't really like Dragon magic. It's kind of confusing." Sylica pouted, then perked up a little. "But I can make us run faster."

Thea nodded. "I know. And that's better than running at a normal speed, right Ulfgar?"

Ulfgar muttered something under his breath and rubbed his shins. Daisy jumped up and licked his face.

"Well?" Thea asked.

Ulfgar sighed and wiped his face with the back of his hand. "I guess we keep running."

It was a long day, even with magic to stave off exhaustion. Restday was all but gone when they reached the banks of a river. Its water was dark and deep, flowing at a smooth, relentless pace that swept along anything in its path.

Thea looked up and downstream, but the river cut directly across their path. Somehow they would have to cross.

Ulfgar grunted. "Well, we've made it to the end of the Deorcian, it seems."

Thea stared at the flowing water with new interest. It did look like the great river that bordered the southern edge of the Deorcian. "Then we've come very far!" She looked with relief at her companions. "At this speed, we might make it to the Resistance tomorrow!"

Ulfgar nodded pensively. "I don't relish that river crossing, though." The thin dusting of snow had melted during the warmer measures of staph, but the air was still bitterly cold. He glanced at Sylica. "Don't suppose you can get us across with that magic of yours."

"I used all my magic juice." Sylica's forehead scrunched up into a frown. "I wanted us to go as fast as we could."

"We were going fast," Thea assured her. "We just have to get across the river now."

"You both have magic too," Sylica offered.

"Not like your magic. I can't bless us across the river, or charm it into letting us cross. Transportation isn't a part of Allulien's magic. I don't suppose it's a part of Micai's either."

Ulfgar shook his head. "I could smite the river, for all

the good that would do." He sighed. "I guess we're getting wet."

Thea spread her oilskin cloak on the ground, carefully wrapping her bow and quiver in the water-resistant fabric.

Ulfgar tightened the straps on his oversized pack. "Anyone got a rope on them?"

"No." Thea's heart sank. "Roland has mine."

"Yes you do, Thea," Sylica objected. "You have Hwasan's rope. I saw you take it."

Thea's heart ached. She'd forgotten she had Hwasan's bag. Gingerly, she pulled it out of her pack. It was a simple leather satchel and didn't have much in it. A sleeping mat, a bit of dried food, the empty brazier, and the rope he had used to lead them up the cliffs on their way to the Dragons. Nothing that told her much about the lonely Minathril's life, or why he had chosen to serve the Fallen General.

Thea handed the rope to Ulfgar. He untangled it and tied one end to his waist. Breathing warm air on his hands, he eyed the flowing water with an unimpressed glare. "Shield it is," he muttered.

Thea felt the surge of magic, and the air around her didn't seem as cold as it had a moment before. She followed it with her own surge of magic. A blessing couldn't lift them across the river, but it could make the crossing easier.

Ulfgar jumped into the river with a massive splash. Quickly he surfaced again, swimming with quick, powerful strokes as the current swept him downstream.

Thea could only just see him as he pulled himself up the far bank.

"Oi!" Ulfgar's voice drifted back to them over the

murmur of the river. "Cold cold cold brrr cold."

The rope had only just been long enough. Slowly, he picked his way back along the bank of the river and tied the rope around a largish tree.

"You go ahead, Sylica," Thea offered. "I'll go last."

Sylica tied Daisy to the end of the rope, then splashed into the water. "Ulfgar!" she wailed, "I thought you shielded us!"

"I did." Ulfgar grumbled. "Would be colder if I didn't."

"I can't feel my toes!"

"Hurry up, then."

Sylica splashed noisily across the river, as Daisy whined and paced beside Thea. The water reached Sylica's waist, but pulling herself hand over hand, she propelled herself through the current.

"Come on, Daisy," Thea muttered. Hoisting her oilskin-wrapped bundle over her shoulder, she grabbed the rope and stepped into the river.

It was cold. The rushing water swept past her legs, threatening to pull her along with it. Setting each foot with care, Thea struggled forward. The rope jerked back and forth as Daisy continued to pace the riverbank, but it remained secure enough for Thea to keep her balance, even as the numbing water reached her waist.

Shivering, Thea finally pulled herself up on the far bank. Unrolling her oilskin, she wrapped it tight around her shoulders.

"Good girl, Daisy!" Sylica called across the river. "You can come now!"

With a splash, Daisy leapt into the water and sank like a stone.

Sylica's eyes widened. "What if Daisy can't swim?"

"Come on," Ulfgar grumbled. "Let's pull her in."

Grabbing the rope, Ulfgar and Sylica pulled it hand over hand. Before all the slack had been pulled in, Daisy emerged from the water at their feet, scampering up the bank like an excited puppy. Ulfgar scrambled out of the way, but Sylica wrapped her arms around Daisy's wriggling form in an enthusiastic embrace.

"You made it, Daisy!" Sylica gasped. "But you're so cold! Poor little dragon!"

Ice gleamed on Daisy's metallic surface, cracking and falling to the ground as she jumped and cavorted around Sylica's feet.

"She doesn't seem to be hurting for it," Ulfgar grumbled, stamping his feet. "Let's walk for a bit. Get ourselves warmed up."

Quickly coiling the rope, Thea followed Ulfgar through the trees, with Sylica and Daisy tramping along behind. They walked until the light of day faded from the sky, then huddled together for the night, shivering beneath Ulfgar's magical shield and Thea's magical blessing. Slowly warmth crept once again over Thea's senses, and she sank into a deep sleep.

Thea woke to the sound of snoring in her ears, wedged tightly between Ulfgar and Sylica. The blue-green light of night was tinged by the first golden rays of morning. Gingerly, she tried to extricate herself from between her companions.

"Hmm?" Ulfgar grunted. "Morning already?"

"It seems so," Thea replied. "Sorry to wake you."

Ulfgar grunted again and heaved himself into a sitting position.

The world outside of the huddle of blankets was crisp

and cold. Thea shivered.

Ulfgar frowned. "What's that?" Staggering to his feet, he stomped over to the foot of a nearby tree. "There's footprints here."

"Faun prints?"

"No. What do you make of these?"

Thea went to see. The footprints looked like something made by an Elf, or maybe a human, but they were larger, and whatever had made them hadn't been wearing shoes.

Ulfgar eyed her thoughtfully. "Do Elves come in bigger sizes than you?"

"A little bit, maybe. I'm average-sized. Roland's a bit taller."

"Big enough to make prints like this?"

"No." The prints might have been made by something as big as a Minathril, or bigger, but they didn't look like the clawed, lizard-like feet of the Minathrils.

"What made these, then?"

"I don't know. Did it come when we were asleep?"

"The ground's frozen. Must have been during staph, when things thawed a little." Ulfgar frowned and eyed the forest, silent in the early morning light. "We should follow them."

Thea hurried back to where Sylica lay curled up next to Daisy. "Wake up, Sylica. We're going to check in, then we need to go."

"Morning, Thea," Sylica mumbled, stretching sleepily.

Thea knelt and waited to hear what Allulien might say. The warm glow of magic returned, and with it a sense of urgency that filled every part of her body. They needed to go. Now.

Finishing her check in more quickly than she ever had before, Thea got up and returned to where Ulfgar still waited by the tracks. "Ready to go?"

Ulfgar nodded. Sylica trotted over to join them, shoving her blanket back into her pack.

Just beyond the tree, the set of tracks was joined by another. Then the two were joined by another two. A few paces later, they crossed another set of tracks. Ulfgar knelt to examine them.

"Same kind of creature," he muttered. "Looks like five or six of them." The two trails went separate ways through the trees.

"Which ones do we follow?" Thea asked.

Ulfgar frowned. "Don't know. Let's try that way." He led on, and the others followed.

After a while they lost the trail, then found it again. By a small creek they found dozens of prints, left in its muddy banks. The tracks scattered through the forest, moving in groups of three or four.

"They're everywhere," Thea muttered. "Why are there so many?"

Ulfgar scanned the forest with a dark frown. "And what were they here for?" He glanced at Thea.

Her heart sank. Whatever they were, they were looking for the Resistance. She had to find them before it was too late.

"Come on." Thea hurried through the trees. "If they were everywhere, there's no point following the tracks. We need to find the Resistance before they do."

But where was the Resistance? There was no way to contact them, and they moved their camp so often there was no way to know where in the forest they would be.

"Keep looking for tracks," she urged the others as they hurried on. "Especially Faun ones. Maybe we'll find a sign from Thabani or one of the others."

The forest stretched on as they continued their search, but there was nothing but more and more tracks of the strange, large creatures. If only there was a way of contacting Thabani, they wouldn't be wasting time trying to comb a forest that took days to cross.

"Look." Ulfgar gestured to the ground not far away. A dented trail of tracks crossed in front of them, all moving in the same direction. A large group of the creatures had gone this way—twenty or thirty at least.

Changing course, Ulfgar followed the new trail. It moved straight as an arrow through the trees, gathering more tracks as it went. Thea's heart sank. Where were these creatures going? They must have found some sort of destination, or some sort of target ...

They stepped out of the trees into a clearing. It had once been a camp. Pine branch bowers hung broken and limp. The trampled ground was red with blood and littered with the bodies of Fauns.

Chapter Two

A deathly silence filled the air. Thea stared in horror at the devastation before her. Bodies lay everywhere, bloody and dismembered. The ashes of the fire had been trampled, the small huts beneath the trees torn apart and left in half-deconstructed heaps. Broken weapons and charred scraps of wood lay strewn across the blood-soaked ground.

Thea crouched by the body of a Faun where he lay, mangled and covered with blood. She recognized his face, though she had never learned his name. The head of another Faun lay beside him, severed and bloody.

Ulfgar stumped around the clearing, his face dark with anger. "A bloody massacre. Look at this." Beneath the tatters of the bower, the lifeless form of a Faun was clutching a pan of half-chopped root vegetables. "No warning. They didn't have a chance."

Tears filled Thea's eyes. The Fallen General had done this, and he'd found out because of her. Gently, she touched the curly head of the Faun that lay beside her. "I'm so sorry," she stammered, her voice a hoarse whisper. She was too late. Was there any Resistance left to save?

"Thea," Sylica's voice was small. Thea looked up into her large, troubled eyes. "I think there's something out there."

As Thea got to her feet, magic surged, exploding

from the far side of the clearing. Throwing her own magic into a counterspell, Thea stared as five large creatures charged out of the undergrowth, weapons raised. Metal gleamed in the light.

Ulfgar grabbed his great axe and leapt to meet the intruders.

Thea drew Raybow. Where was the caster?

Ulfgar's blow struck the first creature on the side and it crumpled to the ground with a clang.

There—the furthest of the creatures. As magic swelled again, Thea shot, and the caster collapsed.

The next creature struck Ulfgar with a massive broadsword, sending him stumbling back. Beside him, Sylica braced herself and took a blow to her shield.

These creatures almost looked like Elves, but they were larger—like Minathrils in size. Their bare skin shone with a metallic gleam. One of them snarled, baring its sharp, fang-like teeth, and charged at Thea.

Thea shot and the monster dodged out of the way, the arrow nicking its arm. It lunged at her, green blood oozing from the wound.

Thea dove behind Sylica. Metal clanged as something struck Sylica's shield. The monster roared.

Thea scrambled back to her feet. Ducking out from behind Sylica, she shot again. The monster knocked her arrow aside. Daisy's teeth were sunk into its leg, but it didn't seem to notice, dragging the small metal dragon along as it advanced.

Blades crashed as another monster forced Ulfgar back, step after step. Ulfgar staggered, his sleeve red with blood.

"Ulfgar!" Sylica yelled, bracing her shield against another powerful blow. "Get back when I yell three!"

"What—" Ulfgar yelled.

"Three!"

Thea threw herself out of the way as Sylica jumped back. The ground where they had stood turned as soft as mud. The monsters slipped and began to sink.

Thea shot again. The arrow struck its mark, and the monster collapsed.

Another monster roared, flinging a handful of mud that splattered across Sylica's face. "Hey!" Sylica yelled, ducking behind her shield.

The monster facing Ulfgar struggled to pull itself out of the mud.

Ulfgar stepped back and staggered slightly. His grime-smeared face seemed very pale.

Metal flashed. A throwing axe struck Ulfgar's chest with a sickening crunch. He stumbled back and fell.

In an instant, the monster was on top of him, swinging its sword for the kill.

Ulfgar yelled, knocking the blow aside at the last possible moment. The sword plunged deep into the ground.

The monster kicked Ulfgar in the groin and wrenched its sword up and over its head.

Thea shot, striking the monster in the chest. It collapsed on top of Ulfgar with the crack of breaking ribs.

A metallic crunch rang across the clearing.

"Daisy!" Sylica cried.

Sudden fire burst out of Daisy's mouth, engulfing the final monster. It yelled, its skin glowing molten red. Sylica swung her mace and smashed its head. It collapsed to the ground.

Thea ran to Ulfgar. It was almost impossible to see

him beneath the massive bulk of the monster. Dropping Raybow, she tried to shove the monster out of the way.

"Ow," Ulfgar groaned. "Careful with that."

"Are you alright?" Thea gasped.

"No," Ulfgar growled. "That hurt."

Putting her shoulder against the lifeless form of the monster, Thea pushed. Slowly, it fell to the side. Beneath, Ulfgar was soaked with its strange, green blood.

Gingerly, he pushed himself into a sitting position.

Thea stared at the body of the strange, Elf-like monster. "What are they?"

"Don't know. Never saw one before. Damn, I hurt all over."

Thea touched its metallic skin. It was cold and hard. "It's metal ... at least it feels like metal. I never heard of a metal-skinned creature before, just stone-skinned creatures, like Elves and trolls." The monster's long, canine fangs protruded from its mouth. Its large feet matched the kind of footprints they had been following. "Whatever they are, they killed the Fauns."

"And we saw footprints for a lot more than five," Ulfgar muttered, attempting to struggle to his feet.

"Careful," Thea urged him. "Where are you hurt?"

"My shoulder and chest, mostly. Ow—careful!"

Thea withdrew her hand. "Sorry. Shouldn't we get you cleaned and bandaged? There's blood all over you!"

"No time," Ulfgar muttered. "Only fourteen bodies here. The rest of the Fauns are out there somewhere. Got to find them." He staggered to his feet.

Thea glanced around the clearing.

Sylica crouched on the ground not far away, her little metal dragon in her arms. She looked up at Thea with an expression of horror. "They hurt Daisy."

Thea hurried closer. The little dragon's back was caved in, dented by a blow from the monster.

"What do we do?" Tears filled Sylica's eyes.

"Seriously?" Ulfgar grumbled. Shaking himself, he put a grubby hand on Sylica's shoulder. "Look. We get ourselves back to the forge at Thea's house, and I'll put that right in no time."

"Really?" Sylica sniffed.

"As good as new."

A gleam of light moved in the corner of Thea's vision. A Faun was creeping out from the trees, crouched with a spear in her hand. Two more Fauns followed. They froze as they spied Thea and her companions, then wide smiles spread over their faces and they hurried forward.

Thea cast comprehension.

"Thea! You came back!" The foremost of the Fauns embraced her warmly.

"Just not soon enough," Thea replied. "I'm so sorry."

The Faun gestured for her companions to keep moving. Approaching the collapsed huts, they began pulling them apart as if they were searching for something.

"Can't stay long." The first Faun spoke with a grim smile. "The enemy's everywhere now." She glanced at the bodies of the monsters. "I see you've met them."

"I think they were hiding here in case anyone came back. They attacked us almost as soon as we got here."

"Waiting for us, I imagine." The Faun frowned. "We came back for bandages and food, but anything we do, it seems they're one step ahead."

Thea stared at the monsters, their strange green blood staining the ground beneath them. "What are they?"

The Faun gestured helplessly. "Never saw anything like them. Just appeared out of nowhere and ... that happened." Her gaze turned to the bodies of the Fauns, scattered across their decimated camp. Pain clouded her face. "And we have to leave them like that."

Three more Fauns emerged from the trees. One of them had blood dripping down his face. The other two were limping.

"We'll come with you." Thea offered the Faun a reassuring smile. "Allulien sent us to help."

The Faun nodded her thanks. "I'm Noxolo, by the way."

"Do you know where Thabani is?"

"No. We're the only ones I've been able to find. I don't know who else survived."

Thea glanced at the Fauns, still searching through the heaps of branches that had once been huts. "Can we help you find what you're looking for?"

Noxolo nodded and gestured for Thea to follow. "There should be some dried food we can take. I don't think anyone else had time to grab it." They approached the remains of the bower. Moving branches aside, they dug until they uncovered some broken jars and crushed baskets. Noxolo rooted through them, handing Thea bits of dried meat and crumbled biscuits.

One of the other Fauns approached. "We found the medical bags. We should go."

Noxolo nodded to Thea. "That will have to be enough."

They returned to find Sylica rooting through her pack.

"We need to go, Sylica," Thea urged her. "Can this

wait?"

"But they're hurt." Sylica pointed to the injured Fauns. "We need to help them."

"We will," Thea assured her, "but not here. We need to find somewhere safe."

"Nowhere is safe." Noxolo's voice was low. "Not with those things out there."

"I know a safe place. We just have to make it there." Thea glanced from Sylica to Ulfgar. "First we need to find as much of the Resistance as we can."

Noxolo nodded.

One of the Fauns stepped forward. "I'll scout." Shifting into the form of a cougar, they padded silently away.

Leaving the clearing behind, Thea and the others followed the Dryad through the shadows.

"Do we want to travel fast?" Sylica asked.

"No. We don't want to miss anyone." Thea scanned the forest around them. It was eerily silent. "And we might need your magic if we encounter more of those monsters."

As they hurried east through the forest, Thea watched the ground for hoofprints and strained her ears for any sound of the scattered Resistance, but there was nothing. Quickening her pace, she fell in step beside Noxolo. "Do you know of anywhere we should look?"

Noxolo's face was grim. "I checked everywhere I could think of, but if there's anyone nearby, Dark Paw will find them."

A shadow crossed the sky. Thea froze. With a rush of feathers, two giant eagles dove through a gap in the trees overhead. One was brown, the other was pure white.

As they landed, the white eagle's form shifted into a human with pure white skin and hair. Their face spasmed in pain.

"Ember!" Thea cried, rushing forward as the Dryad staggered.

Ember gave her a wan smile as the Fauns crowded around. Dark Paw emerged from the shadows, shifting back into Faun shape to join them.

One of Ember's legs was bloodied and maimed.

"Sylica!" Thea called. "Ember's bleeding!"

Throwing her pack on the ground, Sylica rooted out some long bandages and elbowed her way past the Fauns.

"Where's Thabani?" Noxolo asked.

Everyone looked from Ember to Kaji. The giant eagle was Thabani's companion. She rarely left his side.

Ember's face was drawn in pain. "I don't know. I wasn't in camp when the ambush happened. Kaji came and found me. I've been looking everywhere."

Noxolo stroked the giant eagle's back. "What happened, Kaji? Where is he?"

Kaji made a low clicking noise and leaned closer to Noxolo for a scratch.

"She doesn't know," Ember replied. "Suddenly he was gone, but she doesn't know why. We've flown the forest north to south, but wherever we went we were too late. The enemy had already been there. You're the first part of the Resistance we've found alive."

Sylica finished wrapping the bandage around Ember's leg. Bloodstains were already seeping through.

Ember turned to Thea. "But now you're here, and just when we need you most."

Thea's heart sank. "Yes. Allulien sent us."

"Where's Zanele?"

Thea knew the question was coming, but that didn't make it any easier.

"She's dead." Thea's gaze fell to the ground beneath her feet. "There was a spy that joined us as we travelled to the Dragons. He killed Zanele and told the Enemy about the Resistance. That's how he knows about you now."

"And Roland?"

"He's gone. He went to help his people, and I have come to help mine." She looked again at the cluster of Fauns and Dryads around her, their spirits bright with the light of the Deity. These were her people. She belonged here with them.

"We are glad you came back to us." Ember smiled and took her hand.

"Thank you," Thea whispered.

"We need to move," Noxolo interjected. "Ember, can you walk?"

"I'll do my best." Ember moved their leg and grimaced. "I don't think I can shift again for a while."

"Here." Thea offered an arm of support, which Ember gratefully accepted. With their other arm stretched over Kaji's back, Ember hobbled forward.

Dark Paw shifted back into cougar form and slunk into the shadows as Noxolo hurried everyone on as fast as they could go.

As they walked, Thea watched the surrounding forest with a worried frown. How much more of her magic would she need before the day was through? Could she spare some to bless their travel and make it easier for those who had been hurt? Ulfgar's sleeve was still red with new blood. The Faun with the head wound was still unbandaged, and two of the Fauns were limping. If they didn't have a chance to rest soon, someone's injuries were going to get worse.

Dark Paw appeared out of the shadows and shifted into Faun shape, speaking with Noxolo in a low, urgent voice.

Thea hurried to join them. "What's going on?"

"Enemies ahead," Dark Paw hissed. "Coming this way."

"How many?"

"Six."

Thea glanced around their small band of Resistance fighters. Three of the Fauns were injured. Ulfgar's fighting arm was immobile, wrapped in a very rough sling, and Ember was in no shape to be fighting anything. That only left five of them still able to fight.

Noxolo gave a grim smile and gripped her spear. "Let's show them what the Resistance can do."

"Wait!" Thea hissed. "You can't just run at them, they'll kill you in an instant! We have to make a plan."

Noxolo frowned. "We never made plans before."

"Well maybe it's time now." Thea glanced at her companions, thinking quickly. "Sylica, your shield seemed to hold them back. Does anyone else have a shield? Then try to find something. With shields and long range weapons we have a chance."

"Right." Ulfgar swung his axe over his shoulder, then flinched in pain.

"No, Ulfgar, you're hurt. You too, Ember, and all of you." Thea gestured to the injured Fauns. "We need to hide you somewhere you won't be seen."

A murmur of protests erupted.

"Enough of that," Noxolo snapped. "Thea's right and

we don't have time to argue. Get down and stop complaining."

As Ember urged the injured Fauns into the undergrowth, Thea turned back to the fighters who were still standing. One of the Fauns held a short curved sword in one hand and a thick, rotting branch the other. Noxolo gripped her spear. Between them, Sylica stood gleaming, mace and shield in hand. Dark Paw shifted back into cougar form and slipped into the shadows.

Tramping footsteps grew louder. Thea put an arrow to the string of her bow. There—the monsters emerged, their metal skin gleaming in the mottled shadows.

Dark Paw leapt from the trees overhead. That instant, a monster swung its sword, and the Dryad fell with a scream.

Thea shot. The monster staggered back, her arrow in its chest.

With a shout, Noxolo charged. Her spear skidded across her opponent's skin with a spine-shuddering screech.

Kaji dove at the monsters, talons extended, knocking her target to the ground.

The Faun with the branch dodged a cudgel blow. With a flick of his curved blade, he sent the cudgel tumbling to the ground. The monster drew a dagger from its belt, striking faster than sight. The Faun collapsed with a gurgling cry.

Thea shot, but the monster ducked into a crouch. Turning its fierce gaze on Thea, it growled and sprang towards her.

Thea scrambled back, then stared as the monster ran past her, straight into the place where the injured were hiding.

"Hey! Stop!" Thea yelled.

A Faun appeared out of thin air, standing just beside Thea. Magic surged, and the monster disappeared.

"Get down!" the Faun yelled.

As Thea threw herself to the ground, a tree exploded, splattering green blood and body parts across the surrounding forest.

As soon as the fragments had settled, Thea sprang to her feet again. The tree that exploded had been close to the monsters. At least two of them lay beneath the tree's twisted remains. Another got to its feet in a daze. Drawing an arrow, Thea shot it in the head.

A heap of branches shifted, and Noxolo crawled out.

Sylica poked her head out from behind her shield. "What was *that*?"

"That wasn't you?" Thea stared in surprise.

"That was me," the new Faun replied. He seemed a little shaken. "I knew that would work, but I didn't know it would work that well. Is everyone alright?"

Noxolo pushed her way through the carnage. "Msizi? Since when were you a caster?"

The Faun gave a wry smile. "Since today, apparently. Enkeli said I was needed."

Thea stared. "You're serving beneath Enkeli?"

Msizi nodded. "Orders to get the survivors of the Resistance together, as fast as possible."

"Those are my orders too!"

Msizi smiled. "Good. I have twelve Fauns and two Dryads so far, and most of the Faunlets. They're on their way here now. We heard the sound of fighting so I transported myself on ahead."

"That's how you appeared out of nowhere?"

Msizi nodded. Out of the undergrowth, Ulfgar emerged and stared at the mess of splintered wood, dripping with green blood. "What the—"

"Ulfgar!" Thea hurried to his side. "Is everyone okay?"

"No." His face fell. "That monster came right for us. Got one of the Fauns before it … disappeared?"

"I transported it," Msizi explained.

"And exploded a tree?" Thea stared at the carnage.

"I transported it *into* the tree. When two things occupy the same space, the results are dramatic. At least, that's the way Enkeli put it. I wasn't expecting it to explode quite like that." He wiped his face with his arm, but it only smeared the splattering of monster blood.

Ember limped out from the undergrowth, the lifeless body of a Faun held in their arms. "That monster got her before we had a chance. It happened so fast."

Tears stung Thea's eyes. "I'm sorry, Ember. I didn't know it was going to run past me like that. How did it even know you were there? You were all hidden."

"They knew Dark Paw was above them in the trees too." Noxolo's face seemed tired. "I looked for Dark Paw, but there's no body."

Thea's heart ached. The Dryad was no more, and their seed had returned to the ground like Arl's had, waiting for the day when a new Dryad would grow.

Slowly, the last two Fauns emerged from the undergrowth.

Gripping Raybow, Thea took a shaky breath. "We need to keep going. If there is anyone left to find, we have to find them."

Msizi nodded. "The others should be here any

moment now." As he spoke, Fauns began emerging from the surrounding trees. Soon the small clearing was crowded with Fauns and Dryads, embracing each other and offering greetings in low, hurried voices. At their heels, two foxes padded silently. A falcon rested on a Faun's wrist, and a raven sat on another Faun's shoulder. Faunlets were underfoot everywhere, tugging on the older Fauns' hands or peering curiously through the trees.

Msizi scratched his head. "I guess I should mention—there's about fifty of those monsters chasing us. We should probably get moving."

Chapter Three

The word spread through the Resistance fighters: "Time to go." The Dryads that had come with Msizi shifted into large forest elk to carry those who had difficulty walking. Faunlets were lifted up for piggybacks and shoulder rides. Msizi gestured for everyone to get moving.

After making sure that Ulfgar and Sylica were alright, Thea fell in step beside Msizi. He was a thin, wiry Faun with dark skin and small, sharp horns that poked out through his curly black hair. Thea watched him with interest. She had never met someone who served beneath Enkeli before. As far as she was concerned, the Elves didn't count.

"Enkeli wanted you to save the Resistance?" she asked as they hurried on through the trees.

"As many as I could find." Msizi nodded. "Nineteen strong now. That's not bad."

"Is there anywhere you haven't looked yet? I'm supposed to find survivors too."

Msizi grinned. "Nice how the Generals work together, isn't it? Not sure how much time we have left. Enkeli said we have to be out of the forest by eclipse tonight."

Thea stared at Msizi. "But it takes days to cross the forest!"

"That's what Enkeli magic is for."

"Enkeli magic helps with travelling?"

"The transportation magic does. It's just what we need to get us out of here."

Thea considered this. "What else does Enkeli magic do?"

"Comprehension and messaging."

"Messaging?" Thea almost jumped with excitement. "Can you contact the rest of the Resistance?"

"I was. That's how I found so many of us, but I need to save the rest of my magic for getting us out. You've got comprehension magic, right? We can use that to see if there's anyone else nearby, then we need to get out of here before those monsters catch up."

Thea blinked in surprise. Why hadn't she thought of doing that? As they hurried on, she cast her comprehension magic—not to understand languages this time, but to comprehend whether there were any other Fauns nearby.

There—she could feel one! "This way," she gestured to Msizi and veered slightly off course. "There's a Faun this way!"

"Just one?"

Thea nodded. Her spirit sight tingled and she paused. There was something dark, something that felt like a monster up ahead, right where her magic had located the Faun.

"Tell everyone to wait," she whispered. "I'll go first." Grabbing Raybow, she put an arrow to the string and crept forward. She only felt one monster. If she got one good shot, that would be enough.

The undergrowth was thick, but there seemed to be some kind of clearing ahead. Thea crept as silently as she could, peering through a gap in the branches.

A monster stood alone in the middle of the clearing, its gleaming metallic skin streaked with green blood. In its arms was a baby Faun.

Thea froze. As she watched, the baby laughed and grabbed the monster's nose. It was Inyoni, Ayanda's baby.

Carnage filled the clearing. Dead monsters and Fauns lay covered in blood, surrounding the lone monster who stood with the baby in its arms.

The monster closed its eyes and spoke.

Thea cast comprehension.

"I know you are there." The monster's eyes opened and stared straight at Thea. "Come out and take the child. Then kill me."

Thea's mouth went dry. Lowering Raybow, she stepped into the clearing.

The monster stared at her. A shudder ran across its strange, metallic skin.

Darkness filled the monster's spirit, like every other monster Thea had seen, and yet ... it was a different darkness. It was not the darkness of evil, it was the darkness of hopelessness and despair.

Cautiously, Thea approached the monster and stared up at it. It was larger than a Minathril, strong, with thick limbs and bulging muscles. Its eyes were empty and cold.

"You did not kill the child."

The monster spoke, and its voice was like a growl. "*Kill.* Those were my orders, but I will not kill a child. Take it. Its mother is dead."

"Did you kill her?"

"Yes. My war band would have killed the child too, but I said no. They would not listen. So I killed them."

A large axe lay on the ground by the monster's side. It was stained green with blood.

Thea hardly dared to breathe. "What are you?"

"I am an orc, the elite of my war band. My name is Ulga."

"What are orcs?"

"We are weapons. We have come to kill."

Thea stared up at the orc. Jagged tusks protruded from its mouth. Two swords hung from a belt around its waist. A bundle of javelins hung across its back. Its metallic skin was like armour, gleaming in the light. "But you did not kill the child?"

Darkness filled the orc's eyes. "Take it." She held the child at arm's length towards Thea.

Gingerly, Thea accepted the child being thrust into her arms. Inyoni giggled and clung to Thea's side.

The orc sank to its knees. "Kill me now. We have heard of your bow. You will only need to shoot once." Baring its chest, the orc waited.

Ayanda's bloodied form lay motionless at Thea's feet. Just like the bodies of the Fauns, scattered across their decimated camp. Just like Zanele's lifeless body, killed by a servant of the enemy.

With a pounding heart, Thea bent down, and set Raybow on the ground.

The orc stared at her, confusion filling its face.

"The Deity is not like the Fallen One you serve." Thea's eyes did not leave the orc's face. "We offer mercy, not revenge, even to those who have done us so much harm. The only one who cannot receive mercy is the one who does not want it."

The orc's face was immobile, but there was pain in its eyes. "I was made for one purpose and I cannot do it.

There is no reason for me to live."

Inyoni dug her little hooves into Thea's side. The murmur of voices in the distance was growing louder. Thea turned back to the orc kneeling before her. "I travel with the last remains of the Resistance. There are many children with us, like this little one, but the orcs are not far behind. Here is a purpose for you: come with us and protect the children."

Determination sprang up in the orc's eyes. "I will come."

Standing, the orc sheathed its axe and turned to the dead bodies of the orcs that surrounded it. Rooting around, the orc retrieved two javelins and another axe. Clipping the axe to its belt, the orc turned to Thea. "I am ready."

Thea stared at the orc towering above her. She hadn't thought about orcs being male or female before—they had just been monsters—but this orc was certainly female. "You said you have a name?"

"Ulga."

"Pleased to meet you, Ulga. I am Thea, and this is Inyoni. Would you like to carry her again?"

Ulga held out a hand, and Inyoni scrambled up the orc's arm to perch high on the orc's shoulders.

Thea tried to steady her shaking hands. "Come with me. There are some people I'd like you to meet."

Thea stepped out of the clearing and found Msizi, Ulfgar, and Ember waiting for her. They stared in shock as Ulga emerged behind her. Ember crouched and Ulfgar's hand went to his axe.

"Wait!" Thea gestured. "This is Ulga. She saved Inyoni from the other orcs and she wants to come with us." Thea took a deep breath. "*I* want her to come with us."

A smile crept across Msizi's face.

"What?" Noxolo stepped out from the trees, her spear raised.

Thea held up a cautioning hand. "Ulga loves children. She wants to protect the Faunlets."

"Oh." Noxolo frowned. "Doesn't everyone love the Faunlets?"

"Even one of the orcs, it would seem. Noxolo, would you go and explain that to the others?"

Noxolo nodded and disappeared back through the trees. Inyoni laughed, drumming her hands on Ulga's smooth head.

"We should keep going." Msizi spoke in a low voice. He glanced up at Ulga. "Welcome to the Resistance." Turning, he led the way.

"You!" Ulfgar turned on Thea, shaking his fist. "Of all the hairbrained things—at least take me with you next time!" He stomped off after Msizi, muttering to himself.

Ember set a hand on Thea's shoulder. "Well done, Spark."

Joy welled up inside Thea. Yes, she was the Spark, and even a monster could find mercy. Offering Ember her arm, she helped the Dryad limp back towards the others. Another one of the Dryads joined them, in the form of an elk, and Ember accepted a ride.

"Everyone stay close together," Msizi called. "I'm going to speed up our travel, and we don't want anyone left behind."

A distant clang of metal echoed through the trees.

"Orcs are coming," Ulga growled. "I will fight them."

"No, Ulga. Not yet," Thea urged her. "We need you with us."

Ulga frowned. "I will fight and they will not follow you."

"What if we run into other orcs on our way? There must be hundreds out there."

"Thousands."

Thousands? Thea stared. The sounds of pursuit grew louder behind them.

"Come on, Ulga." Thea gestured as Msizi quickly cast his magic.

The orc relented and followed as they set off through the trees.

As they ran, the forest streamed past them, faster and faster. Thea jumped and dodged past obstacles, her mind and reflexes quickened just as much as her pace.

When they finally stopped to catch their breath, the sounds of pursuit still rang through the forest behind them.

Thea looked at Msizi in dismay.

He sighed. "They must have a caster with them, using magic to match our speed."

"That's no good," Ulfgar frowned. "Why run if we'll have to fight them anyways?"

Ember nodded. "If we set up an ambush—"

"No." Ulga stepped beside Thea, comprehension magic still allowing them to understand her words. "You cannot ambush them. Orcs can see every one of you. You shine like torches with the light that is in you."

Thea looked at Ulga in surprise. "You mean the light of the Deity? Orcs can see that?"

"Yes. That is how we were made." Ulga stared towards the sounds of pursuit, growing ever nearer. "It lets us find our targets very well."

"But does it help them spot trip wires tied between

the trees?" Msizi's eyes twinkled.

A grim smile spread across Ulga's face. "With their prey so close, they may not notice that. If we stop them, the children will be safe."

Msizi scratched his head. "I don't suppose either of you have any wire on you?"

Thea shook her head. She didn't have anything that could stop the orcs, but—

"Sylica! Can you make a trap?"

Sylica trotted over to join them. "What kind of trap?"

"I don't know, a pit or something. For the orcs to fall in. You've made a well before, why not something like that, just bigger."

Sylica grinned. "Sure. I could do that."

With a rumble, a huge portion of the ground started to cave in. Fauns and Dryads hurried to get out of the way.

"We need to keep going," Noxolo urged them. The sounds of the pursuing orcs were closer every moment.

"Just a breath." Sylica gestured at the pit and it disappeared, as if it had never been there.

"What—" Noxolo began.

"Oh it's still there," Sylica grinned, "but reality wants it to look like that, so it was easy to cover it up. Come on!" She scampered off through the trees, and everyone else ran to catch up.

Moments later, a chorus of shouts and cries erupted from the forest behind them, with a rumble of collapsing dirt and stone.

The Resistance hurried on. When they stopped again to catch their breath, the forest behind them was silent.

"Oh good," Noxolo grinned. "We lost them."

Ulga turned to her with a frown. "Do not

underestimate my people. We were made to do one thing, and we do it very well."

Msizi stared thoughtfully through the trees. "We can probably afford to slow down a little. The Faunlets are getting tired."

"It's not just the Faunlets," Ulfgar muttered, sinking down onto a moss-covered log. He rubbed his bandaged shoulder and winced.

All too soon, Msizi urged them on again.

As they settled into a more sustainable pace, Ulga strode beside Thea with Inyoni in her arms, taking one stride for every two strides of the Fauns.

Thea watched her with interest. "You said you are the elite of your war band. What does that mean?"

"I *was* the elite of my war band. Now they are dead. I killed them." Ulga walked in silence for a moment. "The elite is the one who has defeated all the others in combat. I was also head of the elites, because I beat the other elites in combat. I did not beat the chief in combat, or I would have been chief of my tribe."

Thea stared in surprise. "You've only fought in one combat that you've lost?"

"You misunderstand me. I did not beat the chief in combat because I did not want to." Ulga's gaze looked far away. "I had too many questions. If I was chief, they would know. I did not want them to know."

"What kind of questions?" Thea ventured.

"If the one who created us is good, why did he create soldiers to kill all who oppose him? If the bright ones are the enemy, why were we ordered to kill all those we meet, not just the bright ones? Those are the tactics of someone wishing to dominate by fear, not someone seeking to make things right." Darkness clouded Ulga's face. "Those questions were very ... dangerous. When I realized I could not follow my orders, I knew my life was over."

Thea looked up into the orc's brooding gaze. "It's not over, you know. It might just look a little different."

Ulga's frown sank deeper. "There is no other life for an orc."

"Perhaps." Reaching up, Thea ruffled Inyoni's curly hair. "Or maybe that's another question you weren't supposed to ask."

Staph stretched into restday, and the remnants of the Resistance pressed on through the endless trees.

"So, where are we going, anyways?" Noxolo asked, quickening her pace to trot along beside Msizi.

"Good question," Msizi grinned. "I'm just getting us out of the forest. After that, I'm not sure. Thea?"

"We will go to my house," Thea replied. "We will be safe there."

"Nowhere is safe from the orcs." Ulga's weapons rattled against her metal skin as she walked. "Wherever you go, they will follow until they make their kill."

Thea glanced over her shoulder. The forest behind them was still silent. She turned to Msizi. "Head towards Gedwyld. My home is just north of the city."

"Gedwyld. Target 4."

Thea looked up at Ulga. "Target 4?"

"We were given four targets. The Spark, the Resistance, the House, and Gedwyld. We should not go there. It will be surrounded very soon."

Fear rose in Thea's heart. "Msizi, we have to warn them!"

Msizi nodded. "Swift Wing!"

A Dryad with a bright red streak of fur down the back of their head and neck trotted over to join them.

"The orcs are going to attack Gedwyld. Can you fly ahead and warn them?"

"Sure," Swift Wing nodded. "Who do I tell?"

"Go to the lord of the city, if you can," Thea supplied. "If he's busy, find the head of the healers. She serves the Deity under Raphea and she will listen to you. My home is north of the city, along the coast. You can meet us there."

Swift Wing nodded. Shifting into the form of a hawk, the Dryad took to the sky and was soon out of sight.

Kaji ruffled her feathers.

"Not this time, my friend," Ember murmured, stroking the giant eagle's back.

Msizi swung a Faunlet up onto his shoulders. "Well, we'd better keep moving."

As they set out again, Thea could feel Ulga's keen stare. She looked up at the orc. "The house you mentioned, is it the house of the Spark?"

"Yes."

Thea's heart sank. More danger for the Resistance. Still, if they made it there before the orcs, they would be safe.

Ulga strode at Thea's side. In her arms, Inyoni was asleep, her curly head resting on Ulga's shoulder.

Thea considered her in silence for a while. "You said one of your targets was the Spark. Do you know who that is?"

"Yes." Ulga's keen gaze pierced Thea again. "We were given a description, but that was not necessary. Your spirit is brighter than anything I have seen. It almost hurts to walk so close to you." Ulga's expression became thoughtful. "Somehow, that pain seems good."

Thea looked away. How could her spirit be bright like that when she had failed and caused so much hurt?

Around her, the Resistance stumbled on, fatigue showing on every face. Thea glanced at Ulga again. She was so used to seeing other people's spirits. It was strange to think that someone could see hers.

"What's that?" Noxolo hissed.

Thea listened. Stamping feet and the rattle of weapons on metal drifted through the forest before them.

"More orcs." Noxolo's face was grim.

Ulga drew her axe. "Someone hold the child."

"Wait," Msizi gestured. "I still have magic. If we go fast enough we can get around them. Come on."

The Resistance raced through the forest, sped by the magic of Enkeli. Two more times they had to change their course to avoid other parties of orcs, but as Micai grew large in the sky, they found themselves on the banks of the river.

Msizi glanced at Thea. "Do we cross here?"

Thea nodded. "If we can. Further downstream it will only get wider."

Msizi turned to Sylica. "What kind of bridge can you make me?"

Sylica stared around the riverbank. "Branches and river weeds."

"Good enough," Msizi grinned.

Thea stared as the logs, branches, and weeds that lined the banks of the river began to move, knitting together into a makeshift bridge floating across the surface of the water.

"I'll try it first!" Sylica cried. Sliding down the

riverbank, she raced across the bridge with Daisy at her heels. The bridge bobbed and swayed beneath her, but it didn't come undone.

One by one, the Fauns followed. The golden-eyed Dryad, Fell Claw, hovered overhead in case someone fell in the water.

Kaji carried Ember across the river, then flew back. Nudging Ulfgar with her giant beak, she waited until Ulfgar had scrambled onto her back, then soared across the river again.

A clattering rumble echoed through the forest. Thea turned as a company of orcs erupted from the trees behind her.

"Look out!" Noxolo yelled.

In the distance, Ulfgar yelled. A glimmering golden shield appeared, flashing between the Resistance and the charging orcs. With a clatter, javelins struck its shimmering surface and fell to the ground.

Dark magic surged, and the shield disappeared.

Casters. Thea reached for Raybow, but Ulga shoved Inyoni into her arms.

"Go," Ulga ordered. "I fight."

Noxolo flourished her spear. "Keep crossing!" she yelled, gesturing the other Fauns towards the bridge.

With a sweep of her axe, Ulga beheaded the first orc. Noxolo charged the second.

Clutching Inyoni, Thea backed towards the bridge.

She blessed Noxolo's spear, and it sank deep into the orc's stomach.

Ulga dodged a blow and struck another orc on the shoulder, severing their arm.

A blow from an orc's mace struck a Faun and he stumbled back, collapsing at the top of the riverbank.

Fell Claw dove, snatching the Faun in their claws the moment the orc's killing blow came sweeping down.

"Go!" Ulga yelled, waving Noxolo back towards the river.

Holding Inyoni tight, Thea slid down the slope and ran across the bridge. It swayed and shifted beneath her. Branches and clinging bits of river weed came loose, drifting away downstream in the relentless current.

"Here!" Ulfgar reached his good arm down the slope and grasped her outstretched hand, helping to haul her up the steep riverbank. Noxolo followed close behind.

Ulga stood alone at the far side of the bridge. Several orcs lay dead at her feet, but more and more pressed down on her.

"Ulga!" Thea called. "We're all across! Come on!"

Giving an extra wide sweep with her axe, Ulga jumped back and skidded down the slope, thundering across the bridge towards them.

Magic surged. Thea counterspelled, and one of the orcs winced. For a moment, the magic wavered, then it exploded across the river.

The bridge disintegrated. Ulga leapt for the bank, scree sliding beneath her feet as she scrambled to the top.

Weeds erupted from the river. Wrapping themselves around Ulga's legs, they dragged her back towards the water.

Shoving past Thea, Ulfgar grabbed Noxolo's spear, and with a surge of magic, threw it across the river. It struck the caster with an explosion of light.

"Ha!" Ulfgar yelled. "Get smite!"

"Hey!" Noxolo protested. "That was *my* spear!"

The caster staggered, then tumbled down the slope into the water.

The weeds entangling Ulga fell limp. She vaulted up the bank and wheeled to face the orcs, a javelin in her hand.

The caster in the water did not move. The rest of the orcs slunk back out of throwing range, talking to each other in low voices.

"Come on," Msizi gestured. "While they're still thinking."

Ulga hesitated, then handed her javelin to Noxolo.

The Resistance ran on, away from the river. Slowly, the endless trees gave way to half-forested hills and scrubby grasslands. Faunlets were passed from arm to arm. Shadows deepened, and the green-blue light of night fell across the land. The fitful breeze bore the smell of salt in the air.

Through the trees ahead, a sudden red light flared. Screams tore through the silence, drowned out by an orcish roar.

Ulga shoved Inyoni into Thea's arms and drew her axe. All around her, the Resistance grabbed their weapons and started running towards the sound.

"Fell Claw!" Ulfgar shouted. "Got a lift?" As Fell Claw shifted into the form of a giant eagle, Ulfgar jumped on their back, diving like an arrow towards the flames that rose higher and higher.

Thea ran. Emerging from the trees with the rest of the Resistance, she saw an old split rail fence, and beyond it, a house and barn in flames.

With a shout, the Resistance burst into the farmyard, still hastened by Msizi's magic. Orcs wheeled to face them and were thrown to the ground by the force of their charge. Ulga swung her axe, smashing orc heads left and right.

The door of the house hung on its hinges, wreathed in flames. Ulfgar's voice yelled over the roar of the fire, and a chair smashed through a window, tumbling to the ground in a shower of glass.

A slight figure climbed out of the broken window. As soon as its feet touched the ground, Kaji swooped down and grabbed it, soaring off into the night. Ulfgar scrambled out of the window, a child clinging to his neck.

Setting Inyoni by the fence, Thea ran to Ulfgar and took the child in her arms.

The child writhed and fought. "The baby!" she shrieked. "Get the baby!"

"Where?" Thea demanded.

The child pointed at the burning house.

"Ulga!" Thea screamed. "There's a baby inside!"

Ulga wheeled and charged into the flames.

Thea stared in horror, shielding the child in her arms. The house shuddered, and a corner of the roof caved in. The flames leapt higher. Thea stumbled back from its heat, afraid to tear her eyes away.

The wall exploded and Ulga leapt through, crouched over a tiny bundle held tight in her arms. The house collapsed into a raging bonfire behind her.

The child tore herself out of Thea's arms and ran to Ulga. The orc placed the bundle in the child's outstretched arms and sank to her knees. Her back glowed as red as iron in a forge.

"Ulga!" Thea gasped.

Ulga gestured her away. "Take care of the child."

Thea forced herself to turn away. Tears streamed

down the child's face as she clutched the baby. Thea urged her to move further from the blazing fire. Once they were a safe distance away, Thea crouched down to speak with her. "Your parents. Do you know where they were?"

"Daddy went to the city." The child's words choked in terrified sobs. "Mommy went out the door when the monsters came, but she didn't come back."

Thea stared around the farmyard. Harsh shadows danced across the hard, trampled ground, littered with rubble and the bodies of orcs. Fauns ran back and forth, leading animals out of the burning barn.

"Wait here." Thea ran back towards the remains of the house. If there was any chance the mother survived …

In the shadows behind a crumbled bit of stone wall, Thea found her, prone on the ground, trying desperately to crawl away from the heat of the flames. Her clothes were soaked with blood and she stared up at Thea through swollen eyelids in a bruised and blackened face.

Reaching beneath the woman's arms, Thea tried to help her to her feet. "Ulfgar!" Thea yelled. "Ember! Someone help!"

Msizi appeared from the shadows. Lifting the woman on either side, they half dragged and half carried her beyond the reach of the fire.

Across the farmyard, the slender boy hurried out of the door of the barn, leading a horse by the halter. Behind him, Noxolo emerged carrying a goat that kicked and struggled to get away.

Fell Claw swooped out of a barn window as the flames blazed higher.

"Sylica!" Thea called. "Bandages!"

Sylica scampered across the farmyard. Dumping the contents of her pack on the ground, she rooted around for her medical supplies.

Gently, Thea peeled back the woman's torn, bloody clothes. Her shoulder was badly maimed by some kind of crushing blow.

"I'll help." Ember stepped beside Thea. "The father is here. You should go speak to him."

A man stood at the edge of the yard, staring at the destruction with horror and dismay.

"Daddy!" The girl ran to him, carrying her precious bundle.

"Eleanor!" The man wrapped her in his arms. "Are you alright? Is Brock alright?"

"I think so, Daddy." Tears streamed down the child's face. "Daddy, the monsters attacked us!"

A movement across the yard caught the man's eye. "Jason!"

The boy came running, leading the horse. "We got all the animals out, Daddy."

His father embraced him. "Jason. You shouldn't go back in a burning building. That was dangerous."

"The Fauns helped me, Daddy."

The man stared, as if seeing the Fauns for the first time.

Noxolo approached, the goat still struggling in her arms. She looked up at the man with his stubble beard and shock of brown hair covering half his face. "Your son is brave," she said in a strong Faunic accent. The goat gave an enormous kick, throwing itself out of her arms and scampering away. "Your goat is an ass."

The man stared at her, his mouth hanging open.

Fell Claw swooped towards him, shifting into human

form to land on the ground. "We did all we could, sir. Sorry we couldn't save the buildings."

The man stared at the Dryad as if he had seen a ghost. "You ... you just ..."

"Excuse me," Thea interrupted, stepping beside them. "Will you come? I think your wife needs you."

The man's face went paler than it already was. He followed Thea until he caught sight of the woman lying on the ground. "Melinda!" he cried, rushing to her side.

The woman looked up when she heard his voice. Reaching out, she held his hand, a gentle smile creasing her bruised face.

"I'm so sorry," the man stammered. "I came as soon as I heard ... I should have been here."

Ember laid a comforting hand on the man's shoulder. "Your family is safe now. The orcs didn't have their way tonight."

"I heard there were monsters." The man looked up with haunted eyes. "The news came to Gedwyld and I came as soon as I could ..." He stared. Across the yard, Ulga walked towards them, limping, her axe in her hand.

"This is Ulga," Thea quickly interjected. "She is an orc who decided not to follow the Enemy anymore. Ulga, this is Melinda and ..." She glanced at the man.

"I'm Dunstan," the man stammered. "I don't—I don't understand."

"We are the Resistance," Thea explained. "We fight against evil and protect the people of Raphtova."

Dunstan stared from Thea, to Ulga, to Fell Claw and Noxolo. "Thank you," he whispered. "Thank you for saving my family."

"They're not safe yet." Fell Claw spoke in a grim

voice. "We need to go before more orcs arrive."

Dunstan looked down at his injured wife. "But how—"

"Allow me." Kneeling down, Fell Claw waited by Melinda's side. Gently, Thea and Ember lifted her up, and Fell Claw shifted beneath her into a large, gentle horse.

Dunstan stared, still clinging to his wife's hand.

"Everyone together!" Msizi called. "We're moving out!"

The Fauns gathered together, herding the Faunlets between them. Some led cows, others held chickens beneath their arms.

"That goat is a lost cause," Noxolo grumbled, stepping beside Thea. "And it can stay lost for all I care."

Thea turned to Dunstan. "Do you know of the old stone building, about a measure's walk north of Gedwyld?"

"Aye," Dunstan nodded. "It's not far from here."

"Could you lead us there?"

Dunstan nodded. "This way."

Walking beside Fell Claw and Melinda, Dunstan led the way down the long, winding lane and out onto the road.

Thea walked beside Ulga. "Are you hurt?"

A shudder rippled across Ulga's metallic skin. Her back was cracked and peeled, but no longer glowed hot. "I am not as hurt as any of you would have been." Ulga's face remained impassive. "The children are safe. That is what matters."

"You were very brave to save that baby."

Ulga looked at her with a blank, guarded expression.

"Orcs are not brave. They are just orcs."

"That's not true, Ulga." Thea watched a spark of light flicker deep in Ulga's spirit. "You have shown us there is more to you than that."

Rounding a bend in the road, they came within sight of the old stone house, silhouetted against the night sky. Eagerly, Thea hurried on, ahead of the others.

Stepping through the gate, she found the windows bright with light. A hum of voices filled the air.

The door opened, and a Little stepped out. She wore simple working clothes, and her wild mass of hair was tied back from her face.

"Elora!" Thea gasped. "I'm so glad you're here!"

Elora looked at Thea, then at the crowd of Fauns, Dryads, humans, and animals that poured in through the gate behind her, bloodied and dirty.

"Thea." Elora put her hands on her hips. "What is going on?"

Chapter Four

"Am I not allowed to bring guests to my own house?" Thea grinned and crouched down to Elora's height, giving her a warm embrace.

Elora's smile was grim. "I know the look of people running for their lives. It's not so long since it was my people."

Thea sighed. "I guess it is very similar, isn't it?" She stared at the milling crowd. "They need protection. The orcs are coming."

"I knew something was coming." Concern clouded Elora's face. "That's why we're here. It's the safest place I know."

Another Little stepped through the door. He was a bit taller than Elora, with sandy-brown hair and a gentle face. "Elora, what—" He stared at the chaos that filled the courtyard.

"Kais!" Thea gave him a warm smile. In his arms was the tiniest, most delicate infant she had ever seen.

"Elora!" Thea gasped. "Is that—"

"This is Adi." Elora caressed the baby's tiny head.

"She's ten days old now," Kais beamed. "Isn't she perfect?"

"She's beautiful!" Thea smiled. "Congratulations, both of you."

A shriek rose from the crowded courtyard, and Sylica sprang towards them, with Daisy at her heels. "Is that your baby? Let me see! Oh your baby is the cutest baby ever!" She squealed in delight. "Can I hold it? Pleeeaaase?"

Elora gestured Sylica through the door. "Inside, where it's warm."

Kais turned to Thea. "Will you join us?"

"I will," Thea assured him. "I just have some people to take care of first."

Elora gave Kais a questioning glance.

"Go on," Kais nodded. "I know you want to help."

Elora sprang lightly down the steps after Thea. Fauns milled around the courtyard, while Faunlets scampered underfoot. Ulfgar and a few others were attempting to herd the animals into the stable.

"H'yup!" Ulfgar yelled, smacking a cow on the rump. "On with you!"

"What about the chickens?" Noxolo called, a struggling bird beneath each arm.

Thea and Elora pushed through the crowd. Dunstan stood beside the golden-eyed horse, still grasping his wife's hand.

"Fell Claw," Thea called, "bring her right inside, if you can. Then see if someone can find her a bed."

The crowd parted and Fell Claw moved gingerly up the steps. Shifting just small enough to fit through the door, the Dryad carried Melinda inside. Dunstan followed.

Thea found Eleanor, still holding the baby. Sending them inside, she hurried towards the stable. There she found Jason caring for his family's horse.

Ulfgar hustled down the corridor between the stalls. He nodded to Thea. "Is that all of them then? Oh, hi Elora."

Elora stared at his bloodied armour and arm wrapped in a dirty sling. "Ulfgar! You look half dead!"

"Been worse than that, since I last saw you," Ulfgar grinned and engulfed her in a one-armed bear hug.

"Wait—you've been *worse*?"

A hawk's cry rang out from beyond the stable walls.

"Swift Wing is back!" Thea grinned. "Come on, there's time for the story later."

In the courtyard, Thea found the Dryad with their telltale streak of red hair. "You made it to Gedwyld?"

Now in human form, Swift Wing nodded. "They're on alert now. The gates are closed and they're mustering the guard."

"Any sign of the orcs?"

"Everywhere. At least two companies on the road between here and the city. Homesteads and farms are burning all over the place."

Thea glanced at Elora. "I don't think you'll be getting home any time soon. Is Zaki here with you?"

"No. He didn't want to come." Elora frowned. "But Grandmother is there, if he needs someone."

"Good news?" Msizi asked, joining them.

"The city was warned, but it looks like the orcs are everywhere now," Thea explained.

The Faun nodded. "It sounds like we'll be here for a while, then. How many rooms have you got?"

Thea glanced around the busy courtyard. Faunlets laughed and chased each other across the flagstones. Full-grown Fauns cleaned their weapons. By the gate, Kaji beat her massive wings. "Probably not enough of them."

"I'll show you around," Elora offered, leading Msizi towards the house.

With the animals cared for, Noxolo and several of the Fauns made their way inside. Ember limped around the gardens to find a place for Kaji. The rest of the Fauns did their best to round up the Faunlets and herd them inside.

Thea found Ulga standing alone by the wall. Using the last of her magic, she cast comprehension one more time.

"This is the house?" Ulga asked.

"Yes. This is my home."

"Why did we come here when I said it is a target?"

"It's the safest place I know of."

Ulga stared at it thoughtfully. "It is full of light. Like you."

"Would you like to come in?"

Ulga was silent for a moment. "I will."

Together, they approached the door.

Thea glanced up at the stern-faced orc towering beside her. "My home is your home, for as long as you want it."

Ulga gave her an amused glance. "Are you sure you want to make that offer? Orcs live forever, if they are not killed."

"Really?" A smile crept over Thea's face. "Elves live forever too." She watched the small flicker of light, deep in the orc's spirit. "My offer stands."

Thea stepped through the door. Inside, the great room was full to overflowing. Fauns were everywhere, talking and laughing. Faunlets skipped around the room and hung from the windowsills. Inyoni saw Ulga enter and scampered across the room, waving her arms to beg Ulga to pick her up.

Everywhere Thea looked, there were people. In the

kitchen, Alya, Gili, Tam, and Talia were busy cooking an enormous batch of eggs and sausages on the stove. Ulfgar and Ember leaned on the large counter that separated the great room from the kitchen, having a lively conversation with the Littles.

The human girl, Eleanor, stood by the fire with Kais, each with a baby in their arms. Her brother Jason ran back and forth, carrying things for the Fauns. A large, broad-shouldered woman sat at the table, cloaked in furs.

"Hi Thea!" Sylica weaved her way through the crowd, handing out candies to anyone who would take one. "We put Melinda in your bed upstairs, I hope that's okay. It was the comfiest bed—I tested them all to make sure. Want a candy?"

Without thinking, Thea accepted the candy and slipped it into her pocket. "Is she doing alright?"

"I think so," Sylica grinned. "She fell asleep right away and Dunstan is there with her."

"Good. Want to see if the Littles need any help in the kitchen?"

As Sylica scampered off, Thea went to join those standing by the fire. Ulga followed, with Inyoni clinging to her back.

Kais looked up, startled, as Ulga approached.

"This is Ulga," Thea explained. "She's an orc, but she turned against her war band to save Inyoni, this baby Faun."

"She saved Brock too," Eleanor added. "She went into our burning house to save him." The baby in her arms seemed enormous compared to the delicate baby Little.

Kais held Adi up into the light. "This is Adi." Tender

concern creased his forehead. "No one's had to save her yet."

Ulga's hard, stoic face stretched into a gentle smile. Reaching out a hand that was as large as Adi's entire body, she stroked the baby's head with an outstretched finger. Inyoni hammered enthusiastically on Ulga's domed head.

The broad-shouldered woman at the table nodded a greeting. "You look like a good hand with a blade." She grinned up at the imposing bulk of the orc.

"She's one of the best," Thea replied.

"This is Brandy." Elora crossed the room to join them. "She came a couple of days ago, about the same time Kais and I did."

"Something was going on." Brandy tapped the table knowingly. "The woods and the beasts were acting strange. That's no time to be alone in the wild."

"When did Alya and the others come?" Thea glanced towards the kitchen.

"They were already here when we came," Elora replied. "It makes quite the crowd, doesn't it?"

Thea stared across the room that had once been so empty. This was what her home was meant to be. Humans, Littles, Fauns, Dryads, all talking and laughing together. Most of them were stained with blood and dirt and hadn't bathed in far too long, but it was the most beautiful sight Thea had ever seen.

"Food's up!" Alya called from the kitchen. "Wash your hands, or you don't get any!"

By the time everyone had eaten, it was well into the night. After consulting with Msizi, it was decided that the large meeting room upstairs would be used as a bedroom and nursery for the Faunlets. With a communal effort, the young Fauns were herded upstairs and left with a few older Fauns to watch over them.

The human family was given the use of Thea's room, since that was where Melinda was already asleep. Thea suggested that Elora and Kais occupy the small sitting room attached to her bedroom, since it was the best chance they'd have of any privacy in the crowded house.

One of the bedrooms was already claimed by Alya and the other Littles, and the two remaining bedrooms were given to the Fauns.

Thea was kept busy running up and down the stairs, trying to find enough blankets for everyone. Thankfully the heating pipes the Littles had installed were working well, so none of the rooms were cold.

Ulfgar waved his tankard at Thea as she ran past for the fifth time. "You thought you had a house," he called with a grin. "Turns out you have an inn, and a busy one at that!"

Sylica had declared that she and Daisy would sleep by the hearth in the great room. The Dryads also agreed that this would suit them very well, and Brandy said that a corner by the fire was all that she wanted. Ulga indicated that she would sleep in the kitchen.

Finally it seemed as if everyone was settled, at least well enough. Thea joined Sylica, Brandy, and the Dryads by the fire. Ulfgar was there too, along with Msizi and Noxolo. Ulga sat alone, sharpening her axe.

Elora watched them all with a keen gaze. "I want to know what happened," she crossed her arms, "starting with you, Ulfgar. You hugged me, and you've smiled more in one evening than the entire time I've known you. What's going on?"

"I jumped off a cliff and met Micai," Ulfgar grinned,

gesturing with his tankard. "But honestly," his eyes grew thoughtful, "I'm not afraid anymore. And it's good."

"The Fauns and Dryads are a part of the Resistance," Thea explained. "We met them on our way to the Dragons." She hesitated. Well, she would have to explain what happened sometime. It might as well be now. Briefly, she shared the tale of their journey, their time with the Minathrils in the mountains, and her part in Hwasan's betrayal, with the events that followed after.

Elora nodded. "Where does that leave us now? You said the orcs are close?"

"I saw them on the road," Swift Wing replied. "If they haven't found this place yet, they will soon."

"This house is safe," Thea assured them, "but we should still set up watches."

"The Resistance will keep watch," Noxolo grinned, her hooves stretched out towards the fire. "That's what we do."

Brandy leaned forward. "We will need more supplies if we're going to stay here long. I'll get a hunting team together in the morning, and we can cut heather to make more beds."

Swift Wing nodded. "And we'll make sure the injured get the care they need. That includes you, Ember and Ulfgar."

Ulfgar scowled, but Ember laughed. "Come on, Ulfgar. The sooner you and I are on the mend, the sooner we'll be out there hunting orcs."

"Speaking of being on the mend," Elora interjected, "you all look exhausted and the night's half gone. Go sleep, and we can make more plans in the morning."

Slowly, the crowd around the fireside dispersed.

"Fell Claw, you take first watch," Noxolo called. "I'll whip the others into shape and we can take short turns for tonight."

Msizi and Elora disappeared up the stairs. Brandy pulled a rough woven blanket out of her leather bag and lay down in the corner of the room. Sylica curled up with Daisy by the fire.

Thea stood alone, the adrenaline of the day slowly draining from her body.

"You alright?" Ulfgar stumped across the room to her side.

Thea looked down at his dirt-smeared face and bloodied shirt. "I think I need a drink."

Ulfgar patted her back. "And I know just the spot." He led Thea through the kitchen and the pantry, down the steps into the cool dark of the wine cellar.

"Here." He handed her a mug. "Sit down and have a drink."

Thea sank to the floor and leaned her back against the cold stone wall. Exhaustion swept over her like a wave.

"Been a tough day, hasn't it?" Ulfgar murmured, easing himself to the floor beside her.

Before Thea had finished the contents of her mug, she couldn't keep her eyes open any longer. Curling up on the hard stone floor, she fell asleep.

Chapter Five

When Thea woke, a dim glow of daylight illuminated the stairs from above. Her blanket was tucked around her, but Ulfgar wasn't there.

Slowly, she pushed herself into a sitting position. Every muscle in her body ached and her head pounded. Finishing the contents of the mug that still sat on the ground beside her, Thea forced herself to stand and climb the steep stairway leading up to the pantry.

She stepped out into the kitchen, blinking in the full light of day. The murmur of voices filled the air, but the only person in the kitchen was Ulga. She handed Thea a dish filled with porridge.

"Food. Eat." Ulga spoke in Common, her voice thick with the sounds of the orcish language.

Thea stared, still more than half asleep. "You know Common?"

Ulga seemed to consider this, then hazarded, "Yes?"

"You're learning."

Ulga considered this again. "Yes."

Taking her bowl, Thea stepped out into the great room. It was filled with people. Several large basins from the kitchen had been filled with water, and some of the Fauns were busy washing and bandaging their wounds. Others were cleaning their weapons. Elora seemed to be presiding over the room, giving orders, making sure the water was being changed for fresh, and that the assorted weapons were kept out of the reach of the rambunctious Faunlets.

Thea pulled a chair up to the table, where Kais and Fell Claw also appeared to be eating a late breakfast. "How was the night?" Thea asked the Dryad.

"It was quiet, from what I hear. No orcs yet."

Thea nodded. "Where's Ulfgar?"

"Out in the forge. Fixing something for Sylica."

"Is Sylica there too?"

"Yes. And quite a few Faunlets from what I saw." Fell Claw grinned.

An infant's cry drifted down the stairs, rising above the general hubbub. Kais jumped to his feet.

"Sit," Ulga ordered, appearing beside him. She marched across the room and disappeared up the stairs, reappearing a few moments later with the tiny baby cradled in her hand. Gently, she handed her to Kais.

"Thank you." Kais smiled tentatively. "She's probably hungry." Excusing himself from the table, he disappeared across the crowded room.

Thea finished her breakfast in silence. Where could she go to check in? The room hummed with noise, but maybe silence wasn't always necessary. Bowing her head, Thea closed her eyes and waited.

Well done. Allulien's voice was impressed upon her spirit as the glow of magic returned. *Now rest.*

Rest. Every part of her body ached for quiet, for a place to be alone. Leaving the table, Thea's steps led her through the maze of Fauns and up the stairs. The murmur of voices wasn't so loud up there, though lively chatter from the Littles' room and shrieks of laughter from the Faunlets drifted through the air.

Thea wandered down the corridor and stopped by

Roland's door. It wasn't Roland's room anymore. Remembrance hit her like a punch in the gut. Roland was gone.

A Faun trotted out the door, nodding a greeting to Thea. Thea nodded in reply. Averting her burning eyes, she stepped into her room. Melinda was in her bed. Of course, she couldn't be alone there. The small table Roland had made for her was covered with cloths and bandages. A Faun sat beside the bed, gently washing Melinda's shoulder.

Thea's heart ached. Zanele should have been there. She could have done so much to help. An image of Zanele's body, bloodied and dead, rose in Thea's mind. She turned away, tears stinging her eyes. All of this was her fault. If she had just followed her orders, none of this would have happened.

Thea stepped out into the hallway. Maybe she would go back to the wine cellar. She needed somewhere to be alone.

"Thea?" Ember stood at the end of the hallway.

Thea didn't have the heart to respond.

The snow-white Dryad watched her with thoughtful eyes. "Do you have a moment?"

Thea shrugged.

Ember gestured for her to sit, and sat down beside her in the empty corridor. "It's heavy on you, isn't it?"

Thea stared at her hands. They ached where she had scrubbed the blood off.

"I heard your story when you were telling Elora. It hurts when your actions have such consequences for others."

Tears stung in Thea's eyes. So many Fauns had died, and who could know who else? How many had died on the homesteads and farms where there was no one to save them from the merciless orcs?

"It's like that in the Resistance." Ember rested a gentle hand on Thea's shoulder. "It's life and death. Any mistake we make means danger or death for our friends. I have watched leaders of the Fauns make choices that killed many of their people. It hurt, and sometimes it tore them apart inside. But the best thing they could do for those who survived was to find peace with it, somehow, and have mercy for themselves. Then they could look forward and start to rebuild."

Thea's heart ached. "I don't know how. When it's someone else, that's different, but I should have known better."

"Anyone can make a mistake. Even the wisest people on Raphtova."

Even the Elves. Thea sighed. That hurt most of all.

"Everyone here loves you, Thea. They don't hold anything against you. Will you hold it against yourself?"

Thea looked up into Ember's gentle gaze. "I'll try not to."

Ember smiled.

Downstairs, a door banged. "Get Thea!" It was Swift Wing's voice. "The orcs are coming!"

Jumping to her feet, Thea hurried down the stairs. All around the great room, Fauns were grabbing their weapons.

"Wait!" Thea called. She glanced around the room. "Swift Wing, Fell Claw, Msizi, come with me. Where's Ulga?"

Ulga stepped through the door from the kitchen, her giant axe in her hand.

In the courtyard, they found Noxolo trying to herd

the Faunlets inside. Kaji paced along the wall, making agitated clicking noises.

Casting comprehension, Thea rested a hand on Ulga's arm. "We shouldn't have to do anything, but I wanted a few of us here to make sure."

"Not do anything?" Ulga frowned.

The clang of weapons on metal rang in the distance.

"Is no one shutting the gate?!" Noxolo demanded, one last Faunlet beneath each arm. Pushing them through the door, she slammed it shut and started running for the gate.

"Wait, Noxolo," Thea called. "We don't need to shut it."

Noxolo opened her mouth to protest.

"Obey the Spark," Ulga growled.

Beyond the gate, a company of orcs approached.

"Oh." Swift Wing gave a small laugh. "I didn't see those ones."

"How many are there?" Fell Claw asked in a low voice.

"This place has been surrounded by one hundred orcs at least," Ulga replied in an even voice. "They will be sure that you do not escape this time."

The largest of the orcs drew its sword.

"Um, Thea?" Swift Wing ventured. "That's a lot of orcs."

A command rang out, and the orcs thundered towards the gate, weapons gleaming.

Noxolo grabbed her spear.

Fell Claw shifted into wolf form and crouched to spring.

At Thea's side, Ulga's muscles tensed.

The moment the orcs stepped in front of the gate,

they stopped, as if running into an invisible barrier. Stepping back, they tried running forward again, only to be stopped in exactly the same place. They shouted, they swung their weapons at the air, but they could not move forward another step.

Noxolo's mouth hung open.

Msizi nodded, a smile creeping across his face.

Fell Claw shifted back into human form. "What are they doing?"

"They are trying to get in." Ulga turned and stared at Thea. "Why can't they get in?"

"Come with me." Thea led Ulga back into the great room and gestured at the carvings on the doorframe. "The magic of the Deity is on this place. No evil can enter here, and no one in this place can do harm to another. It is a safe place, beneath the protection of the Deity."

Ulga stared at the inscription. "No evil can enter here?" She frowned. "Then why am I here?"

Thea looked up at the orc towering beside her. "Because you are not evil. The orcs were made by evil, but they do not have to *be* evil. They can choose."

Ulga's eyes scanned the inscription again. "And how does it work? If they climb the walls or tunnel underground, can they get past it?"

"The musharocs could not find a way in, and I've seen the protection include the basement two floors down. I don't think there is any way past it."

"And if someone enters without meaning to do harm, then once inside chooses to do harm?"

Thea considered Ulga for a moment. What would happen? Clenching her fist, she swung it with all her strength towards the orc's stomach. Her arm froze in mid-air.

Around them, the Fauns erupted into cheers.

Ulga gave her an incredulous glance. "That would have hurt your hand much more than it would have hurt me."

Thea grinned. "I guessed as much, but now we know. Even if the orcs get inside, they cannot hurt us."

"They will not leave until they make their kill. That means a siege."

"A siege?" Brandy rose from her seat by the fire. "We don't have what we need to get *five* through a siege. How will we survive it?"

"A siege does not mean we are trapped." Ember smiled. "We Dryads can fly beyond the orcs, to hunt for food and bring news from Gedwyld."

Ulga glared. "The orcs will shoot you from the sky."

"We will be careful."

"And bring back food for how many people?" Brandy raised an eyebrow. "Plus animals?"

"We will do what we have to. I'll go talk with Swift Wing and Fell Claw now."

Thea followed Ember outside. The white Dryad still walked with a limp, one leg wrapped tightly with bandages.

The other Dryads were watching the fuming orcs with expressions of great amusement. Quickly, Ember explained the situation to them.

"I can fly messages to Gedwyld," Swift Wing grinned. "It's hardly any distance at all!"

"We can scout too," Fell Claw suggested. "Then we'll know what the orcs are doing."

"You will not scout." Ulga strode out the door to join them. "Did you not hear when I explained it before?

You are all bright. Your spirits show that you serve the Deity. The orcs will know you are there long before you see them."

"Is my spirit bright?" Brandy stepped beside Ulga.

Ulga considered her for a moment. "No."

Brandy squared her fur-covered shoulders. "I'm no Resistance fighter. Never prayed in my life. But I don't love the Adversary either. If I scout, they won't see me."

"But how will you get out?" Swift Wing asked.

"I can fly her," Fell Claw replied. "If we fly far enough, the orcs won't see my light."

"We are not the only ones who can fly." Ember gave an eagle screech, loud and startlingly real.

Kaji hopped around the corner of the building and sidled up to Ember, nudging the white Dryad with her beak.

Ember ran a hand along the giant eagle's back. "Kaji is good with a rider, but her rider is gone."

A lump rose in Thea's throat. It was strange to think of someone other than Thabani riding her.

"Aren't I a bit big?" Brandy frowned.

"Short distances will be alright. Kaji has carried two of us before, in an emergency. It will be enough to get you over the wall and out of sight. Fell Claw can help you train."

Fell Claw nodded.

"I'll fly down to Gedwyld," Swift Wing offered. "I want to see how they're doing."

Ember nodded and Swift Wing took to the sky, soaring high above the walls.

"Look! Look!" Sylica cried, running to join them from the far side of the house. "Daisy is all better now!" Daisy scampered along at her side. The battered dent had been bent back into shape, and the little metal dragon glittered as it jumped and yapped excitedly. Ulfgar strode after them, his hammer resting on his good shoulder.

"That's wonderful," Thea smiled, giving Daisy a suitable amount of admiration.

Sylica beamed with delight, showing off Daisy's newly repaired back to anyone who would look.

Excusing themselves, Fell Claw and Brandy disappeared around the side of the house. Kaji hopped after them.

Thea stared at the stable with a thoughtful frown. It would be one thing for the Dryads to bring in enough food for all the people, but collecting fodder for the animals would be an entirely different matter, and with the Great Sleep upon them, it was only going to get harder.

"Sylica," Thea called, interrupting her in telling the tale of Daisy's injury for the third time, "if there's any hay or dried grasses nearby, do you think you could transport it into the stable? We need food for the animals."

Sylica cocked her head. "Oh. Sure, I could do that."

Thea watched her with interest. Sylica had done something like that before, collecting wood to make a funeral pyre. A startled whinny rose from the stable.

Thea hurried to open the door. The stable was filled from floor to ceiling with hay.

"Um, Ulfgar?" Thea called. "Could you help me with something?"

It was at least two measures before the stable had been emptied of excess hay, and the heaps of fodder had been carried away for storage in the other outbuildings.

There was an enormous pile of chicken feed too, which was shovelled into baskets and placed aside for later.

Exhausted and dusty, Thea stumbled back into the house. Ulga caught sight of her and looked her up and down. "Sit," she ordered, pointing to a chair by the fire. Thea sank into it gratefully and closed her eyes.

When she opened them again, the room was quieter than it had been. From the courtyard, she could hear Noxolo's voice raised above a murmuring hubbub.

Msizi watched Thea from across the hearth. "Training," he grinned.

Thea rubbed the sleep from her eyes. "That's good. Sorry I was asleep, I was just so tired."

"That's alright." Pulling up a chair, he joined her by the fire. "I thought you'd like to know that there aren't many bodies at the farmsteads around here. It looks like most everyone escaped to Gedwyld."

Thea frowned. "How did you—?"

Msizi grinned. "Enkeli is good at getting people into places they're not supposed to be."

Thea considered this. "I always thought Enkeli was the General of wisdom and knowledge. That's what the Elves teach."

"That's a part of it. But what good is wisdom and knowledge if you can't share it? That's what the messaging and transportation are for."

A thought grew in Thea's mind. "You can message people. Have you tried to contact Thabani?"

Msizi looked down into the crackling flames. "Enkeli told me not to. Other things are more important."

Thea's heart sank. "So who is leading the Resistance now?"

Msizi shrugged. "Someone usually steps up when the

last leader is gone. It looks like it's Noxolo this time. She was already doing a lot with Thabani."

"What about you?"

"Oh, I'm no leader." Msizi made a wry face. "I'm no fighter either, for that matter. I'll just take my orders from Enkeli."

Ulfgar joined them, shaking bits of hay off his shirt. "Well, Thea, it might be a good time to get out those trollsbane weapons, what with an army setting up camp outside the walls."

Thea nodded. "You know, I think that's a good idea."

Getting up, she gestured for Msizi to follow, leading the way to the old lean-to with its newly-finished toilet rooms. Pulling an inconspicuous rope down from the ceiling, Thea looped it through a small hook on the floor and pulled. A portion of the floor rose, revealing steps that stretched down into darkness.

Fetching a lantern, Thea led the way down the stairs and along the stone-lined corridor below.

Green light shone in the shadows ahead. Cautiously, Thea ventured forward, stepping through the door into the old workshop.

Two lanterns cast their green luminous glow, hanging from hooks in the ceiling. Alya, Gili, Tam, and Talia looked up in surprise as she entered.

Thea stared. "What are you doing here?"

"Making things," Alya grinned, gesturing to the workbenches and tables that filled the room.

"I can see that," Thea stammered, "but this is a magical workshop. It could be dangerous."

"Pipers are used to working with dangerous things. If there is a workshop, it should be used."

"But how did you find it at all? You didn't come

down here before."

"We were having trouble getting the tub upstairs," Alya explained. "The knives you gave us came from down here, so we came down to see what other tools there were." She glanced around the cluttered workshop. "There are lots."

"We finished with the tub," Tam grinned, "then came back to see what else we could make."

"Look at this," Gili piped up, holding a small jar. "There are two powders in it. If you shoot it with an arrow, I think it will blow up."

Msizi deftly slipped the jar from Gili's fingers. "Very interesting." His eyes glittered. "Don't want to try that down here, but it might be useful later."

"Whatever you do," Ulfgar shook a finger at the Littles. "Never tell the Faunlets this is here."

"We won't," Tam grinned. "That's why we come in through the tunnel." He pointed at the tunnel leading out to the forge on the far side of the garden.

"Whenever you make something, tell me first." Msizi watched the Littles with a thoughtful expression. "I want to know."

Cheerily, the Littles agreed. Leaving them to their tinkering, Thea stepped back into the corridor and entered the small room where rows of weapons and armour lined the walls.

Msizi's eyes glittered. "Wait till Noxolo sees this."

"I'll bring her down later," Ulfgar offered. He strode along the wall, tapping the metal of the blades experimentally. "These weapons are trollsbane—strong enough to cut a rock in half. Pretty effective against orcs too, from my experience."

"I've never seen armour like this." Msizi fingered one

of the mail shirts.

"It's all Elvish work," Thea explained, "and made in the magical workshop by someone who used to live here."

Msizi shook his head. "Sure would have helped the Resistance, having gear like this."

"I know." Thea sighed. "But all the special equipment in the world didn't help the Elves when they decided to abandon the war and leave for their island."

"That's why you need the Fauns." Msizi winked. "We don't give up."

Thea smiled.

Climbing back up the stairs, they closed the trap door once again and stepped out into the great room.

Dunstan stood by the fire. Thea went to join him.

"How is Melinda doing?"

"Much better." The worry lines creasing his face were not as pronounced as they had been.

"I'm glad. Do you think she'll be strong enough to get up soon?"

"She's already up and in the kitchen." Dunstan gestured. "Couldn't keep her in bed any longer." He gave a helpless smile.

Thea went to look. Melinda sat in a chair in the middle of the kitchen. Her shoulder was bandaged and her arm was in a sling, but her eyes were bright and her face didn't show any pain. Bare-topped, she was nursing Brock while ordering Ulga around the kitchen. The massive orc collected bowls and measuring cups and the various ingredients that Melinda called for.

Inyoni hung off Ulga's back, giggling and trying to poke her hand into the food. Adi was tucked in the crook of Ulga's arm.

"You take the flour—no, the *flour*," Melinda ordered. "Those are eggs. The *flour*. There you are. Now the salt. *The salt*. Give it here. Thank you." Balancing her infant on her bandaged arm, she demonstrated to Ulga the proper way to measure a pinch of salt.

"I could cast comprehension," Thea offered.

Ulga shooed her away and turned back to watching Melinda.

Remembering Ulga's interest in learning Common, Thea grinned and returned to the fireside.

Excited voices clamoured out in the courtyard. A few moments later, Swift Wing stepped through the door in human form and waved to Thea. "I bring messages from Gedwyld for you and Elora!"

"I'll get Elora," Dunstan offered.

As Dunstan disappeared up the stairs, Swift Wing stretched. "The Lord of Gedwyld sends his regards. The farms have been evacuated and everyone is behind the walls. They're planning to keep everything closed up until the orcs get tired of waiting and leave. I told them what Ulga said about the orcs not giving up, but at least they have the sense to stay behind their walls and not try to fight. He'd like me to bring news every day, if I can."

Thea nodded. "As long as it's safe, I don't see why not. It would be good to know if Gedwyld is having any trouble."

"They're well-supplied for the Long Sleep, from the sound of things, but their walls are just walls. There isn't any magic keeping the orcs out."

"At least they have a guard." Thea frowned thoughtfully. "I'm not sure how well they're trained, though."

"I brought back a couple of fish," Swift Wing added with a grin. "Fell Claw is gutting them now."

Elora hurried across the room to join them, with Kais following behind. "You have a message?"

"Sami was up at the castle when I was there. She says not to worry about them, and that you'd be glad to know all the folks from the farms have places to stay."

"Is Zaki doing alright?" Kais asked.

"Sami thinks so. Apparently he went up to talk to the lord of the city last night, but he didn't say why. Just something about an idea for defence."

"He's always had lots of ideas." Worry creased Kais' forehead. "His parents were like that too. We missed them after they died."

"Zaki won't get himself killed." Elora set a reassuring hand on his shoulder. "He's a quick thinker. Anyways, he never leaves his room."

It wasn't long before Melinda called from the kitchen to announce that the evening meal was ready. The Fauns tramped in from the courtyard, and soon the great room was full to overflowing.

When the meal was finished, Noxolo's voice rang above the chaos. "Right, first watch! Get yourselves outside and keep your eyes open!"

Other Fauns helped clean, or attempted to round up the Faunlets and herd them back to their room upstairs.

"Excuse me," Dunstan approached Thea with a shy smile. "Would you mind if I told a story? That's what I love to do, and it seems like a good evening for it."

"Of course!" Thea smiled. "That's a wonderful idea."

Dunstan stood by the fire, the dancing light gleaming in his eyes. "There's a story to tell," he said. His voice was low, but it carried through the room. "A tale from so long ago, it might have been yesterday ...”

Fauns, Littles, and Dryads gathered around to listen. Jason and Eleanor sat on the hearth, listening with shining eyes alongside the most obstinate of the Faunlets, now rewarded for their stubbornness.

Warmth filled Thea's heart. This was her house. Her "inn". Home for the Resistance, and a place where the races could be together, just like she'd always wanted. If only there weren't people missing ...

She drove that thought from her mind.

Everyone seemed content, or quietly busy with their tasks. She wasn't needed anymore. Slipping away, Thea returned to the only room where she knew there would be space for her. Surrounded by the fragrant shadows of the wine cellar, Thea wrapped herself in her blanket and fell asleep.

Chapter Six

Thea woke in shadow, but light trickled down the stairs to meet her. Across the wine cellar, Ulfgar snored. Softly, Thea slipped past him and climbed the stairs.

In the kitchen, Sylica was cooking a giant pot of porridge, while Ulga watched with an expression of concern. Daisy seemed to be doing all she could to ensure that she was underfoot as much as possible.

Bidding them all good morning, Thea slipped out the kitchen door and into the silence of the gardens. A chilly mist hung in the air, just beginning to glow yellow with the light of day.

Wishing she'd thought to grab her cloak, Thea wandered down through the gardens to a corner that was beyond the view of the house's many windows. She wanted to be alone for a while.

Kneeling on the cold, wet ground, Thea waited.

Allulien's golden light shone around her, bathing her in its warmth. With a smile, she looked up into her General's face.

Something about Allulien's expression made Thea pause. It wasn't the stern face of rebuke, or the joy-filled face that saw the best she could be. Instead, Allulien's eyes seemed thoughtful and preoccupied.

"What are my orders?" Thea asked, when the silence had stretched on for a very long time.

Allulien considered her for a moment longer, then

replied. "Enkeli has asked to borrow you. Until further notice, you will take your orders from them."

For a moment, Thea was speechless. "But ... but *you're* my General. I'm supposed to get my orders from you!"

"Enkeli wants you for something, and it will be much easier if they borrow you for it. Beneath Enkeli's orders, you will have access to Enkeli's domains of magic, not mine, and you will obey Enkeli as you would obey me. Those orders will come today."

"Today?" Thea stammered. "But I don't ... I don't *want* to serve under Enkeli! I never wanted that!" Images flooded Thea's mind of vast halls, stained glass windows, and dusty tomes.

Allulien's eyes flashed. "What is most important is that you are serving the Deity. Which General you answer to is of little consequence, compared with that."

Thea bowed her head. "Yes, Allulien."

"When Enkeli has finished with you, you will return to my command again." Amusement flickered in Allulien's eyes. "You do not need to worry about that."

Thea nodded, trying to quell the anxiety that gnawed in the pit of her stomach.

"Goodbye for the present," Allulien smiled. "Though I think I will be seeing you again soon enough."

Allulien disappeared. The warm glow of magic that Thea was used to feeling was absent. Silence rang in her ears.

"Enkeli?" Thea whispered. "You have orders for me?"

"Right. Orders." A voice drifted through the air. It was followed by a figure, like Allulien's in form, but this figure seemed to be carrying an armful of papers, shuffling through them hurriedly. "Here." Enkeli drew one of the papers from the pile and squinted at it.

There was something familiar about Enkeli. Thea stared, unable to understand why.

"In one measure you will leave for the ship," Enkeli read. "Be ready for transport." Shoving the incorporeal paper back in among the others, Enkeli turned to go.

"Wait!" Thea called. "What ship? How am I getting there?"

"Magic," Enkeli replied. Continuing to shuffle through their papers, Enkeli stepped through the garden wall and disappeared.

"But where is the ship going?" Thea called. Silence drifted on the early morning breeze. The glow of magic poured through her, like Allulien's, but this magic tingled in her veins. It made her want to move, to run, to do something.

She glanced around the empty garden. She had one measure and then she was going. Going somewhere. On a boat. She ran back to the house as fast as her feet could carry her.

Grabbing her pack, Thea sifted through its contents. What would she need? She still had Hwasan's rope and one of the Littles' lanterns. There was Raybow, of course, but she was getting low on arrows. She hadn't had a chance to fletch any more.

"What are you doing?"

Thea looked up to see Elora watching her, hands on her hips.

"I need to go." Thea swallowed. "Enkeli's orders."

"Do those orders say you should have friends with you?"

"Oh, Elora." Thea took her friend's hand. "I think it's just me. But everyone here needs you. Look after them while I'm gone."

"And where do you think you're going?" Ulfgar muttered, stalking across the room.

"I don't know," Thea admitted. "It must be important if it's taking me away from here."

Her eyes took in everything around her. It had just started to feel like home, and now she was leaving again. She looked down at the stocky man beside her. "You'll take care of my 'inn' for me, won't you, Ulfgar?"

Ulfgar nodded. "As long as this is where I am."

Thea smiled. "Thanks. I'll miss you both."

Ulfgar's frown was thoughtful. "I'm not the one leaving this time. That's different."

"Is there any way we can help?" Elora asked.

"I don't have many arrows. Could you see if there's any that will work for my bow?"

Elora nodded and slipped away.

Upstairs, Thea found Ulga in the Faunlets' room, with four Faunlets hanging off her shoulders. As soon as she saw Thea, she lowered them gently to the ground. "You need me?"

Not wanting to rely on Ulga's limited knowledge of Common, Thea cast comprehension. There was one similarity between Allulien and Enkeli, at least.

"I wanted you to know that I'm leaving. It's very sudden, I'm afraid, but I will come back as soon as I can."

Ulga frowned. "Where are you going?"

"I'm not sure, but I have orders from Enkeli to leave very soon."

"The orcs will kill you."

"I'm taking a boat. The orcs won't be able to follow me."

Ulga seemed to consider this.

"Who's taking a boat?" Sylica scampered into the room, with Daisy at her heels. "I want to take a boat too! Boats are so much fun!"

"Sorry, Sylica," Thea smiled. "It's just me. Everyone else is staying here."

"No." Ulga frowned. "Where you go, I will go."

"I'm sorry, Ulga. It's really just going to be me. We need you here."

Ulga bowed her head. "I follow your orders."

"No, it's not like that," Thea protested. "I'm not ordering you, I just can't take anyone with me. Enkeli is using magic to take me to the ship. That's all I know."

"Taking *us* to the ship," Sylica grinned. "I'm coming too!"

"No, Sylica, you're staying here. I told you that."

Sylica pouted. "But I *want* to come."

"I know. But I don't even know where I'm going, and we need you here. You can help keep everyone safe with your magic."

Sylica's face brightened. "I like using my magic! The Big Book says magic is like a shiny thing, and shiny things are even better when they're helping people. Did you know that? And Daisy likes shiny things too, don't you, Daisy?" Chatting cheerfully with her little dragon, she wandered out the door.

Leaving Ulga to watch over the Faunlets, Thea went back downstairs and into the pantry. Its shelves were worryingly bare. After a long, thoughtful silence, she walked away empty-handed. Wherever she was going, she would have more chances of finding food than the others would.

Collecting her gear, Thea pulled her oilskin cloak

around her shoulders. Something small caught the light, tumbling to the ground with a clatter.

The brooch from Roland.

Thea stared, loss aching in her chest. The little silver flower had meant so much to her. Gingerly, she picked it up and held it for a moment. Then she pinned it to her cloak. For memory's sake.

"Here." Elora joined her, holding out two black arrows. "I had some feathers ready, so I made these."

"Thanks, Elora." Accepting the arrows, Thea added them to her quiver. With her bag over one shoulder and her baldric over the other, she made sure Raybow was secure in its place on her back. "I think I'm ready to go."

Across the room, Msizi waved a farewell.

Elora smiled. "Stay safe out there."

Around Thea, the walls faded into open sky. The floor beneath her jerked and pitched—the deck of a boat on cresting waves. Salt spray dashed through the air as Thea staggered and grabbed the rail. Above her, a black sail creaked in the wind.

"The blazes are you doing here!" a voice exploded behind Thea. She turned. It was Svetka. Around her, the Raven surged across the waves, driven by the icy wind.

Svetka wasn't glaring at Thea, but at Sylica, standing by her side with a big grin spread across her face.

"And you!" Svetka turned her glare on Thea. "I expected you to turn up one of these days, but next time some warning would be nice!"

Thea stared. The Raven ... Svetka ... *Sylica?* How was that possible?

"Sylica!" Thea finally managed to gasp. "Did Enkeli send you too?"

"Nope," Sylica grinned. "I sent myself."

"But how ... why ..."

"Hate to interrupt," Svetka interjected, eyes blazing, "but you damn well better tell me what you're doing here, and why there's a bloody dragon dive-bombing my ship!"

"Oh!" Sylica grinned. "Hi, Daisy!"

Daisy landed with a clatter at Sylica's side, her large leather wings flopping wildly.

"This is Sylica," Thea gestured to her friend. "She's kind of an Elf, and this is Daisy, her metal dragon ... pet."

"*Friend*," Sylica corrected.

"Sylica, this is Svetka. She's the captain of the Raven."

"Oh!" Sylica grinned. "I remember the story! You won the race with the—"

"Shut up," Svetka glared. Salt spray glistened on her grey granite skin. "Let me guess. This is Khariton's doing."

"Enkeli, actually," Thea ventured.

"Oh. Khariton's boss. Figures." Svetka scowled. "Never know when someone's going to drop in out of nowhere. Bloody disconcerting, that's what it is. Ready about!"

Around her, the crew of the Raven sprang into action.

Thea clung to the rail, memories of her flight from Lyudmyla crowding her mind. The Raven appeared unchanged. It was like travelling back in time.

Far to port, distant shadowy mountains stretched across the horizon, but in every other direction was nothing but the vast grey expanse of the sea.

"Oh, that's shiny!" Sylica poked at some of the

navigational instruments fixed to the deck.

"Don't touch those." Svetka shot her a glare.

"But I was just wondering what—no, Daisy!"

Daisy froze, her tongue plastered to one of the instruments that gleamed gold in the salt spray.

"Leave it," Sylica scolded.

As Daisy slunk away, Sylica tried to wipe the slobber off with her sleeve. "There we go," she grinned. "That looks a lot better now—oops!" The instrument tumbled to the deck with a crash.

Svetka lunged after it, grabbing it just before it rolled off the side of the ship. Returning it to its place with the other instruments, she glared at Sylica. "Don't touch it."

The Raven surged on through the wind-swept sea. The spirits of the crew reminded Thea of the Minathrils she had met—the spirits of those working for good, but who did not directly serve the Deity themselves.

"So you're just dropping in, or ..." Svetka eyed Thea with a sardonic expression.

Thea shrugged. "I don't know what I'm doing. Just that I'm going somewhere."

Svetka snorted. "I guess you're along for the ride then." Her keen glance took in Thea's attire. "Still have the cloak, I see. Glad it got some use."

"I have the knife too," Thea offered, remembering once again how much she owed to the captain of the Raven.

"And the compass?"

"A crox stole it."

"Thieving buggers." Holding a line, Svetka stood up into the wind. "Two out of three. Not bad."

Thea watched Svetka's muscular form, braced against the dashing spray. "Do you really work for my uncle now?”

Svetka frowned and swung back down to the deck. “Kicked out of the league, what else were we supposed to do? At least we get to sail. We’ve gone further than we ever did with the league, so I guess it’s not all bad.”

Svetka’s first mate, Demyan, nodded a greeting to Thea. “Glad to see you again, and to meet your friend.” He turned to Sylica. “What did you say your name was?”

“I’m Sylica, and this is Daisy, my best friend in all the world.” Sylica grinned. “I like your boat, it’s a really pretty boat. Oh, is this where you steer it?”

“Don’t touch that,” Svetka glared.

“What, you don’t want to let her try?” Demyan’s face was innocent, but his eyes twinkled.

“Oh, can I?” Sylica squealed.

“*No.*” Svetka’s glare shot daggers through her first mate. “Demyan, why don’t you show Sylica the hold? I think she’d love it down there.”

“Ooh! Your boat has a downstairs?” Sylica squealed in excitement as Demyan ushered her away, with Daisy trotting unsteadily after her.

Svetka shot them one last glare and returned to her work.

Thea stood by the rail and stared out at the horizon. The mountains that spanned the western sky didn’t seem familiar to her at all. “Where are we?”

“The inner sea between the continent and Arvera. A scouting trip for Mykyta, though it sounds like we’re cutting it short for some reason. Got the message to head north just a couple days ago.”

Head north? An uncomfortable feeling grew in Thea’s mind. “So where exactly are we going?”

“Don’t you know?” Svetka gave her a keen glance.

"We're going to Lyudmyla."

Thea's heart sank. Lyudmyla? Images of the great capital city of the Elves rose in her mind. Lyudmyla, that had once been her home. Lyudmyla, where she would have sworn to never go again, if it hadn't been for a promise ... and now, orders from Enkeli.

"You weren't expecting that?" A wry smile lingered at the corner of Svetka's mouth.

"No." Thea sighed. Maybe she should have guessed. It seemed like everything kept pointing her back to the one place she didn't want to go. Salt spray dashed across her face and she shivered.

Svetka shot her a glance. "I'm surprised Roland isn't with you."

Thea felt her face stiffen. Roland. Did this mean she would have to see Roland? She stammered. "He—he already left for Lyudmyla. He doesn't know I'm coming."

"Oh, going to surprise your lover boy, then?"

"He's not my lover boy." The words leapt out, stronger than she intended.

Svetka raised an eyebrow. "Had a fight, did you?"

Thea stared down at the churning waves. It was more than a fight. She could still see the hurt in his eyes when she'd called him nothing but an Elf. Deep down, they were all the same, the Elves. She wanted nothing to do with them.

So why was Enkeli sending her back?

"Do I need to give him a talking to?" Svetka's eyes gleamed with the light off the glittering waves. "I will, you know."

"No." Thea sighed. "It was my fault, really."

"He can be a bit of a dumbass," Svetka reflected. "I'll

talk to him."

"No, I'd really rather you don't." Thea looked at the captain in alarm.

Svetka laughed. "Alright. If you say so." She shook her head and shot a glare at several members of the crew loitering nearby. "What are you staring at? Make yourselves useful if you have nothing better to do."

Thea watched the windswept waves roll by, grey with the shadow of the clouds overhead. There was nothing she could do. She was going to Lyudmyla, and by Enkeli's orders.

A chorus of laughter rose from below deck. Thea froze. Sylica was down there. With a horrible sense of misgiving, Thea hurried to see what she was doing.

There was hardly any room below deck, just a few narrow bunks and a small table, but several members of the crew had crowded around Sylica. Thea ducked and squinted through the gloom. It appeared that Sylica was attempting to build a small tower of candy on the table, but every time the boat pitched or swayed, the candies went tumbling to the ground. The sailors watched with amusement and some confusion.

"Sylica," Thea ventured, "I don't think they want their floor covered in candy."

"But I almost did it—oh, it fell down again. I know I can do it, though. Just one more try!" She snatched another handful of sweets from the bag that teetered precariously on the edge of the table.

"Careful, you'll spill your bag," one of the sailors laughed.

"Oh, that doesn't matter," Sylica grinned. "See?" Grabbing her bag, she dumped it over the table. Candy poured out, in a quickly-growing heap.

The crew laughed, then their eyes widened as the candy continued to pour out onto the table.

"Sylica," Thea watched their growing alarm, "I think you should stop now. That's enough."

"But there's lots of candy for everyone!" Sylica grinned.

"They don't need lots of candy!"

The hubbub grew louder as the sailors stared in disbelief. The endless stream of candy continued to pour out of the bag and skitter across the table, tumbling to the floor below.

Suddenly everyone was silent. Thea glanced over her shoulder.

Svetka stood behind her, staring at the chaos. "What are you doing to my ship?"

"Just sharing some candy." Sylica grinned nervously, glancing down at the drifts of candies that covered the tiny floor. "It's kind of a mess, isn't it?"

"You think?"

Sylica flinched. "Sorry."

Svetka's eyes narrowed. "Clean it up." Turning, she stormed away. Thea hurried after her.

She caught up to Svetka at the stern of the ship where she stood alone, staring out at the turbid water. Svetka didn't acknowledge her presence.

"Sylica means well," Thea ventured. "I'm sorry. She wasn't supposed to come with me, but—"

Svetka shot her a piercing glance. "If you don't explain what just happened down there, I will throw you overboard."

"Oh, that was Sylica. She has a magical bag of candy that is never empty."

Svetka raised an eyebrow.

"Her Uncle Bob made it. He was an artificer, from what I understand."

"Huh." Svetka pursed her lips, her eyes scanning the horizon. Far to the south, a shadowy shape stood out against the sky.

Svetka nodded towards it. "That ship's been back there for two days. It keeps changing course to follow us, but we've kept it far to stern." A smug smile flicked across her face. The Raven was fast, and she knew it.

Thea stared at the distant sail. If it had been following the Raven for two days it wouldn't have anything to do with her ... would it?

"Demyan!" Svetka glared sharply at the first mate who was passing by.

"Yes?" Demyan waited attentively.

"What are you eating?"

"A candy." A flicker of amusement crossed Demyan's eyes.

"And you didn't bring one for me?"

Sauntering across the deck, Demyan dropped two candies in Svetka's outstretched hand.

"Go on," Svetka ordered, gesturing him back to his work. Shooting Thea a wink, she popped the candies in her mouth and turned away.

"Look!" Sylica grinned, poking her head up through the hatch. "Now I have a whole bucket of candy!"

Thea spent the rest of the day doing her best to keep Sylica out from underfoot. It seemed that whenever she turned around, Sylica would reach out to touch something or Daisy would trip someone. Still, Thea reflected, it could be worse. Sylica hadn't tried to start a dance yet.

Finally, they shared the crew's simple meal and were

offered two of the bunks for the night. As Sylica's snore rose above the creaking and swaying of the ship, Thea breathed a sigh of relief.

Leaving her bunk, Thea climbed back onto the deck. The wind had blown the clouds away, and the planet Micai filled the sky overhead. Thea leaned on the rail and watched its green-blue light shimmer on the rolling waves. Every measure that passed carried her closer to Lyudmyla and further from the place that she really wanted to be.

It was her home now. Ulfgar and Elora were there, and Ember and the others, doing their best to save the remnants of the Resistance. She should be there with them. Instead, she was sailing for a city of wealth and comfort, far away from dangers her friends were facing.

Svetka leaned on the rail beside her. "Looks like you're having a good day."

Thea sighed. "I can't believe I'm going back to Lyudmyla. That's all."

Svetka shot her a wry glance. "I can't believe I'm working for the Chancellor, but here I am. It's a strange old world."

"But I don't want to go back to the Elves! They're so proud and dead. All their stuffy ritual and hypocrisy has killed them inside. I hate it."

"I hear you. Can't choose your family, though."

Thea looked at Svetka's sea-worn face. "My family locked me up and tried to stop me from obeying the Deity."

Svetka nodded. "They're still your family, though. Funny how that is. We're Elves whether we like it or not."

Thea stared down at her amber diamond skin,

smoother than it used to be. It wasn't soft like a Little's or hairy like a Faun's. She couldn't change form like a Dryad or change colour like a Minathril. She was an Elf, and she would never stop being an Elf. Maybe Sylica wasn't the only one who didn't want to face who she really was.

Thea sighed. "How long will it take to get there?"

"From here? Two or three spans, most likely."

Thea froze. She hadn't considered that it could take so long. It was bad enough that she had to go, but she'd been hoping to at least get it over with so she could go back home!

Her surprise seemed to amuse Svetka. "We have to sail around the far north of the continent to get to Larsya. That's no short distance."

Thea's heart sank. Of course, it had taken her more than two cycles to walk all the way to Gedwyld, but what about her friends, defending themselves against the orcs? What about Svetka and her crew, with two more people to house and feed on their tiny ship? Thea's eyes widened. What trouble could Sylica get into during two or three spans at sea?

Svetka gave her a wry smile. "Welcome aboard."

Chapter Seven

Thea woke in the shadowy hold of the Raven, wedged into one of the narrow bunks. Gingerly, she extracted herself and sat up. She was alone, but voices drifted down from above, along with the creak of ropes and the sound of dashing waves. Around her, the ship lurched unsteadily.

Waiting in the shadowy darkness, Thea bowed her head and waited to hear what Enkeli would say. The sounds of the ship continued, but within there was silence. Maybe there wouldn't be any new orders until she reached Lyudmyla.

Making her way up onto the deck, she found Sylica talking cheerfully with the crew, who appeared to be enjoying her account of the fight with the stone golem.

Svetka nodded a greeting. "Sylica is full of interesting tales, it seems. I look forward to hearing Roland's version."

Thea shifted uncomfortably. If they got to Lyudmyla soon enough, maybe Roland wouldn't even be there yet. After all, she had made it back to the Resistance much faster than she should have because of Sylica's magic.

Sylica's magic! Thea looked eagerly at her friend. If Sylica could make them travel fast, it wouldn't take as long to get to Lyudmyla!

Waiting for a pause in Sylica's tale, Thea pulled her aside. "Could you use your magic to make the Raven go faster?"

Sylica blinked in surprise. "Sure, I could do that. I still have most of my magic juice for today."

"Wait—" Thea's eyes widened in alarm. "Have you already used magic juice?"

"Of course I have. I'm using it to talk the Elf language."

Thea stared. Of course, ever since they arrived on the Raven, everyone had been speaking Elvish. Why wouldn't they? She'd never known an Elf who had learned another language. You didn't need to, when you only ever spoke with Elves. It had been so familiar to Thea, she hadn't noticed.

"It's a nice language." Sylica nodded thoughtfully. "You know, I never thought about using my magic for talking before, but it makes so much sense! Then I can talk as much as I want and I don't need a translator!"

Thea thought of all the times she'd chosen not to cast comprehension while Sylica was talking. There was no safety for her hapless audiences now.

Across the deck of the Raven, Svetka stared at the southern horizon. The sail was still there. Was it larger than it had been? Thea couldn't say for sure.

She hurried to Svetka's side. "If we could make the Raven sail faster, would you agree to that? We'd leave that ship behind and we'd get to Lyudmyla sooner."

"In a rush now, are you?" Svetka gave her a keen glance.

"Just to get things over with."

"Hmm." Svetka thought for a moment. "Come here."

They walked together to the bow of the ship. The western mountains still spanned one side of the horizon, but now Thea could see a second, smaller range of mountains to the east.

"We're approaching a narrows, of a sort. Not too dangerous, but we'll have to watch for rocks. Save the extra speed for once we're through."

Beneath the shadows of the western mountains, a dark shape moved across the water. Thea frowned. "Is that another ship?"

Svetka stared with narrowing eyes, then turned to Demyan. "We have company."

The first mate sprang to the helm, as all around the Raven the crew took their racing stations, waiting for Svetka's command.

The new ship was ahead of them, sailing towards the narrows on a parallel course. Svetka eyed it with a calculating glare. It was too far away to know what its intentions were, but she clearly didn't trust it.

As the narrows grew steadily nearer, the unknown ship maintained its position ahead of the Raven. One of the crew gave a shout and pointed off the starboard bow as another ship shot into view, leaving the shelter of a wide river mouth. Under full sail, it swept towards the narrows.

"Two ships ahead, and another following behind." Svetka glanced at Thea. "Who's after you this time?"

"I can't think who it would be," Thea protested. "*I* didn't even know I was coming, so who else could have known?"

"Whoever they are, they're trying to intercept us, and they're aiming for the narrows." Svetka watched them with a calculating gaze. "They're fools if they think the Raven will be caught that easily." A smile crept across her face. "It's racing time."

"Oh, are we racing?" Sylica squealed in excitement.

"I love racing!"

"Demyan," Svetka's eyes didn't leave the approaching ships. "Would you take care of our guest?"

With a clang, the door to the hold swung shut and Demyan returned to his post.

Thea clung to the rail as the narrows surged closer. The two ships ahead of them drew closer too. They were bigger than the Raven, with trolls and humans crowding their decks. Weapons were in their hands.

A wild light gleamed in Svetka's eyes as the Raven leapt over the waves.

"Steady!" Svetka roared.

Magic surged, coming from both ships at the same time.

Thea threw her own magic into a counterspell. One surge ended, but on the other ship the sails grew larger, propelling it forward to match the Raven's speed. As it swept closer, grappling hooks sailed through the air, crashing onto the Raven's deck. Shouts of alarm tore through the icy wind as the crew rushed to throw them off.

Magic surged again and the grappling lines were pulled tight, slamming the Raven against the side of the enemy ship. Thea tried to counterspell, but another surge of magic swept over her and the Raven shuddered beneath her feet.

Two casters. She couldn't stop them both at once.

Humans and trolls leapt onto the Raven's deck. Weapons flashed. Shouts and cries rang out.

Where was Sylica?

Dodging a swinging sword, Thea grabbed the door to the hold, pulling with all her strength.

As the heavy door swung open, Sylica grinned up at

her. "Hi Thea! Can I come out yet?"

"There's casters," Thea gasped. "I can't—"

Magic surged. One of Svetka's crew staggered past, ropes coiling tightly around their body.

"Hey!" Sylica yelled, pushing past Thea. "That's not nice!" With Daisy at her heels, she stormed towards the ship that gripped the Raven's side.

Thea turned to face the other ship, drawing an arrow. Where was the caster?

Around her, the fight raged on. Blades clashed. Cries and screams tore through the racing wind.

Svetka stood frozen, a curved sword in her motionless hand. She glared at the distant ship, nostrils flaring wide. "Damn you," she hissed. "Get out of my head!"

There—Thea caught a glimpse of the caster's dark spirit. The ship was sweeping further away. She couldn't make a shot like that.

What about magic? She couldn't cast charm anymore. What could she do?

What could Msizi do?

With her own surge of magic, Thea cast transportation. The caster reappeared a stone's throw away from the ship, and with a scream, plunged into the churning water.

Svetka staggered.

Demyan grabbed her before she fell. "You alright?"

Svetka nodded and gripped her sword. "I'm going to kill something."

Demyan let go.

Svetka plunged her sword into the closest human, then kicked him off the deck.

Lashed side-to-side, the two ships swept through the

narrows at an alarming speed. Before them, the channel narrowed—the swirl of the waves betraying the presence of rocks just below the surface of the water.

Thea stared. "Svetka!"

As she took in the danger sweeping towards them, Svetka's eyes narrowed. "Demyan!"

Demyan kicked his opponent in the chest, then turned and raced for the hold.

"Steady!" Svetka yelled.

People stopped and stared. A hubbub broke out on the deck of the boarding vessel. Shouts of "Rocks!" rose over the wind as the enemy crew scrambled to cut the lines that bound them to the Raven.

"Hold on!" Demyan's voice rang above the chaos.

Thea clung to the rail as the Raven listed wildly and the enemy ship fell astern. The churning water of the shallows was all around them, racing past in a shower of spray.

The Raven shuddered, lurching Thea to her knees. Sounds of splintering wood and cries of dismay filled the air.

With a rush, the sea fell away from beneath them. Thea clung to the rail and stared. The Raven was flying!

Below them, the shallows surged past, while on the Raven silence fell, as if they were being carried on a cushion of air. Swooping lower, they touched down in the channel beyond the shallows, with hardly a splash.

The crew stared in disbelief.

"The blazes?" Svetka thundered. "What just happened to my ship!"

Thea glanced at Sylica as astonished cries rang out around them. She looked very pleased with herself.

Svetka stormed over to them. "And just what was

that? Even Khariton hasn't pulled something like that on me yet!"

"That would be Sylica." Thea gestured apologetically. "She has Dragon magic."

"*What* magic?"

"Magic juice!" Sylica grinned.

"And just what—"

"Captain!" one of the crew shouted, gesturing across the straight. The other enemy ship shot into view around the point.

"Damn." Svetka's mouth set in a thin, hard line.

"We're taking in water!" Demyan's voice rang out from the hold.

"Stuff your shirt in it," Svetka snapped. "We have bigger problems. All hands to your weapons!"

"Is that ship one of the problems?" Sylica ventured.

Svetka glared. "They happen to be trying to kill us."

"Should I make them go away?"

"*Yes!*"

The churning water in front of the enemy ship disappeared. With cries of dismay, the ship plunged down into the gaping hole before them and was gone.

The crew on the Raven stared. Water rushed to fill the hole in a torrent of waterfalls, sweeping the Raven off course. Thea clung to the rail as shouts of alarm rang out around her. Beneath them, the Raven listed dangerously in the turbulent water.

Light crackled for one blinding moment, and the roaring waves became calm, as if nothing had happened. The sea moved on with the surge of the tide, carrying the Raven with it.

The enemy ship was nowhere to be seen.

Svetka looked at Sylica with a thoughtful stare.

"Remind me not to make you mad at my ship." She turned and walked away.

Around her, the crew sprang into action, tying ropes that had been cut, pulling down the torn sail.

Svetka crouched by the door that led down to the hold. "You swimming down there?"

"Not yet," Demyan replied.

Svetka glanced at Sylica. "I don't suppose you can do something about the hull." Without waiting for an answer, Svetka climbed down into the shadows.

Thea followed. In the hold, she found Demyan, now shirtless, standing ankle deep in water. Svetka crouched beside him.

A tentative clatter made Thea glance over her shoulder.

Sylica blinked at them with wide eyes. "Is it broken?"

"It's mostly one board that's damaged," Demyan sighed, "but it's a steady leak. We'll be pumping it out all the way back to Lyudmyla."

"Oh." Sylica fidgeted uncomfortably. "I ... I don't think I was very careful with my magic juice. It's all gone now anyways, but I probably shouldn't do any magic for a while."

Svetka eyed her for a moment, then shrugged. "Well, we'd better start pumping." She climbed past Thea, shouting orders to her crew.

Sylica sat on one of the bunks, pulling her feet up beneath her. "Sit, Daisy. Lie down." Daisy lay down in the murky water. "Over a bit. There. Now you're on top of the hole. Good girl, Daisy."

Thea hesitated. "Are you coming, Sylica?"

"Daisy and I are going to stay down here. We'll fix the hole tomorrow."

Leaving her friend in the shadowy hold, Thea returned to the deck.

With a fitful wind at their stern, the injured Raven limped on through the straight. Thea did her best to stay out of the way, watching from her place by the rail as the crew worked, subdued and silent.

After a while, Svetka joined her.

"So, what were those ships after?"

Thea sighed. "To be honest, I think it was you and the Raven. A spy from the enemy joined us as we were travelling through the mountains. He used Roland to find out about the Resistance, and he learned about the Raven too. I don't think this is the last you'll see of ships like that."

Svetka snorted and stared out across the narrows.

"I knew the spy was trying to contact the enemy, but I chose not to stop him in time." Thea stared down at her hands. "It's my fault that you're all in danger now."

Svetka sighed. "There are many things that have happened in my life because of you. This is not the worst."

Thea opened her mouth, then shut it again.

Svetka raised an eyebrow. "You think I like working for the Chancellor? I can handle a few sea battles."

The next morning, Sylica used her magic to fix the crack in the hull, and the Raven surged forward again, with mended ropes and sails.

Thea used her transportation magic to speed their travel, and Sylica cautiously contributed her own magic too. It was hard to tell how fast they were actually going—the rush of the wind and the waves seemed the same as they had always been—but from the landmarks on the horizon, Svetka said they were making very good time.

The next day they rounded the northernmost point of the continent and set their course south-west for Larsya.

Thea didn't have much to do. They hadn't met any other hostile ships, and they probably wouldn't at the speed they were travelling. Thea sat near the rail, watching the mountains on the southern horizon. Her mind played over and over again the events surrounding Hwasan's betrayal. She could still feel the weight of his lifeless body and see Zanele's bloodied form. She could see the anger in Roland's eyes and feel the ache his absence had left behind.

"At least you could stop being a wet blanket." From her place at the helm, Svetka glared at Thea. "You've done nothing but sulk all day. Still pining after your lover boy?"

"I'm not pining." Thea's face grew hot. "People died, okay? Because of what I did."

The whole story poured out of her. Hwasan. Roland. The Resistance. Everything that happened that horrible day in the cave.

After she finished, Svetka was silent for a long time.

"So that's what your fight was about?" Svetka's mouth pressed into a thin line. "He really is an idiot."

"That's not what this is about!" Thea protested.

"Yeah. You screwed up. You said that." Svetka's gaze took in the far horizon. "Everyone screws up. Get over it."

"But—"

"People died. Sure, be sad about that. Death sucks." She shot Thea a keen glance. "You still have to face

Roland, though.”

Thea stared down at the surging waves. “I don’t want to.”

Svetka seemed amused. “You’re going to Lyudmyla. You think you can avoid it?”

“Maybe he won’t be there.”

“And you’ll never see him again for the rest of time? It’s better to sort it out sooner than later. Trust me on that one.”

“But I don’t know how! I should have told him about Hwasan, but I didn’t. That’s it, and it doesn’t make sense. Of all the Elves, he’s the only one who’s always been there for me. I don’t know why I couldn’t trust him.”

“You probably had a good reason.” Svetka shrugged. “What was it?”

“I don’t know!”

“Yes you do. You knew when you first set foot on this ship. If you hadn’t, you would have asked him to go with you.”

“But—but of course he wouldn’t have gone with me. He had to go back to the Eagle.”

“Well, there’s your answer.”

“But sailing was his life!”

Svetka rolled her eyes. “Exactly. That was what he actually cared about.”

“He still loved me though,” Thea stammered. “He said so.”

Svetka gave her a sharp glance. “He actually said that? Damn. I owe Demyan two silver.”

Thea blinked. “What?”

“The point is,” Svetka tapped Thea with a forefinger, “there were other things he loved, more than he loved you." She stared up at the great black sail, billowing in the wind. "He's an idiot. But we're all idiots, in our own way. Doesn't matter how good a thing is, if you're stuck on it." She sighed. "But just because people are idiots doesn't mean they don't deserve another chance. After a good tongue lashing."

Thea watched the waves churning along the side of the ship. "I guess I should try to see him, if I can, and say that I'm sorry."

Svetka shot her a keen glance. "Sorry for what?"

"For not telling him about Hwasan."

"You didn't need to tell him anything. You're his commanding officer."

Thea hesitated. "What?"

"You're the Spark, aren't you? You were the one who got the orders. Roland didn't have anything to do with it."

Thea opened her mouth, but found no words to say. She'd never thought about it like that before.

Svetka watched her with an amused expression. "I trust my crew with my life, but I damn well don't tell them everything."

The Raven surged on through the rolling waves. Sea salt glittered on the captain's grey granite skin.

"So." Svetka leaned against the helm. "Why didn't you tell Roland?"

"Because ... because I looked at him and I just saw an Elf."

"Very observant. He is an Elf. And?"

"Elves don't serve the Deity. Not really. They're slow and stuck in their ways and care more about their own ideas than what the Deity wants. Roland would have sent Hwasan away, I know he would have, even though the Deity wanted him to be with us. I couldn't trust that he would actually set aside what he wanted, to do what the Deity wanted us to do."

"You're right." Svetka's gaze didn't flinch. "He wouldn't have."

Thea took a long, slow breath. She was right. Relief faded into an ache deep in her spirit. She hadn't wanted to be right.

Svetka turned her attention back to the ship. "Am I an Elf?"

"No."

Svetka arched an eyebrow and lifted her arm, examining its stonelike surface with mock solemnity. "Interesting. I rather thought I was one."

"I mean you're not like that. You don't care so much about your own comfort or things always having to be the same."

Svetka nodded. "I'm an Elf, though. You're an Elf. Everyone on this ship is an Elf. Funny how that is." She gave a wry smile. "Elves are Elves, but they're not as slow as everyone says they are. They can change very quickly when forced. Sometimes all they need is a kick in the pants."

Even with magic to speed the journey, the distance to Lyudmyla felt long. The days passed and Thea watched the distant landmarks creep by. It had been so long since she had nothing to do but sit and think. It was good, but hard.

Svetka and Sylica appeared to have reached a truce. Svetka no longer threatened to shut Sylica in the hold for measures on end, and Sylica was careful not to touch any of the "shiny things", though her endless chatter still angered Svetka to no end. Generally, Sylica's one-sided conversations ended with Svetka foisting Sylica on Demyan or another member of the crew and storming away to as distant a point as could be achieved on the Raven's small deck. Sylica seemed unaffected by the captain's sardonic manner, however, and soon had exhausted every story Thea was familiar with, though that did not stop her from continuing to talk.

Finally the mountain island of Larsya appeared on the horizon. Passing it to the north, the Raven circled the island, heading for its berth in Rokhov. Thea stood at the rail and stared as the mountain loomed closer and closer. Soon the small town of Rokhov came into view, and beyond, grand houses and estates stretching up the vast slopes of the mountain—her first glimpse of Lyudmyla.

She was back.

Chapter Eight

As the Raven surged into the harbour, Thea stared at the narrow, ramshackle buildings and crowded docks. Sailors and hired hands loaded and unloaded cargo, their breath condensing in the brisk ocean air. Rough-skinned youths wrestled each other, tumbling off the dock to land with a splash in the icy water. Thin trails of chimney smoke drifted up into the clear, cold sky.

There was light in the spirits of those working around the harbour. In some it was only a little, but others were so bright they might actually be in the service of the Deity. Thea stared. It hadn't been like that before. Roland had said something about new recruits, but she hadn't expected anything like this.

She glanced up to see Svetka watching her with an amused expression.

"What happened here?"

Svetka made a face. "You want to be more specific?"

"It's different than when I left."

"You think the Raven is the only ship working for the Chancellor? Almost every ship here has done a run or two for him, and most are employed full time."

"For what?"

"His damn messenger service. There's people coming and going every measure of the day."

Thea glanced around the busy harbour. "I didn't

know his messenger service was that large."

"You know the Chancellor. He never does anything halfway. Apparently he wants to treat Rokhov like his own bloody shipping yard."

Turning, Svetka stormed off to yell at her crew.

Soon they were docked, and Thea stepped onto the wharf. Sylica and Daisy hopped down after her, skidding a little on its icy surface.

"Thank you, Svetka," Thea called, but Svetka had already gone. Demyan gave Thea a nod and strode after the captain.

Thea watched him go. Around her, the bustle and noise of the harbour carried on unchanged.

Now what? She hadn't received any further instructions from Enkeli. How was she supposed to know what to do?

"Look at all the boats!"

Sylica's squeal drew Thea back to the alarming reality that she was not alone. Sylica scampered down the wharf with Daisy clattering along behind her, drawing surprised glances and concerned stares.

Thea hurried after her. "Yes, it's a harbour. That means there are lots of boats."

"Can we go on them? Look at that one there! It's green like me!" Sylica scurried off to have a closer look.

"Sylica—wait!" Thea ran to keep up, trying to keep her footing on the slick boards underfoot.

As Sylica pushed past the Elves who populated the docks, people turned and stared—not at Sylica, but at Daisy scampering at her heels.

"Look! Look!" Sylica knelt beside the indicated boat and held up her arm to compare. "It's a Sylica boat!"

The Elf standing on the deck eyed her with a friendly

but cautious stare. "Look at that. You are about the same colour, aren't you?"

"We're *exactly* the same colour," Sylica beamed.

The Elf chuckled. "Well, close enough for—wait ... you *are* the same ... but my ship wasn't that shade of green!" Leaping down to the wharf, the Elf rubbed her hand along the side of the ship, staring in disbelief.

Thea gave Sylica a concerned glance. Had she just changed the colour of a ship?

Sylica did a little dance of excitement. "Now I have two best friends, a dragon and a boat!"

"Sylica!" Thea interrupted hurriedly. "We need to go now. Come on."

Pushing Sylica on ahead, Thea made her way through the gathering crowds.

"What is that?" another Elf asked, gesturing to Daisy. "Is it some kind of dragon?"

"Yes she is," Sylica beamed. "Daisy is the best dragon in the world! She can fly too, want to see?"

"Sylica!" Thea cried, but it was too late. Daisy shot up into the sky. All across the harbour, people stopped and stared. Shouts of surprise and alarm rang out.

Overhead, Daisy looped in circles, her metallic skin gleaming in the light. All around Thea, Elves jostled and pushed each other, staring in wonder at the glittering sight.

"It's not a real dragon," Thea assured them. "It's made out of metal."

"She is too a real dragon," Sylica glared. "She can even breathe fire!"

"No!" Thea threw herself at Sylica. "Don't you dare do that here!"

Sylica pouted. "I wasn't going to. I was just showing

them how special Daisy is."

Across the harbour, city guards emerged from the crowded streets.

"I think you showed them," Thea hissed. "It's time for Daisy to get down now."

"Oh alright. Come, Daisy!"

Daisy swooped towards the wharf, straight through the rigging of a nearby ship. Caught in the ropes, the little dragon flailed and writhed, winding herself in a hopeless tangle of knots.

Sylica gasped in horror. "Daisy's caught!" She threw herself towards the offending ship. "I'm coming, Daisy!"

Slipping and skidding along the icy dock, Sylica careened head first into a cleaning cart. Scrambling back to her feet, she crashed into a pile of barrels, which tumbled in all directions, splashing into the water and rolling along the wharf, leaving chaos in their wake.

"Hey!" voices shouted. "Watch yourself! What's going on?"

Sylica vaulted onto the deck and grabbed a rope, pulling herself up towards the flailing dragon.

Elves appeared on the deck of the ship, staring up at the tangled mess of ropes, the panicking dragon, and Sylica scrambling higher and higher. "Hey!" they shouted. "Get down from there!"

Thea hurried through the chaos that spread like wildfire around the docks. "Sorry—" She pushed past the overturned cart. "Excuse me. Let me through!"

Reaching the ship, Thea pulled herself up onto the deck.

"You!" One of the sailors stormed towards Thea. "Are you with her?" He gestured to Sylica, high in the tangled rigging.

Thea nodded, trying to catch her breath. Overhead, Sylica tugged at the tangled mass of ropes, hopelessly knotted around the panicking dragon.

"What do you think you're—" The sailor stopped and squinted at her face. "Wait, what's your name?"

"Thea Kirisensk."

The sailor's eyes widened. "Mykyta's niece! What—"

"Let Daisy go!" Sylica's voice rang across the harbour. The rigging froze, then shot apart, untangling in a sudden dramatic flourish. Sylica landed lightly on her feet. Daisy hit the deck with a resounding clang.

The sailors stared, their mouths hanging open.

"Of all the—" one of them finally gasped.

Another Elf leapt onto the deck of the ship. He wore a simple arming doublet over his obsidian skin, a sword hanging at his waist. His piercing eyes took in the disarray of the ropes, the dumbfounded faces of the sailors, and Sylica's conspicuous presence. "Having fun?"

"Khariton!" Thea gasped.

The old drill sergeant turned to look at her. "Look who came back. Took you long enough."

"Hello!" Sylica skipped over to join them. "I'm Sylica, what's your name? This is Daisy. I saved her from the ropes!"

The sailors looked at each other nervously. Thea guessed that they wanted to be angry about the state of their ship, but whether it was her identity, Khariton's presence, or the magic Sylica had exhibited, they seemed unsure about confronting the issue.

"Go on," Khariton gestured the sailors away. "Take it up with Mykyta if you have a problem."

The sailors nodded distractedly and left to examine

the destruction.

Khariton gestured for Thea and Sylica to get down off the ship. "You're coming with me."

The crowds parted for Khariton as he led the way down the wharf. Sylica skipped and slid cheerily after him. "What did you say your name was? I don't think you said your name. There are lots of things I *could* call you, but I think that—whoa!" Her feet slid out from beneath her and she scrambled to avoid sliding off the edge of the wharf. "That was close! It sure is icy isn't it? I was thinking this place would be a lot nicer if it wasn't so slippery. Don't you think so?"

Thea opened her mouth to protest.

In an instant, the ice covering the docks was gone. All around them, Elves stared at the planks beneath their feet, as if they couldn't believe their eyes.

Khariton turned and looked at Sylica, a frown creasing his forehead. "You did that?"

"Yeah!" Sylica grinned. "Now I won't slip and fall into things like I fell into those barrels earlier and they went all over the place but I was kind of in a hurry because—"

"With magic?"

"Of course it was magic! I like using my magic to help people, except I try not to do it too much because Meiling said—"

Two armoured Elves stepped out of the murmuring crowd.

"Khariton." One of them spoke in an irritated voice. "Another disturbance? You've had your third warning."

Khariton shot the guard an annoyed glance. "Savva, I told you what I think of your warnings. I'm on official business."

"The whole harbour's in an uproar!"

Khariton glanced at the milling crowd, still in tumult over the sudden disappearance of the ice. "I've seen worse."

"Now we don't mean trouble, just come along with us until we make sure no harm's been done."

"No time." Khariton brushed past them, continuing up the docks and onto the busy street.

"Khariton," the guard grumbled, trying to keep up. "We've been through this before."

There was a surge of magic, and the guards disappeared.

Thea stared at Khariton. Had he just transported them away?

Khariton snorted. "Nosy bastards." He turned and continued up the street.

Thea and Sylica followed Khariton away from the harbour, turning off the main street into a narrow alley. He pushed open a grungy looking door and led them up the steep, rickety stairs beyond, into a small apartment.

After closing the door behind them, Khariton eased himself onto a bench and folded his arms, looking Thea and Sylica up and down as if they'd come from a different moon. "So, what happened back there? Mykyta said you'd be coming in quiet."

"If we'd known we were supposed to be quiet, that might have been helpful," Thea retorted, a hint of a smile creeping over her face. She had a better chance to look at Khariton's spirit now. It was bright. Much brighter than the small hint of a flame she'd seen in it before.

Khariton shook his head. "You know how much trouble I've had since you left?"

"It doesn't seem to have done you any harm."

Khariton's eyes flashed.

"Is this your house?" Sylica asked, interrupting any reply Khariton might have given. "It's really tiny. It must be like living in a cosy little den like an animal. Once I tried crawling in a rabbit hole, but only my head fit in and the rest of my body was too big so I couldn't fit inside. Do you like animals?"

"On my plate, if I can't avoid them."

"Well *I* like all sorts of animals! Like puppies and squirrels and rabbits and mice and—"

Doing her best to ignore Sylica's endless chatter, Thea glanced around the simple apartment. "I thought you lived up at the Temple."

"With those old windbags?" Khariton grumbled. "Never had a moment's peace living up there."

"So you moved to Rokhov." Thea looked at the old veteran with some surprise. Elves of his age were usually venerable and sedate, slowing beyond any engagement in the happenings of the world around them. If anything, Khariton seemed faster and sharper than when she'd seen him last.

"This hole is all I need. Above the Roosting Rat. Most of the Rokhov sailors drink there." Khariton shrugged. "Their beer isn't the worst I've had."

"Svetka said my uncle sends a lot of business through Rokhov."

"Huh." Khariton snorted. "That's one way of putting it."

"Do you get to go on the ships a lot?" Sylica asked. "I like going on ships. It was so much fun sailing all the way here, even when those other ships attacked us, which wasn't very nice of them. After that I made the ship go extra fast so nobody could attack us, and we got here sooner, so that was nice. Then we got to meet you!"

Khariton's sullen glare spoke more than words. After a long moment, he turned his gaze to Thea. "You still have Raybow." His eyes took in the bow from where it protruded over Thea's shoulder.

Thea nodded. "It's saved our lives many times since I left."

"Well, it can go on doing that." Khariton gave a wry half smile and rose to his feet.

"Do you know why I'm here?" Thea ventured. "Enkeli sent me, but that's all I know."

"I'm sure Mykyta will have something to say on that subject. He sent me down to fetch you."

"He did? When will I see him?"

Khariton cocked his head as if listening to an inaudible voice. "He will see you now."

With a surge of magic, the room around them faded and was replaced by a larger, more ornate room. A stone fireplace dominated one wall, and the rest were lined with shelves filled with scrolls and books. Before them was a large oak desk, and sitting at the desk in a large, comfortable chair was Mykyta.

Khariton, Sylica, and Daisy had not faded with the rest of the tiny apartment. Sylica stared around the room with her mouth open. Khariton gave a stiff, formal bow to Mykyta. "Thea and her companions. As requested."

Mykyta rose from his chair. He was taller than the average Elf, with pure diamond skin and a keen, thoughtful expression. His wiry, copper-coloured hair bore a family resemblance to Thea's. He surveyed the new arrivals with a firm glance. "You made it, I see."

"Hello!" Sylica bounded across the room. "I'm Sylica and this is Daisy. I love your room, it's so big and fancy!"

Mykyta cocked an eyebrow, glancing from Sylica to Khariton.

"Have you read all these books?" Sylica asked, craning her neck to take in the full expanse of the collection. "I only ever really read one book before—the Big Book you know—but I like stories a lot. Why do they go up so high? There's no way you could reach the ones at the—oh, there's a ladder!" Sylica scampered off to investigate, with Daisy at her heel.

"Sylica!" Thea hissed, glancing anxiously at her uncle.

Mykyta's amused glance followed Sylica across the room. "You will also find that if you pull the candlestick beyond the second bookcase, a doorway opens to the room beyond."

Sylica gasped. "Really?" She grabbed the candlestick and squealed in delight as the bookcase swung open, revealing a hidden room beyond. "It's a secret passage!" She sprang through the doorway and Daisy followed, her metal paws scrambling for traction on the polished floor.

Mykyta turned back to the others. "Khariton, you will see to it that our guest is entertained. I have some business to attend to with my niece."

Khariton opened his mouth as if to protest, then seemed to think better of it. Sullenly, he turned and followed Sylica.

Thea avoided her uncle's gaze. His large, ornate desk wasn't cluttered. It never was. There were neat piles of letters, an assortment of pens, and a gilded bottle of ink.

His personal seal rested beside the small bell he used to summon his attendants.

Mykyta sat back in his chair. "Thea."

Thea forced herself to look at her uncle. His spirit shone brightly, but his eyes were stern.

"I hear we have a war on our hands."

Thea's heart sank.

Mykyta leaned forward in his chair, watching her intently. "The Elves are not ready, Thea. The Resistance is small and does not hold any power in Lyudmyla. Our hand is being forced, but we needed more time."

"I—I know," Thea stammered. None of the Resistance had been ready.

Mykyta sorted the letters on his desk with meticulous precision. "Those with authority remain in firm opposition to any interference in what happens beyond the sea. The Elves must be convinced to go to war, and I cannot do that."

"But you're the Chancellor. Everyone listens to you."

"My position is political and cannot be jeopardized." His keen gaze rested on Thea's face. "Someone else has to convince them."

Thea's heart sank even further. "Is that why Enkeli sent me here?"

Mykyta rested his hands on the desk in front of him. "Judgment is coming, Thea. The only question that remains is which side of that judgment the Elves will be on."

Leaning back, Mykyta rang his bell. The great door opened and several servants entered the room. One brought a tray of refreshments, which were set on one side of the desk. Another handed Mykyta several letters. The third stood behind the Chancellor's chair with an attentive expression. Their spirits were bright—surprisingly so—and they all wore the Chancellor's insignia on their official uniform.

Mykyta stamped his seal on a letter resting on the desk before him and handed the envelope to one of the attendants standing by. "For Her Majesty, at her earliest convenience."

Bowing, the attendant took the letter and left the room, closing the door behind him.

Mykyta turned back to Thea. "First, you will speak with the Queen Regent. Your departure from Lyudmyla caused somewhat of a ... disturbance." He gave a humourless smile. "Many influential people had opinions on the subject, especially regarding your direct defiance of your parents and your evasion of those sent to bring you back. For some time, you were a very popular topic of conversation. Some speculated that you would be banished for the impudence, though of course that is ridiculous. You were hardly more than a child at the time. It remains, however, that you did cause a disturbance, and as of yet that has been unresolved. With the Queen Regent's pardon and blessing for your return, those rumours can be laid to rest and you will be free to go about the city as you wish."

"And then what?"

"First things first." Mykyta poured himself a cup of tea. "I took the liberty of arranging an audience as soon as I heard that you were in transit. You will see the Queen Regent today."

"How soon?"

Mykyta arched an eyebrow. "You have no idea how many strings I had to pull to get you an audience so quickly. Fortunately your matter should not take long, and the Queen Regent agreed to let you step in during her meeting with the High Priestess today. The High Priestess herself has a certain interest in your case."

Thea's heart sank. She had been hoping to avoid the priesthood—and Enkeli's Temple—as much as she possibly could, not speak with the High Priestess on her first day in Lyudmyla!

A scrambling clatter announced the approach of Sylica and Daisy. "I smell cookies, do you have snacks?" Sylica skidded up to the desk and peered at the tray. "Oh, sandwiches! Can I try one?" Without waiting for an answer, she snatched one off the plate and popped it into her mouth. "They're so tiny!" she mumbled through her mouthful. "It all fit in at once!"

Mykyta raised an eyebrow, but did not make any comment.

Sylica turned to Thea with a big, food-filled grin. "The secret room was so much fun! There are lots of interesting things in there, like carvings and old weapons and vases and things, and Daisy only ate one silver spoon so I think that was pretty good, considering how many shiny things there were. Hi Khariton, that was fun, wasn't it?"

Khariton stalked across the room.

Mykyta gave him an innocent smile. "It was fun? I am very glad to hear it."

Khariton turned to Thea, a wild look in his eyes. "This young woman is your responsibility. Not mine."

There was a knock at the door.

"Come in," Mykyta called.

A servant entered. "Her Majesty will speak with Thea Kirisensk."

"Thank you, Halyna." Mykyta smiled and stood. "We

should not keep our good Queen waiting."

Sylica's ears perked up immediately. "We're going to see a Queen?"

Mykyta regarded her thoughtfully for a moment. "It is not often that we welcome guests to Lyudmyla. I am sure the Queen Regent would be pleased to greet you. Khariton, go with Sylica and make sure she behaves in a manner suitable for the royal presence."

Khariton glared at the Chancellor. "What crime have I committed this time?"

"You transported the guards again." Mykyta looked through the letters on his desk with measured austerity. "Do you know how much paperwork that makes for me?"

"They deserved it," Khariton muttered under his breath.

"As do you, I am sure." A hint of a smile flicked across the Chancellor's face. He glanced up from his work. "When you have finished, Thea, I will speak with you again."

Chapter Nine

Thea followed the servant out into the long vestibule with its gilded arches. Large windows let in shafts of light along its length. Sylica scampered beside Thea like an eager puppy, while Khariton stalked after them, a sullen expression etching his smooth, ancient face.

The servant led them to an ornate set of doors, carved with images of past rulers of Lyudmyla. The servant rapped on it smartly and swung it open, announcing in a loud voice, "Thea Kirisensk."

Thea stepped inside. It was one of the smaller audience rooms, with space for about ten people to comfortably meet. The Queen Regent sat in a large, ornate chair, with a personal servant standing in attendance behind her. Another smooth-skinned Elf sat nearby on a similar, though less ornate chair, wearing the robes of one of the Keepers of Knowledge. She was attended by a younger Elf whose simple uniform showed that he was a trainee of the Temple.

As Thea entered, the Queen Regent and the High Priestess stopped speaking and turned to look at her. Thea bowed, trying desperately to recall the formalities she had been taught as a small child.

"Greetings, Thea Kirisensk." The Queen smiled. "Who do you have accompanying you?"

"This is Sylica." Thea gave her friend an apprehensive glance, but she seemed to be behaving herself. "She is a friend that I met during my travels. Sylica, this is Her Majesty the Queen Regent, and with her the High Priestess of the Temple of Enkeli."

The High Priestess had stiffened when she saw that Thea was not alone, but at Thea's introduction she nodded her head courteously. "Welcome to Lyudmyla. I trust that you come in goodwill."

"Actually I came in a boat," Sylica grinned. Khariton nudged her and she fell silent.

The Queen turned to the High Priestess. "I am sorry to interrupt our meeting, Aglana, but Mykyta asked if I could offer Thea an official welcome, now that she has returned to Lyudmyla."

"Returned?" The High Priestess glanced at Thea. "Oh, you are Afonya's child. I heard that you had run away. Most did not expect you to come back again."

"*I* did not expect me to come back again," Thea offered. "But here I am."

The Queen looked at her with interest. "Was it so dangerous beyond our borders? The histories tell of terrible monsters and worse."

"There are monsters." Thea considered the Queen for a moment. Her opal skin gleamed in the light of the high stained glass windows that illuminated the audience chamber. Mykyta had said someone needed to convince the Elves. She might as well start now. "There are people out there too. Humans, Fauns, Dryads, Littles, Minathrils. Most of them have never met an Elf before."

The Queen listened with interest. "So many are still alive? We thought they must have died out long ago."

"How would you know who's out there?" Thea demanded. "No one ever goes to look! For all I know, I was the first Elf for hundreds of circles to speak with someone who wasn't an Elf, except for when Davis came here."

"I remember now." The High Priestess spoke, her gaze cutting into Thea. "You are the one who came to the Temple asking about the human. That was when all the trouble started."

"Trouble?" Thea frowned.

"Since that time, there have been certain ... *people* who have taken it upon themselves to cause as much trouble as they can." The High Priestess's glare shot past Thea to the place where Khariton stood, covertly trying to stop Sylica from pulling on the long, velvet curtains that lined the walls.

"I went to the Temple because I wanted to learn more about the Ancient Wisdom," Thea explained, a little testily. "I can hardly be blamed for that."

"Peace, Aglana." The Queen raised a hand. "Thea was hardly more than a child when she left us. If her words or actions caused others to behave in an unruly manner, the fault cannot hers. Let us each be responsible for our own actions."

The High Priestess nodded in deference and settled back into her chair.

"Thea," the Queen leaned forward and smiled, "we were all young once, and the energy of youth can drive us to make choices that we regret. I am glad to hear that you have returned, and I hope that you can find a place for yourself back among your own people, though perhaps you should take a thought for your raiments."

Thea realized, with a start, that while the Queen and High Priestess—and even their attendants—were dressed in fine silks and velvets, she herself was wearing her old, much-mended travelling clothes, complete with her oilskin cloak and Raybow hanging on her back.

The Queen continued. "As second in line for Chancellor after your uncle and your father, I am sure that we could find you some position of interest here at the Palace, where you can start to learn about leadership and politics."

"I'm not staying." The words burst out of Thea before she had a chance to check them. "I'm only here because Enkeli sent me. As soon as I can, I will be leaving again."

The High Priestess's eyes narrowed.

The Queen looked at Thea in surprise. "Leaving? What do you mean?"

"Elves were not made to live away from the world on their own little island. There is a war going on out there and I am going to go help. All the Elves should be helping. Not just me."

"Your Majesty," the High Priestess interrupted, "it is ridiculous that she claims to be sent by Enkeli. Why, she is so young we wouldn't even accept her as one of our initiates."

"Enkeli did send me, just like Enkeli sent Davis." Thea glared at the High Priestess, then turned to the Queen. "Unlike Davis, I'm not here to sing. I'm here to tell you that the people of Raphtova need your help. You can't stay hiding on your safe island anymore. The Fallen General knows that you're here, and if he conquers the rest of the world, he will come for you."

"Your Majesty," the High Priestess interjected. "This is a child's fantasy. You can hardly be expected to take her seriously."

The Queen's gaze did not leave Thea's face. "Perhaps."

"Your Majesty—"

The Queen raised a hand. "We will discuss it at the next Council meeting. If there is no substance to it, so be it, but I will not have anyone say that the Queen Regent did not take seriously a potential threat to her Kingdom."

The High Priestess opened her mouth to speak, but the Queen silenced her with a gesture. She nodded to Thea. "You are dismissed until further notice."

Thea bowed and left the audience chamber, with Sylica and Khariton trailing behind. As the door shut behind them, Thea's hands wouldn't stop shaking. A child's fantasy—the dead bodies of the Resistance scattered across the forest they had died to protect? The Elves knew nothing. They didn't care about the world. But even if they wouldn't go with her, she would go back. She would give her life, just like the Fauns.

"Did you see that?" Sylica chattered as they walked back towards Mykyta's office. "Even the door handle was made out of gold! And the curtains were so soft. I wanted to use one as a blanket, but Khariton said I couldn't. And he said I couldn't sit in the chairs, but there were so many empty chairs! Why couldn't I sit in one?"

"We weren't staying long," Thea offered distractedly. Still, she thought, the Queen did say the Council would talk about it.

There were no servants outside Mykyta's office door to announce them, so Thea opened the door and stepped inside. After all, her uncle was expecting them back.

Thea found him sitting at his great desk, deep in conversation with her parents.

Startled, Thea froze.

Her father looked up and stared. "Thea!"

Her mother gasped.

"H—Hello," Thea managed to stammer. She hadn't been expecting to see her parents so soon.

Her father wore the same formal robes he always wore for First House matters. He regarded her with a stern, though somewhat startled expression.

Her mother's arms moved, as if to reach out, but instead she stepped back and regarded her daughter with a critical gaze, her embroidered velvet gown rustling in the sudden silence.

Her father cleared his throat. "When your uncle said he had news about you, we did not realize he meant in person. Come here, and let us have a look at you."

Thea stepped forward, acutely aware of their piercing stares.

Her father looked her up and down. "Well, you do not look any worse for being in foreign parts."

"Besides being dressed like some vagabond from Svokyie," her mother added, a disapproving gleam in her eye. "I hope that you will change as soon as you've had a chance to wash yourself."

Thea gave a wan smile. "Hello, mother."

"Are these your mom and dad?" Sylica asked, bounding to join them. "Hi, I'm Sylica and this is Daisy."

Unsure of whether to cringe or be thankful for the interruption, Thea turned to her friend. "Yes, Sylica, this is my father and mother, Afonya Kirisensk and Taisiya Kirisensk."

"It's so nice to meet you!" Sylica beamed. "Thea is one of my best friends in all the world, after Daisy and the green boat, of course. Do you live in this fancy house too?"

"Live in the Palace?" Thea's mother seemed to take it as a compliment. "Well, that would be something."

Thea's father cleared his throat. "Thea, you have caused your mother much distress. You disobeyed our orders and left when the ruling of the Chancellor had been requested. That was most inappropriate behaviour, even for a child. Everyone has been talking about it."

"I know." Thea considered her parents' agitated manner. Their spirits were dark with self-absorption and pride. She sighed. "I didn't want to make you upset. I had to go, but I shouldn't have been so disruptive."

"You are First House, Thea," her mother chided. "You have to remember who you are."

"I know who I am." Thea tried to give her mother a reassuring smile. "You will be glad to know that the Queen Regent doesn't think I caused any harm. I just returned from speaking with her now."

A flicker of alarm crossed her mother's face as she regarded her daughter's unconventional attire, but her father seemed to be relieved. "Your uncle said it would be so, and I am glad to hear it. If there is no harm done, your mother can rest more easily." He exchanged a glance with his wife, then added, tentatively, "Will you be home for the evening meal?"

Thea hesitated. Did her parents actually want her to come?

"I think she will be available by then," Mykyta supplied, "especially if I am given the opportunity to finish speaking with her myself. She still has much to account for."

"Of course." Thea's father seemed relieved. "Come, Taisiya. The Chancellor has business with Thea." He turned and strode out the door. Thea's mother followed, her gown swishing across the polished floor.

"Close the door, won't you, Khariton?" Mykyta murmured, sorting through the letters on his desk.

When the door clicked shut, he looked up at Thea. "They were worried, you know. You were putting yourself in danger of being hurt or even killed. That was why they tried to stop you."

Thea gave him a skeptical frown. Why would her parents be worried about her? As far as she'd ever seen, they were only worried about their own reputations.

Mykyta leaned forward in his chair. "Your parents love you, Thea. They're just not very good at showing it."

"Love me?" Thea protested. "They were never even around!"

"I know," Mykyta sighed. "That makes it hard to believe, but I can see it. You know what your spirit sight tells you, and I know what my social sight tells me. They love you very much. They tried to show it by building the best life for you that they could. Maybe it will be easier to understand when you are a parent one day."

Thea stared at the ground, discomfort crawling in the pit of her stomach.

Mykyta drummed his fingers on the desk. "I am afraid that my duties as Chancellor mean that I must have a talk with you, Thea. Alone. Khariton, take Sylica out to see the city. I'm sure that would amuse her."

The expression on Khariton's face bordered on panic,

but he managed to gather his countenance into a scowl. "I am supposed to supervise training today, sir."

"Oh that's right." Mykyta considered this for a moment. "Well in that case I have a better idea." Pulling a piece of parchment from a drawer in his desk, he began to write a letter.

Thea shifted uncomfortably. "Uncle Mykyta, I think that Sylica could just stay with me."

Mykyta continued to write.

"No, Daisy!" Sylica skittered away to intercept the little dragon who was sniffing her way along a shelf of curiosities. "Don't eat the shiny plate!"

Setting his pen down, Mykyta folded the paper meticulously and sealed it. "Khariton, you will bring this letter, along with our guest, to the home of my brother and his wife. I am sure they would be honoured to host her during her stay in the city."

Thea stared. Sylica was going to stay with her *parents*?

"Actually," Khariton interjected, "maybe I will show her the city after all."

"No, I rather think my brother will appreciate the honour." Mykyta gave a bright smile. "If you feel uneasy, perhaps you could check on them, periodically, to see how they are getting on."

Khariton's sullen glance fell to the floor. "Sir."

Mykyta held out the letter until Khariton reluctantly accepted it. "I would particularly recommend the upper market. There are many interesting landmarks in that area."

Thea watched her uncle, aghast. Sylica, loose in the upper market, with Thea's parents trying to keep her under control?

"Uncle Mykyta—" Thea began.

The Chancellor raised a hand. "Trust me." He settled back into his chair. "I believe that it will work well." He rang the bell and an attendant stepped through the door. "Escort Khariton and his charge to the home of Afonya Kirisensk."

The attendant nodded and waited attentively for Khariton to move.

Mykyta turned back to his desk, collecting some of the letters that waited in a tidy pile. He glanced up at Khariton. "Is there anything you require?"

"A drink?" Khariton grumbled.

Mykyta nodded. "Perhaps that can be arranged later." He turned to Sylica. "I hope you enjoy your stay in Lyudmyla. Khariton will bring you to your hosts now." He looked through the letters in his hand with measured gravitas. When Khariton did not move, his glaze flicked upward, ever so slightly. "I would suggest that you do so."

"Come on," Khariton muttered, gesturing Sylica towards the door.

"Okay, let's go!" Sylica grinned, skipping after him. "Daisy and I love exploring new places! There's always so many friends to meet! Did you know that one time I made sixty-three and a half new friends, all in one day? Sometimes Daisy and I—"

The door swung shut.

Thea waited in silence as Mykyta set down his letters and leaned back in his chair.

"I am expected to give you a very stern talking to." A hint of amusement flashed across his face. "So I would like you to understand that I am being very, very stern." He leaned forward and stared coldly with his piercing eyes. "You did well, and I am proud of you."

Thea blinked, unsure of how to respond. Slowly, Mykyta stood and stepped out from behind the large oak desk. Smiling, he held out his hand. "I really am, Theewee. It's good to see you again."

A lump rose in Thea's throat. Carefully, she reached out and took his age-smoothed hand. "Thanks, Uncle 'Kyta." Relief swept over her. "I thought you might be angry with me."

"I could never be angry with my Theewee." Mykyta's eyes twinkled. "Come on, let's sit somewhere more comfortable."

He led her to a pair of large chairs by the fireplace. Thea set Raybow and the rest of her gear on the floor close at hand and settled into the chair's comforting warmth.

The fire's dancing light reflected on her uncle's smooth diamond skin as he sat and looked at Thea with a fond smile. "You've grown up, you know. Hardly the little girl who used to go hill tumbling with me."

Thea grinned. "I could beat you now."

"I'll have to take you up on that challenge," Mykyta gave a sly smile, "because I am only getting faster."

Thea laughed, then wondered how long it had been since she had laughed. It felt like forever. She looked up into her uncle's kind, twinkling eyes. "I wish I could have talked to you before I left. Father wanted me to, but there wasn't any time. I had to leave that day, and I didn't know when you would be free to come."

Mykyta sighed. "I know. You had to follow your orders. And you're right, I was busy and took too long to get to you. I understand now why you left, but I was very worried. Your parents were panicking and I may have acted more rashly than I should have. Once I managed to track down Khariton, he told me what was really going on. To test his claim, I began serving the Deity for myself. It has made all the difference in navigating politics, believe me." Mykyta's eyes twinkled. "Enkeli and I get along very well."

"I am supposed to be serving beneath Allulien." Thea sank deeper into her chair and stared at the flickering fire. "Allulien is my General, but Enkeli is borrowing me right now. I don't know why. I just know that I was sent here."

"And we need you here. The Elves must return to the Deity and they must join the war again. I am Chancellor, but if I push too hard there are others who would gladly undermine me. There needs to be another voice to call the Elves to account. A Spark, if you will."

Thea's face grew hot beneath her uncle's gaze. "I know." She looked down at her hands. "And I'm the Spark."

"Have you seen what has happened since you left?" Mykyta waited for Thea to look at him again. "Several influential people at the Temple have started checking in again. My Messengers are connecting the Resistance across Raphtova. We now have a standing army over two hundred strong, trained by Khariton, with the ships to move them. All of that didn't happen by itself. It started because of a Spark."

Thea took a slow, trembling breath. "And now?"

"Now we need the Queen's permission."

Thea nodded. "She said she would talk about the war at the Council meeting. When is that happening?"

"Next span."

"*Next span?*"

Mykyta raised an eyebrow. "I'm impressed that she is addressing the issue so soon. You must have said something that caught her attention."

"But it needs to happen right away, not five days from now!"

Mykyta regarded her with amusement. "You're not used to Elf-speed anymore, are you?"

"Elves can change very quickly when they need to," Thea snapped.

"I'm glad to hear it." Mykyta smiled and leaned back in his chair.

"I guess I have to stay until the Council meeting." Thea frowned. "What am I going to do, stuck here for a whole span?"

"Just be the Spark. Who knows what will happen then?" His eyes twinkled. "Your friend is here too. I can see interesting things happening from that as well."

"Uncle 'Kyta," Thea turned a reproachful gaze on her uncle. "You really sent Sylica to stay with my parents? How was that a good idea?"

Mykyta rested a reassuring hand on her shoulder. "I think there is a certain ... penance to be paid. It will do them good, and it won't do your friend any harm."

"It isn't Sylica I'm worried about."

"I know what you mean." Mykyta's eyes twinkled. "Trust me. I have waited too long for a chance like this."

"Like what?"

Mykyta fixed Thea with a slow, thoughtful stare. "You know this city. Everything continues as it has for the past thousand circles, or close enough to make little difference. The wheels of policy and protocol move very slowly. You have given me an asset that does not and cannot move slowly. Now we get to see if Lyudmyla can keep up."

Thea watched the mischief twinkling in her uncle's eyes. Did he really know the chaos that Sylica could cause? She had a sinking feeling that he did.

Mykyta smiled. "But now, Thea, I want to hear about everything you have been doing since you left. And first of all—" he shot her a keen glance, "—I want to know why Roland didn't travel here with you."

Thea stared at her uncle, wondering how much he really knew. "To explain that," she ventured, "I think I need to start a lot earlier in the story."

Mykyta nodded and waited for her to begin.

Starting with the day that Davis arrived in Lyudmyla, Thea shared about everything that had happened. As she spoke, her uncle listened intently and asked many questions, though it was the smaller, more personal details of her tale that seemed to really intrigue him.

When she had finished, Mykyta stared thoughtfully into the fire. "I heard about these orcs. A warrior race, formed by evil. That doesn't bode well for the war."

"They aren't like anything I've had to fight before." Thea shifted in her chair. "Everyone in my home is safe, but Gedwyld isn't protected by magic. I don't know how long they can hold them off."

"All the more reason for the Elves to join the war." The Chancellor gave her a grim smile. "They're fast, they're strong, their skin is hard, they live forever, and their eyes see beyond the material world. Sound familiar?"

Thea frowned. "Orcs or Elves?"

"They sound very similar, don't they?"

Thea nodded. "They're just faster than we are."

"Elves are very fast." Mykyta gave her a keen glance.

"We just lose ourselves and need to be woken again."

Thea sighed. "And that's the problem. How do you wake people who don't want to be woken up?"

"Good question." Mykyta's eyes twinkled. "How did you wake Khariton?"

Thea blinked. "I ... I shook him by the shoulders and threatened ... to make him scrub the courtyard."

Mykyta stared thoughtfully into the fire. "Apparently that was effective. I might have to try that next time."

"Uncle Mykyta!"

He winked. "It's worth using all the resources at our disposal."

Thea made a face and Mykyta laughed. "Oh Theewee. I missed you." Reaching over, he held her hand. "Together we'll get this place hopping."

Thea smiled.

In the silence, her uncle's face grew thoughtful. "How long do you think Gedwyld can hold out?"

"I don't know." Thea's heart sank. "I don't think it will be very long. Not with an enemy like that." She looked up into her uncle's safe, comforting face.

He squeezed her hand. "Thea Kirisensk, you are the Spark. You have ignited me. Whatever the Elves choose, First House is with you. You will not go back alone."

"But what can one House do?"

"First House is stronger than you think." Mykyta watched her intently. "What we really need to know is how long we have."

Thea sighed. "I don't know how long we have. I don't even know how they're doing now!"

"Message them and find out. That is one of the domains of Enkeli magic."

Thea frowned. "I haven't tried messaging before."

"It's very useful, especially being able to talk from mind to mind. I do that sometimes, when sending a traditional letter would take too long."

"But they're so far away."

"The distance doesn't matter if you have enough magic."

Thea gave her uncle a sidelong glance. "So you could have messaged me when I was gone?"

"I could have, but I didn't need to. I knew you would come back someday. Besides, I had a messenger boy to send." He winked.

Thea felt her face getting hot again. It had been nice to have Roland with her, but part of her wished he had never come. Now it hurt to even think of him.

"You'll stay at your parents' house while you are here, I imagine." Mykyta gave her a look that told her she didn't have much choice. "Besides, your friend will be there. She might be ready to see a familiar face."

There was a knock on the door.

"Come in," Mykyta called.

The door opened and another attendant stepped inside, wearing the Chancellor's insignia. Thea looked up and stared.

It was Roland.

Chapter Ten

Thea froze.

"Mykyta—" Roland began, then he saw Thea. He stopped and stared with widening eyes. "I ... I didn't ..."

Thea's heart pounded. What was Roland doing here? Of course, he worked for her uncle, but she hadn't expected to see him like this, wearing an official uniform with the Chancellor's insignia. He looked so different.

"You had a message for me?" Mykyta asked testily.

"Y-yes, sir," Roland stammered. Stepping forward, he handed the Chancellor a sealed envelope, but his eyes didn't leave Thea.

Mykyta examined the envelope with a calculated gaze. "Thank you."

Roland bowed and turned to go.

"Roland," Mykyta's voice froze him in place. "I have not finished."

Roland turned to face him again.

"You will stay where you are." Mykyta's gaze flicked from Roland to Thea.

Cautiously, Thea stood and reached for Raybow. "I think you're right, Uncle, I should go to my parents now. They will be waiting."

"Thea," Mykyta's voice had a warning note to it. Thea let go of Raybow.

Slowly, Mykyta stood and turned to face them both.

"I have a meeting to attend to. You will both stay in this room until you have said all that you need to say." Turning, the Chancellor strode away and closed the door behind him.

Thea and Roland stared at each other. Thea's mind was racing. She hadn't been prepared for this.

Shock and amazement still filled Roland's face. "You ... you came back."

"I had orders." Thea's gaze fell to the floor. "I didn't have a choice."

"How did you get here?"

"The Raven."

"You saw Svetka?" Alarm flickered in Roland's eyes.

"Yes."

"I heard she wanted to talk to me."

"Yeah." Thea fidgeted with the hem of her sleeve. "She said something about that."

Silence fell, leaving only the muted crackling of the fire.

Roland took a deep breath. "Thea, I ... I wanted to say you were right." His voice faltered. "I am just an Elf. I love Lyudmyla, and I love my people." He paused, discomfort written across his face. "I like to think that I would have done the right thing if you'd told me about Hwasan, but I can't say that for sure. It was your right to decide what risks to take, and I should have respected that. You are the Spark."

Thea stared at the ground, unsure of what to say.

Roland's shoulders sagged. "I was hurt, then I lashed out at you. That was wrong. I wanted to protect you, but when you were hurting most I made it even worse. I'm sorry."

"I—I shouldn't have spoken to you like that." Thea

forced herself to look in his pain-filled eyes. "I wasn't being much of a Spark. You were hurting, then I tore you down even more."

"I deserved it," bitterness flashed through Roland's eyes, "after the way I treated you."

"I care about you, Roland. I didn't want to hurt you. What I said—I shouldn't have said it that way. You'd just been forced to betray everything you love, and then I yelled at you."

"Two people you cared about just died. Of course you were upset." His gaze dropped to the ground beneath his feet. "I should have been there for you, instead of turning on you like that. You have every right to be angry with me."

"I'm not angry anymore." Thea realized it was true, even as she said it. "I ... I'm just hurting."

"I'm sorry." Tears glimmered in Roland's eyes. "I wish I didn't hurt you."

Thea's heart ached. "And I wish I didn't hurt you." She stared at the dancing flames of the fire. "Everything was so awful, and losing you made it so much worse."

"I know." Roland looked down at the tiled hearth, taking a long, unsteady breath. "This isn't what I wanted to happen. Everything went wrong, and we had no time to make it right again." His hurt-filled eyes met hers. "I didn't think I would see you again, at least not for a long time. I thought you were going back to the Resistance."

"I did." Thea's heart sank even further. "We saved everyone we could. They're sheltering at my house now."

"How bad was it?"

"At least half of the Resistance died."

"Thea ..." Dismay filled Roland's eyes. He reached out as if to hold her, then checked himself. "I should have been there for you."

Thea sighed. "Orders are orders."

"I thought you'd still be there with them."

"Yeah." Thea made a wry face. "I thought that too. I guess Enkeli had different ideas."

"Enkeli?"

"Apparently I have to be here to give the Elves another chance."

Startled pain passed through Roland's eyes. He looked away. "Not that we deserve it."

Thea's gaze fell to the floor. "The Deity gives mercy—not to those who deserve it, but to those who still have a chance to accept it."

They stood in silence, watching the fire burn. A log settled in a shower of sparks.

"We found Ember and Kaji," Thea offered. "We couldn't find Thabani."

"Do you know what happened to him?"

Thea shook her head. "Noxolo is leading the Resistance now. What's left of it. Elora and Kais are there with them too. And Ulfgar." She gave Roland a sidelong glance. "I'm going to message them tonight and see how they're doing."

"Wait—Ulfgar?" Roland stared in surprise. "I thought he—"

"He came back shortly after you left. You should ask Micai about that."

Roland shook his head. "It seems like I missed a lot."

"You did. The Dragon fights were interesting."

"*Dragon fights?*"

Thea suppressed a smile, her gaze roaming around

her uncle's old, familiar study. It was strange that somewhere could seem so much like home and so far from home at the same time. She glanced at Roland. "I didn't want to come back. I only said I would because I made you a promise." Unconsciously she fingered the silver brooch she still wore.

Roland's eyes were thoughtful. "I could have gone with you that day you left on the Raven. I think about it a lot, wondering what would have been different if I had. Maybe none of this would have happened."

"Maybe." Thea looked into his troubled gaze. "But we made our choices and we can't change that. I'm going back to the Resistance as soon as I've finished what I have to do here."

Roland nodded and stared at the fire.

As the silence stretched on, Thea glanced at Roland again. "My parents are expecting me. They're hosting Sylica, so I should probably join them now."

Roland's eyes widened. "Sylica is here?"

"Yes, she is. My parents have been showing her the city. You can thank my uncle for that." Picking up Raybow and the rest of her gear, Thea turned and walked towards the door.

"Thea, wait," Roland called. "Do … do you think you can forgive me?"

Thea stopped. "I can." She turned and looked into Roland's earnest gaze. "And I do. But I can't trust you the same way anymore. For me, the Deity comes first, before anything else. If I'm going to spend my life with someone, they need to have that priority too, and to put me next, before any city, people, or ship."

"I understand." Roland stared down at his hands for a moment before looking up again. "Do you think we can ever go back to the way we were? Before all of this?"

Thea looked into Roland's eyes. They were not the same people they used to be, but beneath all of the hurt she could still see the carefree young Elf she had played with as a child.

"Of course. You're still like my brother."

Roland smiled. "Thanks. And Elves can change, you know."

Thea turned and stepped through the door. "It doesn't matter who you are. If you are serving the Deity, it's impossible not to."

Chapter Eleven

Thea stepped out through the gilded doors of the Palace and into the courtyard beyond. Ice glittered on the trees and bushes that lined the regal walkways. The chill of the air froze her breath in shimmering puffs of ice.

Along one side of the courtyard, a network of stone arches led to the Royal Residence, where the Queen Regent and her family lived. Enormous gilded windows lined the rooms where the past monarchs of the Elves remained in vidlas, slowed beyond the capacity to live in the waking world.

Along the other side of the courtyard, the Palace shared a wall with Enkeli's Temple, a half-open gate the only relic of the days when the Hall of Messengers was filled with the servants of the Deity, in constant communication with the leadership of the Elves.

Overhead, the great planet Micai was already large in the sky, approaching Allumen for its nightly eclipse. Thea crossed the courtyard and passed through the ornate gates in the surrounding wall. The guard on duty watched her with a wary expression, but didn't interfere with her passing.

Outside the gates, the vast expanse of Lyudmyla stretched out below her, filling the slopes of the mountain all the way down to the sea far below. She had often stood here with her uncle or her father at the end of a workday and enjoyed the view glittering below them. It was a magnificent sight.

Cold wind from the sea rushed to greet her. Thea wrapped her cloak tight and set off down the mountain. The broad, cobbled street passed the large manor homes of the Royal House and skirted the courtyard of the Theatre. Passing into the First House District, Thea turned onto the lane that led to her parents' home. Large, dark windows stared down at her as she walked up the front steps and opened the door.

Inside, everything looked the same as it had when she left. The parlour was empty, quiet, and immaculately clean. The table in the dining room was set, with each bowl, plate, knife, spoon, and fork in its proper place.

A household servant bustled in through the door to the kitchen, carrying an armful of linens. Catching sight of Thea, she almost dropped her burden.

"Miss Thea!" she gasped. "You—you're here!" Setting her load on the table, she grabbed Thea by the shoulders. "Just look at you! You look so well! And they said you were never coming back."

"Hello, Grusha," Thea smiled.

The ageing Elf looked her up and down, her jasper eyes shining with delight. "You're so much smoother now, I can hardly believe it. I'm sure you were a rough little thing, just a span or two ago."

Grusha showed no sign of letting her go, staring as if looking away for a moment could make her disappear again.

"Are my parents home?" Thea asked.

"Not at the moment, Miss. They are out in the city with a guest who has come to stay for a while. We expect them back for feast. Oh won't they have a fit when they see you home again!"

"I saw them at the Palace. They're expecting me for feast today."

"Oh how wonderful! I'll tell Cook right away. Everyone will be so surprised you're here! This place was not the same when you were gone, let me tell you. Of all the—"

The front door opened with a clatter of noise that could only be caused by one thing.

"Here they are now!" Grusha beamed. "Oh!" She scooped the linens off the table and scuttled back through the door to the kitchen.

"Thea!" Sylica scampered across the parlour with Daisy clanking at her heels. "There you are! We had so much fun today! I never saw a city like this in my whole life before. There are stores that sell every kind of thing you can imagine!"

Thea's parents followed Sylica into the parlour, walking with quiet, unperturbed dignity. Thea glanced at them with interest, but they did not appear to be unsettled or upset. Was it possible that Sylica hadn't been a problem after all?

Through the door, Thea caught a glimpse of Khariton, staring at the house as if deciding whether to come in. His eye twitched.

"Hello, Thea." Thea's mother spoke in a stiff, yet cordial tone. "I trust that your audience with the Chancellor was beneficial."

Thea smiled privately. "It was. Thank you, mother."

Thea's father spoke to Khariton, and he entered the parlour, somewhat reluctantly. Another place was set at the table, and soon Thea found herself sitting down to eat with her parents, Sylica, and Khariton. Grusha stood nearby to wait on them.

Thea ate the familiar food, feeling strangely both at home and out of place. Her father ate each mouthful with careful precision. Her mother ventured to suggest some items of interest for the following day, starting with a visit to the bath house. Khariton ate with a dogged determination that seemed to indicate his doubt that tomorrow would come at all.

Oblivious to the discomfort around her, Sylica carried on an enthusiastic one-sided conversation, interrupted only by her desire to enjoy as much food as possible.

"—And there were so many statues!" Sylica interjected between mouthfuls. "They were all over the place—right in the middle of the road and everything!"

Thea's father cleared his throat. "Those were people."

"Really? They looked like statues to me. They weren't moving or anything! How can you tell?"

"Tell?"

"Between the statues and the people!"

Thea's father cut a piece of meat with delicate precision. "We do not make statues, for that very reason."

A small noise from Khariton almost sounded like he was choking.

"Well I thought they were very pretty, even if they weren't statues. And I got to climb up to the top of a tower and you could see so far! All the way across the city, I think." She took another enormous mouthful. "Did you know these are the best buns I ever had? You have to teach me how to make them so I can make them all the time!"

"I do not work in the kitchen," Thea's mother replied.

"That would have been Cook, or they may have come from a bakery. Grusha, tell Cook to come out here. We have a question for her."

Grusha did not move. With a strange, creeping sensation, Thea realized that Grusha was staring at her.

"Grusha!" Thea's mother repeated in a sharper voice. When the servant still did not respond, she pursed her lips and rang the bell that sat in the center of the table.

Grusha jumped and fumbled distractedly with the towel in her hands.

"Bring Cook," Thea's mother repeated in a dry voice. "We wish to ask her a question."

Bowing, Grusha disappeared into the kitchen. Thea glanced around the table. Her father ate with even more delicate precision than before. Khariton stared at his plate with determined focus.

A few breaths later, Cook stepped through the door. Her dull grey skin was smoother than when Thea had last seen her.

Thea's mother fixed her with an even gaze. "The buns. Are they yours, or from a bakery?"

"From the bakery. Nikita's, in the upper market."

"They are so good!" Sylica repeated, once again speaking through an over-full mouth. "Can we go there tomorrow?"

"Perhaps." Thea's mother seemed put out. "After the bath house and our tour of the Theatre."

Sylica looked down at the bowl that was now empty. "They're all gone. Do you know how many I ate? I wasn't really counting, but my tummy feels a bit funny. Thea, did you know we had such a big dance today in the place where all the shops were? There were so many pretty flags flapping around that we just had to dance!

Wasn't it so much fun?" She beamed at her hosts. "We should have another dance now!"

Thea's parents exchanged an alarmed glance.

Khariton emptied his wine glass with reckless speed. "Got to go," he muttered, beating a hasty retreat out the door.

Thea's father cleared his throat. "We thought, Sylica, that you would like to see the room where you will be staying tonight."

"Oh! I want to see it!" Sylica jumped up eagerly. "Don't you want to see it, Daisy?" Daisy bounded around her feet, crashing into a tall candelabra, which tumbled to the ground with a resounding clatter.

The Cook stared with mouth agape, until a sharp glance from Thea's mother sent her back to the kitchen.

Thea's father stood. "If you will follow me."

Sylica scampered after him, and Thea's mother followed, leaving Thea alone. Gingerly, she righted the candelabra and tried to tidy up some of the mess.

"Excuse me."

Grusha stood by the door to the kitchen.

Thea smiled. "Yes?"

"Miss Thea, you're different since you went away."

"In what way do you mean?" Was anything about her the same as when she left so long ago?

Grusha hesitated, embarrassment evident on her age-smoothed face. "It's bright inside you."

Thea's eyes widened. "Grusha, you have spirit sight?"

"Well, I never had much time for it." Her hands fidgeted with the corner of her apron. "I had a family to feed."

"A family?"

"Four children of my own. They're having children of

their own now."

"I—I had no idea," Thea admitted. "You were always just Grusha."

"We came from Elilavat, north of here. My husband couldn't work after he got hurt in the mines, so I got a job here and he stayed home with the children. Working long days doesn't leave much time for elf-sight, but in all my circles I've never seen anything like I see in you now. What is it?"

"It's the light of the Deity." Thea stared into Grusha's gentle eyes, so eager to understand. "I started serving the Deity and that's why I left. I was sent to help the people of Raphtova and to learn from them. I've learned so much."

"The Deity?" Grusha frowned slightly, as if trying to understand.

"The Ancient Wisdom. That is our people's name for the Deity."

"Oh, I don't know so much about the Ancient Wisdom." Grusha rubbed her hands across her apron. "I'm no Priestess."

"Grusha," Thea took the old servant's smooth, worn hand. "You taught me songs about the Ancient Wisdom. I remember sitting beside you while you ironed or mended, and you'd sing. I loved those times with you."

"Well, I do like to sing, though you know I don't have much of a voice for it." Grusha smiled. "There's something comforting about those old songs."

"Of course there is. The Ancient Wisdom cares for us and loves us." Thea stared with wonder at the longing in the old Elf's tired spirit.

Grusha gave her a warm smile. "It does me good to see you like this, Miss Thea. So bright and alive. I couldn't be there much for my own wee ones, so you have a special place in my heart."

"Grusha, it's not just me. Anyone can serve the Ancient Wisdom. All you have to do is ask."

Understanding grew in Grusha's eyes, then her countenance fell. "Not anyone. The Fallen House is banned from the Temple."

"Who cares what they say at the Temple? It doesn't matter who you are. I've seen people from every race turn to the Deity, even people whose spirits were dark and hard. What happened in the past can't stop you, it just shows that we all need mercy. I've needed that mercy too."

A small frown creased Grusha's forehead. "It's a lot to think about."

"Then think about it." Thea smiled. "I'll be here, for a while. We can talk about it again."

Grusha smiled. "Thank you, Miss Thea. I'm glad you're back."

"I—" The words died in Thea's mouth. Was she actually glad to be back? Of course she wasn't. And yet ... maybe in a way she was.

"—I think I'll go to my room now," she finished. "It's been a long day."

Concern filled Grusha's face. "I haven't freshened your bed! I'll get some new sheets right away!"

"It's okay, Grusha." Thea offered a reassuring smile. "It will be fine just the way it is." Picking up Raybow and her bag, Thea walked slowly up the stairs. Sylica's singsong voice drifted out from the guest room at the end of the hall. From the distant murmur of voices, it sounded like her parents had retired directly to their own room.

Softly, Thea opened the door to her old bedroom. It was exactly as she had left it. The bedding was crumpled and unmade. The storage trunk was open, and the wardrobe door was ajar.

Setting Raybow and the rest of her gear beside the bed, Thea sank back onto the soft mattress. She had forgotten how comfortable a bed could be.

Surrounded by her old, familiar room, Thea drifted closer to sleep, her mind filled with memories of the young Elf who had thrown everything away because she wanted to serve the Deity. She would do it all again in a heartbeat.

Forcing herself back onto her feet again, Thea locked the door and sat down by the window. How exactly did one send a message so far across the sea? Closing her eyes, she pictured her home: Its dark stone walls covered with trailing vines. The windows bright with golden light. The fire crackling, sending dancing shadows across the long wooden beams. There were people there. Fauns laughing and talking. Dryads pacing by the walls. Humans huddled around the fire, sharing blankets between them. Littles tinkering with bits of wood and metal, humming scraps of song while they worked.

She knew who she wanted to talk to.

Elora?

Thea could feel Elora's surprise. *Thea, is that you? I thought you were Msizi at first.*

It's me, Thea smiled, *I wanted to talk to you.*

Oh. Elora seemed to consider this. *Where are you?*

I'm in Lyudmyla, a long way north of you. How are things going there?

It's fine. The orcs are out there, but they can't get in.

You have enough food?

... Yes. We get what we need each day.

How's Gedwyld?

They are keeping the orcs back, so far. Ulga says the orcs are testing. Once they decide what to do, that will mean trouble.

When do you think that will be?

Thea could almost feel her roll her eyes. *Wouldn't we all like to know that?*

Thea smiled. *I miss you, Elora.*

When will you be back?

The Council is meeting a span from now. I want to convince them to send an army.

How big of an army?

Hopefully big enough. There's a lot of Elves here. They just need waking up.

A span, then you have to travel all the way back. Thea could feel Elora calculating the time.

Enkeli magic can get us there faster. The hardest part will be convincing them to come. Either way, I'm coming back as soon as I can.

When— Elora's thought broke off suddenly. *Damn! No, don't—*

~

Elora ran across the room and grabbed the Faunlet around the waist, lifting him into the air.

He struggled, trying to throw himself out of her arms and through the open door, chattering angrily in Faunic.

"No going outside," Elora grunted. "That's the rules."

With a shout, the rest of the Faunlets thundered down the stairs, charging recklessly towards the open door.

Not again. Kicking the door shut with her foot, Elora wheeled to face them.

Half of the Faunlets threw themselves at her, tugging her to the ground. Others grabbed the handle of the door and tried to wrench it open.

"Ulfgar!" Elora yelled.

Ulfgar opened his eyes where he lay dozing by the fire. "Hmm?"

With a cry of victory, the Faunlets swung the door open and charged outside.

Kicking off the Faunlets who were trying to hold her down, Elora raced after them, scooping up a Faunlet under each arm. "Get back here!" she yelled, but the little Fauns raced onward in their mad dash for freedom.

With a roar, Ulfgar burst out the door. Charging at full speed, he ran for the gate, scatting Faunlets in all directions. Lunging after the furthest miscreant, already halfway over the gate, he grabbed her hoof and dragged her back down, kicking and protesting.

A loud voice boomed from behind Elora. Turning, she saw Ulga standing in the doorway, her hands on her hips.

The Faunlets fell silent, looking up at the orc towering over them.

Ulga wore an apron and held a large mixing spoon in her hand, dripping bits of batter on the doorstep. In a reproving tone, she reprimanded the Faunlets with a colourful mixture of orcish, Faunic, and Common.

Something about respecting your elders, the kitchen, and going back upstairs. Elora only really followed the parts that were in Common, but she'd noticed a kind of sameness between orcish and The Talk. Sometimes she got the idea of what Ulga was saying, in the rare times Ulga wasn't talking in Common.

The Faunlets listened to Ulga, then trooped back through the door, giggling and talking amongst themselves.

Elora breathed a sigh of relief. The Faunlets only listened to Ulga because they loved her. As Elora knew all too well, bossing, scaring, and threats were useless when trying to get the Faunlets to listen to anything.

At the foot of the gate, Ulfgar swore under his breath, gingerly rubbing his shoulder.

"Back to bedrest for you." Elora nodded towards the house. "The last thing we need is that shoulder giving you more trouble."

"I've had worse." Ulfgar grimaced.

"Sure." Elora pushed him towards the house.

A shadow crossed the sky and a snow-white eagle landed beside her. Changing into human form, the Dryad staggered.

"Ember!" Elora glared. "What were you doing?"

"Just a bit of scouting."

"You're supposed to be resting! How is your leg going to heal if you keep shifting all the time?"

Ember limped towards the door. "It's too quiet out there. I don't like it."

"None of us like it, but we all decided *together* that scouting isn't worth the risk. Not after Londiwe almost died."

"I was careful." Ember rested a hand on the

doorframe and glanced back at Elora. "I was getting restless, that's all."

Elora glared. "You think I *like* being cooped up behind walls?"

"I know you don't." Ember limped through the door, and Elora followed. To her relief, the Dryad sat down by the fire. Ulfgar joined them.

Elora shut the door and strode over to the window, staring out beyond the walls to the bare trees, shuddering in the icy wind. If only it wasn't so dangerous ...

"You used to be a scout, didn't you?" Ember asked from their place by the fire.

Elora nodded. Pursing her lips, she turned to face them. "What did you see?"

"Not as much as I was hoping to. The orcs seem to be staying in their blockade, but it was all very quiet. They're up to something."

Elora nodded.

With a patter of footsteps, Alya, Tam, and Gili entered the room, covered with dust and cobwebs.

Alya joined Elora by the window. "We were searching the cellars like you said."

"Did you find anything?"

"More cloth and some tools."

"Nothing we can eat?"

Alya shook her head. "Not unless you count leather."

"Almost done eating, then I'll be off," Brandy called from the kitchen.

Crossing the room, Elora peered over the counter. Brandy crouched by the far wall, eating a bowl of thin soup.

"Food is almost ready," Ulga nodded. "Soon call

everyone.”

Melinda had Brock over her shoulder, burping him. “Ulga’s managed to make a bit of biscuit. There will only be a mouthful each, I’m afraid.”

Brandy set her empty bowl on the counter. “Fell Claw and I will find something.”

Elora looked out the window. “You’re waiting till dark.”

Brandy frowned. “You hunt at dusk, not after dark.”

“It’s safer after dark.”

Shrugging, Brandy pushed past her into the great room. “Fell Claw! Ready?”

The golden-eyed Dryad stepped through the door.

“It’s not fair!” a Faun across the room whined. “How come they get to go hunting but we’re stuck in here?”

“You’re not stuck,” Noxolo countered, “you’re busy training.”

“Thabani never made us train. We did just fine!”

“We weren’t fighting orcs back then. Do you want them to slaughter us again?”

Elora thought for a moment. “Has anyone seen Msizi?”

“No.” Noxolo frowned. “Not since workday.”

Elora glanced out the window, fingering the arrows at her side.

“What do you want him for?”

Noxolo turned on the Faun who sat slouched in his chair. “Musa! Twenty pushups!”

“You can’t make me,” the Faun grumbled.

“I heard from Thea.”

“Really?” Noxolo looked up eagerly.

Across the room, Ulfgar opened his eyes and sat up.

Ulga stuck her head out of the kitchen. “Thea?”

"What did she say?" Ember asked.

Elora took a deep breath. "She's in Lyudmyla and she's trying to get an army of Elves to come help us."

"An army of Elves?" Ulfgar scratched his chin.

Elora nodded. "It's going to take at least a span, though, and then they have to travel all the way here. It might be help, but it's not coming soon."

"The orcs haven't done anything yet ..." Noxolo offered hopefully.

Ulga frowned. "Not that we have seen."

Chapter Twelve

Thea woke in her old bed, in her old room. Outside, the golden light of Allumen flickered as it passed behind the rings of Micai. One by one, the sounds of the city began—rumbling carts, the murmur of voices, bells chiming in the distance.

Thea sat up, her conversation with Elora still running through her mind. She hated to leave them waiting, but what choice did she have? She had to stay in Lyudmyla until the Council meeting was over.

Thea knelt to check in, but Enkeli was silent. Thoughtfully, she walked over to her old wardrobe. There were lots of clothes she could wear now, but she didn't want to. She would wear her simple travelling clothes, the same as she always did, with Raybow on her back. She would be ready, in case something happened and she was allowed to go home.

Leaving the house quietly, Thea stepped onto the street. From her position high in the First House District, she stared out at the sea far below. It glimmered in the icy morning light.

Somewhere beyond that horizon, the rest of the world waited. She would go back as soon as she could.

Ice crunched beneath her feet as she took the broad, winding road back up the shoulder of the mountain towards the Palace.

She found Mykyta sitting at his desk, with

messengers coming and going in a steady stream.

He nodded a greeting as she entered. "You have news?"

"Elora said the orcs are likely preparing for something, but they don't know what it is. So far there hasn't been too much danger."

Mykyta nodded. Sealing an envelope, he handed it to a messenger who stood close at hand, then turned his attention to the contents of the papers on his desk.

Thea waited. Another messenger arrived, bringing several letters which Mykyta added to the collection on his desk.

"If you're not too busy, can I stay?" Thea ventured. "It's nice to see you again."

Mykyta handed two letters to the waiting messenger. Turning over one of the papers on his desk, he began to write on the reverse. "I have five days to mobilize an army for war, while ensuring that no one outside of the Resistance knows what I am doing. I believe I will be busy."

Thea waited until her uncle set down his pen. "Is there any way I can help?"

Mykyta looked up with his piercing gaze. "You can go and be the Spark."

Thea wanted to protest, but she knew he was right.

Engrossed in his work, Mykyta did not look up again. Quietly, Thea left the way she had come. Passing through the Palace gate, she felt the keen stares of the guards. Maybe she would transport herself inside with magic next time, just because she could.

As the slopes of Lyudmyla spread out before her, Thea stopped to think. She could go find Sylica, but that would mean seeing her parents again. What else could she do?

The residents of Lyudmyla bustled past, busy with their daily tasks. It was different here than by the docks in Rokhov, or among her uncle's attendants. The spirits of those on the street were dark and dead, just the way she remembered seeing them.

Aimlessly, Thea wandered from street to street. Her spirit ached inside of her, as if responding to the unspoken cries of the endless people streaming past.

They were afraid, caught up in the cares and worries of the day. They were lonely, unable to truly love or accept being loved. They were tired, trying so hard to find some meaning and purpose in their never-ending lives, until finally they slowed, bowed beneath the weight of time, and gave up.

Her people needed the Deity. They were lost, and they didn't know how lost they were.

As the day stretched on, Thea found herself by the harbour. There was the Eagle, moored in its place among the racing ships. She walked on, past the Harbour Office. Nothing was different from when she left. The same sailors loaded and unloaded barrels and crates. Merchants, servants, and labourers bustled along the crowded docks. The brisk wind off the sea whistled through the rigging of the ships, carrying murmured conversations and the shouts of the workers.

Standing by the docks, Thea watched the life of the harbour carry on around her. If there was something she should do, she didn't know what it was. She'd always liked coming down to the harbour, but that was usually to watch Roland sail on the Eagle.

People glanced at Thea as they walked past, their eyes drawn to her unusual attire or Raybow hanging on her back. One of the Elves looked very familiar.

"Ilya!" Thea waved a greeting.

The Elf stared, a frown wrinkling his sandstone forehead. "I'm sorry, do I know you?"

"I'm Thea. I sat on your balcony to watch Davis the human arrive on the transport. Do you remember?"

Slow recognition crept across his face. "I do remember. Kseniya talked about it for spans afterwards." He squinted at her. "I'm sorry—you look very different than you did then."

"I've been travelling. I just got back yesterday."

Ilya looked at her with interest. "Is it true what they said, that you ran away to the Dark Lands?"

"I did go to the Dark Lands."

As Ilya's eyes widened, Thea suppressed a smile. "They aren't that dark, you know. No darker than here."

"Really?" Ilya seemed interested, in spite of himself. "I thought there were monsters and all sorts of horrible things."

"There are monsters," Thea admitted, "but it isn't all monsters. I've made some wonderful friends, and I'm going back as soon as I can."

"You are?"

"Yes. I live there now, and I want to go back."

"But ... but no Elves go to the Dark Lands." A strange longing gleamed in his garnet eyes.

Thea paused. "Have you ever thought of going to the Dark Lands?"

Ilya shifted uncomfortably. "I have. Not seriously, of course. I just ..." He sighed. "I thought, marrying into Second House, it would be easier to get ahead. I'd get better opportunities, maybe a job that earns more. It hasn't really turned out like that. I'm just doing the same thing every day, at the same job I always had. None of it matters. I've thought about moving to Svokyie. Maybe there's opportunities there for getting ahead." His countenance fell. "Of course, Kseniya would never go."

Thea looked into his troubled eyes. "If you serve the Ancient Wisdom, everything matters."

Ilya frowned. "Temple life? That sounds even worse."

"I don't mean that. There's a whole world out there, with all sorts of people to meet and adventures to have. As we speak right now, orcs are surrounding Gedwyld and we need to go save the people there. Isn't that something that matters? The Ancient Wisdom wants us to help the people of Raphtova, not stay stuck here the way we've always been."

Ilya stared at Thea, hanging off every word she said. His spirit was shifting, right in front of her eyes. Hope grew where there had been none before.

"How—" he stammered, "—how is that possible?"

"The Ancient Wisdom makes anything possible. Who knows? Maybe next span there will be an army leaving our shores, going to fight in the Great War again."

"I ... I think that would be something that matters."

Thea smiled. "I think it would."

Sudden consternation filled Ilya's eyes. "What would Kseniya say?"

"Talk to her about it. You never know." Thea laid a gentle hand on his shoulder. "Sometimes it doesn't take much for the spark to grow."

~

With her razor-sharp axes, Ulga sliced the meat from the scrawny deer that Brandy had shot the night before. In a large pot on the stove, the bones were boiling for broth.

If everyone had two pieces of meat, and one each for the young ones, that would be enough for two meals. Swift Wing had dug some roots. Those would go in the soup.

As her hands worked, her mind continued churning. Something was wrong, and she didn't like that she couldn't identify it. The war bands outside should have done something before now. Either they were stumped—something she didn't believe for a moment—or a plan was already in operation.

"Ulga!" Kais called from outside the kitchen. "Adi wants you!"

A smile creased Ulga's face. That precious little one was such a terror if she didn't get her "Guh-guh".

"Almost done!" she called, returning her axe to its sheath on her back. "There is a blanket by the fire!"

Piling the roots to the side for later, Ulga wiped the counter with an old rag, then washed her hands.

Stepping out from the kitchen into the great room, she nodded to Kais who was already on his way towards the stairs. He looked tired. There was the usual crowd of Fauns, of course. Ulfgar and Elora sat at the table, deep in conversation.

On a blanket by the hearth, Adi wiggled and gurgled, trying to ingest her toes.

Outside, footsteps approached.

Ulga froze. She knew those footsteps. What were they doing here?

The front door opened and three orcs walked inside.

Everyone stared, shock evident on every face. They had been so sure that the orcs couldn't enter because of the magic on the door.

Of course, that wasn't true. Ulga smiled grimly to herself. If it was, she wouldn't be there. It was the intent to harm or do evil that kept things away. She'd wondered how long it would take for the rest of the orcs to discover that. Apparently they already had.

She didn't recognize any of these particular orcs. Of course, the Chief would know better than to send anyone with a connection to her. That would be asking for trouble.

"Get out," Ulga growled in orcish. "We don't want you here."

A smile lingered on one orc's face. "Try and stop us."

With a pretence of indifference, they glanced around the room. Ulga's eyes narrowed. They were taking everything in, that much was clear. What were they looking for?

Elora rose to her feet. "Ulga, what are they doing?" Her worried gaze didn't leave the intruders.

"I do not know," Ulga replied carefully in Common.

"Permission to hit them with my axe?" Ulfgar muttered.

"You cannot," Ulga replied. "No one can be hurt here."

Ulfgar's frown sank deeper. "Permission to try anyways?"

From the far side of the room, one of the Fauns called something in their own language. There was a titter of uneasy laughter from the rest of the Fauns.

Slowly, the orcs stalked through the room, looking this way and that, poking their noses into every corner.

Ulga stood in the doorway to the kitchen.

"Noxolo," Ulga rumbled. "Block the door to the stairs."

Noxolo spoke sharply and three Fauns leapt towards the door, just in time to stop the closest orc from stepping through. The orc shot a glare at Ulga, hatred burning in his eyes. They had been warned about her. To be a traitor was the worst crime an orc could commit. If it was not for the magic of the door, they would certainly try to kill her.

Lucky for them that they couldn't.

"There is nothing for you here." Ulga returned the orc's glare. "Leave. Now."

The orc turned back to the Fauns who barred his way up the stairs. "Get out of the way," he growled in orcish, gesturing for them to move.

The Fauns stared up at the orc towering above them, giving their very best unimpressed stares.

"Huh," one of them muttered, "I'd like to see you try."

The orc tried to push past them, but he couldn't.

Not without showing aggression. Ulga nodded to herself. So far, the magic of the door was working.

One of the orcs examined the fireplace, prodding the stonework with her finger.

"How do we make them leave?" Elora frowned.

"I do not know if we can, without force," Ulga replied. "When they are ready, they will go."

Ulfgar's axe hand was twitching. Ulga shot him a warning glance. If the orcs were simply taking the chance to scout their defences, that was simple enough. If they were looking for something specific, that could mean trouble.

The third orc eyed the frame around the front door with a cautious gaze. Were they here to learn more about the magic?

Movement caught the corner of Ulga's gaze. The orc by the fireplace bent down and with a quick motion, lifted Adi off her blanket on the floor.

Cold fear gripped Ulga's heart.

With a cry, Elora hurtled herself at the orc. "Let go of her!" Her arms froze the moment before they struck the orc's skin. Anger and horror filled her eyes. "No! Give her back!" She tried to grab her daughter, but the orc turned away.

With a roar, Ulfgar sprang from his seat, swinging his axe. Before it struck, his axe froze in midair.

A cruel light gleamed in the orc's eyes, staring at the tiny infant in its hands.

"Block the door! Now!" Ulga ordered. Fauns scrambled to close the door and bar the way.

They can't hurt her. Ulga steadied herself. *They can't hurt her.*

So what could they do? What had she missed? They wouldn't do something like this unless they had a plan. What was it?

The orc closest to the door was watching her with glittering eyes, as if daring her to do something about it.

Ulga stepped forward. "Give her back."

The orc smiled. "We are taking her with us. There is nothing you can do to stop it."

Ulga glanced at the jostling crowd of Fauns in front of the door. The orcs knew they would block the way. They weren't stupid.

Movement caught her eye. Msizi appeared in the entrance of the lean-to, unnoticed by anyone else. His sharp gaze took in the events unfolding before him.

Ulga felt his presence in her mind.

Get ready. Catch Adi on three.

Ulga carefully did not look at Msizi.

One ... two ...

Ulga lunged across the room.

The orcs disappeared, and Adi fell—landing in Ulga's arms.

Chaos erupted across the room. Elora flung herself at her daughter, wrapping her tightly in her arms. Fauns were shouting. Ulfgar raged.

"What was that!" he demanded, his face getting redder and redder. "They can just walk in here and grab—"

"I thought we were safe!" Noxolo pounded her fist on the table. "Then *that* happens?"

Elora was shaking.

Fauns poured out the door, running to secure the walls and search for other intruders.

Kais appeared at the foot of the stairs. "What—"

Elora ran to him, carrying their child.

Red anger surged through Ulga's veins. Unsheathing her axe, she turned to Msizi. "Where did you send them?"

Msizi gave her a sharp glance. "About fifty paces north of the wall."

Ulga nodded. Eyes blazing, she turned and strode out the door. There would be blood. Enough to make them think twice before trying again.

Chapter Thirteen

Thea walked back up the steep mountain streets. Workday was all but past, and she hadn't eaten yet. If she'd thought to ask her uncle for some money she could have bought something, but as it was, she would go back to her parents' and get something from the kitchen.

Avoiding the large front door, Thea circled around to the back of the house and let herself in through the servants' door. No one seemed to be around, so she slipped into the kitchen and helped herself to a large piece of bread and some cheese.

Eating as she went, Thea headed towards her room.

Grusha was cleaning in the parlour. She dropped her cloth as Thea walked past. "Oh, Miss Thea! I didn't know you were home!"

Thea paused in the doorway. "Sorry to startle you."

"That's alright, Miss, but I was supposed to tell you that your father wants to speak with you."

Thea's heart sank. "Did he say what about?"

"No, Miss."

"Is he home?"

"I believe he's at his office, Miss."

Thea took a deep breath. Whatever it was about, she might as well get the conversation over with.

Father? You wanted to talk to me?

Thea could feel the shock in her father's mind. *Thea?*

What—

It's magic, Father. You wanted to talk to me?

... Yes. I'm in my office.

I can come there. See you soon.

Grusha waited, concern wrinkling her forehead. "Would you like me to take a message to him?"

"It's okay, Grusha. I'll just go there myself."

Leaving her parents' house, Thea took the wide, smooth road up to the First Hall. Passing by the rows of marble pillars, Thea let herself in through the large wooden doors.

Inside, the walls were carved with images celebrating the achievements of the First House. The Elf standing behind the desk looked at her in surprise. Around the room, Elves stopped what they were doing and stared.

"Hello, Erast," Thea smiled. "I'm here to see Father."

The Elf shuffled some papers uneasily. "He is not seeing anyone at the moment, Miss Thea."

"He knows I'm coming." Thea swept past the desk to one of the ornate doors that lined the room. Without knocking, she pushed it open and stepped inside.

Her father looked up sharply from the desk where he sat. When he saw who it was, he seemed to relax, but still regarded her with a frown. "You have still not learned to knock, I see."

Thea considered Ulfgar's stance toward doors and figured that she was doing pretty well. "You wanted to talk to me?"

Her father sighed. "Come here, child."

Deciding not to push her luck, Thea approached her father's desk.

He regarded her solemnly. "What exactly did you do, just a few points ago?"

"I spoke into your mind."

"And how did you do that?"

"It was just magic. Right now I am serving beneath Enkeli, and magic from Enkeli can be used to message people, like I did today."

Her father gave her a skeptical glance. "So you can magically message your father when it would be just as easy to send a servant?"

"Magic isn't just for special things. It can be for anything, as long as it's what the Deity wants. I mean, the Ancient Wisdom."

Afonya's hands rested on his desk. "And you claim to know the will of the Ancient Wisdom?"

"I know a lot about it," Thea snapped. "And I know that messaging you was not harming anyone or doing anything else against the teachings of the Ancient Wisdom."

Afonya considered her for a moment, then rose to his feet. "The Keepers of Knowledge say that Enkeli no longer gives magic, and that those who claim to have it are deceiving the people."

"Well, they're wrong. The only reason the people at the Temple don't have any magic is because they aren't really following the Deity at all!"

A thoughtful frown sank deeper on Afonya's face. "That is a very serious accusation, Thea. The Keepers of Knowledge are the representatives of Enkeli to our people. We cannot disregard what they say."

"Can't we?"

"Thea, the Priesthood is a very powerful influence in Lyudmyla. Even the Queen Regent must take careful thought before pronouncing a judgment on them."

Thea watched her father, an idea growing in her

mind. "Would you like to see more magic?"

He regarded her cautiously. "There is more magic you can do?"

"There is. I want to show you, so you can know that Enkeli really sent me. May I?"

Afonya hesitated. "Very well."

Thea hadn't done it before, but she knew she could. Slowly the office walls around them faded, and they found themselves in the parlour at home.

Afonya stared in disbelief.

A startled yelp rose from the door to the dining room, followed by the crash of dishes on the floor.

"Oh mercy!" Grusha cried. "I never know whether you've come or gone!"

Afonya drew himself to his full height and glared at the hapless servant.

"I'm so sorry, Grusha," Thea spoke first. "I was just showing Father some magic. You had no reason to know we were here."

"Oh, I know you don't mean harm, Miss Thea. I'll just clean this up and be out of your way."

Afonya turned his frown on his daughter and waited until Grusha had scurried out of sight. "So you claim that is Enkeli magic."

"Father—"

Afonya raised a hand. "There is much to consider in the current political climate. Without due diligence and research, it is possible to be accused of anything. I need to make sure I understand exactly what is going on."

"Or you could just believe your daughter."

Afonya stared at her, his mouth a firm, hard line.

"Excuse me, Sir. Excuse me, Miss." Grusha came back into view, hurriedly sweeping up the broken dishes. "I'll only be a breath or two."

"It's alright, Grusha," Thea assured her. "I know it was an accident."

Afonya straightened once again. "Perhaps it is time to return to my office." He took one step towards the door and the room around him faded, replaced with his stately office.

He stood motionless for a moment. Shaking himself, he returned to his desk. "That is a very strange sensation."

"You get used to it." Thea watched her father, frustration and sadness vying for prominence in her heart. Was he so determined to reject everything she said and showed him?

Afonya settled himself in his chair and looked up at Thea with an expression of disapproval. "I see you still wear your rough clothing and carry that weapon. You are in Lyudmyla now. I should think it would not be necessary."

Thea considered how to answer. "When Enkeli sent me here, I was transported out of my home, as suddenly as I transported you today. If I am to be sent away again, I want to be ready."

Her father appeared startled. "You expect to leave?"

"I will go wherever my General commands me to go." Her eyes did not leave his face. "The only reason I am here is because Enkeli sent me. When I have finished what I was sent to do, I will leave again. The war is happening, and they need me there."

"War?" Her father's forehead creased in concern. "That is not a safe place for a young Elf to be."

"It's where I have to be." Thea leaned over the desk, willing for her father to understand. "In the presence of the Deity I accepted a position in this war. They need me."

"And your own family and people do not need you?"

Thea hesitated. "I think you do need me. That's why I'm here, for a little while. I'm here for people like Grusha, who need to know that the Deity cares about them, and that there's a way to have a better life."

"Grusha?" Afonya frowned. "What does she have to do with it? The Fallen House deserves its position of disgrace."

"Deserves?" Thea stared at Afonya. "Haven't you ever thought about showing mercy?"

"There is no mercy for what they did. The Priesthood made that very clear."

"If there is no mercy for those who fail, then I wouldn't be standing here!" Thea gripped the desk between them. "Listen. Only a few spans ago I was travelling with someone who was a spy from the Deceiver. I was given very specific orders that would keep him from contacting the Deceiver, but when the time came, I failed to follow my orders. Because of that, the Deceiver learned about me and my companions. He learned about the Resistance, and he learned about the Elves. Roland returned here and I went to help the Resistance, but before I got there more than half of them had been killed by the enemy. I brought the survivors to a safe place, and that is where they are now, waiting for me to return."

Thea leaned closer. "That happened because I failed, but the Deity showed me mercy. Now I'm here, in the hope that maybe you can receive mercy too."

Slowly, Afonya sat back in his chair, gathering himself into what could be called a stern posture. "You said something about Roland? I did not know he was with you."

"My uncle sent him."

Her father considered this. "I would have rested more easily knowing you had a suitable escort."

"If you are ever concerned about me again, perhaps you should speak to your brother about it."

He nodded, eyeing Thea with a troubled gaze. "You have given me much to think about. Perhaps it is time for you to return home. Your mother and Sylica may be there by now."

"What were they doing today?" Thea ventured.

"Your mother was attempting to buy proper Elvish clothes for her."

"I see." Thea watched her father's cold, lightless spirit. Her heart ached. "Father—"

Afonya raised his hand. "That is enough for today. You may go."

Thea nodded and turned away.

"Thea?"

She stopped and looked back. "Yes?"

"Please walk out of my office. Like a normal person."

~

Elora paced the room, her light footfalls hardly making any sound on the smooth wood floor.

At the table, Brandy and Fell Claw sorted weapons. Jason ran back and forth, stacking them in piles. Outside, Fauns watched the wall, their weapons in their hands.

Everything would be different now that the orcs knew how to get in. There would always be people on watch, day and night, ready to drive the orcs back if they ever tried again.

Ulga said they were testing. Testing to see what the magic would let them do. She'd come back covered with green blood, so angry that she could only speak orcish. It had taken Melinda ages to clean and bandage her wounds. Then Ulga had insisted on returning to her work in the kitchen.

Ulfgar and Ember had thrown themselves into the task of defence—planning watches, talking with Alya and her friends about ways to make the gate and the walls stronger.

Elora's pacing didn't slow. How could they know what the orcs would try next? Fear pounded through her body. She had to do something with it.

"Elora!" Two Fauns burst into the great room from the direction of the lean-to. "We found another way in!"

Elora's heart sank. She'd been afraid of that. That was why she'd sent the Fauns to start looking. If there was any other way the orcs could get in, they needed to know about it.

Elora followed the Fauns down the stairs. In the lower cellars, two more Fauns waited beside an open door she hadn't seen before.

"A hidden door." One of the Fauns pointed into the shadows. "It's a tunnel, not more cellars."

"You've explored it?"

The Faun nodded. "Come see."

With her hand on her quiver, Elora followed.

The tunnel beyond the door was damp and cold. Wetness clung to the walls and made the ground slippery underfoot. Silently they passed through long, twisting caves and carved passages, lower and lower. A low roar rumbled in the distance. Eagerly, Elora quickened her steps.

Rounding a bend, the tunnel opened out into a wide cave. Blue light rippled across the rocky ceiling. The smell of salt and rotting seaweed filled the air.

At the mouth of the cave, they stopped and stared out at the rocky shore. Waves swelled. Gulls cried and wheeled overhead.

The Fauns turned to Elora. "Another way in."

Elora nodded. One more way to watch. But it did give them a way out. A way that—maybe—the orcs didn't know about.

Leaving the Fauns to watch the cave, Elora made the long trek back up the tunnel.

As she passed the workshop, Talia emerged with a grin. "Elora! Come here!"

Elora stepped into the workshop, which had become the home of Alya and her friends. Makeshift beds lined one of the walls. A cluttered desk held dirty plates and half-empty cups.

Eleanor was there too, as she often was. Being as tall as the full-grown Littles was funny to her, and she liked helping them with their work.

"Come see this." Alya held up a thin sheet of metal. It had been bent into a strange pattern of bumps and dents.

"It's the shield?" Taking it from Alya, Elora turned it over. "How does it work?"

"All these reflecting bits should make it hard for an orc to see through it."

"So they won't see my—*someone's* spirit if they're

wearing this?"

Tam scratched his nose. "We haven't had a chance to test it yet."

"How do you put it on?"

Eleanor held up a handful of long, thin cords. "I made these. They go through the holes in the corners, see? I measured them on Daddy."

"Thank you." Elora smiled. "I'll show it to Ulga sometime and see what she thinks. What else are you working on?"

"We're trying to figure out what this glass ball does," Alya pointed it out, "and Talia is working on a pipe that lets you see over things."

"Gili and I are trying to make these metal bars stronger," Eleanor grinned. "Maybe we can use them on the walls or the gate."

Elora nodded. "Ulfgar will be glad for that."

Excusing herself, she hurried on.

"Elora!" Swift Wing called, passing her on the stairs. "I'm just heading to Gedwyld. Any word you want to send?"

"The usual update. You'll be able to get past the orcs?"

"I'll fly high," Swift Wing grinned. "They haven't managed to shoot me yet."

Elora nodded. She would tell the Dryads about the way down to the sea, but not just yet. "Say hi to Zaki for me. I'd like to hear more about those machines he was telling you about."

"Will do." The Dryad looked at the strange metal panel in Elora's hands. "What's that?"

"Something Alya and her friends are working on." Elora shrugged, her heart pounding. "Might be helpful."

"That's good." Swift Wing grinned. "Well I should go. It's almost eclipse!" With a wave, the Dryad strode out the door.

No one else had seen her. Elora slipped up the stairs to the bedrooms. A noisiness filled the air, coming from the Faunlets' room—as it always did. Carefully, she opened the door to the living area that she and Kais shared with the human family. Everything was quiet inside.

Adi slept in the makeshift crib Kais had made from an empty crate. Silently, Elora crossed the room and opened the bag she had brought from home. Reaching down to the bottom, she pulled out her black scouting clothes.

Quickly, she changed, stuffing her everyday clothes back into the bag.

Next she pulled out a handful of thin leather cords. Tying one around her arm, she carefully bound her black sleeve tight against her skin. There would be no loose fabric to rustle or catch on branches or brambles. She wrapped her other arm, then both her legs in the same way. Pulling back her hair, she wrapped it tight with the final cord.

That was better. She stretched, feeling the gentle, silent pull of her scouting clothes, as familiar as her own skin.

Now the shield. It shone oddly in the light as Elora held it up, thinking about the best way to attach it to her body. Finally she tied Eleanor's cords around her neck and waist, strapping the shield to her front like a clumsy breastplate. Hopefully it would work.

The kitchen bell rang. Elora listened as a rush of small hooves thundered down the stairs, followed by a few slow footsteps. Everyone would be eating. They wouldn't notice her go.

Her quiver was at her belt, with a knife from the weapons room. She took her bow from where it leaned against the wall.

In her little bed, Adi was still asleep, her face squished up in a half-pout. Her downy baby hair splayed out in every direction with its wispy little curls.

Silently, Elora leaned over the crib and kissed her daughter, then turned and slipped out of the room.

As silent as a shadow, she crept down the stairs, into the lean-to, and down the steps into the hallway below. She passed the sounds of cheerful chatter coming from the workshop and continued down, through the cellars, into the hidden tunnel.

As she followed the winding way lower, the sound of the surf grew louder until the tunnel opened out into the final cave. At its far end she caught a glimpse of the Fauns guarding the entrance.

Hardly breathing, she watched them for a long time. They seemed to be doing their job well, which was good, but not good for her hope of no one knowing where she'd gone. She would have to talk to them.

Elora stepped forward. Turning, the Fauns saw her and grinned.

"All quiet so far!" one of them reported.

Another eyed her scouting outfit with interest. "What are you doing?"

"I'm going to have a look around. If the orcs don't watch this way, the Dryads can use it to get food."

The Fauns grinned, hailing it as a very good plan, especially if it meant more to eat.

Elora nodded. "I'll be back soon." Passing the Fauns,

she slipped out of the cave.

A stiff wind blew off the sea, sending waves crashing on the shore. The rocky cliff stretched high above her, almost straight up, though its crags and ledges wouldn't be too hard to climb. Close by, she saw the winding path that led from the clifftop down to the shore. If anything along the shore was being watched, that would be.

Cautiously, she scrambled along the shoreline away from the path. Eclipse had begun, and the shadows along the cliff face were deepening. Finding a good place for her climb, she looked up at the sky. It would be an overcast night. That was good. The darker, the better.

Reaching for the ledge above her head, Elora pulled herself up. Yes, there was another ledge above her, just within reach. Her fingers gripped the edge of a crack and she pulled herself higher.

She took her time, careful of every step. Pulling herself up the final ledge, she crouched and stared through the shadows. There was no movement here, just the rustling of dead grass in the icy wind.

Making sure her arrows were loose in their quiver, Elora crept forward, circling towards the orc camps.

She had to find out what they were doing.

The light of a watchfire flickered beyond the wizened trees. Elora crept closer. There—the gleam of metal. An orc stood by the fire, poking it with a long stick.

Elora stayed back, creeping low through the undergrowth. Ulga had pointed out six orcs camps around their walls. Six war bands meant three hundred orcs, but from the sky, Swift Wing had seen more orcs coming into the area over the past few days.

Heavy footsteps tramped towards her. Elora ducked

behind a tree, her hand on the hilt of her knife. Orcs spoke to each other, something about an elite and being strong. Something was dead, or was going to be dead.

The footsteps faded into the distance. She should have tried to learn some orcish from Ulga. As it was, she'd have to manage with its sameness to The Talk. With a grim smile, Elora crept on through the trees.

Light flickered in the distance. Lantern light? Moving through the darkest parts of the shadows, Elora crept closer.

It was a lantern, of a sort. Something was breathing nearby. Where was it?

There. An orc sitting on the ground.

Crouching behind a tree, Elora watched. The orc did not move.

What was it doing? Cautiously, she crept closer. The orc sat without moving, staring towards the distant walls.

What was it staring at? It couldn't actually see the wall from this far away, but it was staring as if it could.

Hardly breathing, Elora circled through the undergrowth, trying to get a better look. No orc she'd seen had acted like this. It reminded her of the strange look Msizi sometimes had while doing his magic. Was this orc doing magic?

The orc moved, rising to its feet in one quick motion.

Elora froze, but the orc turned away from her, shouting through the trees.

Magic ... the door ... to break it ... Elora tried to make sense of its words. In the distance, other voices replied.

Magic ... the door ... the magic on the door? Were they trying to break the magic on the door?

Elora's blood ran cold. That magic was the only thing keeping them safe.

Footsteps approached through the trees. Did this orc know how to break the magic? If it did ...

She couldn't risk it.

Silently, she drew her bow.

"Hey!" she hissed. "Tin brain!"

The orc turned. Elora's arrow pierced its eye, and it crumpled to the ground. Dead.

Three more orcs burst into the clearing. They stopped, staring at the lifeless body at their feet. Growling, they glanced around the clearing.

Elora held her breath, staring through her thin screen of branches.

With a cry, one of the orcs pointed at her.

The orcs stared, something like dread on their faces. Their eyes passed over her, searching the air beside her as if they couldn't quite see her.

Slowly, Elora moved her hand to her knife.

The orcs spoke in low voices. *The ghost ... never there ...*

With a last wary glance, they turned and walked away.

Elora watched until they were out of sight. What kind of ghost would an orc be afraid of? She glanced over her shoulder. Clearly they had seen her, but not well enough to know what was really there. Cautiously, she slipped back through the trees. She had seen all she needed to see.

Night had almost passed by the time she made her way back to the cliff and carefully climbed down to the shore. The Fauns guarding the cave nodded to her as she passed on her way up the winding tunnels.

She crossed the cellars and slipped past the lantern-lit workshop where the gentle tap-tap of a lone hammer filled the silence of night.

Soundlessly, she slipped up the stairs, and almost walked right into Kais.

Elora froze, but there was no hiding. He'd been watching the stairs. Waiting.

"What are you doing?" Kais hissed. His gaze took in her scouting clothes, the bow held in her hand.

Elora's heart sank. She'd been hoping to avoid this. Somehow.

"I had to know what they were doing."

Kais glared at her with burning eyes. "They almost take our daughter and then you go out there? You could have died!"

"I know what I'm doing!" Elora snapped. "I came back, didn't I?"

"But what if you didn't?" Kais' hands were shaking.

Dropping her bow, Elora held Kais' shoulders, staring straight into his eyes. "This is what I'm good at. I couldn't sit still anymore. Not when there's danger out there."

Pain filled his eyes. "I don't want to lose you."

Elora sagged. She didn't want to hurt him like this.

"Kais—" She held him close, feeling every shaking breath. "I don't know what's going to happen, but I promise—I will do everything I can to live, for you and Adi."

Kais nodded.

Elora held him until his shoulders stopped shaking.

"She's back?" Noxolo stuck her head out from one of the rooms. "Oh good. Maybe we can sleep now."

"Maybe." Picking up her bow, Elora turned to Noxolo. "I found out what they're doing."

Chapter Fourteen

Thea stared up at the magnificent wall surrounding the Temple. Light glinted on the forms of Tilaryn carved in its shimmering marble. Enkeli's Temple, built in honour of the General of the Elves.

A shiver crept down Thea's spine as she stood before the large, ornate gates. Above its glittering arches were the likenesses of the four Generals, depicted with uncanny accuracy to the way they usually presented themselves.

First was the image of Allulien. The face on the image was stern, staring out over the city below them. She could almost hear Allulien's voice, reminding her that nothing should be placed before the Deity. Nothing—not even a Temple.

The image of Micai was next. She had not often seen Micai as they were depicted here, with stern face and weapon in hand. Instead, her mind was filled with memories of sitting by a campfire, sharing a tankard of beer. Micai had taught her about mercy, and here she was, on a mission of mercy to the people who deserved it the least.

Raphea's image held a long, flowing bandage. A scar was engraved on their shoulder, like the wound Zanele had healed on Ember so long ago. Zanele had challenged the Minathrils, accusing them of abandoning Raphtova. What would she have to say of the Elves?

Last of all, Thea's gaze rested on the General of the Elves, depicted with a scroll. Enkeli, the General of Wisdom and Knowledge ... and yet the magic given by Enkeli was for messaging and transportation, not just understanding. There was more to Enkeli than books and scrolls, hidden away behind marble walls.

With a boldness she didn't feel, Thea stepped through the gate into the courtyard beyond. Leafless trees stood like stately, ice-touched sculptures. The stones beneath her feet wove in an intricate design, leading her though the well-kept garden beds and silent fountains.

On the side of the courtyard adjoining the Palace, the old Hall of Messengers was dark and silent. On the other side of the courtyard, the Hall of the Keepers rose above the gardens, its magnificent windows glimmering with light. Between them, the Halls of Knowledge dominated the skyline. Its walls were ornate, covered with elaborate designs and images. Stained glass windows and archways spanned its breadth, and its massive domed roof gleamed with gold.

Thea didn't know why she was there, just that she felt like she should go. Hardly daring to breathe, she pushed one of the doors open and stepped inside.

Within, the Halls of Knowledge were the same as when she had visited them before. Endless shelves towered above her, filled with scrolls and books of every description. Between the shelves, the Keepers of Knowledge sat at ornately carved desks filled with parchments and dusty tomes. The scratching of pens and rustling of paper filled the air.

Everywhere Thea looked, she saw spirits that were dark.

Should she talk to someone? The Keepers seemed to be engrossed in their tasks. Maybe if there was a student or an initiate ...

Thea wandered through the endless shelves until she came to a door. Peering through, she found a small antechamber. A lone Elf sat by a table, wearing the official robes that marked her as a high-ranking member of the Priesthood—the same Priestess Thea had spoken to the last time she came to the Temple.

The Priestess caught sight of Thea and rose to her feet. "Welcome to the Halls of Knowledge. What knowledge do you seek?" As she approached, she peered curiously at Thea. "Have we spoken before?"

"Yes. I asked you about Davis."

"Oh yes." The Priestess nodded thoughtfully. "You wanted to hear from Enkeli, and I took you to the meditation chamber."

Thea nodded. She remembered it well.

"I know it can be discouraging at first," the Priestess gave a maternal smile, "but over time you will become accustomed to Enkeli's ways and know what to expect."

Thea watched her for a moment. "What do you expect?"

"Nothing, of course. I did warn you that Enkeli rarely speaks."

"But Enkeli has spoken to me."

The Priestess's eyes widened in alarm. "You are one of the insurgents. You were ordered to stay out of the Temple."

"The what?" Thea frowned. "I'm sorry, I don't know what you're talking about."

"There are certain ... *people*," she eyed Thea with a suspicious glare, "that claim to hear from Enkeli and have caused significant disturbances in the Temple.”

“I haven’t been to the Temple since the day you saw me. How could I be one of the people causing disturbances?”

“I suppose so,” the Priestess conceded, “but you must know that it is a very serious offence to claim a new word from Enkeli, when Enkeli has not actually appeared.”

“I understand.” Thea offered an encouraging smile. “I’m actually here because I have a question.”

“Of course.” The Priestess’s countenance brightened. “What knowledge do you seek?”

Thea considered the Priestess’s long, official robes. “Are you a teacher here at the Temple?”

“Yes. My name is Inessa, and I have the privilege of teaching the initiates and anyone who wishes to commit themselves to the service of Enkeli.”

Thea nodded. “I want to know why you teach that Enkeli has stopped giving magic.”

Inessa seemed surprised. “Why does that interest you?”

“I was taught that the Generals give magic to anyone serving beneath them. That’s what my old tutor used to say.”

The Priestess nodded. “*Historically*, that is correct. The Generals used to give magic, because in those early days, magic was needed. The Great War was fought, our city and this Temple were built, and magic was influential in those endeavours. Through Enkeli’s great wisdom, we now find ourselves in a time when there is no need for magic. Our city and our Temple are prosperous, and we have all that we need. What use would we have for magic?”

"I think we could use magic." Thea spoke softly, weaving her own magic into her words to speak directly to Inessa's heart. "We could use magic to find the wisdom to address difficult questions and problems in our city. We could use magic to bring healing to people who have been hurt, and to help make the world a better place. Don't you think we could use magic?"

"Well—" Inessa stammered, then seemed to pull herself together, "—the other reason is simply what we can see with our eyes. Enkeli *has* stopped giving magic, whether we like it or not. We must trust that Enkeli knows what is best."

Thea's eyes did not leave Inessa's face. Slowly she stretched out her hand. "Enkeli has not stopped giving magic." She transported the Scroll of the Ancient Wisdom—the oldest and most revered copy of the tenants of the Deity—from its place of honour at the center of the Halls of Knowledge. It appeared in her outstretched hand.

Fear filled the Priestess's eyes. "Trickery!"

"No. It is not trickery. It is Enkeli." Thea handed the scroll to the Priestess. "Try reading about it sometime."

Inessa's hands shook as she snatched the sacred text away from Thea. "How did you get this?"

Thea spoke directly into her mind. *I am sworn in the service of the Deity, beneath the command of Enkeli. I have magic, and Enkeli has sent me to you to tell you the truth that you have lost.*

The Priestess was visibly shaken. "You claim that Enkeli has appeared to you. Why would Enkeli not appear to us, who have been dedicated in service since before you were born?"

Thea shrugged. "Maybe you were not expecting it."

Inessa stared at the ancient scroll in her hands. "I cannot believe this."

Thea watched her closely. "Why don't you ask Enkeli if it is true?"

"Enkeli will not answer." Inessa's gaze fell. "Enkeli never answers."

"The Generals never turn away someone who wishes to serve the Deity. If you offer yourself in the service of the Deity beneath Enkeli's command, Enkeli *will* come."

"I entered Enkeli's service two hundred circles ago and Enkeli never appeared to me."

"That is because we are not supposed to serve Enkeli. We are supposed to serve the Ancient Wisdom."

Inessa fixed her with an incredulous stare. "So you say that if I had simply changed one word in my oath of service, Enkeli would have appeared to me?"

A small smile crept into the corners of Thea's mouth. "You could try."

For a moment, neither of them moved.

The Priestess's eyes narrowed. "If Enkeli appears, your words are proved true. If Enkeli does not appear, you will be banished with the insurgents."

"Understood."

The Priestess raised a hand.

"No rituals," Thea interjected. "Just say it."

Inessa hesitated, then shot Thea a glare. "Very well. I swear myself in the service of the Ancient Wisdom, beneath—"

Enkeli appeared, materializing directly in front of her. "Good. Glad to hear it."

Inessa stared, then sank to the floor.

"Here, I'll put that back for you." Enkeli took the scroll from her limp hands. "Check in tomorrow morning. I'll be there."

Enkeli vanished, then reappeared a moment later. "Oh yes, Thea's right."

Enkeli disappeared. Thea stared at the place where the General of the Elves had stood. She still hadn't had a clear view of Enkeli's face.

On the floor, Inessa was shaking. Gingerly, Thea tried to help her to her feet.

The Priestess clung to her. "My eyes have seen Enkeli!"

"Yes." Thea smiled. "Remember Enkeli is just a General—"

"A new vision." The Priestess's eyes were shining. "A vision from Enkeli!"

In the distance, a clamour of voices rose to fill the air. Hurrying footsteps approached. Cautiously, Thea stepped back. Something told her she shouldn't be there.

Pulling on her magic, she pictured the courtyard outside—a quiet corner behind the trees—and she was there.

Murmuring voices drifted through the air. To her surprise, they seemed to be coming from the Hall of Messengers. Thea crept closer and peered through one of the windows.

The inside of the Hall was bare and simple. A small group of Elves sat on a collection of old crates, watching something as if it amused them. Thea shifted her position and craned her neck to see.

A Priest with official robes stood just inside the door, glowering at an Elf that Thea instantly recognized as Khariton.

"Get out of here," the Priest ordered. "You've been

banished from the Temple grounds."

Khariton's smile was reckless. "Really? This is the Hall of Messengers, for the people Enkeli sends with a message. Well I have a message from Enkeli, so I have a right to be here."

The Priest glared. "And what is your message?"

"Get your bloody ass out of here, we're trying to have a drink in peace."

The other Elves murmured in agreement.

The Priest fumed. "The High Priestess will hear about this!"

Kharinton nodded. "Sounds like a plan."

Magic surged, and the High Priestess appeared, staring wildly around her. Seeing Khariton, her eyes narrowed.

"Khariton. We have spoken about this before."

"And I said that the Hall of Messengers is for us, not your stuffy Priests."

The High Priestess glared. "Why did you transport me here?"

"A message from Enkeli. You're still being an ass." Khariton's eyes twinkled. "That's it. Bye!"

With another surge of magic, the High Priestess and the Priest disappeared.

"Alright," Khariton grinned, "time to clear out before they come after us."

Chuckling and talking amongst themselves, the Elves dispersed.

Thea watched them go, then crept away from the window. As quickly as she could, she made her way out the gate and into the city streets beyond. Behind her, the Temple courtyard erupted in chaos.

~

The Ghost moved through the forest without making a sound. It was a quiet night. Only the skeletal trees and dead grasses shifted and murmured in the fitful breeze.

There—a sharp intake of breath. An orc scout stared from behind a screen of branches.

The Ghost waited as the scout crept closer, circling around, eyes probing the shadows. What the scout saw wasn't what was there. The Ghost made sure of that.

Closer ... closer ...

The forest around the Ghost faded, becoming a small clearing beyond the scout's sight. The Ghost smiled, and moved on.

There was an orc camp, not far away. The casters wouldn't be there now, since they worked night and day, hardly taking time to eat or rest. They all worked towards the same goal—to understand and break the magic that protected the house.

With the number of casters growing every day, it was only a matter of time.

The Ghost moved silently through the underbrush, following an indirect, winding path that no one could understand.

There—another muffled sound. Two orcs stared across an open clearing with widening eyes.

The Ghost stepped behind a tree, creating a visual message—an image—and transported it out from behind the tree, as if the Ghost had continued walking. The image turned and stared at the orcs with glowing eyes, then walked silently towards them.

The orcs spoke to each other in low, uneasy voices. Before they could decide what to do, the image faded and disappeared.

The orcs stared for a while longer, then turned and hurried away.

The Ghost smiled. Keep them on edge. Keep them guessing. Every measure they delayed was a measure gained.

There—the first signs of the camp through the trees. Becoming invisible as well as silent, the Ghost stepped forward, passing through the guards and the tents.

A group of orcs crouched on the ground, cleaning and maintaining their weapons. None of them noticed as an image appeared in their midst.

"Don't you think it's interesting that they only harm us when we try to harm them?" Comprehension to speak in orcish, and message to send the words out of the mouth of the image.

"Huh," one of the orcs muttered without looking up from their work. "Shut your mouth. That's traitor talk."

"Is it? Sometimes I wonder which side is really the right side to be on."

Glancing up, one of the orcs saw the image and swore.

"The Ghost!" Murmurs rose amongst the orcs. They shifted uneasily, fingering their weapons.

The orcs had learned long ago that the Ghost couldn't be harmed. Slowly, the image faded away.

The Ghost smiled. It was a good name, and a good reputation.

A spy was a dangerous thing. A ghost could do what it liked.

The camp faded and the Ghost appeared in another

clearing, further along the blockade.

They'd given up trying to catch the Ghost. Every time they tried, it slipped through their grasp, fading into the mists of night. That freedom was exactly what the Ghost wanted.

Night after night the Ghost returned, walking among their ranks, talking with them, asking questions they couldn't answer. The orcs were smart—too smart—but they had only been taught to think a certain way. Other kinds of thoughts were dangerous.

With the Ghost's help, some of them might start thinking the wrong kinds of thoughts, like Ulga had.

The light of a watch fire glowed in the distance. Passing like a breath of wind, the Ghost moved on.

Chapter Fifteen

Thea slipped through the front door of her parents' house. Inside, everything was quiet and empty, besides the snatches of song drifting from the servants' quarters.

Stepping into the parlour, Thea was engulfed by the warmth of the fireplace, crackling cheerfully in its grand stonework enclosure. Setting Raybow and her gear by the wall, Thea moved closer to warm her hands.

From one of the large, comfortable chairs, Thea's mother looked up sharply.

Thea froze, just for a moment. "Hello, Mother," she stammered. "I didn't know you were home."

Thea's mother indicated some papers on a small table at her side. "I am writing, currently."

"Is Sylica here?"

"Sylica is not here." She lifted her pen and returned it to the bottle of ink. "Your Father has taken her to see the Temple."

Thea hesitated. "The Temple?"

Taisiya looked at her daughter with amusement. "Why not? It is one of the more magnificent sights in Lyudmyla."

"I—I suppose, but when did they go? I didn't see them there."

Taisiya's glance was sharp. "Were you there?"

"Yes. I just got back now."

Taisiya's eyes widened in horror. "You went to the Temple dressed like that?"

Thea glanced down at her well-worn travelling clothes. "Why not? This is what I always wear."

Taisiya's eyes flashed. "Will you never care about the effect you have on other people? You walk around like a planet, expecting everything to revolve around you!"

"I do not!" Thea retorted. "I just know that there is more to life than fashion and appearances!"

"So you wear what you want and you go where you want." She fixed Thea with a withering glare. "It doesn't matter at all to you that every moment you are changing people's opinions of you and your family!"

"People's opinions of me don't matter! What matters is whether they are serving the Deity!"

Taisiya's eyes narrowed. "Do you know how hard your uncle and father and I work to stop the Priesthood from gaining more power than they already have? When you left it was all we could do to keep your uncle's influence intact, and now that things have finally settled down again, here you are—disregarding all propriety, and ready to make us the laughingstock of the nobility!"

Thea hesitated, her mind drawn to the one thing she hadn't expected to hear. "You ... work against the Priesthood?"

"To protect our city's interests from their power-hungry ambitions? No measure is too small. They have already taken control over far more than their jurisdiction should allow."

Thea's mouth opened, then closed again. "... I thought you just went to parties."

Taisiya shook her head in exasperation. "How else do you build influence in society? You have to be present *in society* and give everyone no doubt that you are superior, given the alternatives."

Thea stared at her mother. All this time ... all her mother's concern for propriety and fashion and people's opinions ... she had never considered that there might be a reason.

Her mother's glare was withering. "Then after all we have done, you throw everything away for a religious life."

"To serve the Ancient Wisdom, not the Temple."

"I see no difference."

"There is!" Thea protested. "The people at the Temple don't obey the Ancient Wisdom. It's all an act, or a habit that's lost its meaning. Serving the Ancient Wisdom isn't about rituals and scrolls, it's about showing mercy, caring for the world, and being faithful to obey."

Taisiya did not seem impressed. "Then why go to the Temple?"

"I ... I think Enkeli wanted me to go."

Taisiya gave her an incredulous look.

"I needed to talk to someone there. It is time for the Elves to follow the Ancient Wisdom again. I had to see if someone there would listen to me."

"If you want someone to listen to you, you should be more careful about how you present yourself. Dressing well is a sure way to impress, rather than mooching around in those old things."

"I don't want to impress people, I want them to serve the Deity!"

"Do you want them to listen to you?" Taisiya looked her up and down with a judicious gaze. "If you do not want to be dismissed as a beggar or a vagabond, you will have to dress better than that."

"I have to travel in these clothes, not attend fancy dinners with a bunch of snobs!"

"I never said wear a velvet gown with gemstones embroidered on it," Taisiya snapped. "Clothing speaks, and if you are not careful it speaks against you and undermines your words. If you want people to listen to you and take you seriously, it is time to think about what you are wearing."

The retort died on Thea's lips. "I … I never really thought about that before."

Taisiya straightened the letters on the small table. "Clothing must fit its intended use. For impressing snobs, the more elaborate the dress, the better. You, on the other hand, need something practical for travel and quick movement, that also shows that you mean business and ought to be listened to." She glanced up at Thea, with what might have been a twinkle of amusement in her eye. "Wouldn't you agree?"

Speechless, Thea stared at her mother. Where she had expected nothing but judgment, here was a strange kind of acceptance. Her mother knew what she was doing and wanted to help, in her own kind of way.

"I think you're right," Thea ventured. "I guess I could look at getting some new things."

"There are a couple of shops that may have just what you are looking for." Taisiya rose to her feet and collected her letters. "Afonya and Sylica should be gone for another measure at least. Shall we take the time to do some shopping?"

Thea nodded. "Thank you."

Taisiya smiled. "It's the least a mother can do."

~

"Zaki!"

Someone hammered on the door. Groggily, Zaki lifted his head off the table where he had fallen asleep. What time was it?

The hammering on the door grew louder. "Zaki! Come quick! A shooter broke!"

Zaki scrambled to his feet, sending tools and bits of wire and pipe scattering in all directions. Where was his fixing bag? There—he seized it from where it lay in a heap on the floor. Jerking the door open, he bolted outside.

Tamir was waiting for him. Together they raced down the street.

As they neared the wall, the clamour of noise engulfed them. Humans and Littles ran back and forth, carrying stones and quivers full of crossbow bolts. Shouts and cries filled the air as a barrage of spears and javelins sailed overhead, striking the cobblestone streets or embedding deep in the woodwork. Archers crouched behind the parapets, bracing themselves. "Fire!" a captain cried, and the archers sprang into the open, shooting arrows or crossbow bolts before diving for cover again.

In their midst, the large shooter sat motionless. Zaki dashed towards it, dodging spears and the scurrying crowds.

Scrambling up the makeshift stairs to the foot of the shooter, Zaki dumped out the contents of his fixing bag in a jumbled heap.

Two Littles crouched beside the broken shooter, struggling with a long, splintered piece of wood.

"The arm broke," one of them gasped. "It won't shoot!"

Zaki glanced over the wall. Beyond, the teeming crowd of orcs surged closer.

Other shooters screeched, gears grinding as they turned on their metal tracks. They could give some cover, but not nearly enough. Every time a machine broke, the orcs got closer.

"Did you try wrapping it?" Zaki ducked back down, sifting through his heap of tools and materials.

"We did, but it broke again."

"Here." Zaki grabbed a long, thin band of metal. He'd been hoping to use it for something else, but this was more important. "Tamir, find Egon and tell him we need a new shooter arm. I'll fix this one for now. Oh, and tell Nora I need her."

Tamir nodded and took off through the crowds.

As Zaki worked, he explained to the other two Littles what to do if it broke again, and made sure they knew how to attach the new arm when it arrived. Finally, he bolted the arm back in place.

The wall beneath them shook.

"Get them back!" The human captain yelled until her face was red. "Get them back!"

People scrambled to help, grabbing rocks and broken bits of wall, throwing them down at the orc soldiers below.

Zaki nodded. The Littles grabbed the handle of the shooter and started to turn. Gears squealed. Chains rattled. *Clonk.* The bolt fell into place and the catch released, sending the bolt screeching out into space.

It worked. For now.

Zaki slumped against the wall as the Littles continued to wind the handle, sending bolt after bolt into the mass of bellowing orcs.

A cheer rose from the soldiers on the wall.

Across the crowded street, Zaki caught a glimpse of the middle-aged Little who was his newest operator.

"Nora!" Zaki scrambled to dump his heap of tools back into his bag. Slinging it over his back, he slid down off the wall. "Ready to check the north gate rock thrower?"

Nora's face split in a wide grin. "Sure am!"

As they made their way through the maze of back alleys, they soon heard the rhythmic *thrum thrum thrum* of the rock thrower.

Rounding a corner, they came in sight of the enormous machine, filling the open space just inside the city gate. Its four long throwing arms spun around, swooping down to scoop up the next large rock, then swinging overhead, sending the rock hurtling out beyond the gate as the next arm scooped up its rock.

Close at hand, its operators kept the flywheel spinning. A whole team of Littles and humans worked to keep its loading chute full.

"Any trouble?" Zaki asked, joining the operators at the wheel.

Thrum thrum THUNK *thrum.*

Zaki frowned. One arm had failed to load its rock. "That happen much?"

"Once every point or two." One of the operators shrugged. "Not bad, really."

Zaki watched the machine at work for a while. "Let's grease the wheel. Maybe that will help."

The operator pushed the lever and the flywheel disengaged. The spinning arms slowed to a stop. "Nora?" Zaki called.

Pulling a jar from an alcove nearby, Nora poured some oil over the turning mechanisms, scrubbing them with a greasy rag.

Zaki ran a hand along one of the arms of his machine. The shooters were good, but he was really proud of the rock throwers. At full speed they threw a rock every breath.

"Ready!" Nora called.

"Start her up."

With a grin, Nora pulled the lever and the throwing arms spun once again.

Thrum thrum thrum.

Nora wiped her hands on the dirty rag.

"Thanks," Zaki nodded. "You good to check the forest gate on your own?"

Nora grinned. "Sure thing." Tucking the rag into her belt, she strode off through the crowd.

Zaki sank down onto a crumbled bit of wall. He had four operators trained for each machine so they could run them in shifts, and now there were two extra operators being trained to run repairs and upkeep. Hopefully that would be enough. Absently, he pulled a bit of wire from his pocket and twisted it back and forth between his fingers.

Trumpets blared in the distance. Another raid.

The captain of the north gate sprang into action. Too often a raid along one portion of the wall had been a cover for an assault somewhere else.

The orcs kept pushing, testing their defences. The city was holding on, but it didn't have much left to give.

The soldiers on the walls were tired and hungry. Most of them had never even seen a monster before the orcs turned up on their doorstep.

The machines helped, but one day the orcs would find a way past them.

A shadow passed overhead. Zaki glanced up to see the familiar form of a hawk, silhouetted against the sky. It saw him and tipped into a dive. Just before it reached the ground, it shifted into the form of a Little about Zaki's age, with a shock of bright red hair.

Swift Wing smiled. "There you are. Elora and Kais wanted me to say hi."

Zaki glanced up at the sky. "It's a bit early, isn't it?"

"We wanted to make sure everything was okay."

Zaki frowned. "What's wrong?"

"Just something Msizi heard. Sounds like the orcs are up to something. We weren't sure if it was up north or down here."

Zaki shrugged. "Nothing new here. Yet."

"A couple more war bands arrived today. I saw them from the sky. Looks like there's some digging too."

"How far away?"

"At the edge of the trees."

Farther than the machines could reach. Zaki glanced at the Dryad. "Elora and Kais are doing okay?"

Swift Wing nodded. "They're worried, but that can't be helped. The orcs have really surrounded the place now. If we didn't have the tunnel out, we'd be starving."

"What if the orcs find it?"

"They won't. Only us Dryads are using it now."

Zaki nodded. "How's Adi?"

"Growing every day," Swift Wing grinned. "She can sure shout when she wants to." Stretching, they glanced up at the sky. "I should head up to the castle. Any message for your folks?"

Zaki fidgeted with his bit of wire. "Just say hi. And that my machines are working."

Swift Wing nodded. "Got it. See you later!"

With a rush of feathers, Swift Wing took to the sky, disappearing beyond the rooftops.

Putting the bit of wire back in his pocket, Zaki slung his bag over his shoulder again. He wouldn't tell them about his new machine. Not yet.

Hurrying through the streets, Zaki kept his head down. Maybe now with more people trained he could actually focus for a while.

The orcs were smart. It wouldn't be long before they made a way into the city. Maybe they were tunnelling to go under the walls. Maybe it would be another way. He wasn't sure how they'd get though, but when they did, he had to be ready to stop them.

The Big Bad wasn't going to win. Just because he hated the Littles and made his own kind of people instead didn't mean they were worthless. Zaki would show him just what the Littles could do.

He would make something even better than orcs.

Shutting the door behind him, Zaki ran up the stairs to the attic. His prototype lay on the floor, almost filling the attic from end to end. Big armour. He made it to stand tall—taller than an orc. It was stronger than steel and fully controllable, as if the armour was a body of its own. The hollow inside was just large enough for the operator and the controls—a vast array of switches and levers controlling the legs, arms, and weapons.

Once the orcs made a way in, someone would have to stand in their way. With this big armour, he had a chance of stopping them.

If not, he would die trying.

A gentle tapping on the door punctuated the silence.

"Zaki, dear," Sami called. "Come get something to eat."

"I'm busy." Zaki bent over his table filled with scraps of paper and bits of twisted metal. In the center of it all was a convoluted mass of gears and wires—the big armour's final piece. To run, it needed power, but finding a way to make and store that much power seemed to be impossible.

He had gears upon gears, wires and magnets, every single trick he could think of, but it still wasn't enough.

The door creaked open and Sami tottered across the room. She set a plate of cookies on the table. "You've got to eat sometime, dear."

Zaki sighed. "No. I need to figure this out. It won't be done in time if I can't get enough power."

"You'll figure it out." Sami smiled and patted him on the back. "A few hiccups never stopped you before."

"This isn't a few hiccups. I'm doing everything I can and it isn't good enough."

"Turned it off and on again?"

Zaki looked up into her twinkling eyes. "I can't do it, Sami."

Sami laid a frail hand on his shoulder. "Then ask the Great Big Big for help. That is where power really comes from. When we reach our end, all we can do is ask for help."

Zaki looked down at the table.

Sami's soft footsteps crossed the room and went back down the stairs, step after step.

Maybe he could attach the wires differently? No.

That wouldn't work. What if he could twist that gear, increasing the tension on the spring? He tried, but it wouldn't twist any farther.

Zaki stared at the mass of gears and wires in front of him until his eyes burned. There was no way. He couldn't see any way.

He put his head in his hands. *Great Big Big, help me. I need to make this, and I can't.*

Nothing changed, but slowly a feeling of peace crept over him. He looked up. Maybe he should try again.

Gingerly, Zaki reached out and touched the gears. They tingled beneath his hands.

Grabbing the biggest gear, Zaki turned it. It went farther than it ever had before. Beneath it, the coil began to glow.

Zaki smiled.

Chapter Sixteen

Thea stared down the length of her arrow. Around her, the brightly-coloured banners of the archery range flapped in the icy wind.

She took three shots, then went to collect her arrows. One was close enough to the mark, but the other two had gone wide.

Thankful that she'd thought to come practice, Thea returned to her place, trying again and again until her accuracy and confidence returned.

Loud voices approached from the street. Thea glanced up as a group of young Elves entered the range, wearing white tracksuits. It was the crew of the Eagle. Dropping their bows and quivers in an untidy heap, they started stretching and warming up.

The captain of the team gave her a curious glance. "Hey, it's Thea! I thought you weren't around here anymore!"

The whole team gathered around her, jostling and talking amongst themselves.

"It's Roland's girl."

"Haven't seen him in ages either."

"Nice bow you've got there."

"Where have you been, anyways?"

Thea did her best to offer a friendly greeting. "I've been travelling," she explained.

"Where'd you go? Rokhov?"

A ripple of laughter swept through the gathered Elves.

"Beyond Svokyie, actually," Thea retorted. They seemed so smug and condescending. How had she ever been glad that Roland was a part of their team? Fixing them with a superior smile of her own, she continued, "I've been to the great human city of Gedwyld and walked through the shadows of the Deorcian where monsters are. I've climbed mountains taller than you've ever seen and sailed further than you've dreamed of going."

The crew of the Eagle glanced at each other.

One Elf gave her a suspicious glare. "All that in just a few cycles?"

"That's not even half of what I've seen and done."

"Huh," one of the Elves ventured. "Sounds like you're full of it."

The captain knocked the offending Elf on the side of the head. "Boasting's all well and good," he grinned at Thea, "but how are you with that bow?"

"Yeah, let's see you shoot."

"Alright," Thea smiled. Slowly she pulled an arrow from her quiver and put it to the string. It was one of the arrows Elora had made for her. Thea sighted along it and let it fly.

It struck the target—a bullseye.

The crew of the Eagle cheered and slapped Thea on the back.

"Look at that!" one of them laughed. "You're better than Yarik!"

The captain looked her up and down. "I'm impressed. You learned to shoot like that in the Dark Lands?"

"I did."

The captain nodded thoughtfully. "It sounds like you had quite the adventure out there."

"Maybe you should try," one of the crew nudged the captain with a wink. "You're always going on about how boring it is here."

"Well," he gave a cocky smile, "I think an adventure or two would suit me just fine."

The crew nodded their agreement.

"No early morning workouts. I'd go for that."

"Hah—you already skip out every time you can get away with it."

A quieter member of the crew watched Thea with wide eyes. "What's it like out there?"

There was longing in her eyes. Thea smiled. "It's different than what we know here. It's a whole world to explore, filled with wonder and beauty and all sorts of people you've never seen before."

"What, you mean Fauns and Dryads and things?" another Elf interrupted. "Like in the stories?"

"Yes. Some of my best friends are Fauns and Dryads. I've travelled with them and fought beside them. They've saved my life and I've saved theirs."

"Wow." One member of the crew seemed to speak for the others. "Sounds a lot more interesting than training every day." The rest of the team nodded in agreement.

"I did all of that because I serve the Ancient Wisdom." Thea looked from face to face. Attentive faces, listening to every word. "Do you remember the stories about the Great War? It isn't over yet. The people out there are still fighting, and they need our help. That's why I've come back, to tell the Elves they need to fight again."

"The Great War?" The crew looked at each other, interest growing in their eyes.

"Now that sounds like an adventure!"

"I've got a good hand with a sabre."

"You all saw that time I beat Arki in a fight."

"We'd get to see all those interesting places."

"And all those strange people!"

The captain slapped Thea on the shoulder. "If the Elves really go to war, you can count us in! No one could turn down an adventure like that!"

The crew murmured in agreement.

"The Ancient Wisdom wants us to fight?" One of the Elves fixed Thea with a curious expression.

"Come on, Nika, that's what she said!" The captain knocked him on the side of the head. "Weren't you listening?"

"I was listening. I just want to know why we haven't been fighting, if that's what the Ancient Wisdom wants."

"Because we haven't been listening," Thea replied. "It's been a long time since the Elves really listened to what the Ancient Wisdom wants."

"That's wrong isn't it?" Nika's eyes didn't leave her face. "We're supposed to obey the Ancient Wisdom."

"Yes, we are."

"Come on, Nika," the captain protested, "that's Temple talk! Our job is winning our next race." He grinned at Thea. "We won the last two races since you went away. You should have seen it!"

Grins and nods echoed around the team.

"That isn't all the Ancient Wisdom wants." Thea wove comprehension magic into her words. They wouldn't all understand, but one or two of them looked as if they might. "The Ancient Wisdom wants people who have offered their entire lives in service. Not like the Temple, but like I did. To serve beneath a General and obey their orders, whether that leads to adventure or war or simply going home. The important part is to obey."

"Well, we all know what it's like when Coach says jump, don't we?" The captain grinned, managing to draw a chuckle or two from the group. "If the Queen decides to go to war, we'll be first in line to sign up. You can count on us."

The rest of the crew gave their hearty assent.

"Now come on!" The captain gestured his team to get moving. "We're here to shoot, not talk."

As the team collected their bows and arranged themselves, the captain approached Thea.

"It's nice to see you again." He flexed his bow and gave her a cocky smile. "I haven't noticed Roland around much lately. You want to come over to my place tonight?"

Thea gave him an incredulous glance. Apparently he was being serious. "No. I'm not interested."

The captain shrugged amiably. "If you change your mind, just let me know."

Trust me, that is not happening. Thea spoke into his mind, smiling to herself as his eyes widened in surprise.

Clipping Raybow onto her baldric, Thea turned and left the archery range.

Around her, the bustling city stretched out in every direction. She wandered towards the upper market, then along the broad, terraced streets that lined the upper reaches of the mountain. It wasn't like she had much else to do. As she walked, her gaze turned to the dark line on the far horizon, her only glimpse of the world beyond Larsya.

Thea? A voice appeared inside her head.

Thea stopped. *Msizi?* She gasped in delight. *I'm so glad to hear from you!*

Msizi's voice was urgent. *Thea, the orcs are breaking the magic on the house. We can't stop them. Whatever we try, their counterspells stop us. It's all I can do to—*

The voice was gone.

Thea froze. *Msizi? Msizi, what happened?*

Icy wind blew past Thea as she waited, heart pounding.

Msizi?

...

Silence.

Chapter Seventeen

Thea hurried up the street towards the Palace. The span was over—finally—and her uncle wanted her to wait in his office until the Council meeting was scheduled to begin.

She'd been on edge ever since the unfinished message from Msizi two days ago. When she tried to message him back, her magic had failed. Whatever was happening there, her magic wasn't strong enough to get through.

Thea clutched the package she was bringing to her uncle and quickened her pace. She just had to make it through this Council meeting, and then she could go back. Hopefully she'd be bringing help.

Her span in Lyudmyla had felt unbearably long, with little to do but wander the streets alone. It hurt, seeing the dull, lifeless state of her people. They could be so much more than that. But they weren't.

She glanced down at the new clothing her mother had bought for her. There hadn't been one outfit, but several, each suited for a different purpose. Today she wore one specifically chosen by her mother for this occasion. It was formal, reminiscent of what court officials wore, while still being practical and suitable for travel.

"If you are speaking to the Council," her mother had said, "the least you can do is dress as if you mean business."

Thea had also promised her mother that she would leave her travel bag behind.

"Your father told me about your magic." Her mother gave her a keen glance. "If you can move things here and there whenever you wish, leaving it should not be an issue. If you need it, you can make it appear wherever you are."

Raybow hung over Thea's back, as it always did. No one was going to convince her to leave that behind.

The guards at the Palace gate seemed to be expecting her. With a nod, they gestured her through. Thea made her way to her uncle's office and knocked.

"Come in!" Mykyta called from beyond the door.

Thea opened it and let herself in. Mykyta sat at his desk, sorting through his seemingly endless stacks of letters. He smiled as Thea approached and accepted the package from her hands.

"Thank you for bringing that, Thea. I expect everyone very soon." Setting the package on his desk, he returned to his letters. "I hear you've been all over the city."

"I don't know how much I really did," Thea ventured. "I talked with a few people, but that's about it."

Mykyta nodded approvingly. "It had just the effect we needed."

The door opened, and Roland stepped inside.

Thea felt herself stiffen, though she tried not to show it.

"Ah, Roland." Mykyta nodded. "Just the person I need."

Roland bowed to the Chancellor, handing him a letter. After Mykyta turned away, Roland glanced at

Thea, his eyes twinkling. "You look like you mean business."

"That would be my mother's doing." Thea gave a wry smile.

"How have you been?" Roland casually examined the leather of his mail bag.

"I am well. Anxious to get back home, though. You?"

"Not bad." He hesitated. "Sorry I didn't get to see you all span. Your uncle kept me very busy."

Mykyta glanced over the contents of the letter. "There's a war on. Of course we're busy."

"That's alright." Thea nodded to Roland. "I had my own things I needed to do."

Mykyta set the letter on his desk. "Roland, if you would just open the package from the bakery, Thea and I have our meeting to attend."

"What meeting?" Thea frowned. "The Council isn't starting yet." She thought she caught an impish smile at the corners of her uncle's mouth.

"It's cookies?" Roland looked at the open package in his hands with a puzzled expression.

"Just hold those for us, won't you?" Mykyta nodded. "There's a good lad."

Thea stared at the cookies. Her uncle wouldn't ...

She glanced around the empty room. "Micai?"

Beside her, Micai appeared, taller and more iridescent than any Elf, but otherwise appearing just the way Thea was used to seeing them.

Thea gasped in delight. "You're here!"

"Hi, Thea!" Micai grinned. "Mykyta said there would be cookies."

Eyes wide, Roland stood at attention as Micai reached into the open bag.

"What are you doing here?" Thea demanded.

Micai took a bite. "Cookies?"

Thea tried to glare, but couldn't help laughing. "You didn't just come for the cookies."

"I could if I wanted to." Micai examined the partially eaten cookie in his hand. "Not the same as Sami's, but not bad."

A golden glow filled the room, and Allulien appeared.

Thea gasped, fighting her sudden urge to fall to her knees before her General. "Allulien!"

Allulien smiled. "Hello, Thea. I told you we would meet again."

Micai nodded a greeting.

Allulien turned to Micai with an amused gleam in their eyes. "Already found the cookies, I see."

"Did you expect any different?" Raphea appeared beside Allulien. "If there are cookies, Micai will eat them."

Micai made a face, reaching into the bag for another cookie. "I can stop if I want to."

Thea stared from Micai, to Allulien, to Raphea. Her mouth went dry. "It's a council of war, isn't it?"

"It is." Allulien stepped forward.

Thea's heart beat faster. They'd had a council of war the night before getting the Littles out of the Deorcian. What were they preparing for now?

The Council meeting. It wasn't just a meeting—it was war. The war for the loyalty of the Elves.

Allulien glanced around the room. "Enkeli?"

Through the closed door, Enkeli appeared. Still carrying folders full of notes, Enkeli shuffled through them, muttering in a low voice. "I think I've got it all. Right. If we just put this here—" Glancing up, they saw that everyone was waiting. "Oh. You're all here."

Thea stared at the fourth General—arms full of papers, looking down at them with an uncomfortable, preoccupied expression. Suddenly she knew where she had seen that face before.

"You—you're my tutor!"

"Hmm?" Enkeli glanced up. "Oh. Yes, I did that for a while."

"How—" Thea stammered, "—how is that possible? You were just a regular old tutor, but it was you!"

Enkeli seemed flustered. "Had to make sure you were taught right. Education these days, you know."

Thea turned to glare at her uncle. At his side, Roland's mouth hung open.

"Did you know that?" Thea demanded.

"I did not, at the time." Amusement gleamed in Mykyta's eyes. "Though I learned it more recently, in my conversations with Enkeli."

"But—" Thea turned to Enkeli—her tutor—who was still shuffling through their armful of papers. "But why?"

Allulien's eyes gleamed. "Because Enkeli had a plan."

Thea stared around the room at the shimmering beings surrounding her. Allulien, her General, who had encouraged her and rebuked her as she learned what it meant to be a servant of the Deity. Micai, whose gentle companionship had taught her so much during those first days away from home. Raphea, who had shown her that it was possible to be faithful to the Deity, even as an Elf. And Enkeli, who had stepped into her normal childhood to teach her about the Deity and the Great War and the world beyond Lyudmyla.

Because of them, she was the person that she had

become.

They were all watching her.

Thea swallowed. "What's the plan?"

"Right." Enkeli shuffled forward. "Remember this is one piece in the bigger picture, which should all work together at just the right time, and if you look here—" Enkeli pulled a candlestick on the opposite side of the room from the one Sylica had pulled before. The row of bookshelves slid back and moved aside to reveal a large wall, once empty, now covered with scraps of paper, scribbled notes, arrows, and bits of string. Enkeli smiled. "This is the plan!"

Everyone stared at the complicated mess covering the wall. Thea didn't even know where to begin.

"You want to translate that?" Micai asked, munching another cookie.

Thea recognized the look on Enkeli's face. It was the expression she saw when she had been taught something quite simple that somehow she still couldn't understand.

"Well," Enkeli fumbled through the papers they carried, checking one of them and pinning it to a center point on the wall. "This is Lyudmyla, right? All the influential figures are mapped out here. If the Queen decides to go to war, that will set this in motion here."

"And if she doesn't?" Allulien's voice filled the room.

"There's a contingency for that." Enkeli pointed to another set of papers. "Mykyta can pull his influence and send an army of at least two hundred—"

"That is not enough."

"Exactly." Enkeli nodded. "But with the right setup in place, we should be able to double those numbers." Enkeli's hands ran nimbly along the wall, moving pins and notes, scribbling even more words into the margins. "You see here—with the impact of the work in Rokhov, there may be additional forces available, and if they travel through Wyndburh—"

Enkeli's words washed over Thea. Layer upon layer. Plan upon plan. She listened to the mind that worked fifty steps ahead of everything else, preparing for anything, taking risks and calculated gambles that, if they worked, would lead to even greater outcomes.

She stared at the giant map of ideas and connections spread out before her, and slowly the pattern began to make sense. That—that was the Littles and their influence in Gedwyld, somehow making the city stronger than it had ever been before. She saw the scattering of the Resistance and the war bands of orcs spreading across the land.

Through it all ran a golden thread. Wherever it went, things started happening, spreading out in a network of scribbles and possibilities. It passed through the Deorcian, through Gedwyld. It passed through the forest where the Resistance had been, even reaching high to the home of the Minathrils in the mountains. Last of all it led to Lyudmyla. It was the Spark.

"Enkeli." Allulien's voice cut through the silence like a knife. "You always have a plan, but this does not resolve the deeper issue that must be addressed. The Elves must return to the Deity. We have been patient. We have given the Elves time to repent and have shown them mercy again and again, but still they cling to false worship in their abomination of a temple. Time is running out. The temple must fall, and if they do not renounce it, the Elves will fall too."

Fear rose in Thea's heart. She knew that stern gleam

in Allulien's eyes. The Elves had failed in their service to the Deity, and judgment had to come. She herself had said it was no more than the Elves deserved. And yet ... her mind held new images now. Images of spirits that were lonely and afraid, spirits that were restless, that knew the Temple was wrong, that knew they were meant to do more with their lives than stay in Lyudmyla forever, cut off from the rest of the world. The Elves could change. They just needed more time.

Thea turned to Allulien. "What needs to happen?"

"First, the Elves must return to the war. After that, they must end their worship of the temple."

Thea nodded. "Today we will convince them to join the war."

A startled look passed through Allulien's eyes.

Thea glanced at her uncle. "Won't we?"

Mykyta smiled, pride gleaming in his eyes. "That is our intention. Enkeli says the pieces are in place. There is a chance it will work."

Allulien fixed him with a keen stare. "If it does not, judgment is coming."

Mykyta nodded. "I understand."

Thea glanced at Micai. Surely there would still be room for mercy ... but Micai's face was hard and set. The line had been drawn, like it was for Hwasan. The Elves had to choose whose side they were on, and if they still wouldn't listen ... sometimes mercy looked like judgment.

Not today. The Council would listen to her. They had to listen to her.

Raphea stepped forward and raised a hand. "The Deity's blessing be on you, Thea, and on you, Mykyta, as you undertake this task. Bring new life to this race that has been sick for so long."

Thea bowed her head. When she looked up again, Raphea was gone.

"Good luck, Thea," Micai grinned and tousled her hair. "Show them what you've got."

"Thanks." Thea smiled up into Micai's gentle face. She wondered about the missing tankard—but of course, Ulfgar had that now.

Strolling over to Roland, Micai lifted the bag of cookies out of his unresisting hands and gave a curt nod. "Good job, Roland."

With a wink, Micai disappeared.

Enkeli continued to make notes on the wall.

"You have your chance." Allulien's eyes gleamed as they watched Enkeli closely.

Enkeli nodded. "That's all we need."

For a moment, Allulien's gaze rested on Thea, then Allulien disappeared.

Mykyta joined Enkeli by the map. "You spoke with Khariton?"

Enkeli nodded. "He'll be there, as long as he keeps out of the High Priestess's line of sight."

"Good. I'll have Roland ready to run messages for me. We might need to move fast. It all depends on what the Queen decides."

Thea watched them—her uncle who she knew so well, and Enkeli, the General of the Elves. Her uncle carried himself with confidence, as if knowing that every word he said had the power to move mountains. Enkeli mumbled and squinted at the plan laid out before them, but there was no doubt that Enkeli was greater. It was as if Enkeli didn't care for anyone to know that, though. Enkeli was just Enkeli, whether crafting a plan to win the war or teaching history to a little Elf who wasn't interested in her lessons.

They looked up and saw her watching.

"Enkeli," Thea ventured, "what is happening at my home? Is everyone there alright?"

Enkeli frowned. "There's too much magic around it to get communications through. Not without doing more harm than good." Enkeli stared at the plan. "It hasn't fallen, though, and I think—I think there is time."

Thea took an unsteady breath. She just had to convince the Council to help.

"Here, um, you might need some extra magic today."

A surge of power tingled through Thea's body.

Enkeli's gaze turned towards her. "Glad you came." A smile twinkled in their eyes. "See you later."

Enkeli's form faded and disappeared.

Mykyta twisted the candlestick, and the bookshelves slid back into place. With a nod to Thea, he returned to his desk.

"Roland," Mykyta turned to his assistant who still stood as if frozen at attention. "Take your station in the Green Room. If I need a runner, I will message you."

Bowing, Roland turned and left the room, closing the door behind him.

Mykyta's thoughtful eyes rested on Thea's face. "Understand that I am not going to say anything. Not at first, anyways. I need to appear impartial, the one who will lead them into the best course of action at the proper time. They're going to push you hard, but don't back down. I'll be there for you when you need it." He smiled. "You've come a long way, Theewee, and now's your time to shine. Enkeli thinks you can do it. So do I."

Mykyta picked up the folder of papers that lay on the

desk in front of him. "I will go to my seat in the council chamber. Wait in the antechamber until you are summoned. There are some routine matters the Council must address before hearing your report."

The door closed, and Thea was alone. Taking a deep breath, she stepped out of the office, making her way to the antechamber where she was to wait. The murmur of voices drifted through the door leading to the council chamber.

How long would it be until her turn came? Thea paced the small room, back and forth, as one measure passed, and then another.

At last the door opened and a herald stepped through. Bowing to Thea, she flourished her feathered cap. "If you will follow me ..."

Turning, the herald led Thea through the door and onto a circular platform. Surrounding the platform were several magnificent chairs, decorated with the symbols of the Elvish Houses. The Queen Regent held the position of authority in the Royal Chair. On her right sat the Chancellor, in the chair of the First House. Around the circle, the Head of each of the houses sat in their official seat: Second House, Third House, Rokhov, and Svokyie. To the left of the Queen, the High Priestess stared at Thea with narrowing eyes.

Beyond them in every direction sat the rest of the Council. Every house had six or seven of its most influential members in attendance. Thea caught a glimpse of her father sitting among the nobility of the First House. Roland's mother, the Head of the Merchants' Guild, sat among some of the other prominent citizens of Lyudmyla, many of whom Thea recognized from attending city events with her uncle or her father. A great number of Priests and Priestesses filled the rest of the seats.

The room was silent. Everyone was watching her.

"Thea Kirisensk," the herald announced, and stepped aside.

Deity help me, Thea prayed, staring around the waiting faces. To her spirit sight, Mykyta shone like a beacon in a sea of darkened spirits. Behind him, she caught a glimpse of Khariton, waiting out of sight.

"Welcome, Thea." The Queen Regent spoke in a clear, ringing voice. "You bring news from beyond our lands that may be of interest to the Council. I invite you to share that with us now."

Thea drew herself up to her full height and addressed the Council. "You have all heard of the Great War, when the Elves fought long ago. Though the war was not over, the Elves abandoned the fight and retreated to this island, leaving the other people of Raphtova to fare as they may. The Elves were gone, but the war continued. To this day, the people of Raphtova fight against the Deceiver, but their plight has become desperate. An army of orcs is spreading destruction across the land, burning homes and killing everyone in their path. The people of Raphtova need our help."

A murmur rose from the ranks of officials.

The Queen Regent watched Thea closely. "Explain what you mean by 'orcs'."

"Orcs are a new kind of creature, formed by the enemy. Their skin is made of metal, as hard as any armour. They are fast and strong and very intelligent. Their one purpose is to destroy all those who serve the Ancient Wisdom, wherever they may be found."

Around the council chamber, murmurs of concern

and skepticism rose to fill the silence.

The Head of Second House frowned. "They have metal skin, but they can still move?"

"Just as much as our skin is stone and we can move," Thea replied in an even voice.

"How big is this army?" The Head of Svokyie leaned forward in her chair, watching Thea intently.

"From the numbers I saw evidence of, there are at least two thousand orcs surrounding Gedwyld as we speak. There may be more."

Concerned murmurs filled the room.

"Where's Gedwyld?" a council member asked. Several others appeared relieved that they hadn't been the one to reveal their ignorance.

"Gedwyld lies south-east of Svokyie, beyond the Deorcian."

Though her mention of the Deorcian did not seem to clear any confusion, other members of the Council nodded in approval.

"That is far from here, then." The Head of the Bank settled back in his chair.

"True," the Head of Second House smiled. "Even if Thea is right, does it matter? It will not affect us at all."

"It wouldn't hurt to strengthen our military presence, just in case," the Head of Third House offered. "It is a long time since we saw the need for a standing army."

"Why bother with an army?" the Harbour Master called. "We are on an island. With the size of our fleet, nothing will come near us."

"Excuse me," the Head of Svokyie glared. "*Not* all the Elves live on Larsya. If there is a threat, I demand that troops be stationed in Svokyie."

"Who needs Svokyie?" someone from Second House

retorted. "It's time you lived on Larsya anyways."

"You think you would survive without Svokyie? We provide almost all the raw materials you use here in Lyudmyla. Without us, this city would crumble."

"There's no need to get defensive," the Head of Third House countered. "We don't even know if there's a threat!"

"So you would wait to find out when there's an army on our doorstep?"

"She makes an important point, though," the Head of the Merchants' Guild interjected. "How secure is our supply chain? Any number of things could threaten our resources coming from Svokyie. Have we considered the best way to protect our investments?"

Thea watched in silence as the debate carried on around her, moving on to security programs and coastal patrols. They were distracting themselves. They didn't want to hear her message.

Message. Drawing from her well of magic, Thea spoke. Her voice was soft, but her magic carried her words clearly to every ear in the room.

"If the Deceiver wins, do you think he will stop? If he levels Gedwyld and every other human city to the ground, will his army turn around and go back where they came from? They will come for you next, and you will not be able to stop them."

A hush fell across the council chamber.

"You have to face them now. This is what the Ancient Wisdom is telling you to do."

A murmur of concern swept across the room, but the Priesthood looked startled and angry.

"Enkeli has not told us this." The High Priestess spoke in a voice that stilled the room once again. "We do not accept any word unless it comes from Enkeli."

"The Ancient Wisdom can speak in many ways." Thea fixed her gaze on the Priestess. "Today, I am one of those ways."

"We serve Enkeli," the High Priestess snapped. "The General of Knowledge and Wisdom has brought all this wealth and prosperity upon us and for that our loyalty is undivided. Why listen to any other way?"

Thea stared, a chill creeping down her spine. "Enkeli is not the Ancient Wisdom. Enkeli is just a General and nothing more."

"How dare you insult the Great Enkeli," the High Priestess glared.

"Never mind religious stuff." The Head of Second House leaned forward in his chair. "How do we know this isn't just a sham from start to finish? The Great War ended long ago. Everyone knows that."

Murmurs of agreement filled the room.

Mykyta stirred in his seat. "It seems to me, my Queen, that Thea is the only Elf who has travelled beyond our borders for many hundreds of circles. What is our most reliable source of current information? Records from a thousand circles ago? The world does not go unchanged. Perhaps we should listen to the one who has been there to see it."

"She is a silly young Elf, just looking for attention," the High Priestess snapped. "There is no need to listen to a thing she says."

"She is second in line for Chancellor." Mykyta spoke in a low voice. "And she is a member of First House. Do not disrespect her."

Uneasy murmurs rippled across the room.

"What proof does she have?" someone called.

"Yes," another agreed. "Where is the evidence of this war? Is it real?"

They wanted proof? Thea closed her eyes, calling to her mind all that she had seen—the clearing in the forest littered with the bodies of the Resistance, the homestead destroyed and in flames, the hatred gleaming in the eyes of the orcs as they burst out of the trees with a war cry.

With a surge of magic, she sent the images into every mind in the room.

Gasps of shock and surprise filled the council chamber. Elves stared at each other, grasping the armrests of their chairs. The members of the Priesthood stared at Thea with horror and rage.

The Queen Regent stood. "Thank you for your report, Thea. You will leave now."

Thea opened her mouth to protest.

Go. Mykyta's voice appeared in her mind. *This is about to get very messy.*

Preserving an appearance of dignity, Thea bowed to the Queen and turned away. The moment she stepped through the door, a tumult erupted from the council chamber. Shouts and angry voices tumbled over each other, cut off abruptly by the door slamming shut.

Thea looked up into Allulien's blazing eyes.

Chapter Eighteen

Allulien's terrifying anger filled Thea's senses. They were not staring at her, but at the door behind her.

"It is enough." Allulien's voice shook the air. "They will not listen. The time for judgment has come."

Thea stepped back, panic coursing through her veins.

Raphea stood beside Allulien, a hand laid on their shoulder.

"Are you certain that it is time?" Raphea spoke in a low voice. "Once it has been decreed, there is no turning back."

Allulien's gaze stared past Thea as if the door was not there. "Ever since they first spoke Enkeli's name as an object of worship we knew that destruction must come. We have given them time and they still refuse to turn back to the Deity."

"The Council has not finished." Standing on Allulien's other side, Micai raised a cautioning hand. "There is still the chance for mercy."

"Is there?" Allulien's eyes blazed. "They have sent Thea from the room. They have no more interest in hearing what she has to say."

"Let me try again!" The words burst out of Thea. She stared up at Allulien, heart pounding. "Maybe they will listen to me!"

Anger smouldered in Allulien's eyes. "I have given them one more chance again and again. What can you say that will convince them? They have all the knowledge they need and they have rejected it. They have abandoned Raphtova, giving lip service to the Deity while worshipping their own temple and their own glory. For this, the Elves will die." Allulien's eyes pierced through Thea. "Move aside. The Elves deserve their judgment."

Thea's heart pounded as she stared up into Allulien's unflinching gaze. She knew it was true. The Elves did deserve it, and she had said so herself. She knew her General well enough to know that if she stepped aside now, that would be the end.

She couldn't do it.

Thea braced herself and stared up into Allulien's piercing eyes. "If the Elves must die, then you will kill me too."

An indefinable expression filled Allulien's face. "You have chosen the Deity, Thea. You do not have to stand with them."

"I choose to stand with them. They are my people."

Silence filled the antechamber as Allulien watched Thea's face.

"You have one measure. Save them if you can."

Thea's hands were shaking. Beyond the Generals standing before her, she caught a glimpse of Enkeli standing alone. Somehow she understood—she was Enkeli's gamble, and everything had come down to this.

Turning, Thea grabbed the handle of the door and yanked it open.

A flood of noise poured over her—Elves bickering and yelling, shouting to be heard over the turmoil that had engulfed the council chamber.

Thea stepped through the door and closed it behind

her. Taking a deep breath, she sent her magic cutting through the noise.

"LISTEN TO ME."

Silence fell. The sudden weight of every gaze in the room turned on Thea, filled with shock and disapproval.

Thea froze. What should she say? There hadn't been time to make a plan.

Images of the Resistance rose in Thea's mind. The Fauns never made a plan. If Zanele was here now, she would say the truth, and that was all.

Thea stared at the Elves surrounding her. "You have one measure. If you do not renounce the Temple and turn back to the Ancient Wisdom, the Elves will be destroyed. This is your last chance."

Pandemonium erupted across the council chamber. Councillors leapt to their feet, cries of outrage filling the air.

Thea glanced at her uncle. He sat in his chair beside the Queen Regent in a thoughtful manner, but Thea saw the startled look that passed through his eyes. Behind him, Khariton slipped from the alcove where he had been waiting and stepped out a nearby door, closing it behind him.

The High Priestess gestured for silence. As the turmoil subsided she turned a scornful look on Thea. "Does this child have no respect for authority? She was clearly ordered to leave this room and yet she returns uncalled for, with such impertinent words that it is impossible to take her seriously."

"I speak the words of the Generals." Ignoring the High Priestess, Thea turned to the Queen. "If the Elves do not repent and return to the true worship of the Ancient Wisdom, they will be destroyed. Enkeli has sent me to give you your final warning."

"Enkeli has done no such thing!" The High Priestess drew herself to her full height. "This false prophet should be thrown out of the room at once!"

"I am not a false prophet. Some of your own people in the Temple have heard from Enkeli and can confirm that they sent me. Just ask Inessa."

An uneasy murmur rippled through the robed figures that clustered behind the High Priestess.

"That heretic has been removed from the Priesthood." The High Priestess's eyes were cold. "She was found guilty of fraternizing with insurgents and speaking lies in the name of Enkeli. There can be no doubt of what you really are—a false prophet, sent by the Deceiver himself!"

Around the High Priestess, chaos erupted once again. Horror settled over Thea's spirit. She had seen the works of the Deceiver, seen dark spirits fully given to his power and control. Were the Elves so deceived? To them, light was darkness, and darkness was light.

A hush fell as Thea's father rose to his feet. Bowing to acknowledge the attention of the Council, he turned to the Queen. "The accusation laid against Thea is a serious one that must be addressed. It is true that Thea is young and may not have a full understanding of the Scrolls or the current situation, but these are not suitable grounds for judgment. What the High Priestess neglects to bring to your attention is the fact that Thea has done magic. You have all seen it, and it cannot be denied. All magic comes from somewhere. Either her magic comes from the Ancient Wisdom, in which case we would do well to listen to her, or it comes from the Deceiver, which is what the High Priestess would claim."

Afonya paused as a low murmur rose around him. When it died down, he continued. "In the days since Thea's return, I have spent much time in the Halls of Knowledge, reading the Scrolls. In my reading, I learned something which I am sure is well known to the members of the Priesthood, familiar as they are with the Scrolls of the Ancient Wisdom. For those who may not be aware, it is written that each General can only grant access to certain domains of magic. While some domains are granted by more than one of the Generals, the domains of message and transportation are only given to those beneath Enkeli, and both of these have been demonstrated by Thea in my presence. The Deceiver does not—and has never had—access to those domains."

An excited murmur filled the room.

The High Priestess waved her hand for attention. "Do not underestimate the cunning of the Deceiver! Who knows what kinds of enchantments he may have devised to mimic the works of Enkeli? May he know this day that we will not be deceived by his illusions!"

Something about the straightening of Afonya's shoulders drew everyone's attention back to him again. "If it is true that the Deceiver can disguise his works as those of Enkeli, how can any servant of Enkeli prove their legitimacy? I would like to draw the attention of the Council to the ancient belief that the proof of authenticity for those who serve the Ancient Wisdom is the magic that they carry. Where is the magic of the Priesthood? They claim that Thea is false, but where is the proof of their own faithfulness?"

Nodding to the rest of the Council, Afonya sat down

again. All eyes turned to the Priesthood.

The High Priestess gave a condescending smile. "He is her father. Of course he defends her."

Murmurs of agreement rose around the room.

Thea stared at the High Priestess with narrowing eyes. "You would call me a deceiver? You sit in your Temple speaking about the glory of Enkeli and the wisdom of the Elves, but you have turned your back on the Deity that Enkeli serves and the Ancient Wisdom from whom all wisdom comes. You fill your halls with copies of the ancient scrolls, but you do not live by the words that they say. *Worship belongs to the Ancient Wisdom alone*, but you worship the created rather than the Creator, even worshipping a building made of marble and gold. *The will of the Ancient Wisdom is to care for others and heal the hurts of the world*, but you have abandoned Raphtova and only care about yourself. You claim to be wise, but you have fallen prey to the Deceiver yourself."

Thea was shaking. She stared around the room, seeing every single face, acutely aware of all that hung in the balance. She pointed back at the door she had entered through. "All four Generals are outside that door, waiting to see what you will choose. If you choose yourselves and your own comfort, the Elves will die. If you choose the Ancient Wisdom, you will return to the people of Raphtova that you abandoned for so long. You must choose who you really serve. You do not have long."

Noise erupted across the council chamber.

"Lies!" the High Priestess screamed.

"This is absolutely preposterous," a richly dressed merchant scoffed.

"What if she's right?" another voice cried out.

"We have to listen to her!"

"She's a false prophet—you can't trust her!"

"Just listen to the child! She comes in here and tries to tell us what to do? Throw her out of here!"

A wave of magic swept past Thea with such strength that she almost staggered.

Slowly Mykyta rose to his feet. "The First House will obey the Ancient Wisdom." His voice rang across the room. "We will march to aid the peoples of Raphtova. Our army and navy are ready. We await our General's command."

A murmur of surprise passed from Elf to Elf. One of the doors of the council chamber burst open and a palace guard appeared.

"Your Majesty!" he gasped. "An army just appeared outside the Palace walls!"

"An army?" The Queen looked at him sharply. "What kind of army?"

"An army of Elves!"

"Ready to embark for the Dark Lands," Mykyta replied in an even voice. "Two hundred strong."

The Head of Second House stared at Mykyta, greed glimmering in his eyes. "Are you undermining the authority of the Queen?"

"I speak of the resolve of the First House. I am head of First House, am I not?"

"You won't be for long, acting like that! Enlisting an army and a navy without the Queen's permission? Declaring that you will go before a verdict has been given? I tell you, if you go you will not be coming back, and there will be a new First House in your place."

The representatives of First House leapt to their feet,

protesting loudly.

Afonya raised a hand. When silence fell, he spoke. "I do not agree with everything that has been said or has been done, but the First House will be united. We will not make the same mistakes as the First House that fell. We stand with Mykyta."

The rest of First House shifted uneasily, but they did not challenge him.

"Svokyie will stand with you." The Head of Svokyie rose to her feet. "Why do we build walls to keep the world out? We can help them, and they can help us."

Protests erupted throughout the council chamber.

The High Priestess's eyes blazed. "Anyone who dares to march to war will be cut off from the Temple!"

"Hah," the Head of Second House scoffed. "Let them go. Lyudmyla will be stronger without them."

"You think you are so special," the Head of Rokhov's voice dripped with contempt. "Rokhov will show you we are not afraid of a fight."

"And go against the orders of the Priesthood?" The Head of Third House gasped. "Don't you know that's political suicide?"

"Well the Priesthood can stick it up their—"

"SILENCE!"

Sudden silence fell as the Queen Regent rose from her throne. Her blazing eyes dared anyone to be foolish enough to interrupt her.

"You will all sit down."

Everyone sat. The Queen's steady gaze took in every face in the room. "I am still Queen. I have listened carefully to all that has been said, and I will give you my decision. Thea has come here, calling for loyalty to the Ancient Wisdom. Thus far, it is good. Any one of us would say that we wish to be loyal to the Ancient Wisdom."

Complete silence filled the council chamber. The Queen continued. "Thea also says that the Elves have not been faithful. Perhaps this is so. I cannot speak for the spirit of each person in this room, I can only speak for my own. All my life I assumed that since the Temple stood, the Ancient Wisdom was honoured. I myself have done nothing to show honour or loyalty to the Ancient Wisdom. Perhaps Thea is right, and it is the Priesthood that has led us astray."

The High Priestess opened her mouth to protest, but the Queen raised her hand.

"Finally, Thea insists that the Elves return to the war. As Mykyta has said, none of us know anything of what is happening beyond the land of the Elves, but it cannot be denied that we are strong and secure. Surely it would be in our best interest to send aid to those who find themselves in danger."

The High Priestess rose from her chair. "Our King ordered the retreat from that battle. Who are you to negate his words?"

The Queen's eyes flashed.

"You are Regent," the High Priestess continued, "nothing more. You cannot decide this, it is a matter for the entire Council."

"So I do not have a Queen's authority?" The Queen's eyes gleamed dangerously. "If not I, then who? Certainly not the Priesthood. You overstep your position!"

The doors to the council chamber burst open and an Elf stepped through. His perfectly smooth rhyolite skin gleamed in the light. Curly, mosslike hair stretched down his neck to cover his broad shoulders like a cloak.

From behind him, Khariton's voice rang out, "His Majesty, Ruslan Nevimna, King of the Elves."

Every Elf stared as complete silence fell across the council chamber.

The King stood, motionless, his glittering eyes passing over every person in the room, one by one. He was an Elf more ancient than any Thea had seen, and yet his face was unmistakable, depicted in honour throughout the city—the first King of the Elves.

Mykyta rose from his chair and bowed to one knee. "Your Majesty."

All around the room, the Elves followed suit, bowing to their King. Slowly, the King strode forward to stand before the royal throne. Trembling, the Queen Regent bowed.

Taking her hand, the King raised her up again. "You did not expect to see your old great-grandfather here." A glimmer of amusement flashed through his eyes. "I did not expect to see myself here either, but I have been woken and I believe that I have been called for." His keen glance swept across the room. "I was the one who ordered the retreat, and I now reverse my order. The Elves will go to war."

The King looked at Thea. Her heart leapt into her throat as she realized that she alone of all the Elves had not bowed before the King. His gaze seemed to pierce right through her.

Before she could respond, the King bowed in deference. "What other command do you bring from the Ancient Wisdom?"

Thea stared in surprise.

"That Elf is a false prophet!" the High Priestess cried.

"Do not listen to what she says!"

"Is she?" The King turned the full force of his burning gaze on the High Priestess. "Is she, when her spirit is as bright as the staph-light of Allumen, while yours is as dark as a pit beneath Raphtova?"

The High Priestess gaped.

The King's gaze took in the host of finely dressed Priests and Priestess who filled a full quarter of the council chamber. "I was there when your order was formed. It was never meant to be what it is today."

Deep beneath their feet, the ground trembled.

"Evacuate the Temple." The words burst out of Thea, her heart pounding in her ears. "The Elves may be saved, but the Temple *will* be destroyed. Get everyone out of there. Now."

The members of the Priesthood looked at each other in horrified uncertainty. To obey meant that they gave credence to her words, but they clearly feared what might happen if they did not.

"Well?" The King's eyes gleamed dangerously. "Do you still claim that she is a false prophet, or does she speak the truth?"

"There is nothing in what she says." The High Priestess's voice rose high above the turmoil. "They are lies, nothing more."

"Then go stand in your Temple." The King's voice was low, but it echoed across the room. "If she lies, go to your Temple and prove it."

"I will." Turning on her heel, the High Priestess strode from the room. Many of the Priests and Priestesses followed her. Others glanced nervously over their shoulder and slipped out by a different way.

Mykyta approached the King and bowed. "If I may,

Your Majesty?"

The King nodded.

Mykyta turned to the milling crowd. "Council is dismissed! Go and see to it that your Houses prepare for war, and pray that the Ancient Wisdom shows you mercy."

As the Council scattered, the King turned to Mykyta. "You are the current Chancellor?"

"I am, Your Majesty."

"Good. Khariton said you have an army?"

"Yes, Your Majesty."

"Then let us go see it."

As the King turned towards the door, Mykyta glanced at Thea. Light twinkled in his eyes, but his face was serious. "Will you come?"

Thea nodded and found herself walking between the King and the Chancellor, with the Queen Regent following behind.

They stepped out of the Palace doors to find the courtyard in utter confusion. Palace guards ran back and forth, harried by smooth-skinned dignitaries wearing robes of all colours and descriptions, demanding to know what was going on.

Passing through the commotion, Thea followed the King through the gate.

Outside, the army stood at attention. It was larger than the two hundred her uncle had claimed. Much larger. It filled the street, stretching further than she could see in every direction. Every Elf in its ranks had skin as smooth as Khariton's, or even as smooth as the King's. Hair had grown over their shoulders and backs, but their armour gleamed like it was new.

An Elf Thea didn't recognize stepped forward,

wearing a commander's uniform. She bowed deeply to the King.

"We are here, Your Majesty. Two thousand, one hundred and forty-three strong. Ready to fight again."

"Thank you, Darya." The King nodded. "The time to fight has come."

"That's my Commander." Khariton stepped beside Thea, speaking in a low voice that only she could hear. "Old Darya—worked me harder than I ever worked in my life, but she knows what she is doing."

Thea stared in wonder. "This is the army that fought in the Great War?"

"What's left of 'em. Some of them were in there deep, but there's nothing like a drill sergeant's voice to get the blood flowing again." He gave a wry smile.

"You woke them all up?"

"It was time." Khariton's eyes seemed to stare at something far away. "We are the ones who turned our back on the war. It's time to pay our dues."

From the surrounding crowds, a voice rose through the ruckus. "What is going on here?"

The Queen Regent turned and stared. "Father!" she gasped. "I—I mean, Your Majesty."

"Did someone call?" An Elf with pure amethyst skin stepped out from the crowd.

"Grandmother?" The Queen Regent's eyes widened in alarm.

The Elf frowned. "What has happened to this place? You stay in vidlas for a few hundred circles and everything is in shambles!"

The King stepped beside her. "Is something wrong?"

Surprise filled the old Regent's face. "Your—Your Majesty!" She curtsied deeply. "I ... I did not mean ..."

Around them, chaos filled the streets. Officials in formal robes bickered and argued.

"You think I am supposed to listen to you? I am Head of Second House!"

"No, I was Head of Second House before you were born!"

"You abdicated! I am in charge now!"

"Where is the King?"

"Which King?"

"Not that Regent, the other Regent!"

In the midst of it all, the army stood at attention and waited. There were other Elves, too, who stood and watched in the midst of the chaos. One of them looked remarkably like Thea's father, only much older.

Beneath their feet, the mountain rumbled.

Thea froze. Her uncle put a steadying hand on her shoulder. "The Deity's will be done." He gave her a reassuring smile.

The rumbling grew louder. All around them, people stopped and stared, concern turning to alarm as the ground began to shake. The wall of the Temple compound shuddered. Its marble images cracked and crumbled. Then, with a rumble like thunder, it collapsed.

All across the Temple courtyard, pillars and monuments fell as the paving stones buckled and cracked. Screams and cries filled the air as windows shattered and masonry collapsed.

The ground beneath the Temple caved in, and the Halls of Knowledge crumbled.

In the street, people panicked and ran. Dust and debris billowed up, darkening the sky until it was almost impossible to see. Thea staggered, covering her face with her arm as she tried to breathe. Everything was shaking. The thunderous rumble of collapsing stone filled her ears.

Slowly, the trembling subsided. Thea steadied herself and took a deep breath as the cold wind off the sea cleared the air.

Silence fell across the crowded street. The Hall of Messengers still stood, squat and covered with dust. Where the rest of the Temple had been, nothing but a heap of rubble remained.

"Don't worry." Khariton spoke low in Thea's ear. "We got out everyone that we could. Saw that coming a long way away." He stared at the ruins with a glimmer of sadness in his eyes. "Anyone who was still in there wanted to be. The rest, you saved."

Thea stared around her at Khariton, her uncle, and the growing collection of past Kings and Queens of Lyudmyla, wiping dust from their faces with their ornate, embroidered sleeves. Thea stared at the crowds, sober and shaken. Close by, the army still stood at attention. Beyond them, the city of the Elves stretched out below them as it always had. Only the Temple had been destroyed.

She was shaking and she couldn't stop.

Her uncle placed a hand on her shoulder. "I'll take things from here, Thea. Go home to your parents for a while. I'll let you know when the ships are preparing to sail."

Thea nodded. Turning away, she walked slowly through the crowds, away from the Palace, away from the ruins of the Temple.

Finally, she left the crowds behind and turned onto her parents' street.

"Thea!" Roland appeared around the corner and hurried to catch up.

Thea stopped. He knew what had happened, she could see it in his face.

He was no King. No lofty official or Priest. He was just Roland, and he gave her a hug.

In his familiar, comforting presence, all the fear and horror dissolved into tears.

"You did it, Thea," Roland whispered. "I knew you could."

Chapter Nineteen

Gently, Thea opened the door of her parents' home and slipped inside. The latch clicked shut, closing out the clamour that spread like wildfire throughout the city. Inside, everything was quiet.

Passing by the parlour, a movement caught Thea's eye. Her parents stood in front of the fireplace, their heads bowed close together. Glancing up, they saw her.

"Thea!" Her mother stared as if she had seen a ghost.

Feeling strangely shy, Thea stepped towards her parents. "Hello, mother." She managed a timid smile. "I don't think the Priesthood will be much of a problem anymore."

Taisiya looked from her daughter to her husband. "You said the Temple is gone. I felt the shaking. I didn't know ..."

Images of the destruction played again before Thea's eyes. "It's gone. The Hall of Messengers is all that's left."

Her mother was trembling.

"Thea said it would fall, and it did." Afonya spoke slowly. "The King honoured her as a prophet in front of the entire Council."

Thea felt very small beneath her parents' stares.

"A prophet," her mother ventured after the silence had stretched on a very long time.

"Her words to the Council were from the Ancient Wisdom."

Taisiya's eyes did not leave her daughter's face. "There has not been a prophet for hundreds of circles."

"It seems ..." Afonya spoke haltingly, "we were wrong to try to stop her from leaving. We should have listened, and tried to understand." There was an expression on his face that Thea had never seen before as he turned to face her again. "I am sorry, Thea."

A lump grew in her throat. "I'm sorry too. When I first got my orders from Allulien I never even thought of telling you. I should have found you right away and explained what was going on. I didn't want to disobey you or leave you worried about me."

Afonya glanced at his wife. "We are used to taking things slow. It seems that the Ancient Wisdom sometimes does things quickly, whether we are ready or not."

Thea watched her parents, standing so regal in their official robes and finery. Her father looked tired.

"Thank you for standing up for me during the Council meeting today."

Afonya stared into the glowing fire. "The High Priestess should not have made foundless accusations like that. I was only doing my due diligence."

"It was more than anyone else did, besides my uncle." She met her father's reticent gaze. "I'm glad you're my dad."

Afonya's gaze dropped to the floor. Taisiya put her arm around her husband. "I never thought we would have a prophet in our family," she gave her daughter a tentative smile, "but it seems to suit you, Thea."

Thea smiled. "Thank you." She glanced around the empty room. It was too quiet. "Where's Sylica?"

"Grusha brought her home to meet her

grandchildren."

Thea sighed. "I'm glad. I think I need some quiet for a while."

"I can understand that." Afonya glanced at his wife. "It sounds like things are only just beginning."

Leaving her parents in the parlour, Thea climbed the stairs up to her room. Shutting the door, she leaned against it and closed her eyes. Now what? In her mind, she replayed the events in the council chamber again and again. Had she really done what she had been sent to do?

It was not her time for checking in, but an overwhelming need to check in filled her mind. Kneeling on the floor, Thea bowed her head.

There was no word from Enkeli or any other General, but slowly the fear and adrenaline faded from her body, leaving behind a deep feeling of peace.

Thea opened her eyes. On the floor in front of her was a crumpled scrap of paper.

She picked it up and smoothed it flat. The paper was blotched and stained, but she would recognize the messy handwriting anywhere.

You did me proud.
—Enkeli

Warmth flooded Thea's heart. She could see the smile on her tutor's face—Enkeli's face—just as she had during her lessons so long ago. Right now, that approval was the best reward in the world.

Thea?

Thea startled as Mykyta's voice spoke in her mind. She glanced over her shoulder, but she was still alone.

Yes?

Emergency meeting at the Theatre. Come in the stage door. Roland will meet you there.

Bracing herself, Thea jumped to her feet and opened the door. *I'll be right there.*

Avoiding the worst of the crowds, Thea made her way to the rear entrance of the Theatre. It was locked.

As soon as she knocked, the bolts were drawn aside and Roland opened the door. He grinned when he saw her. "Mykyta said you were coming. We're almost ready to start!"

He led Thea through the maze of rooms. "There's too many people to fit in the council chamber, so we have to meet here. They've saved a seat for you."

The distant hum of voices grew louder.

Moments later, they stepped through a door and onto the stage. The noise of the crowded auditorium swept over Thea like a wave.

On the stage, an array of chairs had been set, with the King seated in the position of authority. The Chancellor was there, as well as the Commander of the Army and the Queen Regent. There was a seat for the Head of each House, but with the leadership of many of the Houses still in turmoil, most of them were empty. It was clear, though, that there had been no debate among the leaders of First House. Mykyta was Chancellor, and no one challenged his authority.

Roland led Thea to the seat that had been reserved for her between the King and the Chancellor. Tentatively, she took her seat, staring out at the vast auditorium filled with the leaders and dignitaries of her people.

Soon a herald appeared and announced the

commencement of the meeting. It began with an opportunity for the leaders of the city to present their concerns. The King listened to each question that was raised, turning to Mykyta to fill in the details of the current situation.

After this had gone on for some time, the King rose from his seat. "That is all of the questions this day will permit. If you have further concerns, you may address them to the Queen Regent as you have always done, starting tomorrow. Now we must focus our attention on the departure of the fleet. We sail today, at the time of the great feast."

A dignitary in the front row gasped. "Today?"

Cries of protest filled the Theatre.

"That is so soon!"

"How will we be ready in time?"

The King raised his hand and silence fell. "We sail today. Every measure we delay puts more lives at risk." He turned his piercing gaze on Thea. "Tell us about the battle going on as we speak."

Thea swallowed and rose slowly to her feet. Thousands of gemstone eyes stared at her. Even the boxes of the nobles were filled with faces. "The city of Gedwyld is under siege. An army of orcs has surrounded it, and surrounded my home which is north of the city. Humans, Fauns, Dryads, and Littles have taken refuge there, but the orcs are using dark magic to undermine their defences and cut them off from help. If we do not hurry, it may be too late."

Silence filled the Theatre as Thea returned to her seat.

The King nodded his thanks and turned to the Elves that filled the auditorium. "Gedwyld is a coastal city—something that is greatly in our favour. We will send our army in two waves. One will sail to Wyndburh and travel overland. The other will arrive at Gedwyld by sea. The first wave will embark today, and the second will embark as soon as further provisions can be acquired. For those who sail with us, go put your affairs in order. For those who do not sail, I charge you to examine your heart and do all you can to aid those who go. May the Ancient Wisdom speed our journey and grant that we reach Gedwyld in time."

The King turned and left the stage. Mykyta and the Commander of the Army rose to follow, and Thea hurried after them.

In the courtyard, she found the King waiting. He smiled as she approached. "Well, Thea, it seems there are at least some who wish to fight with us." He gestured to a large group of Elves, crowding around a table where Khariton and one of Mykyta's assistants tried to bring some semblance of order. Others hurried by, carrying boxes and crates. Officials poured over folders of paperwork.

"Darya will command the overland force." The King nodded to the Commander who stood some distance away. "Roland will command the force that travels by sea, and Svetka will be admiral of the fleet. Mykyta recommends them both."

For a moment, the King watched the busy scene before them.

"I will travel with the overland force, as will all those who remain of the first army of the Elves. We will bear the greatest risk, since we may meet the enemy long before we reach Gedwyld." His expression became thoughtful. "Will you travel with us? You have been that way before, and know better than any the dangers we will face."

Thea looked at the spirit of the King, bright with the light of the Deity. The mosslike hair covering his shoulders was all but gone and his eyes were clear and alert. He was not going to be lost in vidlas any time soon.

Thea smiled. "Yes. I will come with you."

The King nodded his thanks. "The Queen Regent will continue to rule in my absence, and Mykyta will be here to deal with any problems that may arise."

The crowd of Elves in the courtyard was growing larger.

Thea turned to the King. "I have a friend with me here. Her name is Sylica. Could she travel with us too?"

The King smiled. "I have heard about Sylica. She would be very welcome to travel with us if she wishes to."

A woman's voice rose above the clamour. Following the sound with her eyes, Thea caught a glimpse of Ilya pushing forward through the crowd. Kseniya hung off her husband's arm, her eyes wide with fear.

Thea slipped closer.

"Don't you dare!" Kseniya cried, trying desperately to pull Ilya away. "You are no soldier! Just what do you think you are doing!"

"Kseniya." Ilya held his wife's shoulders and stared into her panicking eyes. "Listen. I know you're scared. I've never done something like this because I've been stuck, doing the same meaningless things every day. Now I have a chance to do something. Something that really matters. If I don't go now, I'd hate myself forever."

"But what about me?"

"You can come too."

"What?" Horror filled her eyes. "On a smelly boat? With no servants to do ... my ..." She stared up into the face of the King. "Your Majesty!" She gave a grand, sweeping curtsy, trembling beneath the weight of his stare.

At her side, Ilya bowed.

"What is your name?" The King's voice did not rise above the surrounding chaos, but Thea heard it clearly.

"I am Ilya, Your Majesty, and this is my wife, Kseniya."

"Ilya, I see that you intend to join the army."

"Yes, Your Majesty."

The King's smile was kind. "Ilya, I would like to claim your service as my personal attendant for this expedition, if your wife will allow you to go."

Ilya's eyes widened.

Kseniya gasped. "The personal attendant of the King! Oh my darling, I am so proud of you!" She flung her arms around her husband's neck.

The King shook Ilya's hand. "I will take that as a yes."

"Oh Your Majesty!" Kseniya let go of her husband to curtsy again and again. "We would be so very honoured! My own husband, the personal attendant of the King!" She clasped her hands. "What will the society ladies say now?"

A look of consternation crossed Ilya's face. He bowed. "Thank you, Your Majesty. I would be honoured."

The King turned. "Darya!"

The Commander strode across the courtyard to join them. "Your Majesty?"

"I have just accepted Ilya as my personal attendant. Take him to the Palace and get him a uniform."

Darya bowed and gestured for Ilya to follow her.

Ilya gave his wife a quick kiss and followed the Commander out of sight. Soon Kseniya had also disappeared, hurrying off in a flurry of excitement.

The rest of the day passed quickly. As evening approached, Thea was summoned to her uncle's office.

The King was there, along with his new attendant. Mykyta and the Commander were deep in conversation, while Roland stood close at hand. Sylica skipped cheerfully around the room, poking with interest at anything that caught her eye. She wore an ornate velvet dress that Thea had not seen before, presumably bought by Thea's mother. It would have been very flattering on her, if the effect hadn't been spoiled by the armour she insisted on wearing over it. Daisy trotted cheerfully by her side.

Knowing that they were to leave straight from Mykyta's office, Thea had already said goodbye to her parents. For their part, they had embraced Thea warmly and wished her well. She could tell they still didn't understand why she'd chosen the life she had, but this time she got to say goodbye, and she had their blessing. That meant more to her than she had ever realized.

The door of the office opened, and Khariton entered. Approaching the large oak desk, he bowed to Mykyta. "The ships are ready. We await the King."

"Good. Thank you, Khariton." Mykyta straightened the papers on his desk. "Where exactly is the King's ship?"

"Central dock, Lyudmyla Harbour."

"In plain view of everyone crowding the harbour district to see them off?"

"Yes, sir."

"When I requested that the ship be docked out of sight so we could transport everyone down quietly?"

"... Yes, sir."

Mykyta's keen glance met Khariton's shameless smile. "I see."

"It will give them something to talk about, sir."

"Indeed."

A clatter drew Thea's attention. Across the room, Sylica was standing on Daisy's back in an attempt to reach a stained glass vase, high on one of Mykyta's bookshelves.

Thea stared. "Sylica!"

"I just want to see it close up!" Sylica wedged one of her feet on a shelf, boosting herself a bit higher. As she reached, her elbow bumped a golden figurine. It teetered, then fell to the floor with a resounding clang.

Daisy lunged for it. With a shriek, Sylica lost her balance. Books and ornaments tumbled as she scrambled to keep herself aloft long enough to look at the vase.

"Very pretty!" Sylica smiled. "Oops!" Losing her grip, she tumbled onto the carnage stretched out below her, landing in an undignified heap.

Everyone stared.

Sylica righted herself and put her hands on her hips, glaring at the small metallic dragon. "Daisy, give it back."

Daisy lowered her snout, staring up at Sylica with large, puppy dog eyes.

"Drop it!"

Daisy hacked and coughed, regurgitating the figurine which landed on the floor with a metallic thud. Sylica scooped it up. "Good girl, Daisy!" With gentle precision, she set it back on the shelf—upside down.

Mykyta rose from his chair. "Khariton," he gave him a sidelong glance, "you are aware that Sylica is sailing with you."

Khariton didn't move, but his eyes widened slightly.

A hint of a smile crept over Mykyta's face. "Make sure you keep an eye on her. We wouldn't want her getting in too much trouble."

Khariton glared at him. "You can't make me."

"Can I not?"

"I've had all I can take of that ... that agent of chaos!"

Mykyta raised an eyebrow. "On the contrary, I am sure that you will get along very well."

Stepping out from behind his desk, Mykyta approached the King. "The time for departure is here. You have all that you need?"

"All that I need and more." The King smiled and shook Mykyta's hand. "Thank you for all you have done."

"It is an honour, Your Majesty." Mykyta bowed. "In a moment, I will transport you to your ship."

The King turned to Ilya. "You have said your farewells?"

"Yes, sir. She'll be there to see me off."

"Good."

Mykyta stepped to Thea's side, wrapping his arm around her. "Well done, Theewee," he whispered in her ear. "I am very, very proud of you."

"Thanks, Uncle 'Kyta." Thea held him close.

"Message me when you can. I'll be glad to hear from

you."

Returning to his desk, Mykyta raised his hand in farewell. "The Deity's blessing be on you all, for safe travel and success in battle."

Thea glanced at Roland, standing alone by the door.

"Goodbye, Thea," Roland smiled. "See you at Gedwyld."

Thea nodded.

Around her, the walls of Mykyta's office faded and disappeared, replaced by the gently swaying deck of a large ship. It was the Osprey, the transport she had planned to take the first time she left Lyudmyla. Mykyta and Roland were gone, but the King, Commander, Ilya, Khariton, and Sylica still stood around her. All along the deck of the Osprey, its crew prepared to set sail.

Beyond the ship, the docks and harbour buildings stretched all around them. The streets were filled with people. Gasps and cries of amazement rose as the crowds saw the King and his company appear. Somewhere in the distance, trumpets played a fanfare.

Thea scanned the buildings that lined the harbour. There—the balcony where she and Roland had watched Davis arrive, so long ago. Kseniya stood there now, waving a white handkerchief.

"Transportation magic that precise is very difficult to master." The King glanced at Thea. "I think your uncle was showing off."

"You think?" Khariton muttered.

The clang of the harbour bell filled the air, and the Osprey slipped away from the dock. All around them, people waved and cheered. Sylica waved back, beaming from ear to ear.

Slowly the Osprey sailed past the great lighthouse

and onto the open sea. Thea stared up the vast expanse of the mountainside city. Its villas and halls gleamed in the light. Her eyes traced the route from the harbour and markets, up the steep mountain streets to the First House District, and beyond to the Palace towering above it all. Lyudmyla. The home of her people. Overhead, Micai was already large in the sky, approaching Allumen for its nightly eclipse.

Thea's gaze settled on the empty space high on the mountain where the Temple had once been. Lyudmyla would never be the same again.

Around her, the Osprey creaked as icy wind filled the sails. An entire fleet surrounded them—thirty ships or more—rushing through the surging tide. Salt spray dashed through the air.

Sylica was still waving at the receding shoreline.

"Did you enjoy your time in Lyudmyla?" Thea asked, joining her by the rail.

"Oh yes!" Sylica beamed. "Everyone was so nice and we had so much fun!"

"You got along with my parents?"

"Of course I did! They are very nice parents. Not as nice as *my* parents, but I give them second place as parents."

"By your parents you mean the Littles who raised you?"

"Of course. They are my parents, just like I'm a Little—I mean, not really, but they are still my parents of course."

The island of Larsya grew smaller on the horizon.

"It was a funny thing." Sylica stared down at the churning water, a thoughtful look in her eyes. "Being in Lyudmyla was different than anywhere else I've been before, and I don't know why."

"It is a bigger city," Thea offered, "with a lot of money."

"It wasn't that." Sylica frowned. "It was like I was more invisible. Normally everyone stares at me. There were still people staring at me, of course, but it was always because I did something strange, not because I *was* something strange." She looked at Thea. The salt spray glimmered on her green, stone-like skin.

"That's because you're like us, Sylica." Thea watched her friend's thoughtful face. "You're not exactly like an Elf, but you're more like an Elf than anything else I've met."

"But my mom and dad are Littles." Sylica frowned. "It's all very confusing."

Thea opened her mouth to respond, but Sylica's face suddenly brightened. "Look, there's Khariton! We had lots of fun in Lyudmyla together!" She scampered off across the deck to say hello.

Khariton met her with a less-than-enthusiastic glare.

Sylica didn't seem to notice. "Isn't this fun?" she grinned. "Now we get to go sailing! This boat is a lot bigger than the last boat I was on. So many people can fit on it!"

"Look here." Khariton turned to face her with his arms crossed. "You don't get in trouble, and I won't make your life harder than it has to be. Deal?"

"Okay!" Sylica grinned. "I don't get in trouble very much anyways. Right, Daisy?"

Before Khariton could reply, Sylica turned and skipped away.

Thea stayed by the rail, staring out across the churning waves. The dark line on the horizon grew closer.

"We're coming, Elora," Thea whispered. "We're coming."

Chapter Twenty

There were many Enkeli casters among those who had served in the first army of the Elves. With magic to speed their way, it only took a day of sailing to reach the mouth of the long inlet leading to Wyndburh. Mountains towered up on either side of it, disappearing into the clouds that hemmed in the sky.

"Look at that!" Sylica stared up at the rugged, snow-covered slopes. "Are those the mountains where the Dragons live?"

"No, we're much further north than that." Thea leaned on the rail beside her. "We still have to sail south to Wyndburh, and the Deorcian is beyond that. We'd have to go all the way through the Deorcian and into the mountains south of there to get to Meiling's Caverns. Anyways, these mountains aren't nearly as tall as those ones were."

Sylica frowned. "They look pretty tall to me. Look at how snowy they are! I think it would be fun to—"

"To get to Gedwyld and help our friends, right?"

"Yeah!" Sylica grinned. "Daisy and I are going to—what's that?"

Thea glanced at the shore, but couldn't see anything unusual. "What?"

"There's a person over there! Look!" Sylica pointed and waved excitedly.

Thea squinted at the dark smudge Sylica had

indicated. "Isn't that a tree?"

"No it isn't. It's a person!"

"It's too big. Just look at it. I'm sure it's a tree."

"No, it's a great big person, waving at us!"

Khariton, who was pacing the deck, glanced at Sylica sharply. "A what?"

"A great big person on the shore there. Look!"

Khariton strode to the rail, and a surge of magic burst out across the waves. His expression of alarm faded into annoyance. "It's a tree."

"No it's not!" Sylica pouted. "I'll show you."

Thea sighed. "The ship isn't going to change course just so you can look at a tree, Sylica. We're trying to get to Wyndburh."

Around them, the world shifted. Suddenly the towering mountain was much, much closer. Waves dashed on the rocks.

"Sylica!" Thea gasped.

Shouts of alarm rose from the crew around them.

"Rocks!" The lookout shouted. "Rocks!"

Feet thundered across the deck. Thea staggered as the ship turned in a dash of spray.

Sylica clung to the rail, staring at the shoreline that rushed past at an alarming speed.

"There!" she cried triumphantly, then her face fell. "Oh. It's just a tree."

"Sylica!" Thea yelled. Another sudden turn of the Osprey sent her staggering. "Get us out of here!"

The world shifted again. All around the Osprey, the crew stopped and stared as they found themselves once again a safe distance from the shore.

Khariton swore under his breath and stormed away.

Thea tried to calm her pounding heart. "Sylica, don't

do that."

"Don't do what?" Sylica glanced around, her gaze taking in the subdued atmosphere surrounding them. "Oh."

Cautiously, the crew returned to their work, glancing warily at the now-distant shoreline.

Sylica's thoughtful frown turned into a smile. "I know how to fix it, I'll give them candy!" She scurried off, leaving Thea alone by the rail. To her relief, there were no more incidents for the rest of the day.

When Thea returned to the deck the next morning, she found that the two great mountain ranges had drawn closer, towering above the deep waters of the fjord. Dark patches of forest hugged their lower slopes, petering out to meet the rocky, barren coastline. It looked remarkably familiar.

As she watched, a cluster of small stone huts swept into view. A rutted path led down to an old, rotting pier where a few small fishing boats drifted on the turbid water. Thin wisps of smoke disappeared in the icy breeze.

It was the village where she had her first encounter with humans—besides hearing Davis perform. Past the small, dirty houses, she caught a glimpse of the barn that had been her prison. Pale faces peered out from behind rocks and wizened trees.

Thea watched in silence until they disappeared from sight.

Laughter rose from below deck, interspersed with snatches of song. Sylica's voice rose above the rest in an endless stream.

Khariton joined Thea by the rail.

"What is she?"

Thea blinked. "Sorry, who?"

"Sylica. What is she?"

Thea stared at the old Elf beside her. His smooth, obsidian skin gleamed in the light.

She sighed. "I don't know."

Khariton frowned. "Look, I know magic. That magic she does isn't Deity magic."

Thea stared down at the churning water. "You're right. It's Dragon magic."

Khariton looked at her sharply. "Dragon magic."

"The same kind of magic that Dragons do. She isn't a Dragon, though."

"I can see that." Khariton shot her a withering glare. "Where did it come from?"

"I don't know. Even the Dragons don't seem to understand it."

Leaning on the rail, Khariton stared at the passing shoreline. A pack of crox erupted from a distant copse of trees, cawing loudly.

"Where is she from?"

"I don't know exactly. Somewhere across the sea east of Gedwyld. She was raised by Littles there."

"Littles?"

"You know—little people, like small humans."

"She's not a Little."

"No." Thea gave a wry smile. "It took her a long time to accept that."

"Who were her parents?"

"She doesn't know. As far as she's concerned, the Littles that raised her are her real family."

"So she never knew her parents."

"No. She never did."

Khariton stared across the waters of the fjord. "A bloody Elf with Dragon magic, raised by Littles."

Thea nodded.

"I've seen a lot in my life." Khariton shook his head. "Never saw something like that before."

Thea suppressed a smile. "She's special, that's for sure."

"Bloody chaos, that's what it is." Khariton turned away. "She's lucky she hasn't killed someone yet."

"Oh, she has."

Khariton froze.

"Only when she's meant to, though."

Khariton gave Thea a sharp glance. "That is not a comforting thought."

After staph, the wooden fortifications of Wyndburh came into sight, tucked along the eastern shore. The inlet had become narrower over the course of the day, and what had once been large mountains surrounding it were now gentle hills. Beyond Wyndburh, the first trees of the Deorcian stretched dark towards the southern horizon.

The docks were far too small for the size and number of ships that sailed with the King. As Thea watched, anchors were lowered and the long process of ferrying the army and their supplies to shore began.

The stockade surrounding the town remained dark and silent.

Khariton watched it with a thoughtful gaze. "That was just a few huts the last time I saw it."

Thea shot him a sidelong glance. "Funny how things change when you're gone for a thousand circles."

Khariton's eyes narrowed, but he did not venture a

reply.

"We will speak with the ruler of Wyndburh if we can." The King strode across the deck with the Commander at his side. "They may have news, and we can learn more of the road ahead."

As soon as the King's company had fully come ashore, they approached the gate of Wyndburh. It was closed, with no one in sight. The King ordered a fanfare blown, and the blast of the horns rang out across the empty fields.

Thea glanced at the distant trees that marked the northern reaches of the Deorcian. Along the shore, supplies were stacked and sorted. Banners and pendants marked the companies and officers. Close at hand, the banner of the Royal House fluttered in the icy wind.

With a grinding creak, the gate opened—just a little. One lone human stumbled out, his eyes wide with terror. The gate slammed shut behind him.

The human wore armour, of a sort, but carried no weapon. He stared at the glittering host of Elves, his mouth opening and closing like a fish.

A herald of the Elves stepped forward, accompanied by a swell of magic.

"His Majesty, Ruslan Nevimna, King of the Elves," the herald cried in a loud, official voice.

"D-d-d-d—" the human stammered. "Wh-wh-wha—"

"The King comes in peace," the herald continued, "and wishes to have an audience with the ruler of this town."

The human nodded. Turning, he hammered on the gate, calling through a crack in the old, weathered logs. After a few breaths, he turned back to face the Elves.

"The—the Governor will see you," he stammered, "but—but—"

"Fyren!" Sylica burst out of the ranks of the Elves, careening straight towards the human who panicked and scrambled to get back through the gate—unsuccessfully, since it was firmly closed.

Sylica threw her arms around the hapless human. "Hello, Fyren! I haven't seen you in so long! Did you miss me? This is my new best friend Daisy!"

The man recoiled at his sudden sight of the small metal dragon.

"Isn't this so much fun?" Sylica beamed. "Where's all my other friends?" She stared up at the gate that towered above her. "Hellooooo! Anybody home?"

Slowly, the gate opened a crack. "Sylica?"

"Ashie!" Sylica jumped up and down in excitement. "It's me and a bunch of my friends!"

The gate opened a fraction more and a head with tousled brown hair appeared. "It's really you?"

"Of course it's me! Don't be silly!"

The gate opened a fraction more, then the emerging figure saw the host of Elves stretched out before them. They blanched and disappeared back through the gate. It would have slammed shut, but Sylica stuck out her foot.

"Hey! I'm coming in! I want to see all my friends!"

A muffled voice replied from out of sight.

"No, they're not scary," Sylica protested. "They're actually very nice."

The muffled voice didn't sound convinced.

"At least let them talk with Alda, okay? Does she want to come out or should they come in? No, not all of them! Well, they can all come if you want."

The muffled voice rose in protest.

"Okay just the King and his friends, how does that sound? Okay?"

Nodding, Sylica skipped back to where Thea waited beside the King. "They'll talk with you now, but not all of you because I don't think everyone will fit inside."

Amusement flickered in the King's eyes. "Five of us would be sufficient." After having a private word with the Commander, the King gestured for Thea, Ilya, and Khariton to follow him. Together with Sylica, they approached the gate.

The human Sylica had called Fyren still stood with his back pressed against the gate. He stared as the King and his companions drew near. "You're ... you're the only ones?"

The King smiled. "We would like to speak with your ruler."

"I ... I suppose ..." He turned and whispered through a crack in the gate. Turning back to the King he bowed nervously. "The Governor will see you. Just ... just step this way ..."

Slowly, the gate swung open. Inside, a crowd of humans stared at them. They wore mismatched armour, much of which was rusty. Swords, spears, and pitchforks were clutched in their trembling hands.

"Go on," Fyran muttered, gesturing them back, "move over, they're goin' to the Governor."

Cautiously, the crowds shuffled aside, allowing them to pass. Ilya stared with wide-eyed wonder as they passed through the fearful crowd. Khariton walked with a hand on the hilt of his sword, but the King followed Fyran with a confident stride.

Sylica bounded ahead, greeting every third or fourth

person by name with a beaming smile.

Fyren led them to a building that was arguably less dingy than the others they had passed. Pushing the door ajar, he poked his head inside. "Governor! The leaders of the army want to talk to you."

A voice inside replied, and the door swung open. Inside they found a room of moderate size, its high ceiling supported with large timbers. The air was thick with the smoke from a smouldering fire that burned on a hearth in the center of the room. Beyond it, a middle-aged woman sat on a large chair, its age-stained wood carved with a simple motif. Guards stood on either side of the chair, with spears in their hands.

Comprehension magic surged from the King as Fyren bowed formally. "Alda Barton, Governor of Wyndburh."

Sylica scampered forward. "Hi friends!"

Khariton glanced at her sharply, but it was too late. She bounded past the fire, with Daisy galloping behind her.

Eyes wide with terror, the guards scrambled to defend the Governor.

"Sylica!" Thea cried.

Magic surged.

Sylica and Daisy disappeared, reappearing beside Khariton. As Sylica looked around in surprise, Khariton grabbed her shoulder. "Just because you know someone," he hissed, "doesn't mean you get to go first."

The Governor and her guards stared in astonishment.

"I believe Sylica is known to you." The King spoke with a smile, his Elvish words becoming Common in Thea's ears. "I am Ruslan, King of the Elves. I travel with my army from our lands in the north to the aid of Gedwyld, which is currently under siege. We mean no harm to you or your people."

The guards looked at the Governor, as if uncertain of what to do.

Slowly, the Governor rose from her chair. Her clothes were plain and serviceable. Only her fur-lined cloak spoke of any prestige that would set her above any other person in the town.

"If you come in peace, you are welcome." She turned to Fyren. "Tell Graulf we have guests."

The King and his company were invited to sit around the fire as food and drink were brought.

The Governor spoke with the King. "We have heard reports of an army of monsters south on the road. You know of this army?"

The King gestured to Thea at his side. "Thea has come from the lands surrounding Gedwyld and she brought us a report."

The Governor frowned. "No news has come from Gedwyld. You say it is under siege?"

The Governor's spirit was dark. Thea glanced uneasily at the King, but he did not seem concerned. They both waited for her to speak.

Thea nodded. "It is under siege. We mean to reach Gedwyld before it falls."

The Governor eyed the King shrewdly. "Why does an army of Elves appear now? We haven't seen an Elf for hundreds of circles."

The King glanced at Thea. "The peoples of Raphtova are meant to fight together against evil. The Elves forgot that for a long time, but now we have come to make that right."

The Governor seemed to consider his words. "Better coming as an ally than an enemy. Forgive our cold reception, but with reports of an army of monsters, we did not know what to expect."

Amusement flickered in the King's eyes. "You will see more of the Elves in the circles to come. There used to be trade routes, long ago. Perhaps Wyndburh would be interested in a trade agreement with the Elves?"

The Governor's gaze took in the regal attire of her Elvish guests, an eager glint in her eyes.

The King handed her a letter. "This outlines some of the resources that Elvish trade has to offer. You can send a representative to Lyudmyla if you wish, or I can arrange for a delegate to come to Wyndburh by ship. I can foresee a significant increase in traffic through your port in the coming circles."

Across the fire, Sylica sat between Ilya and Khariton, with Daisy at her feet.

"—And then I want to go see Harold, because I haven't seen him for such a long time!" Sylica's continuous chatter seeped into Thea's consciousness. "He always has such yummy meat pies, and one time I found a wishbone in my pie so of course I had to make a wish and you know what? My wish came true the very next day and then I—"

"Listen," Khariton snapped. "Just because something comes into your head doesn't mean you have to say it."

Sylica seemed taken aback. "Then how are people supposed to hear what's in my head?"

"They don't."

"But—" Sylica protested.

"Elves think fast. The older they are, the faster they think. No one says every thought in their head. They have to choose which ones they want people to hear."

"But I want people to hear *all* the thoughts in my head! They're so interesting and they all go together so quick that I just have to—"

"If you say all of yours, you don't get to hear mine."

"Oh." Sylica stopped. A slow frown crept across her face.

"You're not the only person with interesting thoughts," Khariton concluded, a wry gleam in his eyes.

Sylica blinked, clearly trying to process this unexpected revelation. "What would happen if you said all your thoughts?"

Khariton stared down at the fire. "There'd be a lot more swearing."

An unusual silence fell across Sylica's side of the fireplace.

Thea watched from the corner of her eye as another thought occurred to Khariton and he turned to Sylica.

"If you're talking with someone and don't care what they say, then go ahead and derail the conversation as much as you like."

After the meal was finished, the King and his company returned to the army outside the walls. The ships with their crews were preparing to depart, along with most of the Enkeli casters. It had been decided that the King and his army would travel by the road without the help of transportation magic. Through consulting with the Governor of Wyndburh and Thea's experiences on the road, they guessed that it would take about two spans to make the journey to Gedwyld.

The ships would return to Lyudmyla as quickly as possible and prepare themselves for the long journey to

Gedwyld by sea. Svetka, Roland, and the rest of the second army would depart from Lyudmyla within the next couple of days, and with magic to speed their journey, they should be able to reach Gedwyld about the same time as the overland force.

Unwilling to impose on the hospitality of the small town, the King and his army set up their camp in the fields for the night.

As Thea watched the ships depart, Ilya joined her. His face was creased in concern.

"Do all humans live like that?"

"Like what?"

Ilya frowned. "Everything was so dirty. There was muck on the streets and the house was filled with smoke. The floor was nothing but dirt."

Thea stared out across the makeshift harbour. "They live like that because they're poor. They haven't had the peace and security the Elves have had." Thea glanced at the shadowy trees that filled the southern horizon. "In some places the humans are more prosperous, like in Gedwyld, but in Wyndburh they live under the shadow of the Deorcian. It isn't an easy life."

Once the final Elvish ship had sailed, Thea returned to the King's pavilion. A fire had been lit, and the smells of food being prepared drifted across the Elvish camp.

"You were uneasy about trusting the Governor of Wyndburh," the King commented as Thea joined him by the fire.

She shifted uncomfortably. "Her spirit was dark, Your Majesty. I wasn't sure how much we should tell her about our plans."

"You may call me Ruslan when we are talking," the

King smiled. "I hear 'Your Majesty' quite enough as it is." His eyes grew thoughtful. "The Governor's spirit was dark, you are right. Her motivations, though, were only to protect her people." His gaze took in the bustling army around them, preparing their camp for the night. "The brightness of a spirit is important, but if you use spirit sight to help discern someone's character or motivations, that can provide helpful insight. I trusted her to do what was best for her people, which was all I needed to trust her for."

Thea listened with interest. "I didn't know you could use spirit sight for other things like that."

"The longer you have had your sight, the more you learn. In nearly two thousand circles I have not found its limits. There are always more depths to explore." A shadow crossed his face. "That is the danger, and the gift."

Thea glanced down at her skin, so much rougher than the King's. "I haven't had my sight very long at all."

The King smiled. "Walk beside me on the road tomorrow. We may not have much time, but I will teach you what I can." His gaze seemed to look deep inside her. "Your spirit is the brightest I have ever seen. I am honoured to count you among my company."

Thea's face grew uncomfortably hot. "Just because someone's spirit is bright doesn't mean they don't make mistakes."

"I know that very well." Ruslan's gaze met hers. "From what I have seen, though, you have more than atoned for yours."

Chapter Twenty-One

At first light the next morning, the King and his host broke camp and set out on the road to Gedwyld.

From her position beside the King, Thea watched the endless ranks of Elves stretched out before and behind them. Sylica scampered up and down the column, making friends, telling stories, and sharing candy with indiscriminate enthusiasm. Somehow, she always ended up by Khariton's side again, pestering him with questions or telling him all about her latest adventure—a development that seemed to frustrate Khariton enormously.

As the days passed, the King learned all that he could from Thea about Gedwyld, its defences, and the orcs. When they weren't speaking of the road ahead, he taught Thea about spirit sight or shared stories from the days of the Great War.

They hadn't seen any sign of the enemy yet, or any other traveller. As Thea walked, her gaze scanned the surrounding valley where Elvish scouts flanked the road, on constant alert for any sign that the passage of the Elves had been seen.

Keep your eyes open. You will meet someone today.

Enkeli's words from that morning's check in ran through Thea's mind. Who could Enkeli mean? They were still many days from Gedwyld. Had someone escaped and come to meet them?

"Your Majesty!" One of the scouts appeared before the King, breathless, her eyes wide with alarm.

In an instant, the Commander was beside them. "What did you see?"

"A company is approaching from the south!"

"Where?"

The scout pointed to a gap in the hills. "We heard the sound of weapons. They are marching very fast!"

The Commander's face was grim. "Call a halt at once. No trumpets—send runners. I will take the King's Guard and cut them off from behind."

"Don't attack!" Thea cautioned. "Not till we know who it is."

The Commander frowned.

"You know of this company?" The King turned to Thea.

"I might. Don't attack until I know for sure."

The Commander seemed to relent. "Stay with the trumpeters. At your signal we will attack."

Quickly, runners were sent the length of the army. Swords were drawn, bows were strung.

In the distance, a faint tramping of footsteps echoed through the hills.

Thea stood beside the trumpeters, her heart pounding. Whatever was coming didn't sound like a few people, it sounded like an army.

The King's Guard slipped into a nearby copse of trees and disappeared from sight.

Moments later, a host of soldiers marched into view. They were tall, with strange, lizard-like faces. The orange of their scales gleamed in the light.

Thea recognized their leader at once.

"Jeewon!" Thea gasped. Running across the space

that still lay between them, she threw her arms around the suddenly transparent Minathril Captain.

Behind Jeewon, the Oreum crew stood at attention.

Thea cast comprehension, unable to tear her gaze away from the glittering host. "What are you doing here?"

"Looking for you," Jeewon replied, her scales a vibrant tan as she removed herself from Thea's embrace. "Raphea told us we would find you here."

No longer outfitted as a scouting party, the Oreum carried spears and shields. Every crest was erect, and determination gleamed on every scale. A Minathril stepped forward from the ranks and bowed.

"Ssen!" Thea embraced the Sergeant warmly. "It's so good to see you! Is Sungy here?"

"I am here." Sungy joined them, her scales a brilliant yellow. "I would not be left behind."

As Thea embraced her friend, the King stepped forward. "It seems that we are witnessing a meeting of old friends." He stared up at the glittering Minathrils, standing a head taller than any Elf.

"Yes," Thea smiled. "Your Majesty, this is Oreum Jeewon, the Captain of the Oreum crew. Jeewon, this is Ruslan Nevimna, the King of the Elves."

Jeewon bowed. "I bring greetings from my Dragon and the rest of our crews."

"How are you here?" Thea asked, still hardly believing her eyes. "I thought you stayed in the mountains."

"That is how we used to be. Since the Spark left us, some have said that the Spark was right and we were wrong." A golden sheen crept across Jeewon's scales. "I was one of those people. My crew has received our

Dragon's blessing to come and fight this war with you."

Thea's heart leapt. In the Minathrils standing before her, she saw a new kind of light that she hadn't seen before. The Elves were returning to the war, and now the Minathrils were too.

"You are happy." Ssen's scales gleamed yellow. "I remember how to tell."

"Yes, Ssen," Thea beamed, "I am very, very happy that the Oreum is here. You are most welcome."

Among the Oreum, Thea recognized Tayhyang, their healer, and many other faces. She counted about eighty in their ranks.

"We travel to Gedwyld." The King looked up at Jeewon. "Will you march with us?"

Jeewon shouted a command to her crew. Drawing together in a close formation, they marched onto the road, turned sharply, and stood at attention.

"We will march," Jeewon's golden scales gleamed in the light, "and we will fight. We will not be cut off from the world anymore."

As they resumed their travel, Ssen marched at the head of the Minathrils, while Jeewon walked with Thea.

"After you left the Caverns, we lost our Shindahs." A strange sort of amusement gleamed on Jeewon's scales. "Because you and your party called us to account, those in the service of the One were ordered to go out into the world until they have compensated for their neglect. What seemed strange to me was that it was only the Shindahs who were made to pay this penance. All of the Minathrils are guilty of serving our Dragon before serving the Deity. Why should only the Shindahs have a reparation to make? I set my mind to follow after you, and because of that, our Shindah was permitted to remain with our crew."

"Meiling did not oppose you leaving?" Thea watched the Minathril Captain with interest.

"No. We received the Dragon's blessing, even to allow others a leave of absence from their own crew if they wished to march with us."

"And some actually came?"

"Some came. The Caverns are different because you were there."

Among the Minathril ranks behind them, Sylica eagerly reacquainted herself with her Minathril friends.

Curiosity rippled across Jeewon's scales. "What has happened to you since you left us? I have not seen a certain Minathril among your party."

Thea's gaze fell to the ground. "Hwasan chose to betray us to the Enemy. Because of that, I had to kill him."

Jeewon's scales faded to a thoughtful grey-blue. "I have thought much about the way you and your companions treated Hwasan. I hoped that he would find the way to change, but I see that was not so."

Thea nodded. "He had the chance. That's all we could give him." Sadness ached in her chest, and yet as she looked around her, she saw the Elves and Minathrils, ready to help the people of Raphtova once again. When given their chance, some had chosen to take it.

As evening fell, the Elves and Minathrils set up camp for the night. Jeewon and Ssen were invited to join the King and his companions as they ate their evening meal. The King cast comprehension magic across their company, and soon Jeewon and the King were deep in conversation about Minathril culture and military experience.

Ssen sat beside Thea. "Is Roland with you? I was hoping to see him."

"Roland isn't here, but you will see him. He's sailing with the rest of the Elvish army and will meet us at Gedwyld."

Ssen's scales gleamed yellow. "I am eager to fight beside him. I hope we will meet soon."

Thea smiled. "I know Roland would like that too."

From her place by the fire, Thea watched the Minathril crew. They remained alert and disciplined, without any of the humour or laughter she had witnessed while living among them in the Caverns. Now they were on duty, and they took that very seriously.

Among the host of the Elves, Khariton strode from company to company as he did every evening, reviewing the day's travel and ensuring that each company had all that they needed.

Sylica followed him like a puppy, greeting everyone by name and listening to their accounts of the day. Her presence seemed to embarrass Khariton, but he never sent her away.

Thea looked up at Ssen. "I heard you speaking Common earlier. You've learned a lot since I saw you last."

Ssen bowed. "Thank you. Kureum Noonie has been teaching me."

Thea stared out at the Elvish banners fluttering in the breeze. "I'm afraid that most Elves don't know how to speak Common. They haven't had a reason to learn it before now."

"I did not have a reason either, until I met you and Roland. Thankfully there is magic, and friends to translate for us."

Khariton returned from his evening rounds and went to report to the King. Sylica scampered after him.

"Hi, Thea! Hi, Ssen! I checked on everyone and they're all doing great! Aleks did complain that there isn't any salt for putting on his food, but Khariton said he was salty enough and everyone thought that was really funny but I didn't see any salt on him so I licked him just to check and he didn't taste salty at all! But Khariton said that I should really ask people before I lick them so I learned something new today. Sometimes Daisy licks me without asking, but Khariton says that's different because people don't expect Daisy to follow the same rules that people follow, which I think is very—"

Across the fire, she caught Khariton's eye. Checking herself, she glanced around apologetically. "Oh, right. Someone else can talk now."

Khariton gave her an encouraging smile and turned back to the King.

Ilya had been watching Ssen with wide-eyed fascination. "Excuse me," he ventured. "You are a Minathril?"

"I am." Ssen bowed.

"I never met a Minathril before. I only heard about them in stories."

"I would have said the same of the Elves, before Thea and her companions came to the mountains."

Ilya stared at the stern-faced Minathrils standing guard around their camp. "You look like you are prepared for anything."

"They have to be!" Sylica grinned. "They fight Dragons!"

Ilya's eyes opened wide. "You fight Dragons?"

A hint of embarrassment flashed over Ssen's scales. "It is the Dragons who fight Dragons, but we do need to be prepared to defend ourselves in the event of a Dragon attack. Training is very important to us."

"I joined the army the day we sailed from Lyudmyla." Ilya's gaze fell to the sword that hung at his side. "I haven't had any training at all."

Gold gleamed on Ssen's scales. "If your King can ever spare you from your duties, come spend time with us. I would be glad to teach you."

"Thank you." Ilya smiled.

Across the fire, Khariton had finished giving his report. Thea waved for him to join them.

"Ssen, this is Khariton. Khariton, Ssen is one of the Sergeants of the Oreum crew."

Khariton nodded a greeting.

"I am glad to meet you." Ssen bowed, then turned to Sylica. "Is Khariton your family? I see he acts like a father to you."

A look of horror crossed Khariton's face.

"Oh no," Sylica shook her head, "Khariton isn't my dad. He's just teaching me about how to be an Elf. My real mom and dad live a long way across the sea. You have to take a boat to get there."

The King joined them, turning to Sylica with interest. "I had been meaning to ask you about your family. As far as I understand, no Elf has lived so far from Lyudmyla since the Great War began. How did your family come to be there, so far across the sea?"

"Oh, my parents aren't Elves, they're Littles. There's

a lot of Littles that live across the sea, you know. It's kind of strange that I ended up being so much like an Elf."

Thea glanced at the King. "I'm guessing she was adopted, but she doesn't know anything about her birth parents."

"My what?" Sylica frowned.

"Your parents that you were actually born to. Something must have happened to them when you were very young, and then the Littles raised you."

"Does that mean I get to have *four parents*?" Sylica's eyes lit up in delight. "I can't wait to tell them! My mom and my dad are my favourite people in the world, besides Daisy of course. I haven't seen them for such a long time!"

Thea watched her friend with a thoughtful expression. "How long has it been since you left home?"

"Oh, I don't know. Ages and ages, I think. Probably two or three hundred circles by now. It's kind of hard to keep track. Maybe I'll go back and see them someday. That would be fun!"

Thea's heart sank. "Sylica, you know that Littles only live for a hundred and fifty circles. I ... I don't think your parents will be there anymore."

"Of course they're there," Sylica retorted. "They never really travelled much. That's why they sent me out to see the world!"

"I don't mean that. I mean ... if you've really been gone for that long, I think they would have died by now. Elves live forever, but most other people don't."

Sylica's gaze dropped to the turf beneath her feet. "I know," she ventured in a quiet voice. "They were getting old when they sent me away. Everyone was getting older, except me. I know they're dead, but in my head they're still alive. That's how I want them to be."

Thea reached out and took Sylica's hand. "You're with your own people now. We'll still be here, no matter how much time goes by."

Keep your eyes open. The words from her General echoed through Thea's mind as she walked alongside the King the next day. What had Enkeli meant this time? Were they going to meet someone again?

She kept her eyes open, but nothing unusual appeared.

Jeewon and the Commander seemed to get along well. Thea overheard snatches of conversations about tactics and siege warfare. Behind them, the Minathril crew marched in perfect formation, their scales gleaming in the icy light.

As staph approached, the road passed through a small patch of forest. Snow drifted down from the trees overhead and Thea glanced up. Someone crouched above her in the branches, staring down at her.

Thea gasped. Before she could react, the figure vaulted down to the ground, landing lightly on its hooves. Turning to Thea, the Faun gave an elaborate bow.

Thea stared. "Thabani!"

Thabani grinned and gave a shrill whistle. From the trees all around them, Fauns leapt down in a shower of snow and ice. Cheers and laughter filled the air.

"Lady Thea," Thabani smiled, "we are honoured to meet you once again."

Sylica squealed with delight and threw herself at the Fauns, with Daisy scampering excitedly beside her. The rest of the Elves and Minathrils stared in surprise.

Thabani's large, ram-like horns had nicks and cracks they didn't have before, and there was more silver in his dark curly hair, but his eyes still twinkled with light.

"What are you doing here?" Thea demanded. "We all thought you were dead!"

"I thought that too, on at least a couple of occasions. Getting past those orcs is like dancing through a hornet's nest."

Thabani's Fauns gathered around, smiling and jostling. Despite the cold, they had nothing but their own fur to warm them. One Faun carried a falcon on her wrist. Another had a ferret on his shoulder.

"They sure came suddenly." A shadow crossed Thabani's face. "The Resistance scattered. These are the only ones who made it out with me."

"I got some of the Resistance out too." Thea placed a hand on Thabani's shoulder. "Msizi and Noxolo helped me. Sixteen Fauns, and most of the Faunlets. Ember and Kaji are there too."

"They are?" A smile filled Thabani's face. "That is great news. Where are they now?"

"They're at my house near Gedwyld. We're on our way to help them."

"Good." Thabani glanced around, taking in the host of Elves and the crew of Minathrils. "You've got quite the company."

Feeling the King's presence beside her, Thea turned and cast comprehension. "Your Majesty, this is Thabani of the Resistance. He is a dear friend of mine. Thabani, this is the King of the Elves and Jeewon, the Captain of the Oreum."

Ignoring the Minathril Captain, Thabani smiled

broadly at the King. "Micai told me your host was on its way, Sir King. My Fauns and I would be glad to fight beside you in the war against the orcs."

The King looked down at the Faun whose head was about the height of an Elf's shoulder. "Thank you, Thabani of the Resistance. Mykyta has spoken to me of the valour of the Fauns. We will be glad to have your assistance when the battle comes."

"We'll help you before then too," Thabani winked. "There's twenty of us, and every one a caster. I'm with Micai, but many of them have signed up under Enkeli. We can get you where you're going. Fast."

As the army continued on its way to Gedwyld, Thea found herself walking between Thabani and Jeewon. Looking from the Minathril towering above her on one side to the Faun's nimble form on the other, she almost felt like she was in a dream.

"I saw Sylica of course," Thabani chatted amiably as they walked. "Can't miss her! Where's the rest of your party got to?"

"Roland is coming on the ships with the rest of the Elvish army," Thea explained. "Ulfgar is with Ember and the Fauns that we got out of the forest."

"Good." Thabani nodded.

Thea hesitated. "Zanele died to save me as we were leaving the mountains."

Thabani stared down the road that stretched out before them. "Faithful until death," he said in a low voice. "I knew you needed her."

"We did need her." Thea looked down at the tender-hearted old Faun. "I don't think I'd still be alive if she hadn't been there."

Light twinkled in Thabani's eyes. "But now the Spark lives."

"Yes." Thea glanced up at the Minathril Captain. "Zanele wasn't just there for me. She was there for the Minathrils too."

Amusement flashed across Jeewon's scales. "She certainly threw our healers into chaos."

"Good for her," Thabani grinned. "We all need a good dose of chaos."

"Sometimes, perhaps." A hint of brown crept over Jeewon's scales. "In my experience it often causes more heat than light."

"Good thing both are important, then." Thabani smiled to himself. Throwing his dirk in the air, he caught it with a flourish.

Jeewon broke the silence. "I hear the Fauns have been having trouble with orcs."

"You could say that." Thabani shook his head. "We scattered, but they came after us like hounds."

"I would have thought that if you worked together you could have made a better defence."

"If a dead defence is the best kind, then I'm sure you're right."

Confusion showed on Jeewon's scales. "I do not think that is true."

Thabani winked. "Well there's your answer."

"If you disagree, it would be simpler to say so."

Thabani shrugged, giving Jeewon an impish glance. "Surprised to see you down here. I thought Minathrils' knees couldn't walk downhill or something."

"We are perfectly capable of walking downhill," Jeewon replied, her scales flaring reddish-orange, "which you would have known if you gave it any thought. Anyone who cannot walk downhill should not live in the mountains."

Thea looked from Jeewon to Thabani.

"Excuse me," Jeewon said stiffly. "I must go speak with my Sergeant."

"Hmph," Thabani muttered to himself as Jeewon turned and walked away. "Someone needs to lighten up."

"Thabani, I don't think—" Thea began, but Sylica bounded up to join them.

"There you are, Thabani! You have to come meet everybody! I've made so many friends since we saw you before. First there's Khariton and then there's Ssen, and then there's—"

Pulling Thabani by the arm, Sylica dragged him out of sight.

Thea was left alone.

That evening, Thabani and his Fauns joined the King's company around their fire. Beneath their exuberant influence, jokes and laughter flowed freely, and the fire blazed higher than ever.

One of the Fauns had a small wooden flute, and soon a dance was begun, to the astonishment of the Elves. Sylica jumped and leapt in the middle of it, her face beaming with happiness.

Jeewon sat stiffly at the edge of the revelry, her scales showing her discomfort. As politely as she could, she excused herself and returned to the Minathril camp.

Thea watched as more and more of the Elves were swept into the dance. She didn't feel like dancing today. Instead, she sat in the flickering shadows, alone with her thoughts.

"Excuse me," Ilya ventured, joining her beyond the firelight. "What is going on?"

"The Fauns started a dance. It's not unusual for them."

Ilya stared at the leaping Fauns. "Why?"

"Why not?" A smile creased Thea's face. "Does there need to be a reason to dance?"

"I guess not." A perplexed frown still lingered on his face.

"They only live for thirty circles." Thea spoke in a low voice. "They need to fill them with as much living as they can."

"Thirty circles?" Ilya stared. "No wonder the light bounces off them strangely. There is so much life inside them they must be practically vibrating."

His foot started tapping to the music.

"You should dance." Thea gave him a sly grin.

Consternation filled his face. "I don't know how to dance."

"This isn't the kind of dance you can do wrong."

Ilya hesitated.

Gently, Thea encouraged him forward into the circle of light. A Faun noticed him and grabbed his hand, pulling him into the dance.

As the night stretched on, Khariton waded through the spinning Fauns and pulled Sylica away.

"Hey, it's not fair!" Sylica pouted. "I want to dance!"

"It's late," Khariton countered, "and you haven't eaten yet."

"Oh." Sylica considered this. "I am hungry."

"Go eat, then." Khariton gestured her off through the shadows. "I saved some food for you. It's by my kit."

As Sylica scampered off with Daisy in hot pursuit,

Thabani joined Khariton by the edge of the firelight.

"She is your Faunlet?" Thabani smiled, watching Sylica disappear through the shadows.

Khariton frowned. "My what?"

"Faunlet. A Faun who's too young to care for themselves. You know, a child."

Khariton shifted uncomfortably. "She's not mine."

"You're caring for her, though?"

Khariton stared out through the shadows. "I guess so." He shrugged helplessly. "Someone has to do it."

Thabani watched the dancing of the flames. "Fauns don't worry about parentage too much. The Faunlets belong to all of us, and we raise them together. Sometimes, though, there is a Faunlet who needs more care than the others do. When that happens, a Faun with a special connection to the Faunlet chooses to call them their own and cares specially for them." He glanced at Khariton. "I think Sylica is that kind of Faunlet."

Khariton shrugged. "Maybe she is." He glanced furtively through the shadows. "I should go check my kit. Make sure Daisy hasn't swallowed anything."

Turning, Khariton left the circle of light.

Thabani watched him go, then came to sit beside Thea. "Why aren't you dancing?"

Thea sighed. "I was thinking about the last time I was at a Faun dance. So many of the Fauns that were there are dead now. Roland was there too. That was a special time with him."

"You miss Roland?" Thabani smiled gently.

"I miss what we had."

Thabani's eyes twinkled. "Lovers' quarrel?"

"Not lovers anymore." Thea watched the flickering

shadows. "We're still friends, he just loves other things more."

Thabani stared thoughtfully at the fire. The Fauns danced and twirled, careless of the night that was slipping by. Their song's haunting tune drifted away through the cold night air.

Thea stared at her hands. "I didn't want to hurt your people, Thabani. I'm sorry."

Thabani gave her a thoughtful glance. "You messed up, did you?"

"I let a spy contact the enemy. That's how the orcs knew about you."

For a moment, all Thea could hear was the crackling of the flames. Thabani watched her, the firelight gleaming in his eyes.

"When you're a leader, mistakes hurt, because they hurt so many other people. I've been there too." A shadow of pain passed through his eyes. "Once I forgot to check in and didn't get a warning from Micai in time. More than half of the Faunlets died." His gaze fell. "Sometimes you carry those mistakes for a long time. Thankfully, there is still mercy."

The firelight gleamed on the silver in Thabani's hair. His face seemed old and tired, but there was peace in his eyes.

Thea watched the dance whirl round and round. "Allulien told me that because of what I did, I can't follow my own desires anymore. I have to focus all my efforts on saving the Resistance."

Thabani nodded. "Then do that to the best of your ability." A grin spread across his face. "At least you're immortal. Deity willing, you've got time for a lot more than that."

With a wink, Thabani returned to the dance. Thea sat and watched the sparks from the fire fly up into the sky, their tiny points of light shimmering past the gentle glow of Micai.

Chapter Twenty-Two

Eyes open.

Thea suppressed a smile as she rolled up her blanket and prepared for the new day. What did Enkeli have in store this time?

Around her, the icy morning air was filled with the sounds of bustle and clamour as Elves, Fauns, and Minathrils packed up and readied themselves for another march.

Thabani waved to Thea, trotting over to join her where the leaders of the army were gathering.

"Now that we're here, the Fauns can scout for you," Thabani grinned. "Got to be careful now that you're getting closer to the orcs."

Thea shook her head. "Sorry, Thabani, but you can't scout for us. You're all casters. The orcs can see the light of the Deity in you."

Thabani's eyes widened. "Seriously?" He shook his head. "Well that explains a lot."

"We have scouts," the King assured him. "Those in our army with as little light in them as possible."

"I know you have scouts." Thabani made a face. "We could hear them from the next valley over."

"Well, they have been in retirement for over a thousand circles." Light twinkled in the King's eyes.

"A little stiff at the joints, are they?"

"Stiff would be one word you could use for it."

After the King excused himself, Thabani frowned. "The orcs can see our light." He glanced at Thea. "How did you find out about that?"

"An orc friend of mine explained it to me."

"You have an orc friend?" Thabani shook his head. "You really are the Spark, aren't you?"

"It wasn't my doing this time. It was Inyoni."

"With those big eyes?" A thoughtful smile creased Thabani's face. "She could make anyone fall in love."

"Thea, may I speak with you?"

Thea looked up at Jeewon who had been walking in silence beside her. "Of course."

Jeewon bowed. "Thank you."

Thea glanced around. The King had used his magic to allow the leaders to communicate freely, regardless of the language they spoke. At the moment, Thea and Jeewon were alone. The other leaders were walking elsewhere, or deep in their own conversations.

Confusion showed on Jeewon's scales. "I do not understand Thabani. I see that he is your friend, and he is counted among the leaders of this expedition, but he seems to me very irresponsible and thoughtless. Is there something I have missed?"

The sound of tramping feet filled the thoughtful silence as Thea considered how to respond. "First, you need to remember that he is a Shindah. By your own traditions you must honour him for his service to the Deity. I know his manner is different than the Shindahs of your people, but to serve the Deity means to obey. It does not mean being serious all the time."

In the distance, Sylica and Khariton wound their way through the ranks of the Elves that served as a vanguard. A group of Thabani's Fauns joked and laughed as they walked.

"The Fauns have been fighting this war alone for generations." Thea spoke softly. "They are quick to forgive, but they are also quick to speak their minds. Thabani didn't expect you or any Minathril to come. Why would he? The Elves and the Minathrils should have helped them long ago, but we didn't. They had every reason to give up on us."

Jeewon walked in silence for a while, emotions rippling across her scales.

In the distance, Thabani's laugh rang out above the noise.

Thea's gaze followed the sound. "Thabani may seem lighthearted, but he has been leading the Resistance for many circles, while also protecting his people and their children." She gave Jeewon a sidelong glance. "And all of that without a Dragon to help him."

Jeewon nodded, her scales a thoughtful grey. "I see that I have much to learn. Thank you." Turning, she walked back to her crew.

A short while later, Thea found herself walking with Thabani. He hummed a quiet tune to himself as he trotted along, his eyes scanning the hills on either side of the valley.

Thea watched him thoughtfully. "What do you think of Jeewon?" she ventured after a while.

"Hmm?" Thabani glanced at Thea. "Jeewon? Well, I can tell that you respect her. For myself, I don't know what to think. She's so stoic and unemotional. How can anyone live like that?"

"I thought Minathrils were emotionless until I got to

know them. You see, their faces don't work like ours, so they can't show their emotions the way we do. It's the colours on their scales and the way they hold their crest and body that show what they are feeling. Yesterday when you were talking with Jeewon, her scales were grey because she was confused. When her scales started to turn orangish-red she was getting frustrated and defensive, but that was just because she couldn't understand you."

Thabani frowned. "I didn't think there was that much going on. She just said a few things and walked away."

"Minathrils can't understand our emotions very well. It's something they have to learn, just like we have to learn theirs. They take their work very seriously, and I'm not sure if they can understand your sense of humour, or why the Fauns would be lighthearted in such a dangerous situation."

Thabani shook his head. "I don't know how anyone can be so serious all the time. Where's the fun in that?"

"See that Minathril over there?" Thea pointed out a Minathril who had entered their line of sight. "She thinks something is funny. Her scales are yellow and her crest is shaking." Thea pointed out another. "That Minathril has grey scales and his crest is back. That means he's worried about something."

Thabani listened intently, understanding growing on his face.

"Thea!" Sylica scampered towards them. "Thea! Can I go see—oh hi Thabani! You know what I just realized? I haven't shown you any of Daisy's tricks yet!"

Grabbing Thabani by the arm, she dragged him off the road. "Sit, Daisy! Roll over!"

Thea turned to Khariton who had appeared along with Sylica. "What was she wanting?"

Khariton gave an embarrassed smile. "She wants to know if she can go see that lake over there." He gestured across the valley. "I told her she had to ask first, but she got distracted again."

Thea glanced in the direction Khariton had indicated. The lake didn't seem too far away. "I think that's fine, as long as someone's with her."

Khariton nodded and strode to Sylica's side.

"Jump over the stick, Daisy!" Sylica coaxed, waving a bit of branch in the air. "Jump over the stick!"

Khariton tapped her shoulder. "Forgetting something?"

Sylica blinked in confusion.

"Thea says you can go see the lake."

Sylica squealed in delight. "Oh! Right! I forgot!"

Dropping the stick, she dashed off towards the lake, with Daisy scampering at her heels. Khariton had to run to keep up.

On the road ahead, some sort of commotion had begun. An Elf approached, breathless, and bowed to the King. "Your Majesty, we hear sounds of combat!"

The Commander stepped out of the ranks behind him. "Where?"

The Elf saluted. "North of the road, just beyond the vanguard."

Jeewon approached with a bow. "I can take my crew and investigate these sounds."

"The Fauns can go," Thabani offered. "We've got the magic to deal with most things."

The Commander raised her hand. "The King's Guard will approach first."

"No," Thea interrupted, "I am going. The rest of you wait here."

"Lady Thea," Thabani protested, "the Spark should not be unprotected."

"Enkeli wants me to see who it is."

Jeewon nodded. "My crew can—"

"Alright," Thabani grinned. "Charge!" The Fauns turned and dashed along the roadside.

Jeewon's scales flared red. The Commander's mouth hung open.

"Excuse me," Thea muttered. Casting her magic, the world shifted around her and she appeared beyond the vanguard. Shouts and the clash of steel echoed through the distant trees. Thea hurried towards the sound.

Pushing through the tangled undergrowth, she caught sight of two orcs towering above a small, wizened figure. The ground around them was littered with bodies.

One of the orcs turned to face Thea. Snarling, it gripped its spear and took a step towards her.

The wizened figure swung a massive, two-handed sword over its head, striking the orc with a resounding crunch. The orc crumpled to the ground.

With a chorus of cries, the Fauns burst out of the undergrowth.

"Hold it!" the old man cackled. "No interferin' now. This is my fight."

The old man and the last orc circled each other, eyes blazing.

With a lightning quick movement, the orc struck out with its blade. The old man jumped back and swung his massive sword. It struck the orc's shoulder, cutting a rending gouge in its metallic flesh. The orc roared and struck out with its other arm. The old man dodged and swung his foot.

His boot hit the orc's metal shins. Yelping in pain, he dropped his sword.

As the old man bent double, the orc swung its blade.

Light gleamed off the knife the old man snatched off the ground. He drove it up into the orc's midriff in an explosion of green blood and guts. The orc crumpled to the ground.

Slowly straightening his back, the wizened man peered at the circle of Fauns. "Didn't expect an audience."

Thea stepped out from the trees. "Coham!"

"That's the name." The old man cracked a toothless grin. "Say, I know you! How's the adventuring life?" Wiping green blood off his face, Coham went to fetch his sword, limping slightly. "Keep forgettin' their skin's so hard." He shook his head ruefully. "What will Beatrice say?"

With an explosion of noise, the Minathril crew burst through the trees, their shields and weapons at the ready. Seeing that the combat was over, they stopped and stood at attention.

"What is going on here?" Jeewon demanded, her scales blazing red.

"Nope," Coham cackled. "Good guess, though."

"This is Coham," Thea explained. "He was fighting orcs, but he didn't appear to need our help."

Jeewon turned on Thabani. "What were you doing? The Spark explicitly ordered you to stay where you were!"

"Did she?" Thabani grinned. "I recall her telling *you* to stay exactly where you were."

"Darn nuisances," Coham muttered, kicking the lifeless body of one of the orcs. "Ow!"

"Jeewon, Thabani," Thea looked at them sharply, "we will discuss this later." Glancing around the clearing, she saw that there had been four orcs. They were all dead.

Coham limped towards the far side of the clearing. "You coming, or you going to stand there all day?"

"Where are you going?" Thea asked.

"Beatrice's house, just over the hill." Coham grinned. "I'm sure she'd love to meet all you nice young folks."

Thabani glared at Jeewon. Jeewon did not look at him, but her scales were still a pulsing red.

"We will be there soon," Thea replied. "Thank you, Coham."

Turning, she left the clearing and returned to the road where the King and his army waited. After explaining the situation, the King agreed to meet with Coham and his family.

"Another friend of yours, I see." The King's eyes twinkled. "They seem to be appearing wherever we go."

Slowly, the company of the King made their way in the direction Coham had indicated, and a runner was sent to find Khariton and Sylica.

Circling the hill into the valley beyond, Thea and her companions found a small, wood-frame house. It sat by itself on a patch of bare, hard ground. A half-built fence lay along one side and two skinny chickens pecked at the half-dead weeds.

A large woman with thick braids and a green-stained apron stepped out of the door. A sword hung from the scabbard at her waist.

Thea felt the surge of magic as the King cast

comprehension.

"Grandfather!" The woman yelled over her shoulder. "You invite guests for feast the very day I said there wasn't a thing in the pantry?"

"Can't leave them wandering the highways," Coham grinned, his head popping out from behind Beatrice, "not with all them orcs about!"

Beatrice rolled her eyes.

"We will not impose on your hospitality," the King assured her. "We travel with our own provisions. We were hoping, though, that you could tell us about the state of the road from here to Gedwyld."

Beatrice put her hands on her hips. "Well, you'd better come in, then."

Thea followed Beatrice through the door. It was a small, one-room house, with a fireplace, a table, and three chairs. A ladder led up to a sleeping loft above. Every nook and cranny of the small house was filled with wooden things—staffs, stools, bowls, spoons—all elaborately carved with beautiful, swirling designs. An assortment of weapons were arranged on the table, in the process of being cleaned and sharpened. An ornate golden plate hung above the mantle.

A man who looked to be about Beatrice's age sat on a stool by the fire, carving a staff.

"Edwin, dear," Beatrice called to him, "Grandfather brought home some people. They're asking about the road to Gedwyld."

"The road to Gedwyld?" Edwin's hands ran up and down the staff, testing its smoothness. "They must be brave ones." He stopped and listened. "Actually, they sound like they're prepared for it."

Thea moved aside and the King entered, followed by

Ilya.

Edwin did not turn towards the door. "Someone important?"

"This is Ruslan, the King of the Elves," Thea introduced, "and Ilya, his attendant. Darya is the Commander," Thea continued as Darya stepped through the door, followed by Thabani and Jeewon. "And this is Oreum Jeewon and Thabani."

Jeewon bowed.

"Nice little place you have here," Thabani grinned.

"They've done it up right nice," Coham nodded. "Not bad for a first little nest."

"Edwin's done a lot for it," Beatrice beamed, busily moving assorted weaponry out of the way so there would be more places to sit.

Sylica burst through the door, followed by Khariton. "Hi everybody! Did I miss something? The lake was really pretty but there weren't any ducks this time ..." her voice faded into silence. "Somebody else's turn now," she concluded with a sheepish smile.

"This is Sylica and Khariton," Thea finished the introductions.

"Right," Beatrice nodded. "I'm Beatrice and this is Edwin. If you haven't met old Coham yet, that's your own doing."

The small room was quite crowded. Thea's gaze took in all the beautiful woodwork around them. "You're a woodcarver, Edwin?"

"That I am." Edwin's hand ran along the surface of the staff, found a rough spot, and started to smooth it. His eyes didn't move.

"You made all of these things?" Sylica gasped. "They're so pretty!"

Pleasure shone on Edwin's face. "I cannot say that I try to make them pretty, but I carve designs that feel good in my hands, and often that ends up the same." He continued to work as he talked, his small knife moving swiftly over the length of the staff.

"Oh, can I feel them?" Sylica asked.

"Of course," Edwin smiled. "They are meant to be felt."

Jumping up, Sylica grabbed a staff from where it leaned against the wall. "It's so smooth!" She ran her hand up and down its length. "Smooth and swirly!"

Thea glanced up at the glistening plate above the mantle, remembering the last time she saw Coham. "Did you get that from the mountains?"

"Nice little present from the Dragons," Coham grinned. "Worth its weight in gold too, only—" he scowled, "they won't let me sell it. Edwin can't even see the damn thing!"

"But I can hear it." Edwin smiled. "It makes such a beautiful sound whenever we talk around the table. Can you hear it?"

Thea listened. At the edge of her hearing was a faint ringing echo.

Beatrice crossed her arms. "Edwin likes it, and there it's staying." She glared at her grandfather.

"You can't eat pretty sounds," Coham grumbled, sitting down on a stool in the corner.

"We are doing just fine," Beatrice countered. "I can hunt all the food we need and Edwin's work sells in the city. Before the orcs came, his spoons were selling faster than he could make them!"

"Before the orcs came," Coham muttered. "Now the game's gone and we're all gonna chew the soles off our old boots."

"Have the orcs been quite a problem here?" Thea asked.

Coham scowled. "They keep comin' around and making trouble. That's why I'm stickin' around here, t'help out till this all blows over."

Beatrice sighed. "Grandfather, we are perfectly capable of defending ourselves."

"With every homestead from here to Gedwyld burned to the ground?" Coham scratched his balding head. "You're lucky you're so far back off the road."

"How far are we from Gedwyld?" the King asked.

"Two or three days' walk, depending on how the arthritis is doing."

The King glanced at Thea. "With hastening it won't be more than two days. Are the orcs often on the road?"

"Sometimes yes, sometimes no," Coham reflected. "Once you get close to Gedwyld they're all over the place. There's no way you're getting through to Gedwyld now. They're under siege."

"We are here to lift the siege."

Coham snorted. "You and what army?"

"The army outside, I presume," Edwin replied with a private smile. "Can't you hear them?"

Coham opened the door and stuck his head outside. All around the house, the forces of the Elves, Minathrils, and Fauns were setting up camp.

"Huh," Coham muttered, and shut the door.

"The Deity has sent us to save Gedwyld," Thea explained. "We have an army, and we have magic."

"Do you have any advice for us," the King asked Coham, "as we try to approach the city?"

Coham frowned. "Don't trust numbers to get you

through. I've crossed swords with enough of those buggers and they're tough nuts to crack, let me tell you."

The King nodded. "We are not counting on an easy fight. Some of our number have faced orcs before." He glanced from Thea to Thabani. "Our advantage is that they do not know we are coming."

Across the room, Sylica looked through a stack of ornate wooden boxes, peering inside each of them, one after the other.

The Commander leaned forward. "But can we reach the orcs before they become aware of us? As we get closer, secrecy will be difficult to maintain."

"With enough magic we can move pretty fast," Thabani offered. "That would give them a good shock."

"It would also give us no time to scout or form a strategy," Jeewon countered.

The King's expression was thoughtful. "We have one more day of travel before we have to make that decision. Perhaps the way forward will become clear before then."

"Well, there's only one road," Coham offered, "so I can't help you there. Not unless you've got boats in your backpack."

"The boats are coming, but our company will approach on foot."

"You've got guts, that's for sure," Coham grinned. "Can't fault you for that."

The King glanced around the crowded room. "Is there anything else that should be addressed while we are here? If not, we will take the opportunity to rest while we can."

Khariton shifted nervously. "There is something I want to speak with you about. Doesn't have to be now.

Sometime after feast, maybe."

The King nodded. "We could address it now."

"It's just a personal matter. Nothing to do with the war."

The King gave him a sidelong glance. "And?"

"It was just a thought. That I was thinking about. But if it isn't a good time—"

"Khariton. Just say what you want to say."

Khariton took a deep breath. "I would like to adopt Sylica. As my daughter."

Silence fell across the room.

Sylica's head poked up from under the table. "What's going on?"

The King regarded her thoughtfully. "Khariton would like to adopt you."

"What's adopt?"

"When someone chooses to take in a child who is not their own. They become their parent and the child becomes their child."

Slow understanding crept across Sylica's face. "So I would get to have another daddy?"

"Yes, you would."

"Wow!" Sylica beamed. "Now I get to have three daddies! My birth daddy and my Little daddy and my grumpy daddy!"

Laughter erupted around the room.

Khariton stared at the ground in embarrassed consternation. "Don't suppose I could change my mind on that?" he muttered.

Sylica bounded excitedly around the cramped little room, knocking staffs, trays, and mixing bowls onto the floor in a resounding clatter.

The King's eyes twinkled as he turned to Khariton.

"You were asking about the legal paperwork, I believe?"

Khariton nodded.

The King turned to his assistant. "Ilya, could you get my bag with the papers and documents?"

Ilya bowed and slipped out the door.

The King regarded Khariton thoughtfully as Sylica scrambled to clean up her mess. "You don't have any family of your own, do you?"

"No, Your Majesty." Khariton looked at the floor.

"Any land or property?"

"I used to have a house in Enzhelika."

The King nodded. "Enzhelika will be rebuilt. I will ensure the finances are available for restoring your house."

"Thank you."

When Ilya returned, the King spread a series of pages out on the table. His pen scratched busily. "We can transport the papers to Mykyta to be recorded in the—" he stopped himself. "I was going to say 'in the Halls of Knowledge', but I suppose it will have to be recorded wherever such things are being recorded now." He gave a wry smile and set down his pen. "Khariton, please state your intention."

Khariton froze as everyone turned to look at him. Nervously he cleared his throat. "Sylica—"

Sylica looked up from the floor where she had been piling wooden dishes into a lopsided pyramid. "Yes?"

Khariton crouched on the floor beside her. "You've always felt like you're different, or like there isn't a place for you to belong." He looked straight in her eyes. "I want to give you that place to belong. I know we're different, but I think we're more alike than most. I want to be there for you and help you in a way that the Littles or the Fauns can't, because we're Elves, and for us belonging means forever." A gentle smile gleamed in his eyes. "Will you be my daughter?"

Sylica stared at Khariton, her eyes filling with tears. "For real?"

Khariton nodded. "For real."

Sylica flung her arms around Khariton, tears streaming down her face.

The King smiled. "I think that means yes."

Thea watched them, Khariton with his dark obsidian skin, smooth and ancient. Sylica with her vibrant green. Both agents of chaos, in their own way.

Joy filled Thea's heart. Now Sylica had a family and a home.

Khariton held her until the storm of tears passed. After the sobs had turned to sniffs, Sylica wiped her face on Khariton's sleeve and smiled. "I love you, Grumpy Daddy."

Tentatively, Khariton patted her head.

Chapter Twenty-Three

The news spilled out from the small house and through the surrounding camp. The Fauns declared a great celebration, and soon bonfires were lit and a dance had begun.

When the paperwork had been finished and sent by magic to Mykyta, those in the house emerged to join the party.

"It is official." The King smiled and shook Khariton's hand. "Congratulations to you both."

Sylica was already dancing. Thea joined her, letting the music flow through her once again. Around them, Fauns, Elves, and Minathrils joined in, spinning around each other in the unrestrained joy of the dance.

Even Khariton allowed himself to be dragged into the middle of it all. Sylica returned to him, again and again, as if assuring herself that he was really there. Every time he welcomed her with a smile.

From the edge of the trees, Jeewon watched the revellers, amusement gleaming on her scales.

Beatrice sat beside Edwin, her arm resting on her husband's shoulder. His carving knife darted and flashed, as if it too was in time to the music.

There was food and wine—though Thea was not entirely sure where it had come from. People ate and drank, laughter filled the air, and the dance carried on and on.

Thea danced with Ssen, then danced with Thabani. Across the fire, Ilya and Sungy laughed together as if they were lifelong friends.

Music did this. It brought people together like a language they could all understand.

The King approached Thea and bowed. "Could I have this dance?"

Thea smiled. "Of course, Your Majesty."

Hand in hand, Thea and the King returned to the dance.

Any stiffness or slowness the King may have felt, he wasn't feeling it now. Thea laughed in delight as they whirled round the fire again and again.

He was an Elf who was fully alive and present in the moment. Quicker than any Faun, strong as any Minathril. His spirit glimmered and shone with the light of the Deity. With a King like this, her people would never be lost again.

Exhausted at last, Thea left the dance and joined their hosts. Beatrice's foot tapped along to the music, but she seemed perfectly content to watch the revelry from her husband's side. Coham was stuffing his face with as much food as he could eat.

Beatrice nodded a greeting as Thea approached. "Well! I haven't been to a party like this since I was a girl."

Edwin smiled. "Everyone sounds so happy."

Thea watched the dancers whirl around. "The Fauns know how to have a good time, and how to help everyone else have a good time too."

"They sure do," Coham cackled and threw back a mug of wine. "Well, got to get back to dancing. There was one lady Faun who seemed particularly interested."

"Coham!" Thea laughed.

"What?" Coham shot her a wink. "You don't think she can keep up?"

He hobbled off to join the dance, passing Sylica who scampered towards them. Flopping on the ground, she panted heavily. "Hi Thea, isn't this so much fun?"

Thea smiled. "Yes, it is."

Daisy flopped down beside them, nudging Sylica's hand with her nose until she got the attention she wanted.

Sylica's eyes shone as she watched the dance go around and around. Despite the enthusiasm she always showed, there was something steadier in her countenance.

"Sylica," Thea began, "I'm really happy for you."

"I'm really happy too!" Sylica grinned.

"I know you were trying to find a place to belong. I think you've found it now."

A thoughtful look crossed Sylica's face. "It's funny. I never really thought I would." She grinned. "I guess surprises happen every day!"

Thea couldn't help smiling. "You know? I think they do."

Skirting the other revellers, Ilya came to join them. "Sylica, I want to offer you my congratulations. We are cousins now, you know."

"We are?" Sylica blinked in surprise.

"Khariton is from Third House. I was born into Third House too."

Of course! Thea's smile grew. Sylica didn't just have a father, she belonged to a House. The Elves really were her people now.

"That means your name is Sylica Oryzny!"

"It is?" Sylica considered this with a puzzled expression. "How come I get two names?"

"Oryzny is the name for everyone in Third House. My second name is Kirisensk because I'm a part of First House."

Sylica looked around. "Is anyone else here from Third House?"

"There's lots of us," Ilya supplied. "We're a pretty big House."

Sylica's face lit up. "I have *more* family? Where are they?"

Ilya smiled. "Come. I'll introduce you."

As Sylica scampered after him, Thea felt like she'd never stop smiling. Third House wouldn't know what hit them when Khariton and Sylica returned to Lyudmyla.

Edwin leaned closer to his wife. "Is Khariton here?" he asked in a low voice.

Beatrice glanced around. "Khariton!" she bellowed, catching sight of him across the yard.

"You didn't need to call," Edwin muttered under his breath.

"Yes I did," Beatrice retorted.

A little while later, Khariton joined them by the house. "Did you want something?"

Edwin held up the staff that he had been carving. "This is a gift for you."

Carefully, Khariton lifted it out of his hands.

"I carved it with the sounds of the dance and what the music feels like to me, as a memory of this day."

Thea leaned closer. The surface of the staff was covered with curling, twisting motifs, exploding apart and drawing together in an intricate, beautiful design.

She had never seen anything like it.

"Thank you," Khariton replied, staring at the staff in his hands. "I will remember this day." His eyes twinkled. "I don't think Sylica will let me forget it."

Filling the yard in front of them, the dance went on, faster and faster, as Micai grew large in the sky and night fell over the land. In the shadows, Thea caught a glimpse of the Commander's stern face and the glimmer of light reflecting off a spear point. Not everyone was lost in the revelry. Part of the army still kept watch.

The joy and fun were only a reprieve. In the morning, they would continue their journey to Gedwyld.

Beyond the circle of firelight, Coham eased himself down onto an old stump.

Thea went to join him. He cocked his head in greeting as she approached, tapping his hand in time to the music.

"*Dum dum dum*," he hummed along. "Sure is a catchy one, isn't it?"

"It is." Thea watched the dance for a while longer as she formulated a thought that had been lingering in the back of her mind. "Coham, you've fought quite a few of these orcs, haven't you? I saw you hold your own against more than one."

"Hmm well," Coham reflected thoughtfully, "when you've been a blade for hire all your life, you learn a trick or two. I get them where I want them, on my terms, see? You lot are going down to Gedwyld to meet them on *their* terms. That's going to be a whole lot different."

Thea nodded. "I can see that will be different, and there are so many of them." She took a deep breath. "I was wondering if you would come and fight with us.

You have experience fighting orcs, which is something most of our army doesn't have, except for Thabani's Fauns."

Coham's face screwed up thoughtfully. "Well, now …"

"I'll understand if you don't want to. You said it would be much more dangerous."

Coham's eyes sparkled. "A little danger never turned old Coham away. 'Bout time we taught them orcs a lesson." He nodded decisively. "You can count me in."

"What about Beatrice and Edwin? I know you were staying here to protect them."

The old man waved a dismissive hand. "Eh, they will be just fine without me. I taught Beatrice everything I knows."

Thea smiled. "In that case, we would be very happy to have you."

Coham's eyes twinkled. "What you gonna pay me?"

Taken aback, Thea stared at the old man.

"Blade for hire, you know," he cackled. "I don't hire for free."

"Oh … well, I can speak with the King about that. He should be able to offer you something."

Coham winked cheerily. "Never you mind that. If I die it won't matter, and if we win I'm sure someone'll be glad enough to offer me a bit o'something." He stared out into the distance, his eyes glimmering in the firelight. "I'll be there. Someone's gotta be there to help you when your King dies."

Thea froze.

"What … what do you mean, when the King dies?"

Coham shrugged. "He's got the mark of death on him. When you've been a campaigner for a long time, you gets to know these sorts of things."

"That doesn't mean he's going to die!"

Coham gave her a slow stare. "Take it from me. He's got the mark on him, and he knows it. You can see it in his eyes. He knows he's going to Gedwyld to die."

Fear welled up in the pit of Thea's stomach. It wasn't true. The King couldn't die, her people needed him! There was no reason why—

A hand rested on her shoulder.

Thea looked up into the gentle eyes of the King. He looked down at Coham. "I will speak with Thea now."

Coham nodded. "Yessir, Mister King." Easing himself up, he hobbled off towards the house.

Thea found that she was shaking. "It isn't true." She stared at the King, her heart pounding. "You're not going to die, are you?"

Gently, the King took her hand. "I am going to die. I have to pay the price for what I let the Elves do."

"It wasn't your fault!"

"Was it not?" The King's face was gentle, but his eyes were sad. "I was given the care of our people. It was because of my failure that all of this happened. If I had not slowed, I would not have approved the retreat from the war or turned a blind eye as the spirits around me started turning dark. There is a price to be paid for that, and I am not afraid to pay it."

"But if you stay alive you won't let the Elves do it again!"

"*You* won't let the Elves do it again." The King watched her intently. "Some may stay awake and some may not, but I know that you will never fall asleep. I give the care of the Elves to you."

"But—" Thea stammered, "—but I'm not Royal House, and I don't want to live in Lyudmyla!"

"You don't have to live in Lyudmyla. There will still be a Queen or a King ruling our people. From what I have seen of Mykyta, he will never become slow, so you will not be called to fill the role of Chancellor. They will care for the daily lives of the Elves as they always have." Light shone in his eyes, but he regarded her with a solemn, earnest gaze. "I entrust to you the spirits of our people. They will always need a spark."

Overhead, the vast expanse of Micai filled the night sky.

"It isn't just the Elves," the King continued in a low voice. "You are the Spark for all the people, but I charge you to carry the Elves in a special place in your heart. We are the ones who live forever. We are the ones who are supposed to remember."

Thea stared up at the oldest of the Elves, standing beside her. It had been his task, and he was giving it to her. She nodded, her throat constricted to a whisper. "I will."

The King smiled. "Thank you."

For a moment, the nobility and authority in his face seemed to fade. He was just an Elf. His name was Ruslan, and he was her friend.

Tears filled her eyes. Elves weren't supposed to die.

"What about you?" she whispered.

Ruslan looked up at the moons crossing the night sky, the glimmer of memory in his eyes. "I sat at the feet of Enkeli as the Elves were taught at the beginning of time. I learned what it means to be an Elf and our role in the world. I should have known better, but I forgot. It was when I failed that my fate was sealed." He looked at Thea. "In the Palace or on the battlefield, I will die. But this way, more people will live."

In Ruslan's face there was no regret or fear, just a determination that Thea felt she was beginning to understand.

"Enkeli was my tutor as a child." Thea looked up into Ruslan's eyes. "I didn't know it at the time. The Elves failed, but Enkeli gave us another chance."

Ruslan smiled and held Thea's hand. "Mercy, even for the Elves."

Chapter Twenty-Four

That night, the army of the Elves and their allies camped around the little house. Thea, Sylica, Khariton, and the King were invited to sleep inside.

Thea woke as the first pale glimmers of daylight emerged from the eclipse of night. It was warm inside. The coals on the hearth still glowed brightly. Tiptoeing around Sylica and Daisy, Thea knelt by the fire to check in. Soft sounds from the King and Khariton indicated that they were also rising early to check in.

Enkeli was silent.

Careful not to disturb the others, Thea collected her bag and clipped Raybow to her baldric. As she opened the door, cold morning air rushed in to meet her.

She stepped outside and found herself surrounded by a crowd of small people, only half her height, staring up at her with scowling faces. They wore untreated hides and held spears in their hands. The smallest, most wizened of the group stepped forward. A gleaming falcion was in his hand.

Thea stared. "*Big Boss?*"

The goblin leader drew himself to his full height, which wasn't much.

Thea cast comprehension. "What are you doing here?"

Big Boss pointed his sword at Thea, a scowl on his pale, wrinkled face. "We have been following you. You have a big army. Big army and strong magic people to fight the orcs. We do not like orcs. They kill us, break our tunnels. We make a deal with you. We help you kill the orcs."

Thea stared in wonder. "You're here to fight the orcs?"

Big Boss stuck his chin in the air. "Goblins are not afraid to fight. We will fight and kill orcs."

All around Big Boss, the goblins murmured their approval.

Thea stared into his spirit. It seemed just as dark as it had been, but looking as the King had taught her, she saw more than that. Big Boss wanted to help his people. The orcs had been harming them too, and they couldn't win on their own.

"You said you want to help us," Thea reflected, "but what will you want in return?"

Big Boss looked at her with glittering black eyes. "All we want is to see the orcs dead. Then we will go home to our tunnels and you will not kill us."

Thea nodded. "I promise. If you do not harm us, we will not harm you. And you *will* see dead orcs."

The goblins nodded in approval.

All around them, the camp was stirring. Cries of alarm rang out as the sentries realized that a small—but armed—company had entered their camp without anyone seeing them.

Jeewon strode towards them, her grey scales and lowered crest showing her concern.

Thea raised a hand. "They are friends. They are here to join the war against the orcs."

The door behind Thea opened.

"Who's here to—" Sylica began, then she saw the

goblins. "It's the Littles!" She squealed in delight. "Hi, friends, I haven't seen you in so long!" She swept up the closest two goblins in an enthusiastic embrace.

Big Boss watched this development with an apprehensive frown.

Thea turned to him. "If you travel with us, you must understand that certain members of our party will call you Littles. I'm sorry, but there isn't anything I can do to change that."

Big Boss scowled, glancing around his company of goblins. There were about forty of them, from what Thea could see. He frowned up at her. "It is an insult we are willing to tolerate."

The King and Khariton emerged from the house, stopping short as they saw the crowd of goblins.

"Your Majesty, this is Big Boss," Thea explained, "the leader of the goblins."

"We will fight the orcs," Big Boss announced, puffing out his chest. "No one will say we are weak."

"The goblins are really Littles," Thea explained in a low voice. "These ones prefer to be called goblins, but they are still a part of the peoples of Raphtova. They want to fight with us."

The King smiled. "Welcome, Big Boss. I can see that your people are hardy warriors."

Big Boss beamed and held out his falcion. "See the Sword of the Big Boss. With this I will kill many orcs."

"Hi there!" Thabani trotted across the yard, a friendly smile gleaming in his eyes. "It looks like some more folks have decided to join the party!" He winked at Thea, then held out a hand to the leader of the goblins. "Thabani. Pleased to meet you."

Big Boss seemed taken aback, but he shook the

Faun's hand.

"These Littles are my friends," Sylica grinned. "We had so much fun when we got to visit them, and they really like candy too!" Her candy bag was already out, and she was thrusting handfuls at anyone who would receive them.

Across the yard, Ssen stopped and stared at the crowd of goblins, all gathered around Sylica while trying to maintain a posture of tough indifference. With a smile, Thea waved for him to join her.

"These are the goblins you met before?" Ssen whispered as he drew close.

Thea nodded.

"And now they are friends to you?"

"Not exactly friends. They are enemies of the orcs, though, which is why they came. To Sylica they are friends."

Ssen shook his head in wonder. "At least they will fight for us, not against us."

Thea gave him a thoughtful glance. "The orcs were hurting them too. I know you're not used to thinking of goblins as allies, but you'll have to get used to it now."

The Commander stepped next to the King and spoke in a low voice. "They infiltrated our camp without any of our guards seeing them. Does this concern you?"

The King smiled thoughtfully. "It tells me that now we have access to some excellent scouts. That is something we did not have before." His eyes twinkled.

As the companies of the Elves, Fauns, and Minathrils prepared to depart, Beatrice and Edwin came out to say goodbye. Coham also emerged, his large sword hanging over his back and a belt pouch at his side.

"I wish you well." Beatrice gave the King a curt nod.

"Don't let that old codger boss you around," she added with a sharp glance at her grandfather.

"Eh?" Coham shook his head in mock dismay. "Since when did I boss anyone around? I just minds my own business." He tottered off through the assembling army. "Who leads this parade, anyways?"

The King bowed to their hosts. "Thank you for your hospitality. It has been an honour to spend this time with you."

"And it was an honour to have you in our home," Edwin replied, his hand resting on Beatrice's shoulder. "If you return this way, we would be glad to welcome you again."

Soon, the army made its way back to the road, with the goblins following behind.

Jeewon approached Thea with a formal bow. "I had a private word with the King last night. The Oreum will act as your personal guard for the rest of our journey. The Spark must be protected."

Thea wanted to object, but she saw the determination gleaming on the Minathril's scales. She bowed. "Thank you, Jeewon. I would be honoured."

As Thea took her place on the road, Jeewon stepped beside her, and Ssen came to walk on her other side. Behind them, the Minathrils followed, marching in formation.

Before them, the King's Guard surrounded the King and Coham who were deep in conversation. Beyond, Thea caught a glimpse of Thabani and his Fauns.

Sylica had insisted on walking with the Littles, and Khariton joined her. From what Thea could see, it appeared that Sylica was acting as a translator, much to Khariton's amusement and the goblins' dismay.

With the exception of Sylica's perennial enthusiasm, an atmosphere of grim determination settled over the army of the Elves and their allies. The Enkeli casters among Thabani's Fauns continued to hasten their travel, and they all knew that they were drawing closer to their goal. Voices were silent, eyes were alert. They would not reach Gedwyld until the next day, but every step brought them closer.

Around staph, the road approached the sea. Thea could see it, stretching across the eastern horizon. The road turned south, following the coast.

Thea's heart leapt. They were so close! Of course, she couldn't actually see her home yet, and the orc forces still lay in front of them, but soon—very soon—she would be home again.

The army marched on.

There was no sign of any ships on the sea. Thea made a mental note to save some of her magic to message Roland, if she could.

Far above the sea, two dark specks wheeled and dove.

Birds?

They soared high again and seemed to notice the great host as it travelled south along the road. The specks swooped closer, becoming a pair of hawks. Passing overhead, they banked sharply and dove towards the front of the army.

Thea stared. Were those Dryads?

She ran. Leaving the Minathrils behind, she pushed her way through the ranks of Elves towards the place where the hawks had landed.

Passing the King's Guard, she saw Swift Wing and Fell Claw, now in Faun shape, hugging Thabani and their other Faun companions, tears streaming down their cheeks.

Seeing Thea, a smile lit Swift Wing's face and they shifted into human form, running to meet her.

"Thea!" Swift Wing embraced her warmly. "We are so glad to see you!"

The Minathrils pushed their way through the startled Elves, taking their position behind Thea once again.

Jeewon stepped beside her, orange and red flickering across her scales. "We are supposed to be guarding you," she muttered under her breath. "Warn us before you do that next time."

Swift Wing stared at the growing crowd surrounding them. "We hoped you might come soon, but we never dreamed you would come with a host like this! We might have a chance after all!"

"How is everyone?" Thea asked, her words tripping over each other. "Is everyone okay?"

Swift Wing clasped her shoulder. "As okay as we can be. We haven't lost anyone yet, but there's been some close calls. Fell Claw can tell you more about that."

Magic surged as the King stepped forward. "It seems that we witness another meeting of friends."

"Yes." Thea couldn't stop smiling. "This is Swift Wing and Fell Claw. They're a part of the Resistance that's sheltering at my house."

The King turned to them with interest. "You were able to get out? I heard the orcs have you surrounded."

The Dryads exchanged a glance.

"We can get by unnoticed a little more easily than most," Swift Wing grinned. "And the orcs haven't found the tunnel yet."

"The tunnel?" Thea frowned.

"There's a tunnel leading down from the cellars to a cave on the shore."

Memory flooded Thea's mind. "Roland said there had to be another way down to the shore! I'm so glad you found it!"

"It's been a lifesaver, that's for sure," Swift Wing agreed. "Us Dryads can swim underwater to go fishing and get news from Gedwyld without the orcs seeing us."

"What is the news from Gedwyld?"

"If I may," the King interjected, "I think the most important question is how far we are from the enemy forces. Should we be on guard?"

The Dryads considered this.

"The orcs don't often come this far," Fell Claw replied. "You could probably walk another measure or two without too much risk."

The King glanced up at the sky, judging the time.

"How far are we from their primary forces?"

"Around the house? I'd say six or seven measures yet."

The King nodded. "By the time we plan an assault and travel that far, night will be upon us, and we have been walking all day. We will find a secure place to camp and launch our attack tomorrow."

Swift Wing nodded. "We'll help you find a place. Come on!"

The Dryads shifted back into their hawk forms and took to the sky.

With Thabani and the Fauns leading the way, the Elves and their allies continued down the road. Thea allowed herself to be escorted by the Minathrils once again.

After about a measure, the Dryads led the way off the

road and through a dense thicket to a small valley on the far side. Landing, they spoke with the King.

The order to make camp for the night spread quietly from company to company. All around the valley, Elves, Fauns, Minathrils, and Littles—goblins, Thea reminded herself—busied themselves with preparations for the night. There were no fires this time. They did not want to risk unwanted attention.

Ilya joined Thea where she stood among the Minathril crew. "Miss Thea," he whispered. "What are they?"

Thea followed his wondering glance. "They're Dryads."

"What do they actually look like? They keep changing!"

"That's what Dryads are." Thea smiled. "They may have a shape they like best, but they belong to all of them, not just to one."

Swift Wing hurried towards them, shifting into Elf form as they did so.

Ilya stared with widening eyes.

"Coming, Thea?" Swift Wing called. "We want to share the news so we can get back to Elora."

"Coming!" Thea called.

In a small hollow under the shadow of the trees, the leaders of the armies gathered to hear the Dryads' report.

"We're holding on," Swift Wing explained, the comprehension magic cast by the King allowing them to communicate freely. "There's a lot of casters outside the walls, and it's all we can do to stop them from breaking the magic on the door. Every day or two Noxolo and the Fauns have to go out on some kind of raid to break up their work. Fell Claw and I do our best to run distraction. It's getting harder, though. The orcs expect us now. Musa would have died yesterday if Fell Claw hadn't been able to pull him out. As it is, we might have to amputate his arm. The orcs crushed it pretty bad."

"And the situation in Gedwyld?" the King asked.

"They're hanging in there. The machines on the walls have kept the orcs back for the most part, but there's just so many of them. If there's five hundred keeping us in, there's at least three thousand around Gedwyld. At least, that's my best guess from the sky."

The King nodded thoughtfully. "Tomorrow we will break the siege on the house. That will bring relief to your people and give us a secure position to regroup before assaulting the primary forces." He glanced at the Dryads. "Would you be able to make a map for us, with the location of the house and the enemy positions as you know them?"

Fell Claw nodded and crouched on the dirt. Using stones and bits of wood, they started building a map.

Thea glanced around the circle. The King of the Elves watched Fell Claw intently, with Ilya standing close at hand. The Commander stroked her chin as the map came together, piece by piece. Thabani shifted eagerly, the evening light glinting on the silver in his hair. Jeewon stood alert and impassive, though Thea caught a hint of eagerness in the quiver of her crest. Big Boss stood with his arms crossed, a habitual scowl creasing his face. Coham leaned against his massive sword, chewing a bit of twig. Swift Wing darted back and forth, collecting materials for the ever-growing map.

They were all there. In the circle around her, all of the races of Raphtova were represented—Humans,

Elves, Fauns, Dryads, Littles, and Minathrils. They had come together, and together they would fight against the Fallen One.

The King stared at the map. "Explain what we are seeing."

"This is the house and the wall," Fell Claw gestured. "These are the orcs. There's about ten warbands, but between their camps they've made a barricade of guards and watch fires, even on the cliff side. There's casters everywhere, but there are more of them here and here, just out of our range from the walls. The road goes here."

The King nodded and glanced at Thea. "What do we know about orcs as opponents?"

"They are very strong. Their skin is metal and they can see the light of the Deity in people. That will make it hard to surprise them."

"They aren't like trolls or other monsters," Swift Wing offered. "They're smart, as Ulga keeps telling us."

"It's true," Fell Claw agreed. "They know what you're doing, even before you do it."

Thabani nodded. "As we've found, it's best to have no plan at all. Surround them, run at them, keep them guessing because there's nothing to guess."

Frustration flared over Jeewon's scales. "You cannot simply run at them and expect to win. You need defences and strategy."

"Huh," Thabani snapped. "They'll see you marching in your nice straight lines and decimate you before you give your first command."

"Strategy is not marching in straight lines. It is giving careful thought to your strengths and your enemy's weaknesses."

"You can think all you want. The Fauns will be out there, actually doing something."

"And they will kill you, just like they have killed you again and again." Jeewon's scales pulsed red. "Will you never learn from your mistakes?"

Thabani's eyes flashed. "How many of your people have ever faced the enemy or given their lives? This is real war, not a training field."

"Now listen here!" Coham tottered into the center of the circle, giving a sharp glare to both Jeewon and Thabani. "How I see things is that these here Fauns are daring and adaptable, while these here Minathings are careful and calculated. Turns out, both of those are important in a fight, you hear me? If you only have one trick, the enemy's bound to get the better of you some time or other. So now both of you can just shut up and pay attention."

Turning, Coham returned to his place in the circle.

Everyone watched him in silence, waiting for what else he would say. Coham just leaned on his sword with a toothless grin.

Big Boss stepped forward. "The goblins will scout. We can get close to the orcs and lead you by the best way."

Thea nodded. It was true. Not only were the goblins very stealthy, but their spirits were dark. The orcs wouldn't be able to see them.

The King nodded to the Commander of the Army. "The Elves will lead the attack. With transportation magic, we can—"

"You can't," Fell Claw interrupted. "They have that place surrounded with so much counterspell magic you can't do anything within two measures of it."

Thabani leaned forward. "You said there were a lot of casters. Just how many do you mean?"

"Our best guess is thirty. Maybe forty."

Thabani's eyes widened.

A tingle crept down Thea's spine. She knew how much harm one caster could do, never mind so many working together.

Jeewon's scales gleamed orange. "If these casters are a danger, we will be sure to target them first."

"The danger is that *they* will be targeting *us*." Thabani frowned. "Fauns can't be charmed, but other people can."

"They've been focusing all their magic on the house," Fell Claw offered, "so they might not have much available. We should still be careful, though."

Thea nodded. "If we keep our own casters spread throughout the army, there will always be someone nearby to counterspell."

Murmurs of approval swept around the gathered leaders.

The Commander glanced at the Dryads. "What is the risk of reinforcements coming from the orcs surrounding Gedwyld? Do we need to be prepared to fight more than five hundred?"

"Not if we stop anyone from getting away," Thabani grinned.

"You mean circle around and cut them off from the south?" The King seemed to consider this.

"Two forces," Coham interjected, "one from the north and one from the south."

The King nodded slowly. "That could work."

"How will the southern force get into position without being seen?" the Commander asked.

As silence fell, Big Boss stepped forward. "The goblins will get you there."

"More than a thousand soldiers, slipping by unnoticed?" Jeewon's crest was back. "How would you propose to do that?"

"You could have been dead where you slept this morning." Big Boss smiled. "The goblins will make sure you are not seen."

Thea looked at the wizened Little, standing with his hand on the oversized falcion at his side. "Thank you, Big Boss."

The King nodded. "We will divide the Elvish army into a northern force and a southern force. The goblins will scout and lead us into position. If we sleep now we can leave after nightfall and arrive at first light in the morning. "

"Once you're in place, we can get Noxolo to start a raid," Swift Wing suggested. "Then the orcs' attention will be towards her. Fell Claw can give a signal, like we usually do."

"That could work," Fell Claw agreed. "If they haven't seen the army yet, they'll think it's just a normal raid."

"Won't that be dangerous for Noxolo?" Thea asked. "You said the orcs expect you now."

"We can break through to them." Thabani's eyes gleamed with determination.

"The Minathrils will break through to them," Jeewon replied at the same time. Her scales flashed orange.

"A good old one-two," Coham grinned. "Minathrils with the south force, Fauns with the north force, and on the signal they both head for the gate."

Thabani and Jeewon exchanged a glance.

A hint of tan crossed Jeewon's scales. "Oreum is the

guard of the Spark. We will follow her command."

Thea smiled. "I will go with you to help Noxolo."

Jeewon bowed. "Then that is what we will do."

"Where will you go, Coham?" the King asked, a gleam in his eye.

"Well, I reckon I'll go with the southern force. Bound to be a bit more pressure that way, if any of the orcs decide to bolt."

"I was thinking the same myself," the King replied. "Darya will command the northern force." He nodded to the Commander. "I will lead the south."

The Commander turned to Fell Claw. "What will be the signal?"

"It's an eagle scream, usually. Noxolo will know it's mine and start her raid."

The King nodded. "The Elves will begin their advance at the same time, from the north and south."

"What will be the signal for Oreum and the Fauns to join Noxolo?" Jeewon asked.

Thabani frowned. "Do we need a signal?"

Frustration flared over Jeewon's scales.

"If Noxolo's party is holding their own they might not need us at all," Thea interjected. "Is there a way she can signal us if she needs help?"

Swift Wing frowned. "I'm sure we can think of something. If she shouts very loud, or ..."

"I doubt that will carry far enough," Jeewon countered. "Not over the noise of battle."

Big Boss reached into the recesses of his hide jerkin and pulled out a bit of carved bone. "Tell her to blow on this. Everyone will hear it."

Swift Wing accepted the small whistle, then glanced around the circle. "If that's decided, I should get back to

Elora. Noxolo will need time to plan her raid."

As silence fell, the King looked at Thea.

Thea nodded and turned to the Dryads. "You may go. Say hello to Elora for me."

"I will stay here." Fell Claw's golden eyes glinted. "If I travel with the southern force, I will know when to give the signal."

Swift Wing shifted into hawk form once again, gripping the whistle in their talons. With a rush of wings, they soon became a rapidly diminishing speck in the sky.

As the leaders dispersed, Thea stood and stared out over the camp. The atmosphere was subdued and uneasy, compared to the revelry of the previous evening. In just a few measures, the Elves would join the war. This was what she'd wanted, ever since she entered the service of the Deity and learned that the war wasn't over. Now here they were, two thousand Elves, with people from all the other races, ready to fight for Raphtova.

Jeewon waited beside her, as Thea had often seen Ilya standing in attendance beside the King.

Feeling strangely self-conscious, Thea tried to smile. "Thank you, Jeewon."

Jeewon bowed, but did not leave her side, continuing to accompany her as she ate and prepared to sleep.

Ssen remained close at hand too, but when Thea tried to talk with him, he only nodded politely and spoke as little as possible.

The Minathrils were on alert. Their job was to protect her, and they were taking it very seriously.

Across the camp, Thea caught a glimpse of Sylica laughing. Khariton was there, and some of the Fauns.

Not far away, Thabani and Fell Claw were deep in conversation. From a bundle of blankets that seemed all elbows and knees, she could hear Coham's snore.

As Thea prepared her own place to sleep, the Minathrils encamped around her, in much the same way that the King's Guard stationed themselves around the King. Was this his doing?

She stared across the camp to the place where the King sat alone, staring at the windswept sky. He believed that he would die, but he wanted her to live.

Close at hand, Thea noticed a friend.

"Good night, Sungy," she called.

A brief flash of pleasure crossed Sungy's scales, but they quickly returned to their orange sheen and she bowed formally. "Good night."

Thea wrapped herself in her blanket and lay down. Despite the Minathrils' surrounding presence, she felt strangely alone.

In the distance, she could just hear the roar of the sea. She could take a few moments before going to sleep.

Roland?

Thea? She could feel his familiar smile. *It's good to hear your voice!*

It's good to hear yours too. How are you doing?

Really well. It's nice to be sailing again. Where are you now?

We're almost there. Tomorrow we'll try to break through to my house.

Already? That's great. We aren't there yet, but Svetka hopes we'll make it the day after tomorrow.

That's good. That's when we'll need you.

Thea knew she shouldn't linger.

Good night, Roland. See you soon.

Good night, Thea.

As the magic faded, a thought occurred to her. *Oh, Ssen says hi.*

She could feel Roland's surprise. *What—*

Roland's mind was gone, but Thea smiled. With Enkeli's magic, the distance didn't seem as far.

Chapter Twenty-Five

Thea woke to the sound of Minathrils stirring around her. Overhead, the blue-green glow of Micai filled the sky.

Someone approached the place where she was lying.

"Thea, it is time to go." Ssen's scales gleamed orange in the shadowy light.

"Thanks, Ssen."

He bowed and turned away.

Thea shivered in the cold night air as she rolled up her blanket and prepared to go. Around her, the camp was alive with the hum of anticipation.

With Jeewon at her side, Thea returned to the road. A stiff wind blew off the sea, sending shreds of cloud tearing across the night sky. Behind her, the Minathrils began to assemble, their spears and shields gleaming in their hands.

Company by company, the Elves returned to the road, arranging themselves in order of travel.

The southern force went first, with the King's Guard leading the way. The King himself walked with Coham on one side and Fell Claw on the other.

Thea followed next, accompanied by Jeewon and Ssen. The Minathrils marched in formation behind them, determination glinting on every scale.

The northern force and the Fauns made the rear guard, ready to turn aside as they drew closer to the enemy. Khariton was among those assigned to the northern force, and Sylica chose to walk with him.

Big Boss and the goblins were already gone, slipping off through the shadows ahead of the forces of the King.

There would be no transportation magic today. The risk of detection was too great, and the magic would be needed for the assault.

As the measures passed, the landscape around Thea began to look very familiar—the coastline, the woods, the hills in the distance—all cloaked in the shadow of night.

The Elves leading the way stopped as two goblins emerged from the undergrowth. After a hushed conversation, the Elves advanced again, creeping off the road to travel through the woods to the west. Thea and the Minathrils followed.

Glancing over her shoulder as she stepped off the road, Thea saw two more goblins leading the northern force away to the east.

Her heart pounded. They must be getting close.

Walking as silently as she could, Thea followed the Elves that went before her. There was no sign of the orcs, but beyond the rustling of the trees was a distant murmur that may have been voices.

Thea walked with Raybow in her hand. At her side, Jeewon was alert, scanning the forest with her piercing gaze.

A goblin stepped out from a shadow nearby, holding up a hand in a gesture to stay.

Jeewon's grip tightened on her spear.

Overhead, the first rays of Allumen's light flickered through the trees. Time to check in.

Thea knelt on the frozen mud and bowed her head.

She could feel Jeewon's presence beside her, keeping watch. In the distance, a little bird trilled its greeting to the day.

Enkeli didn't speak, but Thea felt the reassuring tingle of magic as it rushed through her body. It was time. Silently, she rose to her feet.

The Minathrils stood close at hand. Waiting. Thea's heart pounded. She noticed now that the goblin's knife was stained green. The forest seemed hazy with a darkness Allumen's light did not dispel.

An eagle cry tore through the silence.

Thea glanced at Jeewon.

The Minathril Captain nodded.

Thea drew an arrow from her quiver and stepped forward through the trees. The Minathrils fell into position around her.

In the distance, a chorus of shouts and cries tore through the silence. Thea quickened her pace.

Something moved in the trees ahead.

Orcs. They turned to face Thea and the Minathrils with a growl, their weapons gleaming.

Thea shot, striking an orc in the chest.

With a shout, the Minathrils lifted their spears and charged. Thea ran in their midst, putting another arrow to the string.

The Minathrils met the orcs with the clash of metal on metal. At Jeewon's command, the Oreum raised their shields and held their ground.

Thea shot again.

Through the trees she caught a glimpse of Elves, their swords flashing in the light. There was a swell of magic. Dark magic.

Thea threw her own magic into a counterspell. The

magic collided and disappeared. Through the melee, her gaze met the caster's. The orc's lips curled in a sneer of hate.

Thea pulled another arrow from her quiver.

The orc shouted.

From the corner of her eye, she caught a flash of movement as an orc with a crossbow turned towards her and pulled the trigger.

Transportation. Thea threw her magic at the approaching bolt as she hurtled herself to the ground.

Her magic disappeared in a counterspell.

The bolt hissed, passing just above her head. Beside her, a Minathril screamed.

Heart pounding, Thea crouched behind the shield wall. Nocking her arrow, she braced herself, ready to spring.

Another surge of magic. Thea leapt and shot. The arrow flashed bright as it struck the caster. The dark magic faded away.

Thea threw herself to the ground again. A crossbow bolt whizzed overhead.

With a grim smile, Thea put another arrow to the string.

Around her, the Minathrils fought on. Orcs died, but even more appeared to take their place.

A whistle's piercing shriek tore through the trees.

Jeewon shouted and the Minathrils drew together, locking their shields in an arrow formation. Ssen stood at its point, his spear in his hand. At a command from Jeewon, they ran.

Thea ran too, hidden within the impenetrable wall of shields.

On either side of them, the orcs were thrust aside

beneath the force of the Minathril advance. Metal clashed as orcs threw themselves at the shield wall, only to be knocked aside or pierced with a spear as the Minathrils continued their charge.

A whistle blast pierced the air again, much closer than it was before.

Adjusting the direction of their advance, the Minathrils ran on. Thea's legs ached, her heart pounded with the effort of keeping pace.

The cries and tumult of combat were all around them.

Jeewon shouted another command and the shield wall burst apart. Fauns and orcs stared at the sudden arrival of the lizard-like warriors in their midst. Before they could react, the Minathril onslaught crashed over them.

"Noxolo!" Thea ran through the melee.

Noxolo dodged a spear strike, crouching low over a bloodied form lying prone on the ground.

With a roar, an orc swung its mace.

Ssen leapt in front of it. With one strike, the mace tumbled to the ground. With a second strike, the orc stumbled back.

Magic surged. Whirling to face its source, Thea cast her counterspell. It wasn't strong enough.

Out of the ground all around them, trails of ivy burst up, winding around their legs, entangling them.

Struggling against the vines, Thea drew Raybow and shot.

With a surge of dark magic, the arrow swerved off course. Thea cast her own spell, directing the arrow straight into the caster's heart.

The tangling vines crumbled into dust.

All around Thea, the Minathrils continued to fight, driving the enemy back in an ever-increasing circle.

Jeewon's voice rang out above the chaos and the wall of shields was raised, an impenetrable circle surrounding Noxolo and her Fauns.

"Whoa." Noxolo stared, staggering slightly. Her shoulder was bloodied and smeared with dirt.

Thea hurried to join her.

In the distance, a chorus of shouts and cheers erupted from the trees as Thabani and his Fauns appeared.

Overhead, an eagle cry pierced the sky and Kaji swooped past them, diving straight towards Thabani.

"Kaji!" Thabani leaped in the air and the giant eagle caught him in her talons. Soaring up above the trees, Kaji rolled, releasing Thabani from her grasp. The Faun soared through the air, landing on the giant eagle's back with a shout of delight.

The Fauns cheered.

A second eagle cry rang through the air as a pure white eagle dove towards the fray.

Someone was on Ember's back. As the Dryad struck a fleeing orc with their talons, the figure leapt, his two-headed axe swinging in a giant arc of light.

"Ulfgar!" Thea yelled.

Ulfgar slammed axe first into an orc, disappearing beyond Thea's sight as the orc crumpled to the ground.

In the distance, an orc roared. Thea turned. Not far away, a rutted dirt lane ran towards a far stone wall. Behind it, the ancient stone house stood dark against the horizon.

The gate was open, and in front of it stood Ulga, wearing a stained kitchen apron. Her hands were on her hips as she glared out at the chaos.

Thea smiled. Pushing past the shield wall, Thea ran to greet her.

A portion of the Minathrils fell in step beside her, escorting her to the gate where Ulga waited.

The orc's eyes gleamed as Thea approached. Bowing to one knee, she lowered her head. "Welcome home."

Thea embraced her. "Thank you, Ulga. It's good to be home again."

Ulga's muscles rippled as she returned to her feet. She stared out towards the distant sounds of combat.

The orcs were scattering. Minathrils and Fauns surged after them, some moving with discipline and order, others rushing impetuously, their weapons swinging over their heads. Ulfgar's roar rang over the chaos.

"You did not come too soon." Ulga gave Thea a sidelong glance.

"I know." Thea looked up at the orc towering over her. "I came as soon as I could."

A flicker of grey ran through the scales of the Minathrils standing close at hand. Thea cast comprehension.

"You can return to the fight if you want. I am in a secure placc now."

The Minathrils stood at attention and did not move.

"Our orders are to stay with you," a broad-shouldered Minathril replied. "We must ensure your safety."

An eagle dove through the distant sky. Thabani's laugh rang out as his lithe figure leapt off Kaji and plummeted into the trees below.

No orcs were visible in the clearing around the walls,

but from the trees beyond, the clash of metal and the cries of battle still rang out.

A shield wall of Minathrils approached the gate, escorting the injured Fauns in their midst.

Stepping out from among them, Jeewon approached Thea and bowed.

"This is Ulga." Thea gestured to the orc at her side. "She is one of my friends. Ulga, this is Oreum Jeewon and her crew. They have been my guard for this fight."

Ulga and Jeewon stood eye to eye, reading each other with piercing stares. Ulga's gleaming metal skin contrasted sharply with the thoughtful grey of Jeewon's scales.

Jeewon bowed. "I am honoured to meet any friend of the Spark."

Ulga eyed the Minathril Captain with grudging respect. "You fought well. I have heard of the prowess of the Minathrils. It was not exaggerated."

Ember soared overhead. As the Dryad banked and swooped towards the ground, Ulfgar leapt off their back, landing with a clatter. His axe and armour were stained with green blood.

Swinging the shaft of his axe over his shoulder, he strode to join Thea, a grin splitting his face. "You don't know how long I've waited to do that."

Thea embraced him, bloodstains and all.

Ember landed beside them, shifting into the form of a pure-white human. "Hello, Thea. We're glad to have you back."

Smiling, Thea embraced Ember. Around them, the Fauns gathered, talking, hugging, and laughing.

"I think that's it, then," Ulfgar grinned. "Those orcs turned tail and ran."

"They have retreated to Gedwyld," Ulga replied. "They will regroup and come back."

"They're trying to retreat, anyway," Thea grinned. "The Elves are there to stop them."

"They retreated to Gedwyld," Ulga repeated. A grim light gleamed in her eyes.

Rounding the wall from the north, a sparkling green figure bounded towards them.

"Hi, Thea! Hi, Ember!" Sylica beamed. "Hi, Ulfgar! Did you miss me? We fought lots and lots of orcs. Some of them didn't like me very much, but I made them go away with my magic. I got to hit some with my mace too. The orcs didn't like that much either. Were the orcs just grumpy today do you think?"

Daisy pranced at Sylica's heels, leaping and yapping in excitement. Khariton strode after her, a slightly harried look in his gleaming eyes.

With a rush of wings, Kaji landed close by and Thabani leaped to the ground. Ember embraced him with a beaming smile.

As the Fauns gathered around Thabani, a company of Elves approached, led by the Commander. "There are no more orcs to the north," she reported to Thea. "Is there any word from the southern force?"

"Not yet." Thea looked around the growing crowd of Fauns, Dryads, Minathrils, and Elves. At the edge of sight, she caught glimpses of goblins lurking in the shadows beneath the trees.

"Listen to me!" Thea called. "Anyone who still has strength to fight should go south and join the King."

Thabani nodded. "Hear that, Kaji?" He ran his hand along the giant eagle's back. "Let's fly."

The Commander turned to the Elves. "We march to

the aid of the King. All who are injured, remain at the house."

"I can help!" Sylica grinned. Bounding off towards the trees, she waved for Khariton to follow. "Come on, Grumpy Daddy!"

Ulfgar patted Ember's back. "Well?"

Ember smiled, and with a rush of feathers, shot into the sky. Grabbing Ulfgar by the back of his chain mail, they soared over the trees. An eagle cry pierced the sky, followed by Ulfgar's triumphant yell.

The Minathrils continued to stand in formation.

Jeewon bowed. "With your permission, Thea, we will remain with you."

Thea bowed in return. "You have my permission. Thank you, Oreum."

Pride rippled across the Minathrils' scales.

"Do you have a medical room here?" Tayhyang approached. "Some of the Fauns are in desperate need of care. I am afraid that my knowledge of battlefield medicine is still very limited."

Thea shook her head. "I'm afraid we don't have a medical room, but we'll find a room you can use." Turning, she stepped through the gate.

Beyond, the house waited. The ivy clinging to its bare stone walls rustled gently in the wind. The windows glowed with light.

As Thea approached, the door opened and Elora stepped out. She wore her scouting black, wrapped tight with leather cords. Her bow was in her hand.

"Elora!" Thea called, hurrying to meet her.

Elora smiled. "Welcome home."

Crouching down, Thea embraced her friend. Elora seemed thinner than she had been. Her face bore the marks of worry and strain.

"How are Adi and Kais?"

"They are well." A businesslike gleam returned to Elora's eyes. "Come inside. Everyone wants to see you."

Thea stepped through the door. In the great room, the human family stood clustered around the windows, along with Alya and the Littles. Several Fauns stood near the door with weapons in their hands. Many of them bore evidence of recent injuries.

Dunstan stepped forward to greet her. "Is the battle over?"

"Almost. The army is doing what they can to stop the orcs from getting away."

"We really won?" Jason asked, a dirk clutched in his trembling hands.

"Yes, we won." Thea rested a reassuring hand on his shoulder. "Next, we will save Gedwyld."

The sound of people in the courtyard drifted through the open door. Thea turned to Elora. "We need to set up a medical room. Where would be best?"

A look of concern crossed Elora's face. "How many have been hurt?"

"Some of the Fauns. Beyond that I'm not sure."

"We could spare one or two of the smaller bedrooms, but the Faunlets are in the larger room and we don't want to let them out yet." Elora made a face. "They're convinced they should be out there fighting too."

Jeewon stepped through the door. "Tayhyang requests permission to bring the injured inside."

"Yes, of course." Thea hurried to the door.

Outside, three Fauns were being carried on rough stretchers. Others limped or wore bandages already soaking through with blood.

Thea gestured the healer inside. "There is some space upstairs, but we might have to use this room too."

Tayhyang nodded, his keen eyes taking in the room with its assortment of improvised furniture. Two Minathrils carrying a stretcher stepped through the door.

"I'll show you the bedrooms upstairs," Elora offered, hurrying to lead the way.

Nearly every Faun in Noxolo's party had been injured in some way. Those in more serious condition were carried upstairs and attended to by Tayhyang himself. The rest stayed downstairs in the great room and Melinda was called to help care for them. Three Fauns trotted upstairs to replace her watch on the Faunlets' door.

When all the injured had been brought inside and at least been given a place to sit, Thea leaned against the fireplace, allowing herself a moment to breathe.

Ulga joined her.

"They would not let me join the raid, for fear someone would kill the wrong orc." A grim light glimmered in her eyes as she stared out across the injured. Nearby, Melinda washed and bandaged a lacerated arm.

"They wanted to protect you." Thea looked up at the orc's sober face. "They care about you, don't they?"

Ulga frowned. "I am not used to this ... this caring. I wanted to protect them."

"I know. Don't worry, there will be more chances to fight."

Ulga sighed. "That is not what worries me."

Ssen joined them, bowing to Thea. "The southern force is returning," he reported. "I thought you would want to know."

"Thank you, Ssen."

Returning to the courtyard, Thea found Thabani's Fauns gathering by the gate. Beyond, Elves gathered in an ever-increasing host. The Commander's voice rang out above the noise, calling for divisions and companies to regroup. Ember soared overhead.

Crossing the courtyard, Thea stepped through the gate.

The King was there, speaking with Thabani. Sylica and Khariton emerged from the trees, supporting a limping Elf between them.

Coham elbowed his way through the crowds, ambling up to Thea with a nod of greeting. "Well I haven't had a scuffle like that in a long time. Made me think of my younger days, fighting in the army."

"You used to fight in an army?" Thea looked down at the wizened old man.

"Nope, never," Coham cackled, "but it seemed like the right sort of thing to say, didn't it?" He squinted up at the gate arched above him. "So this is your old place, eh? I think I'll take a peep." With a grin, he swung his sword over his shoulder and tottered through the gate.

Across the field, Thea caught a glimpse of Fell Claw talking with Ulfgar. Giving them a wave, Thea went to join the King.

"I am glad to see you alive and well." The King smiled, but there was a sober look in his eyes. "I was just saying to Thabani that the Elves will camp outside the walls, but if there is room in the courtyard the other companies should camp where they are protected."

Thea nodded, watching the Elves still emerging from the trees. Many were limping or bloodied. "Send the injured into the house. We'll care for them there."

Big Boss and his goblins watched from the edge of the trees.

Thea approached them with a smile. "Thank you for your help today. I couldn't ask for better scouts."

Big Boss puffed up his chest. "Goblins are the best scouts. We brought you close and the orcs never heard us."

"Well done," Thea smiled. "Now will you come? Set up your camp inside the walls, and there are healers for anyone who was hurt."

"Goblins can do healing too. Goblins will care for goblins."

"At least come within the walls," Thea urged them.

Hesitantly, the goblins followed her through the companies of Elves and into the courtyard. They stared up at the large stone house with apprehension.

"You do not need to come inside," Thea assured them, "but you are always welcome."

Fauns lounged against the stable wall, cleaning and sharpening their weapons. Across the courtyard, the Minathrils were setting up their camp.

Inside, the great room was filled to overflowing. Elora and Kais bustled around, finding crates and barrels that could be used as chairs. Melinda moved from patient to patient with Sylica trailing after her, doing her best to help. Khariton and Ulfgar moved furniture and heaps of bedding to make comfortable places for the injured to lie down and rest.

Swift Wing strode through the door in human form. "We have more stretchers coming in. You want them in here?"

Thea glanced around the crowded room. "I guess so."

"We can use the outbuildings if we need to," Alya suggested, stopping by on her way from the kitchen with a bowl of hot water. "Or we can make beds that hang from the ceiling."

The door opened again and four goblins stepped inside. Big Boss was there, with two goblins Thea recognized as his personal guards. Between them they supported a goblin whose leg was bent at an unnatural angle.

Eyeing the room cautiously, Big Boss approached Thea. "There is one of my people ... if your healers can help ..."

"Of course," Thea assured him. "Alya, could you help us find another bed?"

Alya grinned at Big Boss. "You're new, aren't you? I'm Alya."

Blinking, Big Boss stared at Alya. "You ... you are ..."

"Gili!" Alya called over her shoulder. The younger Little poked her head out from the kitchen. "Go make space in the workshop. We have friends to join us there."

Gili smiled and waved a greeting before scurrying off.

"You ... live here?" Big Boss frowned.

"We live in Gedwyld. Do you come from around here?"

Their dialects were different, but they seemed to be able to understand each other. Thea smiled and turned away.

By the fire, Ulfgar and Khariton held a rather disjointed conversation, relying on Sylica to play translator. Thabani walked among the injured Fauns, joking and laughing. Jeewon stood at attention near the door.

One of the Minathril Sergeants approached Thea. "Some of the Elves are going out to gather the fallen and count the dead. Do we have your permission for a portion of the Oreum to join them?"

"Yes, of course."

The Minathril bowed and turned away.

"Excuse me," Noxolo trotted across the room to join Thea. "The Minathrils friends of yours, right? Do you know how they fight like that?"

Thea smiled. "Why don't you ask them?"

Noxolo frowned. "I tried, but I couldn't understand their language."

Thea gestured for her to follow. "There's someone I think you would like to meet."

Stepping outside, she found Ssen. "This is Noxolo," Thea explained in Common. "She is interested in the Minathril way of fighting."

"Is she?" Ssen's scales shone with pleasure. "I would be happy to teach her."

"You would?" A grin lit Noxolo's face. "I'd love that!"

Leaving them in the courtyard, Thea returned to the house. Jeewon gave a bow of greeting as she entered.

Weaving through the crowded room, Thea found a place to stand by the fire. Slowly, the effects of her comprehension magic faded.

Everywhere Thea looked, Elves and Fauns sat or reclined with bandaged shoulders and legs. The Faunlets had been grudgingly released from their bedroom and scampered eagerly about, managing to always be underfoot, but never enough to get into trouble. All of Alya's friends had emerged from the workshop downstairs and were chatting eagerly with Big Boss, while the cornered goblins shifted uneasily, staring around with wide eyes. Khariton and Thabani helped an Elf with a bandaged leg hobble to a vacant chair, while Sylica enthusiastically fluffed the cushion. In the kitchen, Ulga was chopping fish. Brandy and Ulfgar lifted a cask of wine onto the counter.

The house had been empty, but it was not empty anymore.

As Thea watched and took it all in, Ulfgar came and stood beside her. His well-worn chain mail was dirty and stained with blood, but he leaned against the stonework with a thoughtful smile.

"This is what you wanted, isn't it?"

A deep gladness welled up in Thea's spirit. "Yes. I wanted this room to be filled with all kinds of people, and here they are."

"I thought you were crazy," Ulfgar shook his head, a wry grin creeping across his face. "I guess crazy is catching."

There was peace in his eyes as he watched the bustling scene. "Got to give you credit, your home seems like a good place to be."

Thea's gaze met his. "It's your home too. Whenever you come back, there will be a place for you."

Ulfgar smiled. "Thank you."

At the table nearby, Khariton and Sylica were folding bandages.

"So it's like changing what is real?" Khariton asked, smoothing out a large square of cloth and folding it carefully.

Sylica nodded. "I wanted the orcs gone, so they were gone."

"Just like the time you wanted the ship to be in the middle of the dangerous rocks and it was?"

"Yeah …" Sylica grinned sheepishly.

Khariton set the bandage in the pile and reached for a new one. "Five orcs disappeared, then you said your magic juice was gone."

"Well I *am* pretty small so my magic juice runs out kinda quick."

Khariton gave her a skeptical glance. "I would think that making something completely disappear would take a lot of magic juice."

"I guess so." Sylica frowned, then her countenance brightened. "I can make things appear too!"

"You mentioned that." Khariton's eyes twinkled. "A whole table full of pies, according to one of your stories."

Sylica grinned. "That was fun! Another time I made fireworks too, did I tell you that story?"

Khariton set another bandage on the pile. "Twice, I believe."

"Only twice?" Sylica protested, launching immediately into the tale.

As Khariton worked, he glanced across the table at Sylica, a smile playing at the corners of his mouth.

"You know," he said when Sylica's tale wound itself to a close, "someone once told me that if you want a rockslide, it is easier to move one rock high on the cliff, instead of pushing all of the rocks yourself." He picked up a pile of bandages and set them in Sylica's waiting hands. "If you are careful, I think you could do much more with your magic than you think you can."

Tayhyang approached Thea where she was standing by the fire. Thea cast comprehension.

"I am afraid there is one I could not save." Tayhyang bowed, blue glimmering across his scales. "Where would you like us to carry her?"

It was one of the Fauns from Noxolo's party that had been badly injured. Placing her gently on a stretcher, two Minathrils carried her downstairs and out the door. Thea followed.

Passing between the Minathril camp and the Faun camp, they stepped through the gate. A sombre atmosphere hung over the wide clearing in front of the wall where the bodies of the dead were being laid. Most of them were Elves.

Minathrils and Elves emerged from the trees, carrying more bodies. Laying them down, they returned to the forest again.

There were so many. Thea stared across the rows laid out before her. She hadn't seen many die in her part of the battle, but she had been with the Minathrils. Their shield wall had protected them from the worst of the danger. The rest of the army hadn't had that protection.

The King and the Commander walked through the rows of the dead, speaking to each other in low voices.

Close by the gate, Ilya stared at the dead Elves with a stricken face. Softly, Thea walked over to join him.

"It's hard, isn't it?" She looked into his tear-filled eyes.

"They're ... they're dead," Ilya stammered. "I—I hadn't ..."

"You hadn't seen someone who was dead before." Thea's gaze fell. "I know. I hadn't either, till I left home."

Ilya's voice was a hoarse whisper. "They're really gone?"

Thea nodded. There were so many. So many Elves who would never march home again. For all the death that she had witnessed, she had never seen a dead Elf.

"Elves aren't supposed to die," Thea whispered. "It hurts, doesn't it?"

Ilya nodded, his tears glimmering on his face. "I got to know some of them." He stared at the bodies as if he couldn't tear his eyes away.

"I know." Thea rested a hand on his shoulder. "It doesn't get easier, but it's a pain the rest of Raphtova has had to learn well. It's our turn to learn it too."

The King joined them, a grim light in his eyes. "Most of those who fell were in the southern force. When the orcs decided to retreat, they let nothing stand in their way."

Thea sighed. "Ulga seemed to think that would happen. I wish it hadn't cost so many lives."

The King stared out across the field of bodies. "They all knew the price to be paid, and they were ready to pay it." Tears gleamed in his eyes. "I am proud of them. They gave all that they had to give."

The Commander crossed the field to join them. "Have you asked her?"

"Not yet." The King turned to Thea. "What should we do with the bodies? We cannot leave them here, but we also do not have an excess of time."

Thea's heart sank as she stared at the growing number of dead. "The Fauns usually burn those of their people who die."

The King frowned. "I do not think we could burn so many. Not with the time and resources we have."

Thea stared around them, her eyes settling on the cliffside to the north. High above the rippling sea, the bluffs stretched into the distance, their long grasses waving in the fitful breeze.

"We will bury them," Thea replied, "and they will not be forgotten."

As more Elves returned, the King set them to the task of digging graves.

Thabani came out to identify the Fauns who had died—two from Noxolo's party and three from his own. "We will bury them with the Elves," he said with a sad smile. "There is no time for a pyre today." Picking a feathery stalk of grass, he placed it gently in a dead Faun's hand. "The Elves and Fauns paid the cost for this victory. They can be buried together."

Chapter Twenty-Six

Eclipse was approaching by the time the last of the dead were buried and the Elves returned to their camp. Inside, Swift Wing and Fell Claw found a place to rest by the fire, their skin streaked with dirt from digging graves.

Thabani joined them, his smile more sombre than usual. Ember walked by his side.

It wasn't as crowded in the great room as it had been. Those with minor injuries had returned to the camps outside, and the more seriously injured were moved upstairs.

Noxolo trotted back and forth, gathering makeshift seats from around the room while Elora arranged them into a large circle around the fire.

With a sigh, Coham eased himself into a chair and stretched out his crooked legs. "Well, that's more like it." His gaze turned to Ulfgar who approached with a mug in each hand. "A drink? Don't mind if I do."

The Commander approached Thea. "Is everyone here? If so, I will inform the King."

Thea glanced around the room. Big Boss stood alone with his arms crossed, his face knotted in a frown. Jeewon was there, with Ssen at her side. Ulfgar emerged from the cellars again, bringing more mugs for those gathered around the fire. Ulga stood by the door to the kitchen, sharpening her axe.

Thea nodded. "I think so."

"Come on, Grumpy Daddy!" Sylica bounded across the room with Khariton in tow. "Let's help Ulfgar!"

The King approached Thea. "Do you have any magic left? It will aid our planning if everyone can speak freely with each other."

Thea shook her head. "I don't have much. Enough for one person, maybe."

"Then use your magic for yourself. I will go speak with Khariton."

Thea glanced around the room. She hadn't seen Msizi yet.

"Were we able to find enough magic for everyone?" Thea asked Khariton once they were all gathered around the fire.

"Enough for the King. That was all."

"What about you?"

Khariton shrugged. "If there is something I need to know, I'm sure Sylica will tell me."

The gathered leaders fell silent as the King rose from his seat. "Thank you, everyone, for all that you did to bring about our victory today. The siege on the house has been lifted, and our first objective achieved. This did not come without cost. Four hundred Elves died today, along with five of the Fauns." He nodded to Thabani. "The sobering truth is that we can only account for about three hundred orcs. The rest escaped and joined the larger force surrounding Gedwyld."

Murmurs of concern rose among the assembled leaders.

Coham scratched his chin. "Three hundred of them, but four hundred of us, eh?"

The King's face was grim. "Given the number of orcs

surrounding Gedwyld, those odds are not in our favour. We will have to fight smarter next time." His gaze took in all those gathered around the hearth. "How should we go about doing that?"

Jeewon leaned over to Ssen, speaking into his ear.

Ssen turned to the others and spoke in Common, "We must follow up on our victory soon, before the orcs have time to regroup."

"And we'll do something unexpected," Thabani grinned. "If they can't anticipate it, they can't prepare for it."

"Jeewon says we should act soon, and Thabani suggests doing something unexpected," the King repeated, the comprehension magic on his words allowing everyone to understand him. "But what would the orcs not expect?"

"They're pretty quick on the uptake." Coham gave Ulga a shrewd look. "Any advice?"

Ulga set down her axe. "War is their life. Whatever you do, you will not surprise them. They have studied combat since they could speak and trained since they could walk. They have learned to expect anything."

Khariton gave Sylica a thoughtful glance. "There may be a way of doing something quite unexpected." He spoke in a low voice, words only the Elves in the room understood.

"I heard that a second army is coming on boats," Elora leaned forward in her chair. "When will they get here?"

"I spoke to Roland last night." Thea felt the weight of all the eyes in the room turn onto her. "He said they should be here tomorrow."

The King nodded. "That gives us a place to start. If

we launch an attack first, the second army will arrive and the orcs will find themselves with the fight before and behind them."

Jeewon and Ssen exchanged a few words, then Ssen turned to the others. "It is dangerous to rely on their arrival when we have not seen any sail yet."

"I thought you said we should act as soon as possible," Thabani muttered under his breath.

"So we wait for those ships, then pop down and pay the orcs a visit?" Coham grinned.

"That is one option," the King replied, "but what is the situation in Gedwyld? Will a delay put them in danger?"

"Zaki doesn't think they'll hold out much longer." Elora's face was grim. "The city has done all it can."

The King nodded. "So we must press on and trust that the fleet will join us in time."

Ulfgar gestured with his tankard. "How many soldiers are in this second army of yours?"

"We do not know exact numbers, since it sailed after we were gone, but the fleet can carry two thousand, and we have confidence there will be close to that number."

Ulfgar's eyes widened. "Then we'd outnumber the orcs!"

"Superior numbers mean nothing," Ulga replied. "Not when you are fighting orcs."

Ulfgar shrugged. "Well, it can't hurt."

Big Boss frowned. "Why hurry for a city?"

Elora shot a glare at the goblin leader, replying in her own dialect of The Talk. "If we wait, the orcs might take it."

Big Boss crossed his arms. "Goblins are here to kill orcs, not save a city. Why should we care if it dies?"

"Because there are thousands of people in that city! There are old ones and children who cannot fight!"

"Weak ones," Big Boss scowled. "Goblins will not go into danger because weak ones are afraid."

"They are trapped by thousands of orcs who are there to kill them, and you call them weak for being afraid?"

"No, you are weak," Big Boss sneered. "All you Littles, living in comfortable cities, away from real danger."

Elora's eyes flashed. "Now listen, you—"

Thea laid a warning hand on her shoulder. "Big Boss doesn't understand." She spoke in a low voice. "He doesn't understand mercy, or know all that you have been through."

The King motioned for silence. "Big Boss raises an important question: Why rush to save the city when we could wait for a better advantage? I want to draw your attention to the strategic importance of Gedwyld as a city. Whoever controls Gedwyld controls the lands east of the mountains. If it were taken and occupied by enemy forces, I do not know if we could ever succeed in taking it back again. And we must consider," he spoke to all, but his eyes were on Big Boss, "that if Gedwyld falls, three thousand victorious orcs will turn their undivided attention on us. Gedwyld must not fall, and we must do all we can to ensure that it does not."

The King paused, and let the impact of his words settle over those gathered around him. "If we wait, the orcs will not be waiting. I am certain that they will do all they can to stamp us out or to take Gedwyld before we can come to their aid."

"Both." Ulga's glowering eyes flickered red in the firelight.

Coham scratched his chin. "Some of you seem to be on pretty good terms with the powers that be. Why aren't they helping us out?"

The King's eyes were grim. "Because right now all we are fighting are a few thousand orcs. If Micai or Enkeli entered the battle by our side, do you think the Fallen One would leave that unchallenged? He also has powerful Tilaryn beneath his command."

"If the Tilaryn come, the Dragons would also come," Jeewon added, with Ssen translating. "It would be war unlike anything any of you have seen."

Thea shivered, seeing again in her mind the massive Dragons battling in the sky, the mountain shuddering beneath the strength of their magic. A battle of Tilaryn and Dragons would be a battle that no Elf or human could survive.

"It is a game." The King's eyes glinted in the firelight. "How much the Fallen One can overstep his bounds without the Deity's forces stepping in, and how much strength the Generals can show without the Fallen One unleashing more of his power. Once the escalation begins, it would be very difficult to stop."

Ember nodded. "It is true. We already have our help—the power and magic given to us by the Deity. With it, we need to do what we can."

"That's right," Thabani grinned. "Besides, we have a lot of casters once you add us all together."

"And the orcs are not the only ones who have trained in warfare." Determination glinted on Ssen's scales.

"Who will march with us?" The King's gaze passed from leader to leader. "All are welcome, but each must choose as they see fit for themselves and their people."

"Oh, I'll be there," Ulfgar grinned, "and Ember will

too, I imagine. We've been cooped up far too long."

"Swift Wing and I will go too." Fell Claw's golden eyes gleamed.

Thabani smiled. "The Resistance will fight. At least, those who have journeyed with me."

Noxolo nodded. "The Fauns of the house will fight too."

The King considered this. "Will the Fauns fight as one company or two?"

Noxolo glanced at Thabani. "The Fauns with me want to fight like the Minathrils. Alya and her friends are making shields for us."

Ssen's scales shone yellow.

"Well ..." Thabani nodded reluctantly, "if that's what you want, I suppose it's not a bad idea."

Elora hesitated, then sighed. "I will stay here. I promised Kais that I would."

"Thank you, Elora." Thea rested a hand on her shoulder. "We need someone to watch over this place while we are gone."

"The Oreum will go where the Spark goes." Ssen spoke for Jeewon.

"Thank you." Thea nodded. "We go to the aid of Gedwyld."

Big Boss drew himself to his full height. "Goblins are not afraid. We will also fight."

Ulga approached with heavy steps, her axe resting on her shoulder. "I will go first of all. Then many of them will die before they reach you."

"We went through this before," Ulfgar grumbled from across the hearth. "Those orcs hate your guts. You're going to die if you go out there."

"And they will not try to kill you? Whether you are

light or not," she glanced at Big Boss, "you march with the Spark. They will not spare you." Turning towards Thea, she knelt, her head bowed in deference. "Let me fight. It is what I was made to do."

Thea looked into her troubled eyes. "Thank you, Ulga. You will fight with us."

"Here's an idea," Coham tipped back his chair. "Let's split you Elves in two groups again. The Minathrils go with one group and Noxolo's folks go with the other. Ulga can help them, since they're not so used to shields yet. Thabani's crew can have no plan just like they likes, and everyone else can pick who they want to join."

Thea looked down at the wizened old man. "What about you, Coham?"

Coham grinned. "Heh, you couldn't leave me behind."

Agreeing to assemble again at first light, everyone returned to their separate companies to rest and prepare for the morning.

The King stayed behind, staring into the fire's flickering depths. Khariton waited at his side.

Sylica lay on her stomach on the hearth, humming a song softly to herself.

Thea glanced at Elora. She sat alone, a frown creasing her forehead.

"I could talk to Kais," Thea offered.

Elora shook her head. "Adi needs me. And someone needs to keep the Faunlets from getting out."

Thea squeezed her hand. "We'll do all we can to save Gedwyld tomorrow."

Elora smiled. "I know."

Sylica perked up and glanced around. "They're

finished?" She scrambled to her feet, sending Daisy scampering in circles. "Finally! They were talking *forever!*"

Amusement gleamed in Khariton's eyes. "It can certainly be annoying when someone talks forever, don't you think?"

"Oh yes," Sylica agreed. "Now I can show you around properly! Everything was too busy before." She gestured enthusiastically. "This is the big room and I like sleeping here by the fire. It's so warm and cosy! And over here is the kitchen. Come and see!"

Grabbing Khariton's hand, she pulled him out of his chair, dragging him towards the kitchen door.

"This is such a nice house you know," Sylica continued, as if punctuation was something that happened to other people. "Sometimes in the mornings I make porridge. Maybe I can make porridge tomorrow! I'll have to make more than usual, though, because there's so many people now."

Ulga's grumbling voice informed Sylica, with choice words, that certain people were trying to sleep in the kitchen and would not take kindly to being disturbed any further.

"That's okay," Sylica conceded, leading Khariton back into the great room, "I can show you the wine cellar tomorrow. It's Ulfgar's favourite room in the whole house, you know!"

Elora leaned closer to Thea. "That Elf man really adopted Sylica? She told me, but I couldn't tell if it was something he knew about."

"Yes, he really adopted her," Thea confirmed. "They did the paperwork and everything. It's official."

Elora gave Khariton a skeptical glance. "He must be

brave."

The King laughed. Seeing Khariton's quizzical glance, he translated Elora's comment for him.

Khariton gave a wry smile. "I suppose she isn't wrong. Don't know what came over me, really." He watched Sylica scamper about the room, pointing out the gouge she had made in the floor with her shield, and the beam in the ceiling that was her favourite beam. A gentle smile lingered on his face. "Somehow, I don't regret it."

Chapter Twenty-Seven

A movement in the dark woke Thea. Startled, she sat up and stared around with bleary eyes. The fire on the hearth had burned down to a heap of glowing coals. Sylica lay curled up beside Daisy, snoring softly in her sleep. Beyond her, Khariton slept wrapped in his blanket.

Beside Thea, Jeewon lay silent on her mat.

Something moved.

"Thea?" A Faun stepped out from the shadows.

Thea tried to calm her pounding heart. "Msizi? You startled me." She glanced at the others, but they were still sleeping. "Where were you yesterday?"

"It doesn't matter." Msizi crouched next to her. "I need to warn you. The orcs are coming."

"They're coming?" Thea's eyes widened and she reached to wake Jeewon.

"Wait." Msizi grabbed her arm. "That's not all. They have planned a trap. If the army follows them they will be surrounded and killed."

Shouts and the clash of weapons erupted through the silence of night. All around Thea, people woke and leapt to their feet.

"What do we do?" Thea gasped, but Msizi had slipped back into the shadows.

She scrambled to her feet. "Khariton! Go get the King! Jeewon, get Thabani!"

As Khariton ran for the door, Jeewon bowed and turned to follow.

Ulga strode out of the kitchen, a ladle gripped in her hand. "Should I make them go away?"

"Wait, Ulga. There's some kind of trap."

Footsteps thundered on the stairs as Fauns and Littles emerged. Ulfgar burst out of the wine cellar with a growl, his axe in his hand. Sylica stared around at the chaos with large, startled eyes.

The door burst open and Thabani and his Fauns ran in. The King and Khariton entered close on their heels.

"What's going on?" Thabani demanded. "We should be fighting, not meeting!"

"There's a trap," Thea explained, quickly passing on the news in both Common and Elvish.

Big Boss and his goblins tramped through the door, scowling up at everyone as if they had been personally affronted by the clamour and disarray.

Thabani frowned. "If we can't fight, what should we do?"

Alya tapped Thea's arm. "They are trying to trap us. We should trap them instead."

Thea looked down into the Little's piercing gaze. "Did you have something in mind?"

"Gili made something downstairs. It's a powder that will blow up if you shoot it. We were saving it for an important time, and I think that might be now." Alya glanced at Msizi, who gave a subtle nod.

Big Boss gestured that he wanted to know what was going on. Alya translated for him. When he heard what Alya had proposed, his eyes widened.

Sylica bounded towards them, chattering eagerly in the language of the Littles. Around her, an excited huddle of Littles and goblins began to grow.

"Sylica?" Thea ventured. "What—" Outside the walls, the sounds of combat grew louder.

"Oh, we're just planning how to set the trap for the orcs," Sylica grinned. "Big Boss will help us get it there." Ducking down, she returned to the chattering Littles.

"And what should *we* do?" Thea demanded.

Sylica emerged again. "What?"

"The Elves and Fauns and everyone else. We're being attacked. What should we do?"

"Oh." Sylica considered this, then consulted with the Littles and goblins for a moment. "Keep the orcs busy. Half a measure should be lots of time."

After another moment of consultation, the Littles and goblins set off towards the workshop.

"Come on, Grumpy Daddy!" Sylica called, bounding across the room to seize Khariton's hand. "We're going to make a big boom!"

With a slightly unsure look in his eyes, Khariton followed Sylica and the chattering throng of Littles and goblins, with Daisy bounding excitedly beside him.

Thea turned to the King. "Hold off the orcs. The Littles need time."

The King nodded and hurried out the door, followed by Thabani and the Fauns.

"You good?" Ulfgar asked Thea.

"I ... I think so."

"Right. I'll go find Ember then." With a grin, he strode out the door.

Jeewon and Ssen waited beside Thea.

"What will you do?" Ssen asked. "Will you fight?"

"No." Thea glanced at the shadowy corner where Msizi stood alone. "There is someone I want to talk to first."

"And the Oreum?"

"One of you can stay with me if you want. The rest ... I don't know. Maybe stand watch around the house in case the orcs have something planned we don't know about."

Ssen bowed and relayed her words to Jeewon. After a moment of discussion, Ssen turned back to Thea. "The Captain will stay here with you. The rest of the crew may need someone who speaks Common."

Thea nodded and Ssen strode out the door. The great room was surprisingly quiet again. Thea joined Msizi in the corner where he waited.

Msizi smiled. "You will come with me?"

Thea nodded and glanced at her attentive companion. "Jeewon will come too."

Magic surged and the room around them faded away, replaced by the shadowy walls of the courtyard. An icy wind blew off the sea.

Had Jeewon not come after all? No, she was there, though nearly impossible to see with the camouflage of alarm filling her scales. Thea gave her a reassuring smile.

Msizi put a finger to his lips and pointed. From the forge hut, a trail of Littles and goblins crept stealthily, with Sylica leading the way and Khariton bringing up the rear. Sylica, Khariton, and the Littles wore strange metal panels strapped to their chests. The goblins had weapons in their hands.

When they reached the door overlooking the sea, they huddled together to confer. Silently unbarring it, Big Boss crept through first. One by one, the others followed.

"We will go too." Msizi's voice was lower than a whisper. He gave Thea a wink. "Make sure they don't run into trouble."

Silently, he crept towards the open door. Thea followed, with Jeewon striding after her.

Beyond the wall, they caught a brief glimpse of Khariton disappearing into the shadows. In the distance, the sounds of battle tore through the night sky, but by the coast all was still.

Following Sylica and her assorted Littles, they crept on until the sounds of battle were behind them. Then the Littles and goblins stopped again, gathering in a tight huddle around Sylica.

Khariton whispered something to Sylica, and she relayed it to the others. Whatever was said seemed to excite them. Following Khariton's lead, they crept inland once more.

As they approached a deeper shade among the shadows, Big Boss raised his hand and everyone stopped. Alya pulled something out of a satchel at her side. It looked like a vial—small, even in a Little's hand.

Taking the vial, Big Boss crept into the shadows, gesturing for Khariton to follow him.

Khariton silently took the bow off his back and pulled an arrow from his quiver.

Of course. Thea watched him creep after Big Boss. *Raybow used to be his.* Someone had to be good enough at shooting to hit the vial without being too close.

Thea held her breath. With a surge of magic from Msizi, they came into focus—Big Boss and Khariton creeping through the trees. And the orcs. There were hundreds of them, crouching in the shadows, so intent on the distant sound of combat—was it coming closer?—they didn't notice the shadowy figures creeping behind them.

Khariton stopped a short distance away, but Big Boss crept closer, planting the vial almost in their midst. Glancing over his shoulder to be sure Khariton had seen its location, he crept away.

After a long, breathless silence, Khariton drew back his bow and shot.

Fire erupted in a blinding flash. Its deafening roar tore through the forest, shaking the ground beneath their feet. Screams of pain and surprise filled the air.

Thea held a tree to steady herself. Shadows swirled in her vision, an echoing of images that may have been orc body parts scattering through the trees.

"Are—are they alright?" she stammered. Her eyes managed to focus on Msizi's face. He nodded, a grim light gleaming in his eyes.

"Come on," he whispered.

Thea took a step, and the world moved around her, shifting into the corner of the gardens from which they had left.

There was Jeewon—all but invisible. Thea was shaking.

Msizi laid a hand on each of their shoulders, though he could barely reach Jeewon's. "Let's go inside."

Ulga met them at the door, her hands clenched into fists. "Warn me if you are going out like that." Turning, she stormed back into the kitchen.

It wasn't long before Sylica and her companions arrived, clambering up the stairs from the workshop. They beamed from ear to ear, chattering excitedly amongst themselves, with the exception of Khariton who seemed a little dazed but still in a remarkably good mood.

"We exploded them," Sylica reported in a cheerful voice, "and it didn't take any Dragon magic at all!"

"Could've used some of that stuff up at the Temple," Khariton muttered to himself, his eyes twinkling.

Soon the door was thrown open and others poured inside, shouting and laughing.

"You should have seen it!" Thabani called. "They stared as if they couldn't believe their eyes!"

A member of the King's Guard approached Thea. "His Majesty could not be spared, but he wishes to know if we should press our advantage and pursue the orcs now instead of waiting for dawn."

"Should we go now?" Thea echoed in Common, for the sake of those who stood near. Silence fell across the room.

Thea stared around a sea of expectant faces. Thabani, Jeewon, Khariton, Sylica, Big Boss, and everyone else looked at her as if she was the one who should make the decision. She couldn't see Msizi anywhere.

Thea swallowed. "Ulga?"

The orc looked down with a guarded expression. "Yes?"

"Should we attack the orcs now, while they're recovering from the explosion?"

Ulga stared out the window. "If anything could make them less prepared, it would be that. I think we could try."

Thea nodded. "Then we will try."

The courtyard was filled with a flurry of activity as the

companies assembled and prepared to depart. Thea and Jeewon found the rest of the Oreum standing by the gate, shields and weapons in their hands. Tayhyang joined them, carrying his medical satchel.

Emerging from the gate in formation, they joined the King's company and set out through the shadow of the trees. Khariton and Sylica strode among the archers. Ilya walked beside the King.

It wasn't long before they left the trees behind. The road towards Gedwyld was battered and littered with debris. Voices rose in the distance, a clamour of disarray and confusion.

With the light of Micai glinting on their scales, the Minathrils surged forward, shields locked in formation. The Elves followed in a wave almost a thousand strong.

In the distance, the walls of Gedwyld were dark against the horizon.

Orcish cries rang out. Their shadowy figures filled the field before them.

With a shout, the Minathrils lowered their spears and charged. A volley of Elvish arrows soared overhead as the Minathril formation swept towards the enemy host, meeting with a resounding crash.

Their charge was unstoppable. Orcs were swept aside, trampled, or cut down as the Minathrils carved a path deep into the orcish ranks. The Elves surged after them, filling the gap left in the Minathrils' wake. Blades swung with the clash of metal on metal. Bowstrings sang.

From within the shield wall, Thea shot again and again into the seething masses of orcs. Time blurred into a chaos of shouts, cries, swinging blades and churning bodies.

Reaching for another arrow, Thea stopped as something intercepted her hand. It was Ssen.

"Eat," he said simply, thrusting a bit of dried meat into her hand.

Relief swept over Thea. She hadn't realized how hungry she was. Overhead, the first flickers of daylight gleamed in the sky.

"Ssen!"

Ducking through the Elvish archers who had gathered behind the shield wall, Thea hurried to catch up.

A startled look rippled over his scales as she grabbed his arm.

"It's morning! The Shindahs need to check in!"

Ssen nodded. "Bring them here."

Running through the chaos, Thea found the King. Khariton wasn't far away.

Quickly, Thea passed on her message and hurried back to the Minathrils. Behind the shield wall she found Tayhyang, bandaging a head wound. As Thea gestured that they needed to check in, relief surged across the healer's scales.

Jeewon shouted a command and the wall of shields drew tightly together and stopped its advance. Thea dropped to her knees. It felt terrifying to close her eyes, but she knew she'd never be able to concentrate with them open.

Around her, shouts and cries filled the air. The clash of weapons and shields rang in a deafening cacophony. Close by, a Minathril screamed.

Clenching her fits, Thea braced herself. She couldn't hear anything above the chaos surrounding her, but slowly the tingle of magic filled her again. She leapt to her feet. Close by, Tayhyang hurried to the fallen Minathril with a surge of magic.

Thea nodded to Ssen. "Thank you."

Ssen shouted and the Minathrils fought with renewed vigour. Weapons clashed. Shouts rang out. Daylight gleamed on orcish metal and glinted on scales coloured with determination.

Crouching behind the shield wall, Thea drew an arrow from her quiver. Crossbow bolts whizzed overhead. Leaping to her feet, she returned fire. Her arrow flashed with light and an orc screamed.

She only had a few arrows left.

The Minathrils were no longer making headway through the orcs. Beyond the churning melee, Thea caught a glimpse of Gedwyld in the distance. It was still so far away. Between the forces of the King and the besieged city were far too many orcs.

She glanced at Khariton and Sylica who had stayed behind the shield wall to quickly eat. They seemed to be noticing the same thing.

"Should I do something?" Sylica asked. "I could do something, you know."

"I know." Khariton rested a cautioning hand on her shoulder. "Wait."

Eagle cries pierced the sky.

Overhead, Kaji and Ember wheeled and dove, plummeting towards the orcs below.

With a roar, Ulfgar leapt from Ember's back, his axe flashing with light. He disappeared among the orcs with a crash.

Two more giant eagles dove—Swift Wing and Fell Claw—each with a fighter clutched in their talons. Swift Wing dropped their Faun beside Ulfgar and took to the sky again. Fell Claw dropped Brandy, then shifted into wolf form, teeth bared as they plummeted towards the orcs.

In the distance, a chorus of Faunic cheers tore through the chaos. There they were—dodging through the melee, stabbing and running in an irresistible onslaught.

Thabani's laughter rang above the noise.

With a shout, the Minathrils surged forward again. Arrows hissed overhead as the King's forces renewed their attack, driving the orcs back, step after step.

Thea sighted carefully along her arrow. Every shot had to count. Four arrows left. Three arrows left. Two. One.

The advance pressed on, slowed, and came to a standstill once again.

In the distance, the second host of the Elves fought, surrounded by the orcish hordes.

An archer beside Thea fell, a crossbow bolt in his chest. Tayhyang crouched over an injured Minathril, worry colouring his scales. The ground was stained with blood.

The circle of Fauns was smaller than it had been. Another scream pierced the deafening clamour.

People were dying. If the ships would just come ...

Thea stared towards the distant sea. No fleet had appeared. Roland said they would come today, but the day was still early. Should they try to hold out until they came?

Thea crouched on the ground behind the wall of shields. She hadn't used any magic yet.

Roland? Where are you?

Thea? Roland's mind was hard to latch onto. *I'm

busy. Can it wait?

How far are you from Gedwyld?

Don't know. Ships attacked us. A whole fleet of them. We're trying to—

He was gone.

The sounds of combat rushed over Thea's senses again. The fleet was under attack. Of course—enemy ships had attacked the Raven before. Why wouldn't there be enemy ships now?

Trembling, she scrambled to her feet. The ships weren't coming today. Who knew if they would come at all?

Ducking, she ran through the chaos. Where was the King? There—he was crouched on the ground, trying to help an injured Elf to his feet. Her eyes settled on the bloodied Elf. *Ilya?*

Thea rushed to join them. "Ilya, are you alright?"

Ilya's arm was over the King's shoulder. He staggered as he tried to stand. Blood dripped from a rending gash in his armour.

The King's eyes were grim. "That blow had my name on it, if he hadn't jumped in the way." He gave Thea a sharp glance. "Why aren't you with Jeewon?"

"I had to tell you," Thea fought for breath, "the ships aren't coming yet. Enemy ships attacked them. That's all I know."

The King stared at Thea for a moment, then his eyes took in the battle surging around them. "We can't sustain this. They will harm us more than we harm them." He turned to the Commander. "Sound the retreat."

Thea crouched beside Ilya as the signal to retreat rang out overhead. In the distance, the call echoed among Thabani's troops, and even further away among the second host of Elves.

"Someone get Tayhyang!" Thea called. "Quick!"

"There isn't time." The King ripped a strip of fabric off his clothes and wrapped it hurriedly around Ilya's chest. "We have to get him out."

"I still have magic." Thea looked up at the King.

He nodded.

Around them, the Elves had already begun their retreat. The Minathrils held their line as they moved back, step by step.

With a roar, a massive ball of fire erupted in the distant orc camp. The ground shook beneath their feet. Thea stared. *Big Boss.*

There wasn't time. She had to get Ilya out of there.

Wrapping her arms beneath him, Thea cast her magic.

The chaos of battle faded, replaced by the silent walls of the courtyard. Ilya was too heavy. She couldn't lift him.

"Elora!" she called. "Someone help!"

The door swung open and Dunstan hurried outside, followed by his son. Working together, they lifted Ilya and carried him into the house.

"Melinda!" Dunstan called as they laid Ilya on one of the makeshift cots that lined the great room.

Elora gave Thea a sharp glance as she entered. "You're back."

"We had to retreat. Just for now."

Elora watched her for a long moment. "I see."

Melinda bustled into the room, her arms filled with towels and bandages. "Elora, get hot water. Jason, the Faunlets are asking for you again."

Thea hovered by Ilya's side as Melinda set up her workspace and examined the injury. "Will he be alright?"

Melinda gave a curt nod. "He will if I have anything to do with it." Methodically, she began cutting off his mangled armour with a trollsbane knife.

Leaving Melinda to her work, Thea sat by the fire. Exhaustion swept over her like a wave.

"Are you alright?" Dunstan asked, a worried frown creasing his forehead.

Thea nodded. "Just tired."

"What happened? Did the orcs win?"

"I guess. We were doing well at first, but too many people were dying. Then we learned that the ships aren't coming yet ..."

Across the room, Elora looked up sharply.

"They were attacked by enemy ships. I don't know when they'll be here now."

Dunstan frowned. "So now what?"

Thea sighed. "I don't know."

Soon the retreating army began to arrive, and injured fighters filled the great room once again. Outside, the various companies organized themselves and did their best to account for those who were missing.

Jeewon joined Thea, her scales showing her frustration. Thea guessed that the cause was her disappearance from the battle without any of her guard accompanying her.

"Sorry," she muttered. Jeewon bowed.

"Open the door!" Noxolo's voice rose urgently from the courtyard.

Moments later, Ulga strode inside, carrying a Faun

in each arm. Gently lowering them to the floor, she staggered. Green blood oozed from ugly wounds on her shoulders, arms, and head. Turning she limped towards the door.

"Excuse me!" Melinda blocked the way with her hands on her hips. "You are not going anywhere."

Ushering Ulga to one of the beds, Melinda placed her under the watchful gaze of one of the Fauns. Thea joined them.

"We made it out." Ulga's brooding gaze took in the injured all around her. She shifted, and winced in pain.

Thea offered a hopeful smile. "Maybe the explosion in the orc camp did something."

Ulga gave her a calculating glance. "Like make them mad?"

Gradually, the leaders of the army assembled once again. When Big Boss entered the great room, Alya and the Littles gathered around him, chattering excitedly.

"Big Boss!" Thea called, gesturing for him to join her by the fire. "I didn't know you were going to make another explosion."

"We planned it last night," Alya grinned, "since we had two vials. Big Boss's people snuck the other one in while you were fighting."

Thea turned to the goblin leader. "Thank you, Big Boss. That must have done more than the rest of us did together."

Big Boss beamed. Thea almost didn't need a translation to understand his words.

"He says that his people who took it were very brave," Alya relayed.

"I know," Thea assured him. "It must have been very

dangerous. Did they make it out alright?"

As Big Boss replied, a stunned silence fell over the Littles.

"He ... he says they did not plan to make it out," Alya whispered.

For a moment, Big Boss's expression of bravado faltered. Gili wiped tears from her eyes.

"Many people died today," Thea said slowly. "They were all very brave."

Big Boss nodded. "Very brave."

Reports of the toll began to trickle in. Five Minathrils had died. Thabani and Noxolo had both lost several of their Fauns.

Across the room, Thea watched Brandy storm out of sight, her eyes red as if she had been crying.

"It's Fell Claw," Ulfgar said, joining Thea by the fire. "They didn't make it."

"What?" Thea stared, unwilling to believe her ears.

Ulfgar nodded and slouched into a chair. "The orcs got them while they were shifting. Brandy tried to help, but ..." he shrugged and shook his head. "We'll miss them."

Thea nodded, tears stinging her eyes. The golden-eyed Dryad had given their all, like so many others had that day.

Just over three hundred Elves were not accounted for, the King told Thea when he joined her by the fire.

"Swift Wing has gone to scout, in case anyone lost their way or got left behind," he continued, "so the numbers may be better than that."

Thea nodded, knowing that wouldn't make up for all the other lives that had been lost.

"I think our tactics were better this time." The King frowned, his eyes absent with thought. "We fought longer and had fewer casualties. The explosion may have given us a chance to advance again, but the cost would have been higher. We were right to retreat when we did." His keen gaze rested on Thea's. "We should not try again until the ships arrive. With greater numbers, our chances improve significantly."

"We don't know when the ships will get here. How long do we wait?"

"As long as we have to." He sighed. "It may be for the best. We are tired, and many have been hurt."

Thea nodded, staring out across the crowded room. Tayhyang, Melinda, and Sylica moved from patient to patient, cleaning wounds, bandaging injuries, offering medicine and encouraging words.

Khariton stood beside the King, though his eyes moved to see what Sylica was doing. Laughter seemed to follow wherever she went, along with a trail of candy wrappers.

Slowly, the room began to empty. Those with serious injuries were moved upstairs, and the rest returned outside to the camps. The smells of the evening meal drifted through the air.

Sylica skipped over to join Thea, Khariton, and the King by the fire. "Everyone was really happy about my candy," she grinned. "I like making people happy. Grumpy Daddy says it's one of my special powers, right Grumpy Daddy? Just like Daisy's special power is eating shiny things." She flopped down on the hearth with a satisfied smile. Daisy trotted over to join her and started licking her face.

A smile twitched at the corners of Khariton's mouth.

"That is a good power to have," the King reflected, his eyes gleaming in the firelight.

"That's not my *only* power though," Sylica continued, a thoughtful frown creeping over her face. "We stopped fighting before I could do anything to help."

"You did help," Khariton assured her. "You fought just as hard as anyone."

"I mean I didn't help with my *magic*."

The King glanced at her in interest. "Khariton said you have an unusual kind of magic."

Sylica grinned. "Dragon magic!"

"The thing is," Khariton leaned closer, "we know that, but the orcs don't. The only orcs who saw you do magic are ..." he hesitated, "... not around anymore. Because they're not expecting it, that gives us an advantage. The right time will come for you to use that advantage, and when you do, it will be spectacular."

Sylica blinked. "I'm a secret weapon?"

Khariton smiled. "The best kind of secret weapon."

"Well I like secrets," Sylica grinned, "and I like weapons—like my shiny mace—and I like being the best!"

Khariton tousled her hair. "You are the best. No day's dull when you're around."

The King laughed.

Thea looked up into his gleaming eyes. Here with just the four of them, he seemed more like Ruslan again. An Elf, who was a friend. It was a comforting feeling.

"How is Ilya doing?" Thea asked.

"He's stable." A sober gleam returned to Ruslan's gaze. "He won't be moving much for a few days."

"He saved your life, didn't he?"

Ruslan nodded. "He knows I'm ready to die, but he did it anyways." Firelight glimmered in his eyes. "I'm glad it didn't kill him."

An image of Kseniya rose in Thea's mind, clinging to her husband's arm. She was right, it was dangerous. But Thea knew beyond a doubt that this was where they were supposed to be.

Fatigue surged through her body as a peaceful kind of silence fell across the room. Beside her, Ruslan stared thoughtfully into the fire. Across the hearth, Sylica hummed softly to herself, while Khariton sharpened his knife. The rhythmic sounds seemed to blend with Sylica's little tune.

Thea closed her eyes.

Something jolted her into wakefulness. A surge of darkness held her in a terrifying grip, like a nightmare, but waking up didn't make it go away. She felt it—the darkest presence she had ever experienced. Staring around the room in terror, nothing seemed any different. Sylica slept with her head on Daisy, and Khariton dozed in his chair. The fire flickered on the hearth, filling the room with a soft, comfortable warmth.

Ruslan was not asleep. He stared with narrowing eyes as if he could see, through the wall, something far, far away.

"Ruslan?" Thea whispered, her heart pounding in her ears.

Slowly, he turned and looked at her. A grim light flickered in his eyes. "You felt it too?"

Thea nodded. The oppressive weight of darkness slowly faded, leaving an imprint of dread impressed upon her spirit sight. "What was it?"

"That," the King rose slowly to his feet, "was a Fallen Tilaryn."

Chapter Twenty-Eight

What is that?

Zaki stood above the gate, staring out across the field of battle. Once it had been filled with farms. Now it was trampled and battered beyond recognition. The orcs surged around something—*someone*—that towered over them, too far away for his eyes to pin down exactly what he was seeing.

The Captain of the Guard stood beside Zaki, staring out beyond the walls with narrowing eyes, her hands braced on the parapet in front of her.

The Lord of Gedwyld was there too, with the head of the Pipers' Guild and the other leaders of the city. The clothes visible beneath his armour were wrinkled and unkept. His face was haggard, as if he hadn't slept in days.

None of them had slept in days. At least, not a proper sleep worth anything.

Zaki had stood on the wall with them yesterday, watching as the Elvish army tried to battle its way across the field. He could still feel the fear and dismay that rose all around him as the Elves sounded the retreat and marched away.

And now this ... this *thing* had appeared. Zaki could feel its malice, even from this distance. It stared at the city, unmoving, its dark form flickering in the icy morning light.

"A Tilaryn." Acwellan's voice was low. "The Fallen General sent one of his Tilaryn."

Zaki stared up at the Principal Healer of the city. She still wore her white robes, but now they were soiled and stained. Bits of hair had pulled loose from their binding and waved wildly in the wind. Her face was grim.

Zaki shivered. Even the comforting feeling of his fixing bag slung over his shoulder didn't quell the sensation of dread creeping over his senses.

They were alone, and the Big Bad had sent a Big to kill them.

Not alone. Zaki reminded himself. *They'll come back. Elora won't let them leave us.*

Across the field, something rippled towards them, like a blast of billowing smoke. Hitting the wall, it recoiled, soaring over the city and out of sight. For a moment, Zaki felt a glowing shield, covering the city like a bubble. Then it was gone.

He felt the creature's hiss of anger.

Zaki stared. "What was that?"

Acwellan glanced down at him. "You felt it?"

"Something came at us, but it hit the bubble and flew away."

The Healer's eyes were grim. "It was trying to charm us. If it had succeeded, the battle would be over."

Zaki swallowed nervously. "But now?"

"Now it begins."

Close at hand, the forest gate stone thrower continued to turn. *Thrum. Thrum. Thrum.*

From their position on the wall, they could see each stone's thudding impact in the crater-marked areas where the orcs did not go.

"You are a magic-user too?"

Zaki's hand grasped the bag at his side. "In a way."

Beneath his feet, the wall shook.

"Acwellan," the Lord of Gedwyld's voice seemed to come from far away. "You know something of this new enemy?"

"I do. Somewhat."

"What should we do to prepare for its assault?"

Acwellan's gaze did not leave the distant shadow. "I do not think there is anything we can do."

The wall shook again, the tremors growing stronger and more violent with every passing breath. Cries of alarm rang out from the streets as people ran to see what was happening. Above the rumble of grinding rock rose a creaking and groaning, the scream of tortured wood.

Zaki stared at the rock thrower. Its arms were swelling and buckling, straining against the bands of metal holding them in place.

"Look out!" he yelled, throwing himself down with his arms over his head.

The rock thrower exploded, sending bits of metal and fragmented wood every direction. Screams and cries filled the air.

Cautiously, Zaki raised his head. His arm was bleeding where a bolt had torn through his shirt. Pieces of his rock thrower were everywhere, smashed and broken, filling the street with its ruin.

There were people under the rubble. He heard their cries, saw people frantically digging to get them out.

An orcish call tore through the wind. They were coming. With the rock thrower gone, the ranks of orcs advanced towards the gate.

The gate. Zaki stared as the gate began to twist and

writhe, the metal buckling and folding in on itself, tearing chunks of stone from the wall.

Terrifying certainty flooded over him. This was it.

In the street, people screamed and ran. City guards stared, frozen in fear.

Zaki leapt from the wall, ducking for cover as the gate exploded. Shrapnel shot across the street, embedding itself in the walls opposite the gate.

With a deafening rumble, the arch above the gate collapsed, filling the air with choking clouds of dust.

The wall was breached. The orcs were coming, and there was nothing standing in their way.

Turning, he ran. Down the street, up the narrow alley.

In the distance, screams and cries rose as the news spread like wildfire through the city. Alarm bells rang. Sirens blared.

"Zaki!" Diving out of a side street, Tamir plummeted towards him.

"Get the others!" Zaki yelled. "They're coming!"

Tamir's face was ashen. Turning on his heel, he sprinted back the way he had come.

Zaki ran on.

Bursting through the door, he ran up the steps two at a time.

Nora was there, wiping her hands on a greasy rag. She saw the look on his face.

"It's time?"

Zaki nodded. Pulling the lever by the table, the false wall folded out of the way. Behind it, five suits of big armour waited. They were ready. Every piece was oiled and working perfectly. Now they would face their real test.

Footsteps thundered up the stairs. Tamir, Avi, and Chaya appeared, red-faced and panting.

Zaki knew he couldn't do this alone, that was why he built more suits. He'd had time for five. His operators knew what they were doing, and what the cost would be. They trained together at night, in case the time to use them ever came.

Now it was here.

"Gosh," Avi gasped, trying to catch his breath.

Chaya pulled her cap over her curly hair, hurrying towards the suits. "They're ready?"

Zaki nodded. "As ready as they will be."

Tamir stepped into his suit, clipping himself into the harness. He gave a wan smile. "Ready or not."

Zaki pulled another lever and the wall beyond the suits opened onto the alleyway below. Icy wind rushed in to greet them.

Nora climbed into her seat and shot Zaki a grin. The door of her suit swung shut, closing her in.

Zaki gave one last glance around the attic. It had been a good room.

The others were in their suits now, turning on the power and testing the controls. Zaki climbed into the final one.

Sitting back in the seat, his hand ran along the panel of buttons and switches, finding the ones he needed without pausing for thought.

The door clicked shut and he felt the reassuring hum of power. The viewing window cleared and the limb controls engaged.

Great Big Big, help us.

Reaching out with his suit's robotic arm, he pulled the lever.

Click. Click. Click.

One by one, the hold clips opened and the five machines dropped to the cobblestones below.

As soon as he landed, Zaki ran through his control panel. Everything was working and ready. Now run.

Lurching and rumbling, the five machines thundered down the alley and turned onto the street. Through his fogging window, Zaki saw people running by. Humans and Littles. Terrified faces. Screams and cries rose above the churning sounds of machinery as he turned towards the gate.

He flicked a switch and the siren blared.

There was no slowing now. People leapt out of his way as the ruins of the gate swept closer.

He pulled a lever. Gears whirred as the automatic crossbow lowered into place.

Bloodied figures lay among the rubble. In front of him, someone's head fell off their shoulders. Rolled. Stared up at him.

Focus. There. The orc saw him and stared. Zaki pushed the button.

The suit shuddered as the crossbow bolt ejected, slamming into the orc's chest.

The orc grew to fill his entire view.

Wham.

The world shook, then righted itself. There—more orcs, thundering towards him. Two fell with crossbow bolts in their heads.

Zaki wiped the condensation from his window. Next time he would have to make proper ventilation.

Next time.

Something dark whizzed towards him. His armour shuddered and a red light started flashing. Crossbow arm compromised. Flicking a switch, a series of gears moved to replace the damaged part. Pushing another control, a blade extended from the other arm. It swung, striking the closest orc.

Tamir fought next to him. His blade flashed, cutting deep into an orc's side.

Zaki's hands darted from control to control as the orcs surged towards him.

Another orc fell, and another.

Chaya, Avi, and Nora held the second line of defence. Crossbow bolts whizzed past him to strike the oncoming orcs.

Zaki flicked another lever. A barrage of thick metal caltrops shot out from the front of his suit, scattering the ground in front of the breach with their sharp, barbed points.

The orcs still surged forward, but more cautiously than before.

A blinking light alerted him that his crossbow was ready. A grim smile lingered on his face as he shot again and again. He *could* make something better than an orc, and the Big Bad couldn't stop him.

Through his blood-splattered window, Zaki could still see the distant figure, standing beyond the advancing orcs. Something drew his gaze back to it again and again, even as he fought. Menace flowed from it, reaching towards him like a shadowy hand.

Around Zaki, the walls of metal shuddered, then began to creak and groan. Warning lights flashed across his control panel. *Both* arms were compromised? Frowning, he pulled a lever. His machine responded, but sluggishly.

The shuddering grew worse. Zaki flicked the switch

for the stabilizers. Nothing happened.

The suit lurched, completely out of his control. Alarms blared, warning lights flashed. What was happening?

Metal screeched, so loud it was hard to think. The space around him was smaller than it was before. It was twisting, closing in on him.

Panic rising, he pulled the handle for the collapsing door. It was stuck. He couldn't get out.

Zaki hammered on the window as the machine crumpled around him.

Pain shot through his leg.

He couldn't breathe.

Sudden silence flooded his senses. The dark magic was gone. Not gone—it was still out there, but the shadowy figure had turned.

In the distance, magic surged.

Zaki's head sank onto his crumpled cage of metal. Everything went dark.

Chapter Twenty-Nine

With a surge of magic, the King reappeared directly in front of the Fallen Tilaryn.

The Minathril shield wall surrounded Thea on every side, brought to a halt by the impenetrable ranks of orcs. They had brought the King close enough. Now they had to hold their ground.

Thea stared, unable to drag her eyes away from the horrible being that towered above the King. She thought she had seen spiritual darkness before, but it was nothing like this. This Tilaryn wasn't filled with darkness. It *was* darkness.

The King's sword plunged towards the Tilaryn in a shimmering arc.

The Tilaryn's sword swung to meet it.

"Join the shield wall." Close by, Khariton spoke to Sylica. "I will help the King."

Beyond the Minathrils and the orcs, it was almost impossible to see the King's distant figure, but Thea's spirit sight saw the light within him as clear as day. He seemed small beside the Fallen Tilaryn.

Its terrifying power overwhelmed her senses, sharpened as they were to the spiritual world. She couldn't move. She could only stare as she felt the surge of dark magic begin to grow.

Thorned roots sprang out of the ground, snapping like whips as they surged around the King.

The King's magic flared and he leapt, propelled high above the reach of the tangling roots. He swung his sword over his head, bringing it down in a sweeping strike that cut deeply into the Tilaryn's shoulder.

The Tilaryn screamed in pain, a terrifying sound that seared through Thea's consciousness like a red-hot iron.

She stared. How could a sword hurt a Tilaryn? Somehow the sword itself glowed with light, as if it existed just as much in the spiritual world as in the physical one.

The Tilaryn struck the King with the butt of his sword. The King staggered back.

For a moment they watched each other, crouched, ready to strike.

With a surge of magic, the King lunged forward, his sword swinging faster than sight.

A counter-surge erupted from the Tilaryn and the King staggered to the side.

The Tilaryn thrust with its sword, striking deeply into the ground as the King rolled out of the way.

Dark magic surged, and the King's sword glowed red. It clattered to the ground as his hand recoiled from its heat.

The King's magic surged and a sudden cascade of water appeared out of the air, drenching the red-hot sword in a deluge that exploded into a cloud of steam.

Wrapping his hand in some cloth, the King grabbed his sword once again, dodging out of the way as the Tilaryn's blade came sweeping through the dissipating mist.

Khariton was there. Thea saw his light darting behind the King. With a clash of steel, he struck a nearby orc. Another orc leapt towards the King, and

Khariton cut it down.

The Fallen Tilaryn and the King locked eyes, reading each other, the air crackling with the intensity of their stare.

The King leapt. That same breath, dark magic surged and the ground beneath his feet crumbled and gave way.

With his own surge of magic, the King disappeared, reappearing immediately behind the Tilaryn. With a lunging strike, his sword cut deeply into the shadowy figure.

The Tilaryn screamed. A surge of magic lifted a wave of dirt, pushing the Tilaryn and the King apart. Darkness oozed like blood from its gaping wound.

Slowly, the Tilaryn raised itself to its full height, malice glinting in its eyes. As magic surged, the sword in the Tilaryn's hand grew and burst into flames of pure darkness, sucking the light and colour out of the air as they flickered up and down the darkening blade.

The Tilaryn seemed to grow larger too, and stronger. It towered over the King with an overwhelming force of evil and hatred.

The King stared up at his opponent, his eyes glittering with light.

The Tilaryn swung its blade, cutting a sword-shaped arc of darkness where no light could exist.

The King swung his sword to meet it and the blades struck. An explosion of light crackled through the air.

The King and the Fallen Tilaryn circled each other, the clashing of their swords sending bursts of light and darkness streaking across the sky. They dodged and struck, parried and attacked.

With surges of magic, the ground shifted beneath

their feet, back and forth.

The King stumbled.

As the Tilaryn swooped towards him, the King leapt, his blade gleaming with light.

The Tilaryn took the full force of the blow on its chest. Lunging forward, it plunged its sword into the King's shoulder.

The King convulsed as streaks of darkness shot through his body, wrapping around him like tentacles.

Shadow dripped from the wound in the Tilaryn's chest, soaking into the blackening ground beneath its feet as it wrenched its sword from the King's shoulder and swung it back for another strike.

The King staggered, his muscles straining to lift his sword. As the shadowy blade sped towards him, the King's magic surged once again.

The Tilaryn's blade exploded, sending the Tilaryn staggering back, shards of metal lacerating its incorporeal skin.

All around them, orcs yelled and threw themselves to the ground.

The King staggered and collapsed.

With a hiss, the Tilaryn stepped towards his prostrate figure.

Khariton leapt between them. With a surge of magic, the King disappeared.

His limp body appeared within the shield wall of the Minathrils, lying prostrate at Thea's feet. "Healer!" Voices called around Thea. "Healer, quick!"

Thea's eyes were fixed on the Fallen Tilaryn, its horror filling her mind.

Dark magic surged and something rose up from the ground into the Tilaryn's hand. It was the King's sword.

Khariton tried to step back, but a dark spell burst over him with a force that almost made him stagger. His legs were stuck fast where he stood.

The sword in the Tilaryn's hand swung in a glistening arc towards Khariton.

Ducking, he deflected the blow and swung into his own attack. His blade shimmered with spiritual light as it struck the Tilaryn's legs and cut deep.

The Tilaryn shrieked in pain. All around it, stones leapt into the air. Whirling, they hurtled towards Khariton on a wave of dark magic.

With a sickening barrage of thuds, the stones slammed into Khariton, knocking him back, pummelling him to the ground with the force of their impact.

The billowing dust disappeared, and in its place, Sylica stood above Khariton, her body quivering with rage. She glared up at the Tilaryn. "You just hurt my Daddy!"

With a look of scorn, the Fallen Tilaryn stretched out its hand. Dark magic shot out from it, like a whip of black flame. It swirled around Sylica, growing faster as more and more magic streamed out from the Tilaryn's hand, until it swept around her like a dark, unstoppable whirlwind of power.

The Tilaryn stood, arm still extended, but now its face was filled with surprise and growing concern.

Sylica yelled and the Tilaryn's arm moved as if it had suddenly been released. The vortex of power exploded back the way it had come, slamming into the Tilaryn with a force that knocked it back and tore a gaping wound in its chest.

The Tilaryn staggered, its face clouded with shock

and dismay. All around Sylica, orcs stopped and stared.

Sylica crouched, her shield and mace gripped in her hands. "Want to try that again?"

Anger flashed in the Tilaryn's eyes. Dark magic surged as thorned roots sprang out of the ground.

Sylica shouted and the thorns disappeared, transforming into the most beautiful flowers Thea had ever seen. All around Sylica, the trampled broken ground was overgrown by a beautiful, grassy meadow, stretching out in every direction.

The Fallen Tilaryn hissed and thrust its hand towards her with a sudden rush of wind.

Bracing herself against the gale, Sylica leapt, her feet landing on the air as if it was a solid mass. She leapt forward again, higher and higher as if an invisible staircase stretched before her. Behind her mace, a new shape appeared—a spiritual mace, three times its size.

With widening eyes, the Tilaryn stepped back, but Sylica leapt the final invisible stair and struck the Tilaryn's head. Darkness splattered every direction, like blood.

The Tilaryn staggered back and with a surge of magic, disappeared.

"No!" Sylica yelled. Leaving her mace to hang weightless in the air beside her, she reached out, grabbed something unseen, and pulled.

The Fallen Tilaryn appeared again. It staggered, fear and hatred clouding its eyes.

Sylica grabbed her mace again. "Nobody hurts my Daddy!"

She swung her mace, and the Tilaryn exploded in a shock wave of magic.

Silence fell across the battlefield, with small flakes of

dust and ash. Cautiously, the hosts of orcs within the blast range got unsteadily to their feet once again.

Thea staggered, her mind finally free from the overwhelming presence of the Fallen Tilaryn. Across the battlefield, sounds of combat began once again.

In the distance, Sylica crouched protectively over Khariton as the orcs began closing in.

With her magic, Thea reached out to them. Sylica and Khariton appeared in front of her, within the relative safety of the Minathril shield wall.

"Grumpy Daddy," Sylica gestured desperately, crouched over Khariton. "Grumpy Daddy are you okay?"

Khariton groaned and opened his eyes. "That hurt."

Tayhyang hurried to join them.

Not far away, the King lay on the ground with another Minathril healer watching over him. Lines of pain etched his face.

Around them, shouts and cries rang out as the orcs renewed their assault. The Minathrils held their ground, standing firm as the onslaught continued. Orcs surrounded them on every side, stretching as far as Thea could see.

Magic surged. Thea's heart sank. More dark casters? She counterspelled, and felt the magic dissipate. Nocking an arrow, she tried to stare out past the wall of Minathrils. All the spirits of the orcs were dark. Could she find the caster at all?

Magic surged again. She counterspelled, but the caster's magic overwhelmed hers. The ground beneath the circle of Minathrils began to crumble and fall.

No! Thea cast her own magic, transporting the ground back into the place it had occupied before. It obeyed her, but reluctantly.

Close by, a Minathril screamed and staggered back, a javelin piercing her chest. On either side of her, Minathrils moved closer to close the gap in the wall.

There—Thea caught a glimpse of the caster. Sighting along her arrow, she shot.

Dark magic surged again, from the opposite side. Staggering, Thea counterspelled and turned to face it, trying once again to find the caster in the unending sea of orcs.

Around her, the circle of Minathrils grew smaller as the orcs pressed down on them. There was hardly enough room for the injured. Thea reached for an arrow and found that she only had one left.

Fear hammered in her chest. There was no way to get out. Not like this. She could transport one or two people at most, but what about everyone else? Even if the Minathrils could rally to break through, there was no way they could bring the injured with them.

At her side, Sungy crouched on the ground, pain and worry gleaming on her bloodied scales. A crossbow bolt protruded from her shoulder.

Thea!

Roland's voice burst into her mind.

Thea, we're here!

Thea stared, her heart beating loud in her ears.

"Ssen!" she shouted, pulling him out of the shield wall beside her. "Lift me up! Now!"

Startled, Ssen stared at her for a moment, then nodded and dropped his spear and shield. Interlocking his hands, he let Thea step onto them, then lifted her until she was head and shoulders above the Minathril wall.

She stared across the orcish hosts to the sea. There were the ships. Sails of every colour filled the coastline beyond Gedwyld. From her vantage point, she could just see the tumult of battle raging in the distance. The Elves had reached the top of the cliff.

"The ships are here!" she yelled at the top of her voice. "The ships are here!"

All around her, orcs paused to look over their shoulders. Brief expressions of doubt and confusion crossed their faces.

With a shout, the Minathrils surged forward once again, re-establishing their shield wall and attacking with renewed vigour. In the distance, Thea could see the Commander and the rest of the Elves, battling their way towards the gate where the orcs had breached the city.

Tears of relief stung her eyes. The ships had come.

Ssen lowered Thea to the ground once again. As he went to join the shield wall, Thea turned to find Sylica. She was still kneeling by Khariton, who lay propped up by a couple of packs. He was clearly in pain, but a gentle smile creased his face as he and Sylica talked together.

Tayhyang moved from patient to patient, his scales stained with blood and dirt. Beyond him, the King lay alone.

Moving gingerly past the wounded Minathrils, Thea crouched beside the King. His armour had been removed and lay on the ground beside him. His shoulder was red and bloodied.

As Thea joined him, the King opened his eyes. He tried to shift himself slightly, and pain spasmed across his face.

"Do you want me to get Tayhyang?" Thea asked, concern creasing her forehead.

"No." The King's voice was weak. "I told him to care for the others first, especially Khariton. The sword the Tilaryn had ... I saw others like it in the War. Only a Tilaryn can survive the wounds it gives. It—" a spasm of pain wracked his body, "—it's like a poison ... that infects the spirit."

Thea stared. Through her tingling spirit sight, she saw dark tendrils spreading throughout the King's body. Pain throbbed in his spirit.

"Praise the Deity, it was only a lesser Tilaryn." The King's voice was steadier than it had been. "Against a stronger one there would have been very little hope."

Tears stung in Thea's eyes. "But what about you? Isn't there something we can do to help?"

"I am dying." The King looked up into Thea's face. There was a peace in his eyes that she had not seen before. "I have paid for my failure and the failure of our people. We are here, and we have helped those we abandoned for so long."

The King shuddered, and for a moment his eyes closed again. "I—" he forced them open, "I give you my armour. It is made with the finest crafts of our people, taught to us by Enkeli. It changes size according to its bearer, and can change appearance at will. It can suit the noblest courts or the humblest peasant's home, wherever your task may take you."

With a spasm of pain, he moved his arm. Finding Thea's hand, he grasped it tightly. "A gift ... from the King of the Elves to the Spark. Be the Spark for our people, and never let their fire die again."

Thea grasped the King's hand. "I promise."

The King smiled. The hardened lines of nobility faded from his face. He was Ruslan again, and the eyes that stared up at her were gentle and filled with pain.

Within her hand, the pulse of life flickered and began to fade.

Tears glimmered in her eyes. For the first time since seeing Davis's spirit so long ago, she felt glad to be an Elf. "Thank you," she whispered.

Ruslan held her hand tighter as a spasm of pain crossed his face. "Thea," his voice was soft, barely above a whisper, "in the War ... when people were dying ... I used my spirit sight."

Ruslan's eyes drifted shut. His body shuddered. Within him, the tendrils of darkness wrapped tighter, choking the life out of him.

Horror and grief ached in Thea's chest, but she refused to look away. The darkness closed in, but his spirit blazed brighter until everything else faded away and his spirit was free. There was no more pain anymore. The weight of regret was gone.

Light flashed. For one moment, Thea thought she caught a glimpse of somewhere different, filled with light. Then it was gone.

Thea looked down at Ruslan's body lying beside her. He was dead.

Tears ran down Thea's face as she gently rested his hand on his chest.

The King of the Elves was no more. His quest was completed.

Gently, she lifted the King's bloodied armour. Removing her own, she replaced it with the King's, feeling it shift to fit her body as it rested over her shoulders. Wherever she went, she would carry her promise with her.

With an aching heart, Thea rose to her feet. It

seemed that now the injured Minathrils had all been attended to. Sylica was still kneeling beside Khariton. Tayhyang stood at a respectful distance, watching them.

Thea went to join him. "How is Khariton?" she asked the Minathril healer.

Blue tinged Tayhyang's scales. "He is bleeding inside. There is nothing I can do to help him."

"What?" Thea stared.

The healer shook his head. "All of my magic could only give him a few more breaths with his daughter."

As Thea watched, Khariton lifted a hand to Sylica's cheek, gently wiping the tears that coursed down her face. He spoke, his voice low beyond Thea's hearing.

Sylica held his hand as if she didn't want to let it go. "I love you, Grumpy Daddy," she whispered, her tears running over Khariton's smooth, ancient hand.

A hint of a smile played at the corner of his mouth, then faded away.

Khariton shuddered, and did not breathe again.

With a little strangled sob, Sylica bent over his motionless body. Burying her face in his torn, bloodied armour, she cried, her sobs lost in the clash and cries of battle that still filled the air.

Softly, Thea approached her friend and knelt down beside her.

Sylica looked up. Her eyes were red, her face streaked with dirt and tears.

"I'm so sorry," Thea whispered.

Sylica's face crumpled into tears. Throwing her arms around Thea, she clung to her as sobs wracked her body once again.

Thea held her close, the ache of grief throbbing in her chest. She hated war. She hated it. Sylica had just found a family. Why was it taken away from her?

Around them, the Minathrils fought on.

A sudden surge of noise tore Thea's gaze away from Khariton's lifeless form. The shield circle drew back, opening a window to the battlefield beyond. Through it, Elves surged, their weapons and shields gleaming bright in the light of Allumen. Excited clamour filled the air.

From the midst of the Elves, Roland appeared. His armour was bloodied and stained and he had a red gash on his forehead, but his eyes shone with light. Seeing Thea, he stood tall and saluted.

His hand froze in mid-air, his gaze taking in Khariton's lifeless body and Sylica's tear-stained face.

From close by, Sungy laid a hand on Thea's shoulder. "You go," she said in a strong Draconic accent. "I stay." Wrapping Sylica in her arms, Sungy gestured Thea away.

Scrambling to her feet, Thea ran to join Roland.

"You're here!" she gasped. "I'm so glad you're here!"

Shouts of triumph rang across the battlefield. Beyond the shield wall, companies of Elves pressed through the ranks of the orcs. In the distance, the Commander and her troops had reached the gate. Everywhere Thea looked, the orcs were scattered and divided, fighting with angry desperation in their eyes.

Ssen stepped forward and clasped Roland's hand. "It is good to see you." His scales gleamed yellow in the light. "You arrived just in time."

Overhead, Kaji soared, with Ember close behind. Thabani shouted in triumph and leapt, plummeting into another company of orcs. Ulfgar roared, dropping like a stone behind him. A surge of magic rippled through the air.

Roland turned to Thea. "Did I see Big Boss out there?"

"You sure did." Coham strode through the Minathril shield wall, his greatsword slung over his shoulder. "Cunning little rogue, isn't he? I swear every time I'm about to make a kill he pops up and steals it from me." His eyes settled on the lifeless body of the King. "Well, the mark of death didn't lie." A look of melancholy settled across his features. "I'm sorry to see him go. He had a good head on his shoulders."

Murmurs of respect and dismay rose among the Elves who gathered around their fallen King.

Coham rested a sinewy hand on Thea's shoulder. "Seems to me he knew who to trust." He gave her a wink. "Gedwyld is saved. He'd be proud of you."

"It was everyone." Tears glittered in Thea's eyes. "All the races of Raphtova made it possible. Including the Elves."

Roland smiled.

Coham cracked a toothless grin. "Your ol' King knew what was what. I'm glad I got to stand by 'im."

"And now we stand by you." Roland turned to Thea with light gleaming in his eyes. "What do you want us to do?"

Thea stared at the battlefield surrounding them. Orcs still threw themselves at the Minathril shield wall. Their spirits were dark—dark with evil, yes, but also dark with fear and despair.

The weight of the King's armour rested on her shoulders. She was the Spark to all the people, not just the five races, and there were people who needed the Deity's light.

"Ssen!" Thea turned to the Minathril Sergeant. "Lift

me up!"

As her head was raised above the shield wall, Thea cast her magic. Her voice rang out above the chaos of the battle, carried in the language of the orcs straight into the spirit of every orc on the battlefield.

"You do not have to fight. The Deity shows mercy, unlike the master that you serve. Walk away from the fight or put down your weapons and you will live. You can be a part of the people of Raphtova, living with us, not fighting against us. No matter what you've done, mercy is here for you. All you have to do is accept it."

All across the battlefield, orcs stopped and stared. Some looked around in bewilderment, as if wondering where the voice had come from. Some launched themselves into the fray, with more anger and ferocity than ever before.

Others stood nervously, glancing over their shoulders before slipping silently away, disappearing into the distant woods where they were lost from sight. A few lay their weapons on the ground, crouching with their hands on their heads.

Leaping down, Thea turned to Roland. "Some of the orcs have chosen mercy." She smiled. "We will show them what that means."

Chapter Thirty

Thea stood at the foot of the ruined gates, her guard of Minathrils standing around her. Behind them, the battle was all but done. Only a few isolated pockets of orcs fought on; the rest had surrendered, fled, or died.

The Commander and her troops stepped aside to allow Thea to pass. Inside the wall, she stared at the heaps of rubble and twisted metal that filled the street. The people of Gedwyld hurried past, attempting to bring some semblance of order to their war-torn city.

Acwellan strode down the street to meet them. Her robes were dirty and torn, but light glimmered in her eyes as she bowed in greeting. "Welcome, Thea. We hear that our relief is because of you."

"And many others." Thea bowed in return. "I'm glad the city is safe. Did many people die?"

"Not as many as might be feared, praise the Deity. It would have been much worse if it hadn't been for Zaki and his friends." Acwellan rested a hand on a strange, orc-like figure leaning against a pile of rubble. "He called it big armour. With it, they stood in the breach until the Elves reached us."

The metal surface of the armour was battered and dented, but it was still an impressive sight.

"Zaki made that? I didn't know he was so inventive."

"He made most of the defences on the wall, but the big armour is a feat beyond any of that. I believe he may be on the path of becoming an artificer." She looked at Thea with a gleam in her eyes. "An inventor who receives their magic directly from the Deity, since the Innovator fell and no longer holds his place among the Generals."

So that was where an artificer's magic came from! Thea smiled. "Elora will be proud. Where is he now?"

The healer's face became grim. "The Fallen Tilaryn targeted him, before its attention was drawn elsewhere. He was unconscious when the Captain of the Guard brought him in. He woke just a few points ago, and is asking for Elora and Kais. Do you think you could send word for them to come?"

Overhead, Swift Wing soared. Thea waved for the Dryad to join them.

"That was close, wasn't it?" Swift Wing grinned, landing beside them in human form. "At least the worst is over now. I could sleep for days!"

Thea gave the Dryad an apologetic smile. "Do you think you could make one more flight? We need word sent for Elora and Kais to come home. Zaki was hurt in the fight and he's asking for them. I know you're tired, but ..."

"Who said anything about tired?" Swift Wing grinned. "A little flight like that is nothing. I'll be back in no time."

"He is stable now," Acwellan added, "but his injuries are serious and he will need their care for a while."

With a nod, Swift Wing shifted into falcon shape again and took to the sky.

Thea turned to Acwellan. "We will leave a company of Elves to guard the breach until the city is ready to guard it themselves. If there is any other way we can help, you only need to ask."

"Thank you," Acwellan bowed, "on behalf of everyone in the city. We will always remember that we are in your debt."

"You are not in our debt." Thea watched the humans and Littles, picking their way through the rubble-filled street. "We are the ones who were paying our debt, and it was an honour to be able to do so."

Acwellan bowed. "Then you still have our thanks, and our friendship."

"Thank you." Thea smiled. "That is the best gift of all."

Turning, she strode back through the ruined gates.

The Commander stood at attention as Thea approached. "What are your orders?"

"A company of Elves will stay here to guard the gate until the people of the city are able to repair the breach. The rest of your troops will escort the orcs who surrendered to my home where Ulga can speak with them."

The Commander nodded and turned to her troops, her orders ringing loud over the tumult that still filled the air.

Thea strode on, with Jeewon in step beside her. The rest of the Minathrils marched in formation behind them.

Across the battlefield, Elves were gathering in their companies. Fauns trotted about, collecting weapons from the fallen orcs. Goblins were dismantling the orc camps.

In the center of the field, the broad swath of pristine meadow drew Thea's gaze. Its flowers nodded gently in the wind, unmarred by the tide of combat.

"Roland!" Thea called as they approached another company of Elves.

Roland saluted. "Yes?"

"Take your company to start gathering those who died. We will carry them to the field north of my home. That is where we buried those who died before."

Roland nodded. "We will do that."

Thea stared across the battlefield one more time. A steady stream of people moved north along the road, walking and limping. Thea nodded. It was time to go home.

Thea stood by the gate of her house, watching the Elves bury those who had died in the final battle. Offshore, the fleet was already preparing to set sail. They would be carrying the injured Elves home, along with any others whose presence was required there. The rest of the Elvish army would stay behind for a time.

Jeewon stood by Thea, along with Thabani and many of the other leaders of the armies. Sylica stood alone, standing watch over Khariton's body.

The Commander approached Sylica and bowed. "Where do you want your father to be buried? We can carry him back to Lyudmyla to be buried alongside the King he served, or he can be buried here."

Sylica blinked, wiping her hand over her tear-stained face. "I get to choose that?"

"You are his daughter. You can choose where his final resting place will be."

"Oh." Sylica considered this. "I'd like him to be buried here, in the garden. I think it will be pretty there when the Quickening comes."

"Then with Thea's permission," the Commander

smiled gently, "we will bury him there."

Thea helped carry the stretcher through the gate and into the garden behind the house. Ulfgar and Roland found shovels and began to dig in the place where Sylica directed, by the wall where trailing vines blew in the breeze.

"I think those are flowering vines." Sylica looked up at them with a thoughtful expression. "This will be a nice place for Daddy."

Thea stood by Sylica as the hole was being prepared. They had slipped aside quietly from the larger gathering outside. Sylica wanted it that way, without too many people.

Thea's eyes filled with tears as Ulfgar and Roland lowered Khariton's body into the ground. At her side, Sylica cried, tears streaming down her cheeks.

Ulfgar and Roland stepped back. Looking to Sylica, they waited.

The Commander stepped up to the foot of the grave and saluted. "On behalf of your King, well done." She lowered her head, grief glimmering in her eyes. "As your Commander ... well done."

Sylica crept forward and stared down into the hole. For once, Daisy did not follow her.

Sylica knelt by the edge of the grave. "Goodbye, Grumpy Daddy." Her face crumpled as her shoulders began to shake.

Thea hurried to her side. Wrapping her arms around her, Thea held Sylica as she sobbed.

Solemnly, Roland stepped forward again. "Should we cover him now?"

Sylica nodded, tears still streaming down her face.

Daisy crept forward and licked Sylica's cheek.

With one arm around Daisy and her other hand clinging to Thea, Sylica watched as Ulfgar and Roland filled the grave with dirt until all that was left was a rough patch of ground that had once been smooth.

"We will find a stone to put on his grave," Thea whispered. "A beautiful stone."

Sylica nodded. Above the grave, the bare vines began to twist and grow, sprouting buds that burst into small, delicate flowers, glittering with every colour imaginable.

Thea squeezed Sylica's hand. "They're beautiful," she whispered.

Sylica's eyes didn't leave the rough patch of ground at her feet.

Roland came and stood by Thea. "I can't believe he died," he said in a low voice, tears glimmering in his eyes. "The Resistance won't be the same without him."

Glancing up, Thea saw that Tayhyang had joined them. His scales gleamed silvery blue.

"Thank you," Sylica whispered, looking up into the healer's face, "for giving us more time."

Tayhyang bowed. Placing a hand of blessing on Sylica's head, he turned and walked away.

Ulfgar and Roland were gone. The Commander saluted one more time, then returned to the rest of the Elvish forces still labouring outside the walls.

Thea waited beside Sylica, grief aching in her chest.

Sylica stared at the ground, an expression of emptiness and loss etched on her face.

"I've had so many Daddies die," she whispered. "I thought ... I hoped that ..." Tears filled her eyes once again.

Thea held her friend. "I know. Elves aren't supposed to die."

Sylica nodded, wiping her face with the back of her hand. "Now it's just me again."

"No." Thea held Sylica's shoulders and looked into her troubled eyes. "I'm still here. So are Ulfgar, and Elora, and all your other friends. And you are still Khariton's daughter. You have a people and a home. That hasn't changed. For Elves, belonging means forever."

Sylica nodded and took a slow, shuddering breath. Grasping Thea's hand, she stared down at the grave by their feet. "He said he loves me," she whispered, "and that I'm his special girl." A small, quivering smile flickered at the corners of her mouth. "I turned his world upside down."

Thea ventured a smile of her own. "And for Khariton to like that, you really must have been special."

Sylica looked up at Thea. A new light sparkled in her eyes. "I think a lot of people are sad right now. I should give them some candy."

Thea squeezed her hand. "I think that's a wonderful idea."

Outside the front gate, Ulga strode among the surrendered orcs, a kitchen ladle gripped in her hand. The orcs shifted uncomfortably as Ulga spoke in sharp, clipped words, and seemed to regard her with a grudging deference.

As Thea approached, the orcs turned to stare at her. One of them spoke, and Ulga struck his head with a resounding clang, bending the ladle in half.

Stoically straightening it again, Ulga turned to Thea and spoke in Common. "They were surprised that such a small one is chief." Her eyes glinted with something that may have been amusement. The twitch of pain in her shoulder was almost indiscernible. "They will not question it again."

Thea stared at the orc towering above her. "You're telling them I'm the chief?"

"Chief, Spark, whatever it may be. The name is different, the authority is the same." Ulga nodded decisively. "Orcs understand authority. They have many things to learn, but that is a place to start."

By the house, the last of the injured Elves were being assisted on their way to the ships. Thea went to join them, waving a greeting to Ilya, who walked carefully with a Faun supporting him on either side.

Ilya smiled as she joined them. "Goodbye, Thea. I'm told it's time for me to go home."

Thea nodded. "You'll receive better care there than you would here. This is no hospital."

"It's better than a hospital." Ilya glanced up at the ancient stone walls, a smile creasing his face. "I'm not sure what it is, but I'm glad I got to be here."

Within Ilya's spirit, the dull listlessness Thea had seen in Lyudmyla had faded away. In its place she saw light and hope, even though he could barely walk without assistance.

Thea smiled. "What will you do once you are well again?"

"The King offered me a place in Enzhelika, once it is rebuilt. It used to be a magnificent city, I'm told. Kseniya is sure to approve of that." Light twinkled in his eyes.

Sylica scurried by, her candy bag clutched in her hands. She paused as she saw Ilya. "Are you leaving?"

"I am. I'm sailing home with the ships."

"Everyone's leaving," Sylica pouted. "It's not fair!"

"Not everyone," Ilya assured her. "Besides, I'll see you again soon. I hear you have a house in Enzhelika too."

"You live in Enzhelika?" Sylica's face lit up in a grin.

"Not yet," Ilya laughed, "but I will soon. See you there, Cousin."

Sylica gave him an impetuous hug, which sent a spasm of pain across his face, though he hid it with a laugh. Nodding his farewell to Thea, he turned back to his Faun companions, and they continued to make their way down to the ships.

Inside the house, Tayhyang and Melinda were busy attending to the injured who were not leaving. Thea skirted the crowded great room to join Dunstan by the fire.

"Glad you've come back, safe and sound," Dunstan smiled. "Elora and Kais have gone. They left as soon as they got word that Zaki needed them, but they asked me to pass along their regrets of not seeing you."

Thea nodded. "I'm glad they can be with Zaki. Gedwyld isn't far, I'll see them again soon."

"Dunstan!" Melinda called from across the room. "Come hold this for me."

Dunstan nodded to Thea. "Excuse me for a moment." Crossing the room, he went to help his wife.

"Thea!" Ssen strode over to join her by the fire, his scales gleaming yellow. "My Captain has given me permission to sail with the Elvish ships. I go to help them with their training."

"That's wonderful, Ssen." Thea smiled up at the Minathril standing beside her. "I'm glad that all the races can learn from each other."

"Roland made a good start," amusement flickered on Ssen's scales, "but I think they can be even better."

From across the room, Roland came to join them. "Are you ready to go, Ssen?"

Ssen nodded. "I just need my bag. I will get it and meet you at the ships."

"Sounds good," Roland grinned.

"Goodbye Thea," Ssen bowed. "I am sure I will see you again soon."

Smiling, Thea gave him a hug. "You will always be welcome."

After Ssen had gone, Roland turned to Thea. "Permission to set sail? The Admiral is anxious to be going."

Thea nodded. "Yes, it's time for the fleet to go. I'll come see you off."

In silence, they left the house and crossed the garden, past the place where Khariton was buried.

Down at the shore, Fauns bustled back and forth, carrying baskets and crates.

Ssen was there. He gave Thea a cheerful wave as he stepped on board the Raven.

Svetka's crew was almost ready to set sail. In the midst of the bustle and clamour, the captain of the Eagle sat alone by the rail.

"He's with us so we can keep an eye on him," Roland explained. "He hasn't been doing well since the first sea battle."

One of the Fauns dropped her crate with a resounding crash. The captain of the Eagle jumped, his eyes wide with fright.

Thea considered him for a moment. "Make sure he sees a healer when you get to Lyudmyla."

Roland nodded. "I will."

They watched as the final crates were loaded.

"I guess that's it then." Roland glanced at Thea. "I don't suppose you know when you'll be in Lyudmyla again?"

"No." Thea shrugged. "That's up to Enkeli, I guess."

Roland nodded. "I'll come back on the Raven when I can."

Thea smiled. "I'll be glad to see you."

"Oh just kiss her and get going," Svetka yelled from the stern of the Raven. "If I have to be Admiral, at least I'm not going to sit around here waiting."

"Svetka!" Roland glared. "She is my commanding officer!"

"That never stopped Demyan before."

Roland gave Thea an apologetic smile. "Svetka has … opinions."

"Correct opinions!" Svetka retorted.

Thea looked up into Roland's troubled eyes. He was Roland, and that would never change, but he wasn't the one to be more to her than that.

She gave him a wry smile. "Some people."

Roland nodded. "I understand." Untying the Raven's lines from the dock, he leapt on board. "See you around," he called with a grin.

Thea smiled. "Say hi to Mykyta for me."

Roland nodded. "I will."

Thea waved as the Raven slipped away from the dock. All along the shore, the Elvish ships weighed anchor and began their long journey home.

Later, Big Boss approached Thea to inform her that the goblins would also be leaving. When Alya and the other

Littles found out, they gave them an affectionate farewell, insisting that they keep in touch and come to visit them in Gedwyld. To Thea's amazement, Big Boss didn't disagree.

"Next time you want to make something blow up," Big Boss's eyes twinkled, "make sure you let us know."

As they left, Sylica hugged every one of them, bidding them all a tearful goodbye, and sending them with pocketfuls of candy to eat on the way.

"Food is ready!" Ulga called from the kitchen, banging a pot lid with a spoon.

As they ate, Thea, Jeewon, Thabani, and the other leaders that remained gathered around the table.

"It isn't over, you know." Thabani stared thoughtfully at the fire. "The enemy won't give up that easily. This is just the beginning. You can count on it."

The Commander of the Elves nodded. "The difference is that this time we will be ready."

Gold flickered on Jeewon's scales. "We will *all* be ready. For some of us, that means training." She glanced at Thabani, a flash of amusement gleaming across her scales. "I understand that being prepared may look different for different people."

Thabani smiled. "When the time comes to fight again, we will be there with you."

The next morning, Coham approached Thea as she was finishing her breakfast.

"It's about time for me to be getting home," he mused, leaning on the handle of his greatsword. "The weather's due a turn for the worse, and Beatrice will be worried about me."

Thea rose to stand beside the wizened old man. "I

understand. Thank you again for coming with us."

"It was good to get in practice again." He cracked a toothless grin. "Been getting too lazy these days, what with one thing and another."

Thea couldn't help smiling. Somehow, she couldn't imagine Coham ever being lazy. "I'm afraid I don't have money to give you for your help, but you could choose a trollsbane weapon from the armoury."

"Well now, I don't rightly know." Coham's bright eyes squinted just a little. "I've got my old sword and she's done me well. Can't really see getting another girl at this time of life."

From the other side of the table, the Commander rose and indicated that she wished to speak.

When Thea had cast comprehension, the Commander turned to Coham. "On behalf of the King of the Elves, allow me to offer our thanks for your assistance." She held out a small purse. The sound of coins clinked as it rested in Coham's palm. He eyed it thoughtfully.

"If you will not take it for yourself, take it for Beatrice and Edwin. Also this." The Commander handed Coham a sealed letter. "It expresses our interest in establishing trade with Edwin for his excellent carvings. I am sure they would be very well received in Lyudmyla."

Coham grinned. "Well they will be right tickled. Think of Edwin's little knickknacks being sold in a fancy city like that."

Thea walked with Coham to the door. "Say hello to Beatrice and Edwin for us. We'll be sure to see you the next time we are travelling by."

Coham nodded and swung his sword over his shoulder. "We'll stop by too, sometime or other. We like to head down to Gedwyld every now and then, when the orcs aren't too thick."

With a wave, he tottered out the door.

Soon Alya and the rest of the Littles returned to their homes in Gedwyld. They took the human family with them, offering to find them a place to stay until their homestead had been rebuilt.

Slowly, life fell into a new kind of rhythm. Elves patrolled the roads surrounding Gedwyld, and a portion of the Minathril crew kept a constant watch over Thea's house, as a first defence against any new threat from the enemy. A personal guard, led by Sungy, accompanied Thea wherever she went.

Jeewon and the rest of her crew spent much of their time in Gedwyld, training with the Elves, humans, and Littles there. Noxolo and some of the Fauns joined them.

The rest of the Fauns took it upon themselves to watch over the orcs, taking them on work parties to help repair the walls of Gedwyld or rebuild the homesteads that had been destroyed.

The Faunlets, to their intense relief and joy, were finally permitted to run free again, often accompanying the work parties on their expeditions. The orcs grumbled about this, but Thea couldn't help but wonder if they secretly enjoyed it.

When Gedwyld's gate was finally repaired, the Commander of the Elves announced that it was time for the Elvish army to depart. Everyone gathered to see them off. Humans, Fauns, Littles, Dryads, and Minathrils gathered on the walls of the city and lined the road leading north.

The Elves were not the only ones setting out. Faris and several of the other Littles who used to live near Wyndburh chose to travel with them.

"We live with the humans in Gedwyld," Faris grinned, "why can't we live with the humans in Wyndburh too? I'm sure they could use some pipes in their houses, same as we all can."

Thea stood beside the garrison of Elves that was staying in Gedwyld and watched the ranks of Elves setting out on the long march north. A second detachment would remain in Wyndburh, and the rest of the troops would travel on to Enzhelika to help in the work of rebuilding the city.

When the marching columns disappeared into the distance, Thea returned home. It was so much quieter there than it had been. Many of the rooms that had been full were now bare and empty.

Sylica was there. Thea found her wandering around the great room, poking at the air with a set of knitting needles she had obtained from Sami. Daisy followed her placidly as she paced back and forth.

"You're still here." Thea sank into a chair by the fire. "I thought you might have gone with the army, since they're going to Enzhelika."

"Oh I can catch up," Sylica grinned. "I just have to finish this first."

Thea watched, mystified, as Sylica scrambled the knitting needles together in thin air. "What are you doing?"

"I'm fixing the magic." Sticking her tongue out a little, she squinted at the air as if she was really focusing.

"The magic?"

"The safety magic on the house. It was all full of holes, you know. I wanted to fix it before I go away."

Thea glanced at the inscription above the door. "You can do that?"

Sylica waved a knitting needle. "Thea …"

"Silly question," Thea laughed. "Thank you, Sylica."

Wandering out the door, Sylica tackled a bit of air near the gate.

"The magic will be the same as it's always been?" Thea asked, watching her friend at work.

"It will be better," Sylica grinned. "I changed it so reality wants it to be here. It will be really hard to break now."

Ulfgar strolled through the gate, bumping her on his way past.

"*Ulfgar!*" Sylica cried. "You made me drop a stitch!"

"What?" Ulfgar's face creased in a look of complete bafflement.

From the doorway, Ulga watched with an amused expression. "Finish your task, then come eat."

When Sylica finally declared that she was done, the four of them sat around the table and ate together. Sylica chatted cheerily to no one in particular about her plans to stop and see Beatrice and Edwin and then visit all her friends in Wyndburh before going to find Khariton's house in Enzhelika.

After the meal, Sylica collected her travelling pack, mace, and shield. Her gleaming armour twinkled and clattered almost as much as Daisy.

"Bye, Ulfgar!" Sylica threw her arms around his stocky shoulders. "You have to come and visit me in Enzhelika, okay? We're going to have so much fun there! And Ulga, you come too! I'm going to have lots of rooms in my house for all my friends to stay. Okay, Thea? I'll have a special room just for you with lots of pretty things in it, and we can ... we can ..." a strange expression crossed her face, "... go on more adventures, maybe, and ... go visit our friends." Her face crumpled, just a little.

Turning, Sylica picked up the staff leaning by the door. She ran her hand along its beautifully carved surface for a moment, then looked at Thea, tears glistening in her eyes. "I don't like saying goodbye."

"I know." Thea embraced her friend. "I'll see you again soon."

"When?"

"I don't know," Thea admitted, "but there are surprises every day."

Sylica's eyes lit up. "That's right. And I have lots more friends to make in Enzhelika too!"

Thea smiled. "Yes, you do."

Gripping her staff, Sylica turned and strode out the door, with Daisy scampering at her heel.

Watching from the door, Thea waved goodbye as Sylica stopped every two or three steps to turn and wave her farewell.

When she was finally lost to sight, Thea stepped inside again. Ulfgar and Ulga stood waiting for her.

It was their home too. Both Ulfgar and Ulga had expressed their intentions to stay.

"Well," Ulfgar muttered. "I guess that's it then."

"Just the beginning, you mean." Ulga's eyes glittered.

"That too." Ulfgar shrugged. "Anyone want a drink?"

Thea nodded. "I think that's a good idea."

Thea, Ulfgar, and Ulga sat around the fire, its gentle

crackling the only sound breaking the silence. Around them, the house waited.

"It will not be quiet for long," Ulga reflected. "I should start a list of what we need in the kitchen. The pantry is almost empty." Metallic muscles gleaming, she rose from her seat.

Ulfgar nodded. "Thabani and Jeewon should be back soon. I said I'd repair those swords for them." Lifting his hammer from where it rested on the mantle, Ulfgar swung it over his shoulder and stumped out the door.

Thea stood alone. Slowly, she walked up the stairs and down the hallway to her room. It was empty now. Standing by the window, she stared out over the garden and the sea beyond.

Warm light filled the room behind her. Turning, she saw Allulien, their glory filling the room as if it would burst at the seams. Thea fell to her knees. "Allulien ... you're here."

Allulien smiled. "Yes, Thea. Your time of service beneath Enkeli has ended, and I welcome you back again."

Thea stared up at Allulien. Of course, she knew this would happen eventually. It was what she wanted, after all. She'd never asked to serve beneath Enkeli. But she'd thought ... maybe ... she would have had more time.

Images filled her mind, not of a stately form, engraved with long robes and a flowing scroll, but a familiar figure carrying armfuls of paper, shuffling through them eagerly, with plan upon plan for saving everyone in Raphtova.

In the silence, Allulien spoke. "Is there something you wish to say?"

Thea nodded. "I don't ... I don't want to stop serving

under Enkeli."

Allulien watched her with an indefinable expression.

"I—I know," Thea stammered. "I chose you as my General. I just … I didn't know …"

Allulien sighed. "When someone enters the service of the Deity and asks for a certain General, we honour their request. It is better, though, when they do not choose a General, but instead accept whichever General would be best for them."

Allulien paused, watching Thea with their keen, piercing gaze. "We have always known that you are best suited for service beneath Enkeli. You could not accept that at first, because of the anger and fear that you carried, but now I see that you are ready."

Thea stared up at Allulien, her heart suddenly lighter than it had been in a very long time. She could serve beneath Enkeli. She *should* serve beneath Enkeli. It all made so much sense, but she never would have seen it before.

"Thank you," she whispered. "Thank you for helping me until I was ready."

Allulien's gaze was thoughtful. "I enjoyed having you under my care for a time." They nodded. "I will see you again soon, I am sure."

"Me too!" Micai's voice echoed in the distance.

With a smile, Allulien's image faded and disappeared.

For a moment, everything was silent.

"Enkeli?" Thea ventured.

Enkeli looked up from their armful of papers. "Welcome back," they grinned. "You ready?"

Thea couldn't stop smiling. "I think I'm ready for anything!"

"Good." Enkeli nodded, gesturing for Thea to follow. "There's a lot going on, but here's a start. This place is going to be an inn. The Inn. People will come here from all across Raphtova. See these rooms? We'll line them with beds so people have a place to stay. And they'll come from all over, just wait and see."

Moving from room to room, Thea began to see with her waking eyes the plans that Enkeli had. The upstairs meeting room would be a place for the leaders of the Resistance to gather. The great room would be filled with tables and chairs so that many people could come and eat and hear about the Deity. The stable would be expanded and an addition made for a Minathril sentry post. There would be a tower for Dryad scouts and messengers, and the docks would be expanded so that ships from all across Raphtova could find a berth.

"It will take time." Enkeli crossed the courtyard with a purposeful stride. "Right now we have a war to fight, and this place will be the hub for the Resistance. Mykyta's Messengers will use it, and the Fauns and the Minathrils. The enemy knows, so there's no point hiding it now. The best part is, he won't be able to stop it. The fire's been lit, and there is no going back."

Enkeli looked at Thea, eyes twinkling. "In a way, you *are* the Resistance. You're the face that everyone will know, even though it is others who will form strategies and command armies. You're the Spark, and this is your Inn. Anyone who comes here will never be the same again."

Enkeli moved on and Thea hurried to follow. This was the life she wanted. Here, among the people of Raphtova, a piece in the great plan to bring the Deity's light to all the people. What could be better than that?

Thea smiled and stepped through the door of The Inn.

Epilogue

Thea sat by the hearth and watched the bustle that filled the great room. A gentle smile creased her face, as it often did when she had a spare moment to breathe and soak in the panorama of life going on around her.

The chaos of crates and barrels that had once provided seating in the great room had been replaced by proper tables and chairs, and as was often the case come restday, they were all but filled. Local farmers and homesteaders—both humans and Littles—came to get a drink, meet with friends, or hear the latest news. Fauns and Dryads came and went, bringing laughter and snatches of song wherever they went. A group of Elvish traders sat at a table in the corner. It wasn't unusual for passing Elves to choose to stay at The Inn for the night, rather than travelling on to Gedwyld.

Nearly twenty-five circles had passed since Thea had moved into The Inn and made it her home. In that time, The Inn had become a fixture in the community. People often walked or rode out from Gedwyld to stay for a few measures or get a drink. Ulfgar and Ulga had been experimenting with brewing their own beer, and were well on their way to crafting the most popular brew within several days' travel.

A distant crash and muffled voices drifted through the usual cheerful noise. With interest, Thea kept an eye on the kitchen and the entrance to the lean-to. There was a decent chance the noise came from the workshop or the cellar, and either way she'd probably know soon.

Sure enough, Eleanor emerged from the lean-to, an apologetic smile on her face. "Sorry to bother you, Thea, but Zaki broke the ewer again and we've run out of towels. Could we have some more?"

"Of course. There's more in the storage under the stairs."

"Thanks," Eleanor grinned, going to fetch another stack of towels before disappearing downstairs.

Thea watched her go. Eleanor was all grown up now, in appearance looking remarkably like a feminine version of her father. She lived downstairs with Zaki and his apprentices, where they seemed to lose themselves for days at a time, crafting and inventing new and fascinating things. Ulga was sure to send down food for them, since otherwise they might have forgotten to eat at all.

By the door, Coham banged on the table and hollered for another drink. He had become a frequent visitor at The Inn in the circles since Thea had met him, and now he kept himself quite busy training his teenaged great-grandson in the art of being a blade for hire.

Across the room, Ember sat with a new Dryad who had recently joined the Resistance. Ember said they showed promise of being a good scout.

Shortly after the Siege of Gedwyld, Elora and Kais had bought a homestead just across the road from The Inn. They did not have the protection that those within The Inn or Gedwyld had, but the wandering bands of orcs soon grew to fear the Black Scout, and the homestead was left unmolested.

In the circles since they moved, Adi had grown into

an independent young woman, but she still came across to The Inn almost every day to spend time with Ulga in the kitchen.

It was hardest to watch the passage of time for the Fauns. All the Fauns Thea had known during her adventures had died, from war or from old age. Thabani died on a scouting trip with Kaji, going out flying as he had always wanted.

The Faunlets had grown up, becoming new leaders among the Resistance and having Faunlets and Grand-Faunlets of their own. Inyoni was an elderly Faun now, but in her own way she was still quite the terror.

A tramp of feet and shouting voices rang out from the courtyard. The Minathril patrol was arriving.

The Oreum had returned to the mountains many circles ago, and Jeewon had become Lieutenant Commander, the leader of all the crews beneath their Dragon. Now she sent out Liwei's crews on a regular rotation, to patrol the road between Gedwyld and Wyndburh. They kept the trade routes open and provided a safe escort to any who needed to travel but were unable to protect themselves on the way.

A certain measure of safety could be found in the lands surrounding The Inn and Gedwyld, but that was not the case everywhere. The war continued, springing up wherever they least expected it. Orc war bands crossed the land, preying on those who were undefended. Rumours passed through the Resistance of deadly ambushes and sudden attacks, now in the lands to the south, now beyond the mountains, now emerging from the Deorcian, though the Deorcian was safer than it used to be. The orcs who joined the Resistance were sent to fight the monsters there.

Thoughtfully, Thea ran her hand along the King's armour that she always wore. It didn't look like armour at the moment, but instead appeared as simple work clothes, suitable for someone running and caring for an inn. She wore it, though. Her friends insisted on it, for her safety.

Thea's own reason for wearing it was very different. To her, it was a promise.

The bell in the garden tower rang, the signal that a ship was approaching the docks. Running up the stairs to her room, Thea stared out over the sea. There—the black sails of the Raven. Thea smiled. Svetka and her crew would be joining them for feast tonight. Maybe Roland as well. They would bring news about the furthest reaches of the Resistance.

Running back downstairs, Thea leaned into the kitchen. "The Raven's here!"

Ulga grunted. "If Captain Svetka puts her dirty boots on the table again, I *will* throw her out the window."

Across the room, an aging man stepped through the door of The Inn. Although he held a walking stick in his hand, he stood straight and tall, with an eager kind of confidence. A lute was slung over his back.

Thea stared. She would know that spirit anywhere.

"Davis!" she called, hurrying to greet him.

"Hello, Thea." Davis smiled. "I thought I'd come see this Inn that I've heard so much about."

"Come in," Thea urged him. "Can I get you a drink?"

"Thank you." Davis sat down by the fire and leaned his walking stick against the wall. As Thea brought him a drink, his eyes roamed across the busy scene surrounding them. He nodded thoughtfully. "Allulien said it's a good place to be. I can see that it is."

Thea couldn't tear her eyes away from the bard sitting by her side. She had only seen him once, so long ago, but it was still as vivid in her mind as if it had been yesterday. "What have you been doing all this time?"

"The same as I always have. Travelling. Sharing the Deity's song with those who need to hear it."

Davis's face was wrinkled with age and his hair was going grey, but his eyes shone with even more joy than they had when she'd met him before.

"I never got to study beneath you," she reflected. "I would have liked that."

Davis gave her a thoughtful glance. "I already taught you the only lesson that I teach, that day in Lyudmyla. Love the Deity. Everything follows from that."

Thea smiled. "Thank you. I could not have asked for a better lesson."

Davis finished his drink and rose to his feet.

"Won't you stay and eat with us?" Thea asked.

"Not today. I only stopped by for a moment." Davis took his walking stick. "There are still people who need to hear the Deity's song."

Thea walked him to the door. Outside, the Minathril crew was busy disbanding the day's patrol. Overhead, Swift Wing soared, on a message run from Gedwyld. The smell of freshly baked cookies drifted by on the breeze as Adi strode through the gate with a cheerful wave.

Davis wandered through the crowd, the lute on his back gleaming in Allumen's light. Giving Thea a final wave, he turned to go.

"Davis," Thea called.

Davis stopped and looked back.

"You were my spark."
Davis smiled. Turning, he stepped through the gate.

435

"You were my spark."
Davis smiled. Turning, he stepped through the gate.

Ablaze

The Generals sat on the wall of The Inn, staring out across the sea. It was a favourite place of theirs, though very few people ever saw them there.

Micai held a cookie in each hand and was munching them thoughtfully.

Allulien gave them an amused glance. "Adi still brings cookies? She's getting old now, you know."

"Her great-grandmother's recipe," Micai grinned. "The best I've ever had."

"A hundred and ten circles is a long time for many of the races." Raphea stared into the distance with a thoughtful expression. "The Resistance is holding their own, but is there any end in sight? There comes a time when there has been enough pain and loss."

"Just wait," Enkeli nodded. "My final piece is coming soon."

Across the sea, a light flashed, brighter than Allumen in the sky for those who had the eyes to see it.

The other Generals looked at Enkeli, a question in their eyes.

"He's here?"

Enkeli smiled. "Checkmate."

443

Leane Winger is a multidisciplinary creator and recovering perfectionist who always dreamed about going on an epic quest—as long as there would be plenty of snacks. Author of the mountaineering adventure novel, The Door, Leane is thrilled to be diving into the world of fantasy with The Reawakening Trilogy, the first of many stories to be set in Raphtova—a world co-created with her sword-wielding husband Jesse. Together they live in Mackenzie, BC with their growing crew of littles who keep pestering their mom for "the next chapter of the story".

Learn more about Leane's books and other projects at:

www.leanewinger.com

www.ingramcontent.com/pod-product-compliance
Lightning Source LLC
Chambersburg PA
CBHW061540190726
48289CB00004B/1116